BAD BOYS BREAK HEARTS

MICALEA SMELTZER

BAD BOYS BREAK HEARTS
MICALEA SMELTZER

PROLOGUE

RORY

10 YEARS AGO

THE SUN HEATS MY SKIN, BURNING MY NECK. IT prickles and I reach up to scratch it. I should've put on sunscreen like Mommy told me to, but I didn't listen. She says I never listen.

"I now pronounce you husband and wife," my older sister giggles, her eyes darting between me and my best friend Mascen.

"Uh..." I blink. "What's that mean?" I hiss at Mascen.

He cuts his eyes to Hazel. "I think we're supposed to kiss," he whispers back, looking at the grass wrapped around my finger for a ring. Mommy wouldn't let me borrow hers.

"Kiss?"

He nods, puckering his lips.

I'm eight, though, and shouldn't be kissing. Daddy would hurt Mascen if he saw.

But before I can push him away he kisses me. It's so fast I wouldn't think it happened but static burns my lips.

"Ow!" I touch my mouth. "That hurt."

"Kisses don't hurt," he argues.

Hazel runs toward the swing set, bored with this game, and I take off the itchy dress she made me put on over my clothes so that it'd be a *real* wedding.

"You shocked me." Hands on my hips I stare defiantly up at the boy who's only ten but is so big he could pass as twelve. It's annoying.

"You knew I was going to kiss you."

"That's not what I meant." My lips turn down in a pout.

Mascen looks at the blade of grass I put around his finger. "What do we do now?"

"Hazel's gone, so whatever we want." I'm already heading toward the jungle gym.

"We're married. We should do married people things. Like … kiss again."

I shoot Mascen a confused look. "My parents never kiss anymore. All they do is fight."

Mascen stops walking. "Really? Mine kiss all the time. It's gross, but kissing you isn't."

2

I feel my cheeks get hot. "No more kisses. We're not actually married."

"What if I want to be?" He tilts his head, hands on his hips.

"We're too young," I scoff.

Mascen's eyes get bigger. "Fine, when we're older you're going to be my *real* wife."

"Whatever you say. Can we go play now?"

"Sure, Rory."

He grabs my hand and we run the rest of the way to the jungle gym.

That was the last day where my life was simple.

The next, everything went to hell.

ONE

RORY

Staring up at the big brick monstrosity, green ivy climbing up the sides and along the front, I can't help but smile.

I made it here, all on my own. For so long I didn't think college was a possibility for me, especially not one as prestigious as Aldridge tucked into the vast green hills forty-five minutes from Nashville. I worked my butt off to get chosen for a scholarship and I hadn't celebrated that feat until now. I don't think it felt real until I pulled onto campus.

I'm free.

The sun burns bright in the cloudless blue sky. It's a picture-perfect day to welcome me to my new home.

Closing the door on my rickety old Ford pickup truck I inherited from my grandpa when he passed, I go to cross the street to the main building to pick up some things I need, like my schedule and room assignments. Somehow they didn't turn up. No doubt my mother spotted them in the mail and in the trash they went — anything to try to keep me trapped and as miserable as her.

I've barely made it to the middle of the crosswalk when tires screech so loudly my hands threaten to fly up and cover my ears. Turning to my left I come face to face with a bumper.

The massive bronze colored SUV brakes to a stop *inches* from my body.

My breath is gone, my heart is beating too fast to be healthy, and now I'm frozen staring at the bumper with DEFENDER written across it in all capital letters. I have no idea what kind of vehicle it is, but it nearly had my blood splattered all across that too shiny hood. Red and bronze would not look good together.

Trying to compose myself, I stare at the tinted windows, too dark to make out the driver who nearly ran me over.

Before I can catch my breath the bastard behind the wheel honks his horn — or hers, I guess it could be — as if I'm the one doing something wrong.

Anger flares inside my small body and before I know what I'm doing my left hand shoots into the air, middle finger pointed and waving at whatever jackass thinks it's appropriate to honk at someone they almost ran over.

They honk again, and I slam my hand against the hood. It doesn't even dent or scratch but it makes me feel better. With that parting gesture I make it to the other side of the crosswalk unscathed except for my still out of control heart.

The asshole slams on the gas, leaving behind the scent of burnt rubber in his wake.

"Calm down, Rory." I hold my hand to my chest, shaking my head back and forth in an effort to get rid of some of the jitters. "You're fine. You're safe."

But maybe you can slash that prick's tires later. Surely there aren't many of those vehicles driving around here even at this exclusive university.

Entering the massive wooden double doors, my mouth gapes in awe. The ceilings are high, higher than I've ever seen, and dark wood floors extend through the foyer. The walls are comprised of large round stones with sconces inlaid, giving it a medieval castle flare.

Still not recovered from the incident outside, I spot a bench against the wall and sit down. The last thing I want to do is speak to a secretary or anyone in a professional capacity while looking like … well, like I just got run over. I came close to being road kill. The ironic part is that's exactly what I'd be. No one would care about the poor girl who got hit on campus, and my mother certainly wouldn't bat an eye. I think my sister might be hurt, but even that I can't be sure of with our sporadic contact.

Smoothing my hair back, I take steadying breaths.

Once I feel calm enough and my hands are no longer shaking I stand, walking down the hall like I know exactly where I'm going. After I spot someone I get directions for where I need to go so I don't end up wandering in circles. A few minutes later I find myself in the main office.

After explaining the situation the kind lady working there quickly prints off the information and passes it to me. Thank God she doesn't ask why I couldn't access it from my computer. I don't have one, and if I had I'm sure my mom would've stolen and sold it for a quick buck. I was forced to use one in the old library a few miles from our house, which for the longest time I had to walk to until I got Grandpa's truck. Speaking of computer, I'm going to have to buy a laptop to take notes on and for papers. I spent the whole summer working non-stop at the diner a few blocks from the trailer, stashing every dollar I made to cover the costs of necessities since thankfully I don't have to worry about tuition or even my costs of food as long as I eat on campus.

"Thanks so much." I flash her a smile, folding up the papers.

This time I manage to make it across to the parking lot without getting run over—or nearly in this case, but close enough.

Behind the wheel of my truck, I drive around in

search of the dorm listed on the forms. Islebrook sounds like the name of a university in its own right, not a dorm, but I guess everything around here has to sound fancy. More than likely it's named after a donor, one of the rich stuffy families that no doubt have a long-standing legacy here.

Pulling up to the building I park, killing the engine. The exhaust pops and a few students turn, glaring at my clunker. My cheeks flare, because none of the other vehicles are nearly as old as mine. They shake their heads and keep walking.

Adjusting my glasses, I get out, pulling my duffle from the bed.

Everything I own, everything I am, fits into this one small bag. I don't know whether to pat myself on my back for that fact or feel sad that I could never collect anything personal that would be worth keeping.

With one last look at the slip of paper in my hand, I make my way into the building and up to the third floor suite I'll be sharing with two other female students.

It would've been nice to have my own room, I'm a loner, but maybe the forced socialization will be good for me.

Using the card the sweet office lady gave me, I let myself into the room.

My mouth parts with pleasant surprise. The common area is fairly spacious with room for a couch, chair, TV, bookcase, and even a kitchenette. Across from the living area is the open bathroom door and the three bedrooms branching off. Only one door is left open so I head to that one, placing my bag down on the mattress.

There are no sheets or comforter, not even a pillow to speak of. I should've assumed, but in my haste to leave my mother's trailer behind I hadn't bothered to bring those with me.

I blow out a breath, knowing I'm going to have to make a trip to Walmart before bedtime tonight. At least it's not quite noon yet, so I have time.

The murmur of voices carries from the room directly beside mine. I assume my roommates are getting to know each other, or maybe the already do and I'm the odd one out.

Taking a moment to gather myself, I rub my hands on my ripped jean shorts and decide to introduce myself instead of hiding in my room.

Knocking on the closed door, I wait for it to open, revealing a gorgeous Asian girl with the most flawless skin I've ever seen. She smiles upon seeing me.

"You must be our other roomie. I'm Li."

"Hi." I wave awkwardly. "I'm Aurora."

"That's a cool name."

"Thanks, you can call me Rory. Most people do." I learned at a young age Aurora was a mouthful for most people, besides I felt the nickname suited my person-ality better than the flowery princess name.

She opens the door wider, revealing the room to be in a state of disaster as things sit in piles waiting to be put away, but already I can see the personal touches, photo frames, stacks of books, and hints of pink from the bedspread to the twinkle lights already hanging above the bed.

Stepping aside, she nods at the other girl in the room. "This is Kenna."

I smile at the pretty girl with light brown hair and freckles galore.

"Do you guys know each other?" I ask.

Li shakes her head. "Nope, we just met. We're all newbies."

Relief floods me at not being the odd one out.

"This is my room," Li continues, "Kenna's is across the way and I assume you found yours."

"Yeah, it's nice to meet you guys."

Kenna smiles at me. "You don't look like you get out a lot."

Her question takes me off guard. I look down at my loose crop top, high-waisted shorts, and secondhand off-brand sneakers. "Uh…"

"Not your clothes. It's your face." She swirls one of her hands at her own face. "You have this fresh look about you. Don't worry I'll fix that."

I blink at my new roomie. "W-What do you mean?" I lean against the doorway, suddenly wary.

"Nothing bad, but let's go out tonight. I heard there's a bar close to campus that serves minors. You in?" She directs her gaze first to Li then me. Her green eyes twinkle with excitement.

"I need to get out, so I'm game." Li gives a dainty shrug.

I nibble my lip, hesitating. I didn't have time for

partying before. When I wasn't at school I was studying and when I wasn't studying I was working.

What the hell are you waiting for? This is why you wanted to move far away from Mom—education and an actual social life.

"Yeah, sure."

"Sweet," Kenna grins, "do you have anything to wear?"

I think of the bare necessities I packed and shake my head. "I need to run to Walmart and get a few things." More than a few actually.

She wrinkles her nose. "Um … no. You can borrow something from me."

"Oh, um okay. I still need to go out for a bit, but I'll be back later. You guys need anything?"

They both shake their heads, a sweater needing to be hung dangling loosely from Li's fingertips, and I let out a breath.

"See you later, Rory," Kenna calls as I head back into my room.

Swiping up my phone, wallet, and keys I wave at the girls as I head out.

I can do this, I tell myself. *I can be a normal college student. I can make friends. Go out. Live my life. I'm not trapped anymore.*

Then why do I feel like a bird with an open cage who's forgotten how to fly?

TWO

MASCEN

PULLING MY LAND ROVER INTO THE GARAGE OF MY townhouse, I put it in park and find myself sitting there. Despite spending the last few hours on the practice field by myself, working on my pitch, I don't feel any better. My body is drenched in sweat and I need to head inside and shower, but can't seem to make myself move.

It doesn't help I nearly ran over some chick crossing the street on campus as I was leaving. I was in a pissy mood, still am, and wasn't paying enough attention. I could've hit her, which is scary as fuck, but then me being me I honked at her like it was her fault. I can be a real fucking prick. I don't even mean to ... most of the time. There are other times where I get enjoyment out of it. I don't know what that says about me, but it's true.

Being an asshole comes in handy at times, though, especially when you don't want people to get too close. And growing up in a famous family I'm sick and fucking tired of people always in my business. That shit gets old fast. I'm only twenty and I'm jaded by the whole thing. Just because my dad plays drums in one of the most loved bands doesn't mean I want my whole life to be front-page news. But magazines don't care about that shit, they just want a story, and their latest is what sent me to the field. It was some bullshit with a picture of me at a dive bar. The headline?

Underage Mascen Wade spotted at a bar with beer in hand. Is he following in the footsteps of his former alcoholic uncle?

My uncle Mathias, my dad's twin brother and lead singer of their band, wasn't an alcoholic as far as I ever knew. I'm sure from time to time he's drank too much, who hasn't, but the media always liked to make things seem so much worse than they were. Besides, who hasn't had a drink before they're twenty-one?

Still, it pisses me off that people care enough to buy this shit. If they didn't consume it then news outlets wouldn't bother printing it.

Banging the heel of my right hand against the wheel, my mind drifts back to the girl I nearly hit. With her brown hair and wide eyes behind a pair of glasses she looked vaguely familiar. She reminded me of a different life, one before I became so jaded.

Sometimes I really miss those simpler days, the summers spent running through the grassy fields beside my family's Victorian home in Virginia. I always preferred it to our time spent in L.A.

With a shake of my head I grab my workout bag off the passenger seat and head inside.

"Yo, Cole, you home man?" I call out, heading for the stairs.

I don't hear a reply as I go up, but when I reach the landing his door opens. "Where the hell did you go?" he asks, taking in my sweaty appearance.

"Field," I answer, pausing outside the master bedroom door.

He raises a brow, his eyes narrowed. "Didn't know baseball practice began this early. School hasn't even officially started."

"It hasn't." I take off my baseball cap, pushing my sweat damp hair back from my eyes. "Needed to blow off some steam."

He cracks a grin. "You could've used a pussy for that."

"Not in the mood."

"Suit yourself man, and shower while you're at it. You smell like shit."

I chuckle, shaking my head. "That was the plan."

Ignoring whatever dumb thing will come out of my best friend and roommate's mouth next, I shoulder my door open and close it quickly behind me. Tossing my bag on the bench in front of my bed, I head straight for the bathroom. He's right about one thing, I do smell.

Kicking the door closed behind me I turn the knob of the walk-in shower, letting the water heat up. Shucking off my clothes I toss them in the empty hamper. My boxers miss and out of habit I walk over and pick them up instead of leaving them on the floor. My mom hates when dirty clothes are left lying around, and apparently I picked up that quirk from her. Also a penchant for drinking hot tea, but not many people know that. I have to keep my man card.

Stepping beneath the spray, I watch the water swirl down the drain. My shoulders sag with exhaustion from a burden I don't know why I even bother carrying. I know it's pointless for me to care so much about what certain people think of me, and yet I can't stop.

Grabbing my soap, I scrub my body free of dirt and sweat. I wash my hair too and in the end my whole body smells like the Atlantic Ocean, or I assume that's what I'm supposed to smell like according to the label on the bottle. I don't pay much attention to this kind of shit, but my mom stocked me up on all the good smelling stuff for Christmas. I don't know whether she was just being nice or it was her subtle way of telling me I stink.

Despite the fact I'm in the shower, and soapy, I raise my arm to smell my armpit.

With a shake of my head, I rinse the bubbles from my body before stepping out on the rug. Learned shit the hard way when I didn't have one and stepped out and slipped on my ass. Told people I took a baseball to the ass, because it sounded cooler than the fact I slipped on the wet tile floor because I'm stupid.

Grabbing a towel, I tie it around my waist and grab another smaller one to rub over my hair.

Padding over to the sink, my phone vibrates with a text. My nose crinkles when I see a text from Jules, one of my regular hookups from last year letting me know she's back in town and settled in her dorm.

"Not interested," I mutter to myself, blacking out the screen and sliding my phone away.

I'm in too pissed off of a mood to even enjoy getting my dick sucked.

Today, like most days, I find myself wishing I wasn't the son of Maddox Wade.

After putting a small amount of gel in my hair and styling it somewhat, I grab a pair of cotton shorts and tug them on.

Downstairs Cole is sitting on the large sectional couch in front of the flat screen. I head past him to the fridge, grabbing a bottle of water to replenish my liquids.

He looks over the back of the couch at me. "Some of the guys and I are headed to Harvey's tonight. You wanna go?"

I gulp down the last of the entire sixteen-point-nine ounces. "Nah."

Cole arches a brow. "Why the hell not man? It's freshman hunting season. Some beer and pussy will make you feel better."

I think back to Jules' text and scrub a hand over my stubble-free jaw. "Just not in the mood."

It's not that Harvey's is that bad, but I don't really have a desire to sit in a dim bar with loud country music and dancing. I wouldn't mind hanging out with the guys here, but if they're after girls Harvey's is the place to go.

"Fuck you really have had a shitty day." Cole gets up and joins me in the kitchen, grabbing a beer. He pops the cap and hands it to me. "You don't want to go out, that's cool. You can get shit-faced here and maybe you'll be in a better frame of mind."

I crack a half-smile. "That sounds like some bullshit advice." I lift the bottle to my lips, downing a few gulps. Setting it back down on the counter I cock my head. "What do you know, I already feel better. You're a real Dr. Phil type, Cole."

He shrugs, lifting his palms. "I try. You sure you don't want to go? I'm going to head over to Teddy's if you're not going."

"I'm not."

Cole knows once my mind is made up on something it isn't changing, but it doesn't stop him from trying.

"Fine. I'll see you later, man." He claps me on the back, swipes his keys, and disappears down the stairs to the garage.

Dumping the rest of the beer out in the sink, I toss the empty bottle in the trash. I make myself a sandwich, grab another water, and head upstairs.

Getting in bed I stretch my long legs out in front of me and set the plate in my lap. There's something eerie about being in the three-thousand-plus square foot townhome by myself. I guess I've never really liked being on my own all that much, but when you grow up in a large family, with security trailing you everywhere, you're never alone. Now that I have the freedom of being in an empty home it's weird, even though this is the beginning of my third year living here during the school year.

Picking up the remote, I look for something to watch, settling on a rerun of Wizards of Waverly Place.

Cole would give me hell if he caught me, but fuck it, who doesn't like some childhood nostalgia?

Besides, Selena Gomez is hot.

THREE

RORY

A FEW HOURS LATER, I RETURN TO THE DORM WITH bags of goods for my room, including things that weren't a necessity but will make my room more personal. After years of saving and hiding every penny I figure I deserve it. I also picked up some supplies for school, dumb stuff like highlighters, pens, and notebooks. I even swung by the school store and bought a laptop. With the student discount, plus by getting one refurbished, I was able to walk away with a shiny gold Macbook Air. I'm more than a little giddy about it. I'm sure I'll be caressing the precious later.

Depositing everything on the bare mattress in my room I get to work.

Li and Kenna are nowhere to be seen, probably having gone to the dining hall for a bite to eat.

I make my bed first, the white sheets and gray comforter the plainest ones I could fine. Much better than the teal and hot pink options. It doesn't reflect my personality much, but if I'm being honest with myself, I don't really know what that is anymore. My entire life has centered around survival for so long that along the way I lost who I was.

A lot of people say college is a chance to discover yourself and this is more than true for me.

Unpacking the office supplies, I set up my desk with my laptop in the middle.

Next, I string up lights around the window, similar to Li's room because I liked the cozy touch it added. Stepping back, I take in the space. The room is still plain, and I forgot a rug, but it's *mine*. My mom can't touch me here. Maybe the memories won't either.

The door to our suite opens, the girls' voices carrying across the small space.

I poke my head out to find them entering with smoothies in hand.

"Oh, hey you're back. This is for you." Kenna strides across, offering me a cup. "We weren't sure what you'd like. It's strawberry and banana with some kind of other healthy shit in it too."

"Thanks." I take the cup from her, my throat closing up. It's just a drink but I'm touched. No one does anything kind for me ever, except my older sister, but I haven't seen her in person in years. Four years older than me, Hazel grew up even faster after we left Virginia, and with our mom spiraling out of control she dropped out of school at sixteen and left. I know she felt guilty leaving me, but I understood. I wouldn't have stayed either.

We occasionally Facetime and the random card shows up from her with cash shoved into it. Hazel ended up getting her GED after she left, but it didn't stop her from working at a strip club. I don't judge her though, and no one else should either, she makes good money and can take care of herself. It's more than a lot of people can say.

"Did you get everything you needed?" Li asks, dropping her purse on the coffee table and flipping her long straight black hair over her shoulder in the process.

"Pretty much."

I got the necessities, including the toothpaste and hairbrush I forgot to pack.

As the three of us stand there in an awkward circle, I realize I'm not good at this. Small talk, trying to make friends, just being social in general. Hazel was all I had until she fled. After, I didn't see the point.

"So," I rock back on my heels, "do you all know what you want to do?" I realize how dumb I sound and wince. Clearing my throat I add, "I mean, degree wise."

"Graphic design," Kenna answers immediately, her face flooded with relief. I have a feeling she's probably the most outgoing out of all of us, but even then it's sometimes hard to think of what to say to people you've just met and are going to be living with. "I'd love to work with a big company after I graduate designing branding and packaging."

"Wow, that's really cool." I'm not creative enough to even consider something like that.

"What about you?" She sits down on the chair, crossing her legs. She tips her chin in the air, waiting for me to respond.

I swallow, looking away, afraid my eyes might give too much away. "I want to be a child advocate attorney."

"Wow, that'll be a lot of schooling, huh?" Kenna shakes her head. "I don't think I'd have the patience for that."

"Yeah, I have to do four years of undergraduate study before I can apply for law school and then that's another three." I pull my hair over my shoulder. "But that's why I was so happy I could go here. If I get accepted into the law program here I won't have to transfer."

Turning my gaze to Li, desperate to get the topic of conversation off myself, I ask, "What about you?"

"Oh, I want to go into biology. Not sure yet for what. I could always become a professor, but I'm leaning toward the research end."

"Wow, we're all over the place in what we want to do." Kenna gives a soft laugh. "Well, if you guys don't mind, I'm going to get a shower and start getting ready for tonight."

"When are we leaving?"

"Nine," she replies, already edging toward the bathroom.

I look at the time. "It's only five—it takes you that long to get ready?"

Granted, I'm more of the throw my hair in a messy bun, gloss and mascara only, kind of girl but that seems like an unreasonably long amount of time to take to get ready.

"Perfection takes time." She winks, sashaying into the bathroom with a dramatic flourish.

I glance at Li, giving my head a light shake. "I'm going to finish unpacking."

Really, there's nothing left to unpack, but I can reorganize and study the campus map so when classes start on Monday I'll know where to go.

"Me too." Li gives a shy smile, brushing past me to her room.

I've barely closed the door to mine when the shower starts up.

A moment later, Kenna's karaoke show begins courtesy of Britney Spears's Oops I Did It Again.

I close my eyes, exhaling a slow measured breath.

No matter what, I know I did the right thing by coming here.

———

"I CANNOT GO OUT IN THIS."

I stare at my reflection in the floor length mirror. Kenna forced me into a short jean skirt, some kind of lacy bustier body suit, and an open flannel tied above my waist. Completing the look is a pair of cowboy boots.

"This is Tennessee. It's like a religion to dress like this."

I arch a brow. "You sure about that?"

"Uh…" She hesitates, blinking behind me in the mirror. "Definitely."

During our chat while getting ready I learned that she moved here from California. She told me about her family, smiling as she spoke of them. Her dad is a tech genius that owns his own company and based on some of the designer things around her room it's obvious she comes from big money. It's not a total surprise. Aldridge is built to cater to the upper crust of society. I'm nothing but a charity case, but I'm fine with that as long as it gets me to my end game. A law degree with a steady career. I'm fine building my life from the ground up. Not all of us need a springboard in order to achieve great things. Besides, where's the reward without a little bloodshed.

"You look hot," she continues. "Gorgeous, honestly. I wish I had your boobs."

I look down at my B-chest looking much fuller in the push-up bra I only own because Hazel got it for me.

"Thanks?" It comes out as a question, but she doesn't seem to notice.

"What about the glasses, though?" She eyes my tortoise-shell frames. "Can you ditch those?"

I stare at her, lips parted in disbelief. "Only if I want to be practically blind?"

She waves a dismissive hand. "I only mean don't you have like contacts or something?"

"No," I bite out, "I happen to like my glasses."

"Oh," pink flushes her face, "I'm so sorry. I didn't mean to sound rude. I'm really bad about speaking before I think. My dad has tried so hard to break me of the habit. Clearly it hasn't worked."

"It's fine," I mutter, trying not to be aggravated. She's not the first person to make a comment about my glasses and I doubt she'll be the last. The suckiest time was when some girl at my high school told me I'd be a lot prettier without my glasses. Her comment pissed me off so much that even though I normally didn't say a word, I came back with, "Yeah, and you'd be prettier without your judgmental attitude."

She could never make eye contact with me again after that.

"Seriously, you look gorgeous. Just go out and ... be someone else for a night." She gives a shrug, reaching for heels.

Li pops her head in the doorway. "You guys ready?"

She's dressed in a pair of ripped jeans with a flannel tied up just like mine. I long for her jeans though. I'm showing way more skin than I'm used to, but Kenna's words stick with me.

Be someone else for a night.

26

I'm in a new state, at college, where no one knows me and I can finally let go of my past. Being someone else sounds pretty appealing. I don't have a label attached to me already.

"Yep," I answer Li, smiling at my reflection this time. I fluff my hair, curled and hanging down past my breasts. "Let's go."

———

HARVEY'S, the bar Kenna drives us to, looks like a total dive. The kind of place you'd see bikers hanging outside of. Despite the appearance of the building it isn't motor-cycles parked out front. Instead luxury vehicles line the lot like sentinels. You can practically smell the money in the air.

Kenna shuts her car off. You almost can't tell since it's so quiet even when it's on.

"Show time, girls." Kenna rubs her hands together, her caramel eyes sparkling with excitement.

Li leans up from the back as Kenna slips from the car and whispers to me, "She scares me."

Laughter bubbles out of me. "She's something."

Kenna waves for us to hurry and get out, so we do, the headlights on her car flashing when she locks it.

A country song blasts out of the bar as we walk up, Kenna pushing open the doors like a dramatic cop in a western movie. Or maybe it's the outlaw that does that.

Inside, the music is even louder, the lights dimmed. There are booths, a massive bar that's a complete circle in the middle of the room, and a dance floor that's currently heavily occupied by people doing some kind of step shuffle thing.

The atmosphere is vibrant, lively and I find myself smiling.

Kenna grabs my hand and I quickly reach for Li's, both of us letting the other girl guide us through the bar. I think Kenna has become the silent leader of our group.

She locates a booth in a back corner facing the dance floor. It's a little out of the way which she seems disappointed about, but her frown quickly leaves when she announces that drinks are on her tonight and she glides over to the bar with a swish of her hair, leaving the smell of her floral perfume in her wake.

Li sits down, tapping her fingers against her cheek. "This place isn't normally my scene," she says softly, her eyes scanning the building. "I'm not into the whole country vibe thing."

I don't tell her, but this place is a replica of that—all to give the rich college snobs the illusion of being in a real country bar. If this were an actual one there'd be muddy trucks with big tires in the lot, cheap beer, and probably someone getting punched right about now.

Looking around the bar, it's obvious that there are no locals in attendance. The song playing ends and the people on the dance floor clap, some of them heading back to their table and others ready for another dance.

I just want some chicken tenders, but I bet this place doesn't even have those.

My stomach rumbles with my thoughts. "Is there a menu there?" I ask Li, pointing at the end of the table where the ketchup and other condiments are.

She shakes her head. "Nope, I don't see one."

At that moment Kenna reappears with a pitcher of beer that doesn't look anything like the cheap kind, probably some house made brew or local specialty, and three shots.

"Come on, ladies," she passes out the shots, "to college."

She holds up her shot, waiting for us to hit ours against hers.

"To life," Li adds.

"To freedom."

The glass clinks and I knock back the shot, trying not to make a face, I don't succeed because I hear the laughter of some guy and look up. Amber eyes stare back at me and I don't have to look very long to know the guy is hot and fit, probably plays some sport, his skin is a soft brown color and his black hair is buzzed short. Tattoos snake down the entirety of his left arm.

"Having a little trouble there?"

Now, I sputter even more with the newfound audience.

So attractive, Rory. Get your shit together.

Coughing, I grab a napkin, pressing it to my mouth. "I-I'm fine," I choke out.

His smirk tilts up on the corner. "Let me get you some water."

Kenna and Li look from the guy to me and back

again. Then Kenna gives a little shimmy of her shoulders and a wink, urging me silently with a pointed finger to get out of the booth and follow the guy to the bar.

I want to say no, but as soon as I have that thought I toss it to the side. I deserve to let loose and a cute guy is talking to me and all he wants is to get me a water. Honestly, after my hacking show he probably thinks I'm pitiful and truly wants to make sure I'm all right.

"Um, thanks. Water would be great." I slide out of the booth and his hand instantly goes to the small of my waist, his long fingers edging over the denim of the skirt currently hugging my butt.

I feel the burn of eyes following us, all girls when I brave a look, staring on in jealousy. Whoever this guy is, he's a big deal.

At the bar, he signals the bartender and in seconds an ice water is poured and slid my way.

"What's your name?" The guy asks me in his deep voice, a slight southern drawl to it.

"Rory," I reply, wrapping my lips around the straw. His eyes flick down with my movement and a shiver slithers up my spine.

It's been months since I've been with a guy, and none of my random hookups have ever been that great, but the way this guy is looking at me tells me he'd know what he's doing if I gave him a chance. But he's also probably been with the majority of the female population on campus.

Who cares, you only live once.

"What about you?"

"What about me, darlin'? His cocky swagger would normally piss me off, but tonight I find myself not caring. I guess that's what freedom does to you.

"Your name?" I try to hide my smile but I know it shows around the straw.

His amber eyes sparkle. "Cole."

I've never seen eyes that shade, such a unique swirl of gold with an orange hue.

"No last name?" I arch a brow.

"Anderson."

"Nice to meet you Cole Anderson."

"You didn't give me your last name." His grin tips up on the corners and he motions for the bartender again. In a blink a bottle of beer is thrust into his hand, probably one of the 'manly' types that tastes like piss.

"Abbott."

"You gonna dance with me Rory Abbott?" He bites his lip, trying to hide his growing smile but there's something incredibly sexy about it.

"Only if you want your toes stepped on." I wish I could dance, but Hazel inherited all the rhythm genes, all I got was an ability to argue over just about anything.

"I don't mind."

I sip the water, half of it already gone, and he raises the bottle to his lips a challenge glimmering in his eyes.

When the water is gone, I grab his empty hand. "Why not. Show me how it's done, Anderson."

FOUR

MASCEN

I'M BEGINNING TO REGRET MY DECISION NOT TO GO out with my friends. A distraction would be nice right about now, but instead I'm sitting on the couch, legs stretched out on the leather ottoman, watching the History Channel. I have a weakness for Ancient Aliens that Cole never lets me live down since he first caught me watching it. Joke's on him now since I got him addicted to it.

I lift the beer bottle to my lips, finding it empty.

Groaning out a sigh I put it on the side table. As much

as I'd like another, I have to be careful. It's not technically baseball season, but with Coach Meyers there is no true off-season. He runs a tight ship. It's why I wanted to attend here in the first place, to be coached by him, but I worked my ass off to get accepted based on my grades and own merit. Not what I could bring to the baseball team, or what my parents' bank account looks like.

Too many people are content to sit back and let money do the talking, but my family is different.

Both of my parents grew up poor, my dad and his brother were foster kids, and they wanted to make sure that my sisters and I understood that while we were privileged others were not. We learned not only to give back, but to *work* for the things we wanted. We were spoiled in ways, sure, I mean look at my car and this fancy townhouse, but we had a better grasp on things than some people.

I'd been around enough rich pricks for it to put a sour taste in my mouth.

I think that's why I clicked with Cole. We met during freshman orientation, hung in similar circles, and became good friends. He's here on scholarship, the guy is an incredible basketball player, and lucky for me he doesn't give a shit who my dad is.

He's met my parents and didn't bat an eye. It was ridiculously refreshing. I made a comment about it once and he said, "I'm trying to make something of myself out there on the court, your last name isn't going to help me throw a three-pointer."

Rubbing the back of my head, I try to pay attention to what they're saying on TV but I can't focus.

Standing, I swipe the empty bottle from the table and toss it in the recycle bin. I check over things, making sure no dirty dishes are left out—learned that shit the hard way my first year living on my own and ruined four dishes when I had friends over and dinner ended up permanently crusted on them—and turn the security on. Another lesson I learned my freshman year —people are fucking crazy. Or more specifically, girls are fucking crazy. Once they got wind of where I lived they were literally trying to break in and steal things, like as if I would have memorabilia lying around from my dad's band. You'd think it would be women my parents' age going gaga over my dad, but women of all ages are obsessed with Willow Creek. It's fucking crazy.

Taking a bottle of water from the fridge, I also swipe some Cool Ranch Dorito's—my weakness, before turning the lights off and heading up to bed.

Stifling a yawn, I push the door to my room open just as my phone starts ringing in my shorts pocket.

Putting the water and chips on my nightstand I dig my phone out.

Smiling, I answer the Facetime call.

"Hey, Momma."

My mom's smiling, glowing face lights up the phone. Her curly hair takes up most of the screen and her kind brown eyes make my heart ache. I'm a momma's boy through and through.

"How's my baby boy?"

"About to get in bed," I reply, flicking on the light so she can see me better.

"Ah, there you are." She smiles, leaning against the kitchen counter. "What's Cole up to?"

"Out with the guys."

"And you didn't go?" She arches a brow as I yank my bed sheets back.

"Nah. Wasn't in the mood."

She frowns, her brow wrinkling. "What is it this time?"

"The usual." I roll my eyes.

"Mascen," she sighs my name, eyes suddenly sad.

"Don't worry about it, Mom."

Her frown only grows more with my use of the word *mom*. "Your dad means well, honey, he just…"

"Loves Willow and Lylah more," I finish for her, trying not to sound bitter.

She scoffs. "Mascen Zane Wade, absolutely not. Your father loves you all equally."

I give her a narrow-eyed look. "He wasn't even home to say goodbye. He was off with Willow."

"He was stuck in traffic getting back and you know it. *You* wouldn't wait for him to get home."

"He didn't need to take off to Willow's in the first place. So what if the dog got out, isn't that what her fiancé is for?"

Fuck, I sound whiny as hell to my own ears. I can't imagine how I sound to my mom.

The truth is, my dad's absence when I left yesterday to head back to Tennessee has weighed heavily on me, more so than the article I spotted in a small-town gas station when I stopped.

"Mascen." She plops her head in her hand. "Now you're just nit-picking. You and your dad have always had trouble communicating. It's because you're too much alike." I open my mouth to argue that we're nothing alike, and I'm certain that's the real reason we butt heads so often, but she cuts me off. "You *are*, Mascen. He's my husband and you're my son, believe me, I can see it even if you can't. You could've waited for him to get home."

I look away from the screen. She's right that I could have, I know, but I won't say it. There's so much more shit between my dad and me than just him not being there to say goodbye to me yesterday.

I hear a door open and then his voice.

"I'm talking to Mase," she tells him in response to whatever he said.

Suddenly his face appears beside hers, eyes crinkled at the corners, and the tiniest hint of gray at his temples.

A girl on campus yelled across the quad at me last year that my dad's a DILF. It grossed me the fuck out, especially when I recognized her. She'd sucked me off in the bathroom at Harvey's only a few weeks prior.

Clearing my throat, I wave at the screen. "Hi, Dad."

"Did you get there safe?"

"Obviously," I blurt.

He presses his lips together, but doesn't say anything. A little black nose pokes out of the pocket of his shirt and then the whole head of a spiky hedgehog.

36

"Aw," my dad begins, pulling the critter from the pocket. "Quilly Wonka wants to say hello."

"Why's he in your pocket?"

I mean, my dad carrying a hedgehog in his pocket is unfortunately not that uncommon. They're his pet of choice, plus he rescues them, and even breeds them. In his words, "There's no such thing as too many hedgehogs."

I would've been happy with a Golden retriever or something.

But no, we got hedgehogs growing up.

"He got in a fight with Quilliam Shakespeare. I told him he couldn't hog the mealworms."

Running my fingers through my hair, I sigh. "I'm really tired so I'm going to go to bed. Night, guys."

"I love you, call me tomorrow." My mom blows me a kiss.

I catch her kiss, flattening my palm against my chest. "Love you too, Momma."

Staring into my dad's gray eyes I say a simple, "Bye."

"Bye, Son."

I hang up and toss the phone on my bed.

"Fuck." Scrubbing my hands over my face, I finally climb into bed.

Turning the TV on I grab my bag of chips to snack on. In no time my body gives into exhaustion and I pass out asleep.

FIVE

RORY

The pounding in my head can't be normal.

It pulses in time with my heartbeat. A groan rips out of my throat and I squish my eyes even tighter closed. Beneath the warmth of a blanket I do an assessment, wiggling my toes, my fingers, all appendages seem to be intact and functioning. I guess that's good.

Open your eyes, Aurora.

Reluctantly, I crack my eyes open. It's dark in the room, and I look over finding blackout curtains across the window.

Only I didn't hang any blackout curtains in my dorm.

Oh my God.

My head swishes down and I find myself in my bra and panties. The guy beside me is lying on his stomach, hugging a pillow as he snores softly. Not even the smooth muscular contours of his back can calm my racing heart from what I may or may not have done last night.

Things come back in flashes.

Dancing with Cole.

Laughing with Kenna and Li.

Joining Cole's friends.

More shots. Food. Dancing. Drinks. Laughter.

Somehow, I ended up coming back to Cole's townhouse. We made out for a while, I remember rocking against him, and then ... nothing.

"Fuck," I curse, climbing out of the bed.

I stumble around his room, collecting my clothes, well Kenna's clothes. Shuffling into the denim skirt, I search for the flannel but can't find it anywhere. Instead, I swipe a shirt that must be Cole's slipping it over my head. It's big, hanging longer than the skirt.

Stumbling out of his room, I accidentally close the door a little too loud.

I seriously need to empty my bladder, but right now I just want to get out of here, wherever here is, and get back to my dorm.

"No more drinking for you, Rory."

Blinking, I hold a hand to my pounding head. I cannot throw up all over the hardwood floors. That would be beyond embarrassing.

Inhale. Exhale.

That's better.

I start down the hall just as a door flies open.

"Cole, that you?"

Smack.

I collide with wet, hard, male flesh.

Both of our hands shoot out, steadying us before we fall into a pile on the floor.

I stumble back, looking the guy in the face, and holy hell if I thought Cole was hot he has nothing on this guy. Angular face, full lips, sharp nose, slanted eyes. He's an Adonis, carved from stone. Something so perfect he should be in a museum for all to admire. He's also very, *very* close to naked. The thick charcoal towel tied around his waist is barely hanging on to his toned body. His brown hair is wet from a shower sticking to his scalp.

That's when my eyes meet gray ones.

Horror fills me, bile rising up my throat.

I know him, my brain screams, at the same time I also think, *It can't be.*

But it is.

Mascen Wade in the flesh. My childhood friend, the one I never got to say goodbye to. The son of a famous drummer. I've seen his face sprinkled in tabloids from time to time, and I can't believe I didn't recognize him straight away, but I'm blaming my hungover state.

I mouth his name but no actual sound comes out. Recognition flares in his eyes but as quickly as it's there it's gone. It's like shutters close over his eyes, his brow furrowing in anger.

He says something but my ears aren't working from the surprise of standing in front of him again after all these years.

I'm not quite sure I'm awake yet. Maybe I'm dreaming. I've had a few dreams about him over the years, but...

"Why are you wearing my shirt?"

I look down at the large cotton shirt. *Aldridge Baseball* printed on the front with the mascot, a wolf.

"Y-Your shirt?" I stutter. "I found it in Cole's room?" I don't know why it comes out as a question. He has me unhinged, plus I'm still dealing with the effects of what I drank while he's perfectly sober.

"It's mine." He bites out through clenched teeth, eyes full of hate. "Take it off."

"What?" My face squishes in disbelief. "No. I can't find my shirt and—"

His hands sit on his narrow waist, drawing my eyes to the low hanging towel and the *one, two, three*—eight pack he's sporting. "It's my fucking shirt and I don't give my shit away to Cole's hoes."

I flinch. "I ... I can't walk out of here without a shirt." It would be downright degrading to do the walk of shame without even a shirt. His eyes are dark, though, unmoving.

"Should've thought about that before you fucked

him. Give me my goddamn shirt." He opens and closes his hand, signaling me to hand it over.

I open my mouth to say his name, to beg, plead, or whatever, but promptly zip my lips. I won't be degraded by some asshole even if he was my friend once upon a time. He's expecting more of a fight, craving it, I can smell it in the air like a shark senses blood in the water. I remove the shirt, leaving me in just the lacy push-up bra. I won't let him win.

"Here you go, asshole." I thrust it out roughly, my hand practically punching his too hard stomach.

He lets out the smallest grunt of surprise, his big hands grabbing the shirt.

"I know you recognize me," I seethe, leaning into him. His intoxicating scent of something citrus and woodsy threatens to make me dizzy. "You can pretend you don't all you want, but I saw it in your eyes."

His nostrils flare, his glower deepening.

"Nice seeing you again, Mascen," I chirp, even though this is the furthest thing from nice, it's downright humiliating.

And then, because I can't fucking help myself since he wanted to humiliate me, I reach out as I pass him and yank the towel, letting it fall off his body.

I keep walking, not looking, and down the stairs I go.

When I reach the bottom I turn to see if he's still there. Sure enough, he's standing there in all his glory, naked as the day he was born, and I swallow thickly unable to take my eyes away from his half-hard impressive cock. I feel like I can barely breathe from this entire exchange.

"Eyes up here, *Rory*."

I knew it.

I meet those gray eyes that always fascinated me so much as a child. "Only my friends call me Rory. *You* can call me Aurora."

His smug ass smirk grows and he crosses muscular arms over his massive chest. He's *built*, the kind of body that comes from only eating healthy things, never indulging in even a pizza, and lots of exercise.

I turn to let myself out, already bringing up Uber on my phone. I'm not looking forward to riding with a stranger in my bra and a short skirt, but desperate times call for desperate measures.

"See you later then, Princess," I hear Mascen call from the top of the stairs.

I shake my head, ignoring the catch in my breath.

Out of every school in the United States of course I'd choose the one Mascen Wade attends. I haven't paid enough attention to his name on the online gossip sites or I probably would've known it. I *wish* I would've, so I could've been prepared. Though, even if I'd known it's not like I'd have been expecting this encounter.

None of it matters now anyway. I'll be attending school with my old friend, who now looks at me like I'm an enemy and there's nothing else to it. I've endured worse. I won't let this unexpected hiccup ruin my newfound independence.

———

"ROUGH NIGHT?" Kenna asks when I walk in, sitting up on the couch and tossing her tabloid on the coffee table. She looks surprisingly well-rested and not at all hungover like me.

"I don't even remember it," I grumble, locking the door behind me. "I'm going to shower." *And to brush my teeth ten times.*

I keep replaying my short conversation with Mascen over and over, getting angrier each time, especially over him forcing me to give the shirt back. What kind of dick head asshole does that?

Him, obviously.

The look in his eyes—the anger—was nothing like my old friend. I haven't seen him in a decade, a lot happens in that time, but maybe it's selfish of me to think *I'm* the one that should be angry. My whole life imploded and he's been nothing but spoiled by his rich parents, wanting for nothing. He's never had to work a day in his life, but he looked at me like I stole something from him.

"Ugh," I groan out loud, grabbing clothes from my dresser.

Locking myself in the bathroom I shower quickly, washing away the smell of the bar and alcohol from my skin. After drying my hair I quickly braid it and change into my shorts, black t-shirt, and black combat boots.

Stumbling out of the bathroom, I look at Kenna still sitting on the couch.

"Where's Li?" I ask.

"She went to get coffee. We'll meet her for orientation."

"Orientation," I mutter, silently cursing myself since I'd forgotten. I press a hand to my forehead that's still throbbing with the residue of last night's antics. "When do we need to go?"

"Uh…" She picks up her phone, eyeing it. "We should leave in the next ten minutes."

I nod, turning back to the bathroom and grabbing the Ibuprofen bottle. I shake two of the teal colored liquid gels into my palm and swipe water from the fridge, gulping down the pills. I know I need to get something into my stomach so I pop a piece of bread into the toaster and butter it when it's done.

"Let's go," I say, leaving a trail of crumbs behind me to clean up later as I munch on the toast.

Kenna hops up from the couch, following me out and down the hall. Instead of taking the elevator I opt for the stairs. Kenna groans about that, but doesn't stop to wait for it either.

After having to ask a random student for directions, Kenna and I finally find where we need to go and spot Li waiting outside the building, a coffee cup cradled in her hand as she waves us over.

Orientation takes forever, and afterwards we're shuffled off to have pictures taken for student IDs, receiving the laminated cards moments later.

"I can't believe classes start in two more days." Li looks mildly terrified by her own words. It's Friday now

45

with school starting Monday. I have to agree with her. I think a part of me hasn't accepted yet that I'm really and truly here. I might need to pinch myself just to check that this is real and not a dream.

"What did you think you were here for?" Kenna asks, looping her arm through Li's.

I do the same with her other arm.

We met less than twenty-four hours ago, but we've clicked easily. It's more than I could've hoped for.

The three of us stop at a place on campus for breakfast before heading separate ways.

I spend the day exploring campus, familiarizing myself with the various buildings I'll need to go to for class.

I'm on my way back to the dorm when I hear my name yelled at me.

Pausing, my head swings from side to side, looking for the source.

I spot Cole's tall form striding across the sidewalk toward me.

In no time, thanks to his long legs, he's standing in front of me. I didn't realize it last night but the guy is a giant, probably six-foot-six, maybe more.

"I didn't see you this morning."

"Oh, yeah." I bite my lip, blushing. "I had to … um … go."

"I felt bad I didn't get to say goodbye." He shoves his hands in the pockets of his jeans. Again, I'm struck by the unique hue of his amber eyes. "I was having lunch with my friend," he motions over his shoulder and I see Mascen glaring at us from next to a building, a cigarette dangling loosely from his lips, "and saw you."

Tucking an errant hair behind my ear that escaped my braid, I squint up at him, the sun blinding me. "Last night was … fun. Well, I don't actually remember it, but—"

"That's the real reason I wanted to see you." His voice deepens and he touches my arm gently, eyes soft. "I thought you might've run out because you were embarrassed or thought something more happened than it did."

Heat rushes to my cheeks and I have no doubt I'm bright red.

Clearing his throat he says, "I just wanted you to know we didn't have sex. We were both super drunk and I'm not one of those guys to take advantage of that. We made out for a while, but nothing else happened."

"Oh, thank God," I blurt. "Wait, I didn't mean that like *that*, just…"

"I know." He smiles at me.

"Cole!" Mascen yells and he looks over his shoulder, holding up a finger to tell him to wait a minute.

"I hope I see you around again, Rory." He wets his lips, his eyes sliding over me, not in a skeevy way but one that makes my whole body warm like there's a flame beneath me.

"Cole!"

"I gotta go," he tells me.

I stand there, watching him jog across the quad to Mascen. He says something to his friend, but Mascen isn't looking at him. His eyes are on me, and if looks could kill I'd be six feet under.

SIX

MASCEN

THE CIGARETTE TASTES SOUR ON MY LIPS. I TRY NOT to smoke much, and Coach would kill me if he saw, but watching Cole jog over to Rory calls for one. I glare at the white cylinder cradled between my fingers and bring it back up to between my lips, sucking in a lungful of the smoky air.

Catching Rory, fucking *Rory*, in the hallway this morning took me by surprise. Or, I guess I should only refer to her as Aurora now since *we're not friends*. But we were. Back then she was a scrawny little thing, with twig legs, and a nose too big for her face sprinkled with freckles. But I loved her, well as much as a ten-year-old boy can love someone that's not family. She was my best friend and then one day she was just gone. It's not like it's a secret why she left, I remember my parents sitting me down and telling me what happened, not wanting to keep secrets from me even at my young age, but it still hurt losing her.

Honestly, over the years I've forgotten about her. She became a memory, just someone I used to know. But when my eyes lit on her in the hallway I recognized her instantly, but the shock and awe gave way quickly to anger, because she was leaving my best friend's room. It was dumb, childish anger that roared inside me, this primal feeling of *I saw her first* and it hasn't dulled since this morning. It also didn't help when I realized she's the girl I almost ran over yesterday. I don't know how I didn't recognize her then, but I guess I was too lost in my head.

She's got fire in her and my dick should not find that nearly so appealing considering she's done the walk of shame out of Cole's fucking room. I don't have many standards, but I won't do a girl after my friend's had her. That feels way too up close and personal.

Her spunk both surprises and amuses me, especially when she stands in front of Cole looking shy and awkward. She sure was neither when she swiped my towel from my waist this morning. My lips threaten to tug into a grin at the memory, but I force them to stay in a straight line. Especially when we came out of the diner and Cole spotted her across the quad, he smacked me on the shoulder and murmured, "That's the girl."

The one he gushed about this morning, telling me how beautiful and sassy she was. Apparently she's a fucking amazing good kisser too. While he spoke I made non-committal noises in response, my head stuck in the refrigerator so he couldn't see me making faces.

After his, *that's the girl*, declaration he jogged over to her side and the two began speaking. That's when the itch for a cigarette grew too strong and I grabbed the fresh pack from my pocket, the one I'd carried for over a week without opening. Today I broke my streak.

"Cole!" My voice carries across the grassy area, the anger biting. He's talked to her long enough.

The asshole holds up a finger telling me to wait. My jaw clenches and I take another drag from my cigarette.

I narrow my eyes when he grins at her.

This isn't his smug, knows-he-can-get-any-pussy, grin. It's genuine and that kicks me in the gut. I wasn't at Harvey's last night, but clearly whatever happened he really likes her.

And how can I possibly forget that while I was dead ass asleep Cole was fucking her brains out. Fucking the girl I grew up with. The one who lived next door. The one who ran a lemonade stand with me when I was seven and she was five. The one who meant so much to me then and now...

"Cole!" I yell again, my teeth grated.

This time he gets the message and jogs over. I'm not paying attention to him. My eyes stay on Rory—*Aurora*—my lips snarling as I glare at her.

I have no explanation for the hate boiling inside me. Yes, I used to know her, but I don't own her. She can fuck whoever she wants, even my best friend. This feeling has to be just because I'm so surprised to see her, right?

"What the hell man?" Cole interrupts my thoughts. "Stop trying to cock block me. It was a surprise seeing her here. I wasn't going to miss my opportunity."

I slowly swing my gaze his way. "Since when have you wanted a girl for more than one round?"

He looks over his shoulder to where Rory is now walking away in the opposite direction. "Since now." He gives a simple shrug.

I have to fight the irrational desire to punch my best friend in the face.

What the fuck is wrong with me? Ten years, that's how long it's been since I've seen her. She was a little girl then. She's nothing to me now. Nothing.

Maybe if I say it enough to myself I'll start to believe it.

"Are we going to the gym or not?" I toss the cigarette butt on the ground, watching the smoke curl up before toeing the end of my shoe against it. I watch the ash crumble against the concrete so I don't have to make eye contact with Cole.

I'm in a pissy mood—again—and I can't even explain it to him because I'll sound psychotic.

"Yeah, of course." Cole merely shakes his head, used to my mood swings.

The two of us head in the direction of the on-campus gym reserved for athletes only. It's state of the art and usually pretty empty unlike that gym designated for all students.

Cole and I head to the locker area—each athlete is assigned their own—and switch our clothes.

Luckily Cole doesn't ask me to spot him on the bench press, I'd be likely to let him drop the bar on his chest in my current state of mind, and we each head to separate parts of the gym.

Sticking my air pods in my ears, I crank my music up to drown out what's playing over the speakers in the room, and hop on the treadmill. A lot of people hate running, but I love it. When I run I don't think so much, it gives me time to forget about whatever I'm mad about and I usually work up a decent sweat. Plus, working on my endurance helps me with baseball.

Across the room I see Cole working with the free weights.

My thoughts want to drift to the idea of him and Rory, especially if he's serious about liking her, but I chose the treadmill for a reason—to *not* think about this fucked up situation—so I push the button, going faster than I probably should.

By the time I get off my body is drenched in sweat. I wave at Cole to get his attention and once I have it I point to the locker room so he knows I'm going to shower.

Grabbing my soap from the locker I nod at a couple of guys on the football team I hang with time to time.

The showers are empty and I pick one, closing the curtain behind me.

My shower is quick but thorough since I don't want to smell like B.O. the whole fucking day. Leaning my head back, unbidden thoughts steal inside my head. I picture Rory standing on the quad today wearing those fucking pigtail braids. The image changes to another, one of her bent over my bed naked as I fuck her from behind. Those braids wrapped around my fist.

I growl as blood rushes to my dick. It grows and thickens.

Not fucking happening.

The last thing I want is a hard-on because of Rory Abbott.

I switch the water over to cold, the sudden jolt in temperature startling all my senses.

When it doesn't work fast enough I start naming off some of my dad's hedgehogs. That's sure to kill my erection.

Pokehontas.

Quill Smith

Edgar Allen Poke.

Winston Churchquill.

Quillie Nelson.

And my hard-on is successfully gone.

SEVEN

RORY

"No, no, no! You have got to be fucking kidding me!" I yell, bouncing around my tiny room and into a pair of jeans.

It's the first day of classes and *of course* my alarm chose today not to go off on time. To say I'm going to be late is the understatement of the century.

"Shit, fuck!" I curse when my knee slams into the wall during my struggle. I bite my lip from the throbbing pain in my kneecap.

I button the jeans and zip them up, grabbing the first shirt I get my hands on. It's a black t-shirt with a

frowny face stitched over the left breast. How appropriate. Shoving my feet into my boots, I then gather my
un-brushed hair up into a messy bun, push my glasses
up my nose, and grab my bag, slinging it over my
shoulders.

Li and Kenna are already gone, and probably
assumed I was too.

I grab a cereal bar so I can eat on the go. There's not
even time to brush my teeth or drink coffee and I'm a
monster without any sort of caffeine. I'm already late so
I might try to stop at one of the kiosks that dot the lush
campus.

Running down the stairs, I burst out the double
doors into the sunshine.

I keep running, having memorized what building I
need to get to, all the while taking massive, unladylike,
bites of the breakfast bar.

I decide to forget the coffee and get some after class
since if I hurry I *might* squeak into the classroom on
time.

My boots pound against the ground and I get more
than a few funny looks, but I don't care. I stopped
giving fucks about what people thought of me around
the time I turned twelve and realized my mom was
never going to snap out of it and the person she'd
turned into was there to stay.

Just as I'm thinking about how much I don't care
what other people think, the toe of my boot catches on
something and I go crashing to the ground, my hands
and knees scraping against the concrete. I wince from

the burn, fighting tears. All the air flees from my lungs.

Fuck this day.

It's not even eight-thirty in the morning and I'm over it.

Leaning back on my legs, I bring my hands up, studying the gravel embedded in my skin when a pair of sneakers align with my vision.

"Do you regularly fall on your knees in front of guys?"

I look up into the angry, arrogant face of Mascen Wade. He blinks his gray eyes at me. He towers above me even when I'm standing, and now with me on the ground I feel like a tiny ant he could crush beneath his shoe.

"It's where you belong, isn't it? On your knees, legs spread. If you wanted to suck my cock, Princess, all you had to do was ask." Bending his body in half, he growls in a low gravely tone, "The answer would be no. I don't do Cole's sloppy seconds."

Anger courses through my body, erasing the sting of pain in my hands and knees. I shoot to my feet, nearly swaying from the sudden movement. I catch the twitch of his hand, moving to steady me, but he quickly pulls it away and it forms a fist at his side.

"Excuse me?" I hiss, having to tilt my head back to look in his eyes. He's not as tall as Cole, but at least six-foot-something himself.

His lips pinch. "Are you hard of hearing? Should I repeat myself?"

This guy. If anyone said something like he did to me I'd be pissed, but the fact that once upon a time I knew this guy, we were *friends* as children, sends me straight to flat out livid. I don't think I've ever wanted to punch anyone more in my entire life. My hands clench at my sides, digging the gravel further into my palms.

"No, I don't need you to repeat yourself." My tone is mocking, my shoulders nearly up to my ears from anger. "I just can't believe anyone would say what you did."

He arches a dark brow. "Did I or did I not catch you doing the walk of shame from my friend's room in *my* shirt no less?" Somehow his glower grows more pronounced. If he keeps doing that his face is going to be permanently stuck that way.

I don't bother telling him that according to Cole we didn't actually have sex, because frankly it's none of Mascen's business. Besides, it's the twenty-first century and it's about damn time people stopped shaming women for *liking* sex.

"I don't see how that has anything to do with your comment." I cross my arms over my chest, ready to trade more barbs with this guy.

Not 'this guy'. Mascen. The boy you'd spend summers at the lake with. The one you laughed, joked, and ran with.

I push my memories of better years aside, because it doesn't matter. That boy is nothing like the man looking at me with such hatred.

"If you don't get it then you're dumber than I remember, Princess."

"Don't call me that."

"I'll call you what I want."

My hand twitches against my chest, wanting to smack him. People strolling along are starting to stop and stare, but I pay them no mind.

"I have to get to class." And I do, now I really am going to be late.

Mascen steps to the side, sweeping his arm out. "I'm not stopping you from leaving, Princess. In fact, I'm already over this conversation."

Before I can retort, his long-legged stride carries him away. I stare after him, both shocked and mystified.

Shaking my head to clear it free from whatever spell he cast over me like some sort of dark wizard, I hurry on to my class, slipping into the back row of the auditorium seating. The professor gives me a look for entering the room late but doesn't call me out on it.

When all we do is go over the syllabus before being dismissed early, I wonder why I bothered rushing in the first place.

Rolling my eyes as I exit the class into the hall after less than ten minutes in the room, I decide to grab a coffee and a decent breakfast before my next class.

My stomach rumbles, demanding food first.

Entering the dining hall I inhale the scent of food. It's more like a large mall food court, with various areas to pick up and order, than a cafeteria.

I walk around, assessing the various offerings, before ordering an egg sandwich. I wait off to the side for it to be made and once it's done I put the plate on a tray, grab a Coke, and swipe my ID card to cover the cost.

Grabbing a table, I sit down by myself. There aren't many students in the dining hall at this time and there's something peaceful about it. Windows line all three sides of the building where the seating area is, allowing light to flood inside. There's a large outdoor seating area too with umbrellas to block the hot sun. I'm tempted to go out there, but there are more people lingering in that area so I choose to stick with where I am.

Taking a bite of my sandwich I stifle a moan. I haven't tasted anything this good in too long. Digging out my schedule I look over my next class, English, which I already knew but it mentally makes me feel better to check. I'm so thankful for the opportunity to be here and I'm paranoid about fucking it up.

I've worked too hard to get here to mess things up.

Like being late, I silently scold myself.

I groan and a guy at a nearby table looks over, probably wondering what my problem is. Right now my problem is Mascen Wade. Twice, I've seen him *twice*, in less than twenty-four hours and of course both meetings were a disaster.

He was never such an egotistical asshole when we were kids. Granted, he was ten the last time I saw him, but he'd always been sweet and kind. The boy who picked me flowers and tucked them behind my ear just to see me smile.

I never thought our paths would cross again. Not when he's practically a god, or at least the son of one, and I'm nobody now. I fell from grace, a fallen angel if you will, and now he looks at me like I'm the worst of the worst.

I don't get it, but it doesn't mean he isn't wrong.

My family lost everything and my sister and I have paid the most for it.

With my breakfast finished I stuff my schedule back into my bag, toss my trash out, and go in search of the nectar of the gods. Aka coffee, the only thing keeping college kids running since the beginning of time.

I stop at one of the many kiosks across campus and order a black coffee with just one pack of sugar.

"Thanks." I smile at the girl that passes me my coffee cup and drop my change in the tip jar.

Sipping my coffee, I walk around campus since I still have time to kill. I could go back to the dorm for a little while, but it's such a nice day I'd rather be outside, breathing in the fresh air. There's a slight wind, carrying the scent of freshly mowed grass in the distance. Birds sing happily and the sky is a cloudless blue. It's the kind of day that makes my soul happy, one so perfectly sunny and bright that it makes up for all the bad days.

I end up sitting on a bench for a while, watching students walk by to their classes, professors moving about, and just the general buzz of college life.

Checking the time, I finish my coffee and head to my English class, waiting outside the closed door.

Thank God I'm not late this time.

A couple other people join me in wait and I smile shyly at them. None of them smile back, either too busy looking like they hate the world, or they have their face glued to their phone screen. I don't let it bother me.

The wooden double doors burst open, the class before ours emptying out. When the last person is gone I head inside, taking a seat in the fourth row back, close but not *too* close to the front.

Setting my bag between my feet, I wait. I don't see the point in pulling my laptop out. The classroom fills in, only a few seats left unoccupied.

From below, the professor enters from the side door, his back stooped, graying hair, and beady black eyes. He looks around at the room, his lips slightly snarled and turns to his desk, shuffling papers.

Finding the one he's looking for he begins calling out names.

"Aurora Abbott?" He calls out first. I'm not surprised, almost all through school my name was always called first. A few people glance my way when I raise my hand, but they all look bored, none of them realizing I'm one of *those* Abbotts.

Fallen.

Disgraced.

A stain.

The professor moves onto the next name, calling out everyone and checking them off. He then passes out the syllabus, going over it, before going straight into the lesson. I'm thankful to actually have work to do.

Class ends and I continue with my day, not returning to the dorm until three. I've barely closed the door when Kenna enters behind me.

"I'm exhausted," she announces, dropping her bag on the floor before flopping dramatically onto the couch face first. "Can we order pizza?" she mumbles into the pillow.

Grabbing a Sparkling Ice strawberry kiwi water, I turn to face her prone form. "Um, I guess." I think about how much cash I have on me to contribute.

"Awesome!" She hops up, suddenly all smiles. "My treat," she adds and I breathe a sigh of relief. "Where's Li?"

"Still in class, I guess." I give a shrug, sipping the flavored water.

"We should post something with our schedules so we know where each other is."

"That's not a bad idea," I agree.

"I'll text her and see what kind of pizza she wants." Kenna rolls off the couch, heading to her room.

I do the same, leaving the door cracked behind me. I pull out my computer from my backpack, setting it up on my desk.

My phone rings and I smile when I see Hazel's name on the screen.

"Hello?" I answer.

"How's my big famous college-going sister? Haven't forgotten about the little people yet, have you?"

"I miss you," I reply, my tone wistful. It's been too long since I've seen my big sister. "And I could never forget my little people," I joke, tucking a piece of hair behind my ear, perching my butt on the end of my bed.

"See any cute guys?" she asks.

Of course my mind goes straight to Mascen. Despite his hateful attitude and hurtful words, there's no denying he's gorgeous. His face might be sculpted from stone, just like his heart, but it doesn't mean I can't admire the art.

I realize I *should* be thinking about Cole, but...

"No," I answer, keeping my thoughts to myself.

"Just remember, there are a lot of rich guys there — wealthy families, old money, Rory. Mom might've been a piece of shit, but she wasn't lying when she said it's just as easy to love a rich man as a poor man."

I cover my face with my free hand. "Yeah and look where it got her."

"That wasn't her fault." I'd beg to differ, but I keep my mouth shut. "Tell me more," Hazel continues, ignoring my silence. "How are your roommates?"

"I think I lucked out there. They seem pretty great. We're getting ready to order pizza."

"Ugh, I'm jealous. I miss carbs."

Hazel eats healthier than anyone I know, too scared to gain an ounce that she might not get as many tips if she does.

"You could come visit me. We could get pizza together."

"Rory," she sighs, her breath echoing over the line. "I know it's been a while since we've seen each other, but now isn't a good time for me to travel."

I pinch my eyes closed. Of course it's not. "Yeah, it was a dumb idea."

"Rory—"

"I gotta go. Love you."

"Love you, too."

I hang up, tossing my phone on the gray bedspread. I probably shouldn't have ended the call hastily since she did reach out, but it's frustrating when I haven't seen her in person in *years*.

There's a light knock on my door and then Kenna pokes her head in. "I'm not interrupting am I?"

I shake my head, forcing a smile. "Not at all."

"Li gets out of class at three-forty-five so I thought I'd go ahead and order the pizza. It's our first day so pizza and wings seems like the most appropriate way to celebrate."

My smile is genuine this time. "Wings too now, huh?"

She sticks her tongue out. "I'm starving I can't help it. I want all the food."

Looking at her tiny figure I have no idea where she puts everything she eats, but in the days we've been living together I've seen her ingest more than I've ever seen any other human eat.

"I'm hungry too," I admit, having skipped lunch.

"What kind of pizza do you want?" She's already pulling out her phone, eyes on the screen.

"Supreme."

"You got it." She lifts the phone to her ear, walking away.

My phone buzzes on my bed and I pick it up.

Hazel: I'll try to see you soon.

I snort, rolling my eyes. We both know it's a lie.

But it's okay. I love my sister, but a part of me knew when she walked out of the house I'd probably never see her again. At least I get to talk to her and for that I'm truly grateful.

Still, the ache in my chest doesn't ease.

"THIS PIZZA IS DELICIOUS." Li lifts her hand to her mouth, trying to hide her chewing.

"So good," I agree, reaching for a *fourth* slice. Our food is spread over the living space, the TV tuned into a mindless reality show that Kenna says is the worst but best thing she's ever watched. That makes no sense to me, but hey, to each their own.

I have to admit, it feels good hanging out with them. Girlfriends are a luxury I haven't been privy to.

"Thanks for getting the pizza and stuff." Li flicks her fingers over the smorgasbord of other food including wings and brownies.

"No problem." Kenna bounces slightly where she sits, full of energy.

"Yeah, thank you," I echo, even though I've already said it a few times already.

Money wasn't an issue for my family at one point, but I've spent the majority of my life with it being a struggle, tucking away every penny, and sometimes going hungry. I've learned to be extra grateful when I'm presented with a free meal.

"We should make pizza nights a weekly thing."

Kenna beams at the two of us, stretching across the table to grab another slice. "Maybe on Saturdays? Fridays are usually when the parties are and it's the best night to go out anyway."

Li wrinkles her nose. "Maybe Saturdays are reserved to always have dinner together, but not always pizza. I do not want to be one of those people who gains the freshman fifteen when I can avoid it."

"Okay, I'm good with that. What about you, Rory?"

"I'm in," I agree. "I can cook some during the week."

"Thank God, because I can't." Kenna laughs. Staring at her half-eaten slice of pizza she mutters, "Why can't guys be like pizza?"

"Greasy?" I blurt. "Because most already are."

Li hides her giggles behind her hand and Kenna shakes her head. "No, delicious and unfailingly loyal."

I pause, my face wrinkling. "How is pizza loyal?"

"Has pizza ever let you down?"

"Well, no."

"Exactly." She snaps her fingers and digs in for another bite.

"Can't argue with that logic." I reach for my flavored water, gulping down the last of it. For some reason I can't stomach plain water. It's silly since it's literally *flavorless*, but I think it's nasty.

We finish our meal, clean up the leftovers and throw away the trash, before the three of us head into our separate sleeping areas.

I change into my pajamas and climb into bed. Lying

on my back I stare up at the ceiling at the silly glow in the dark stars I stuck up there. They remind me of happier, better times. Ones where my days were filled with laughter and love, before scandal hit and tragedy struck, imploding everything.

Rolling to my side I cup my hands under the side of my head. I made it through the first day, one step closer to freedom.

EIGHT

MASCEN

"DUDE," COLE SLAMS A PALM DOWN ON MY shoulder, "you're quieter than normal. What's up with you?"

I close the refrigerator door and turn around to face him. I don't know what I was searching for in the first place. Some of our other friends crowd the living area, spilling over all the couches. It's the first night we've all been able to hang out since we returned to school.

"Lot on my mind, I guess." I brace my hands on the shiny stone counters, my shoulders nearly rising to my ears in a shrug.

"Like what?" he asks, swiping a beer from the fridge. He offers it to me first but I shake my head. He pops the top off and takes a long swig. "I mean, you're not the chattiest guy to begin with but since you got here you've been…" He pauses, frowning. "Weird."

I take my baseball cap off, gliding my fingers through my hair before replacing it. "Life's been crazy."

He gives me a sympathetic nod. Just today there was an online article circulating a photo of me and an ex from three years ago, although, I wouldn't even consider her an ex. Three dates with the up and coming actress did not make her my girlfriend. But with her headed to rehab for alcohol abuse, suddenly I'm somehow responsible. Go figure.

He pats my shoulder as he passes. "Just try to have a drink. Eat a slice of pizza." He nods at the open box on the counter by the coffee maker. "Chill, man."

I know he's right. I need to stop stressing about things I can't change or fix. School and baseball needs to be my focus, not Rory either, but somehow I still find myself speaking up before he leaves the kitchen. "Have you texted that girl yet?"

"Huh?" He turns back around, arching a brow.

"The one who stayed over?"

"Oh, not yet. I should, though. She's cool. Why?"

"No reason." None that should matter anyway.

He dips his head before ducking out of the kitchen.

Grabbing a beer this time, I lean my hip against the counter as I take a few slow sips. Knowing I can't hide in here sulking forever, I grab a slice and join the guys.

"It's about time you reappeared." Teddy, the short stop on Aldridge's baseball team and one of my closest friends after Cole, spreads his arms wide, nearly falling out of the recliner as he does it.

"You're in my seat, asshole." I kick his leg, not hard enough to do damage but enough for him to make a noise.

"It's mine now. You snooze you lose."

"What are we watching now?" I plop on the couch beside Cole, his friend Andrew, another basketball player like Cole, on his other side. Murray, the third baseman, is asleep on the love seat. The guy can't stay awake for much of anything.

"Godzilla." Okay, apparently Murray was only resting his eyes.

He's not kidding either, it's just beginning and it's the original—aka the best, even with the dubbed over English. I don't know how other guys spend their evenings decompressing after class, but this works for us. Teddy, Murray and Andrew all still live on campus, but end up spending a lot of time here. Can't say I blame them, not with the flat screen my dad set me up with, as well as gaming systems, and the pool table on the bottom level of the townhouse.

Kicking my legs up on the ottoman I finally take a bite of pizza. It's cold now, and greasy, but I'm too lazy to cook something even if I should watch what I eat. I'll have to go on a run tonight, but some sacrifices are necessary.

HOURS LATER, the guys are gone, my run's over, and I've showered the sweat from my skin. Too many times today my thoughts have drifted to Rory.

Aurora, I remind myself, her name grating over my taste buds.

I've only seen her the one time this week, when she happened to fall right in front of me. God, the irony of her falling on her knees at my feet wasn't lost on me. Especially, when ironically I'd had a dream the night before of her in that same position, naked, her luscious mouth wrapped around my cock.

Fuck, even now my dick stirs at the thought.

It's ridiculous how my body reacts to her. After all this time she should be no one to me, a blip, but the fact is back then she was a tether to something more, a solid footing in a world that was nothing but chaos. Then she slipped away, never to be heard from again. Despite everything, she could've found a way to reach out to me, I know it. I tried to find her, begged my parents, but they said it wasn't their place to meddle.

Looking back now I think they were afraid of getting caught in the storm of Rory's family drama, the implications that could blow back on Willow Creek, but I was a boy who just wanted to know his friend was okay.

Scrubbing my hands over my face I let out a groan, the pent-up frustration seeping between my lips.

I need to get Rory off my mind. She's someone I used to know. That's it. She's *no one* now.

"Fuck it," I mutter to myself, swiping my phone off the dresser.

Going to my contacts I click on the first female name in there. Sending a text about dinner this weekend, I'm not surprised when the girl responds in seconds agreeing, a ridiculous amount of exclamation points accompanying her answer.

Do I really think going out and more than likely fucking someone else is going to help my fucked-up feelings over Rory?

No. But it's a start.

NINE

RORY

THE FIRST WEEK OF SCHOOL PASSES AND I DON'T have any more run-ins with Mascen. It was dumb of me to think for even a second that we might have a class together. He'd be a junior so our classes wouldn't intersect. I have heard his name whispered around. I'm learning he's pretty much the king of the campus. He's the guy with connections, the one who apparently throws killer parties, and if what some of the girls have said is true he gives the best orgasms they've ever had.

Stop thinking about him.

Grabbing my truck keys off my desk, I head out to the door.

"Where are you going?"

I nearly jump out of my skin when Kenna's voice breaks into my thoughts. She pops up from the couch like a fucking whack-a-mole.

Placing a hand to my racing heart, I answer her. "I'm going to see if I can find a job on campus or close by. I thought I'd pick up some groceries while I'm out too."

"A job?" She wrinkles her nose like she's never heard of such a thing. "Why do you need a job?"

I blink at her. "For money."

"Don't your parents give you money?"

I know she's not trying to be mean or hurt my feelings, she's literally that clueless. She's grown up rich with everything handed to her and can't imagine anyone else living any other way.

"I'm here on a scholarship, so if I want spending money I need to work."

Luckily, I've saved quite a bit, but I know if I don't get a job I'll go through it quickly and that thought doesn't sit well with me.

Her face falls and she looks truly apologetic. "I'm sorry, I didn't know." Her words are rushed, her face suddenly tinged red.

"I didn't tell you." It's not that I'm embarrassed about it, but at a college catered to children of the rich, famous, and elite, it's not something I want to pass around too much.

"You could have. I wouldn't judge you. I don't think Li would either." She glances to the other girl's closed door.

"I know." I bow my head. "This one is all me. I should've told you guys."

"I want us to be friends, Rory. We're living together and..." She plays with the hem of her sweatshirt tossed over her thin body. "I'm realizing now that my friends back home weren't actually that. It was all superficial bullshit. I don't want that anymore."

My heart softens toward my roommate. "A real friend would be nice. Friends," I amend, looking at Li's door too. "I need to go."

"Right, of course. Sorry." She shakes her head, sitting back down on the couch. "Good luck with the job hunt."

"Thanks." I smile at her before easing out of the room and down the hall.

It's fairly empty this early in the morning, but I can hear voices behind some of the doors.

Pushing the button for the elevator, I wait and head down. Outside the building the sky is a brilliant crystal clear blue with only a few random poufy clouds. As I walk toward the parking lot I inhale the fresh scent of the flowers planted all over.

With the medieval, almost castle-like buildings the campus reminds me of some sort of old school fortress or something from a fairytale. It's ironic, I suppose, considering I'm named after a princess that I'd end up here. Ironic or not, attending Aldridge University is not an opportunity I'm going to scoff at.

Hopping into my truck, I drive around the large campus, stopping at some of the various kiosks, the two bars, and couple of restaurants, but all of them tell me their spots are filled.

"Off campus it is," I mutter to myself, getting back into my truck. Honestly, this suits me better. I'll have to interact less with the student population.

Driving out through the stone arch that marks the entrance to the school, I hop on the highway, heading to the neighboring town. My heart rate spikes in recognition, knowing Mascen's townhome is somewhere nearby. I can't remember exactly where the Uber picked me up thanks to my epic hangover, but I do know I was around here.

I park on Main Street, feeding some coins into the meter. At least unlike on campus my old rickety truck doesn't stick out like a sore thumb.

A breeze stirs my hair, the long brown strands tickle my cheek as I walk down the street looking for any Help Wanted signs.

I come across a restaurant that has a sign posted that they're in need of staff and head inside.

It's large and semi-upscale looking. Photos cover every inch of the brick walls showcasing the history of the town. On the back wall the name of the restaurant, Marcelo's, is spelled out in marquee letters.

There's a bar to the right and I head over there.

A guy a couple years older than me wipes a glass

clean. His dark, nearly black, hair brushes his shoulders and his tanned skin is made even darker thanks to his crisp white button down.

"Hi," I say, cringing at how high-pitched my voice sounds.

He puts down the glass, looking me over and smiles. "How can I help you?" There's a twinkle of mischief in his chocolate eyes.

I toss a thumb over my shoulder. "I saw the sign in the window about hiring."

"Oh, yeah. Let me grab Izzy. Wait a second."

He sets the glass down and tosses the rag over his shoulder, weaving around the bar and through a swinging door. I slide onto a barstool, waiting for what I assume is the manager.

Smoothing my hands down my pants, I exhale a weighted breath, trying to rid myself of nerves. I've done plenty of interviews, but when you're desperate for work you can't help but be a little jittery. If I want to be able to afford groceries and treat myself to the occasional bag of Hershey Kisses then a job is a must.

A minute later the bartender returns, a woman trailing behind him that looks nearly identical in features, same colored skin, black hair, but their eyes are different colors. Where his are brown, hers are a unique shade of green.

"Hello, I'm Isabella, but I go by Izzy." She sticks her hand out and I note her well-manicured fingers.

"Aurora, but I prefer Rory." I shake her hand, smiling at her. She's beautiful, but not intimidatingly so.

78

There's something soft and kind in her eyes that puts me at ease.

"This is my brother Aldo," she nods in the direction of the bartender, "our parents own the restaurant but we're the ones who run it now."

Aldo snorts. "Yeah, and that's why Mama and Papa are *always* in the kitchen barking orders."

Izzy's cheeks turn pink, but she ignores her brother. "Well, then. Why don't we head to the back. I can get you an application and—"

"Please," I blurt out, almost embarrassed by how quickly the plea leaves me. "I need this job. I've done waitressing before. I've never had any issues in the past and I'm a hard worker."

Izzy's eyes stray to her brother and he shrugs. "We do need the help." She bites her lip. "What kind of waitressing did you do before?"

"In a local diner." It was in walking distance from the trailer before I inherited the truck so it was convenient. Plus, the owner Marty was always kind and looked out for me. He slipped more than one free meal my way once he caught on to the fact that I wasn't being fed at home. "I kind of did it all, waiting tables, cleaning up, register."

Izzy nods with each word that leaves my mouth. "Did you use a computer system like this?" She motions me behind the bar to a fancy monitor.

"Not quite this nice, but close enough. I think I could get the hang of it."

She twists her lips, exchanges a glance with her brother yet again, before finally nodding.

"All right, you have the job. How soon can you start?"

"Immediately."

Her eyes widen, but she smiles. "Perfect."

———

HOURS LATER, with all the paperwork filled out, I'm hard at work taking orders and tending to tables. I had to run out and buy proper clothes to wear for the job, changing in the restaurant bathroom once I got back, but I've already made enough in tips to cover the cost. As it moves into evening the restaurant is packed. Apparently it's a favorite with the locals.

Aldo and Izzy's parents showed up around three o'clock and have been keeping an eye on all the food that leaves the kitchen. I've already learned that Marcelo, their father, started this restaurant with their mother, Martina, when both were in their mid-twenties. It makes sense why they're having trouble handing over complete control to their children.

Every so often I catch Aldo watching me from the bar. Whenever our eyes meet he tosses a smile my way. He's definitely more easy-going than Izzy. She's plenty nice, sure, but I can already tell he's more of the goofball type. While he manages the bar, Izzy darts around, checking on tables and making sure the patrons are happy.

I head back to the kitchen to see if an order is ready when Izzy glides up to me. "Is everything going good? You're handling all the tables okay? I'm so sorry you got saddled with so many on your first day. It's not like Heather to call in sick and—"

I know if I don't silence her she'll continue to talk a mile a minute, and honestly if she doesn't take a breath soon I'm afraid she might pass out. "So far so good. If I need help with anything I'll let you know." I hope I don't sound rude, but I don't want her worrying about me when she's clearly already stressed to the max over running the restaurant while her parents oversee from the sidelines.

She lets out a relieved breath. "Good, that's good. I think we lucked out with you walking in here this afternoon."

I smile, pleased by her words. "I'm happy to be here." It may only be day one, but I feel like this is going to be a pretty good place to work.

Izzy darts off again, over to the bar to help Aldo since it's growing increasingly busy.

Grabbing an order for one of my tables from the kitchen I freeze when I walk out, the swinging door nearly smacking my ass. Across from me Mascen enters the restaurant, a leggy blonde in a red dress draped against his side. He says something to the host and then they're brought to a table.

In my fucking section.

I shouldn't be surprised at my sour luck at this point in my life, but of course I silently curse the gods who love to smite me. If they'd been seated just a few tables over they would've been put in Felicity's section, another waitress I only met briefly in passing.

"Rory," Izzy prompts, nodding her head toward my table waiting for the food on the tray I'm holding.

Shaking myself free of the prison my surprise put me in, I breeze to the table, a smile on my face as I set down the orders of eggplant parma and five-layer lasagna.

I have to admit, the lasagna looks fantastic and I'm debating taking some home. Just looking at it makes my stomach rumble.

"Can I get you anything else?" I ask the couple. They both tell me no. "Enjoy your meal. I'll be by to check on you."

Lowering the tray, I force my smile to stay plastered to my face as I walk over to the table Mascen sits at. The girl with him sits right beside him instead of across, leaning her whole body into him. The way her hand moves under the table she's either rubbing his thigh or giving him a handjob.

Please don't let it be a handjob. I do not want to have to clean cum off the seats.

"Good evening, my name is *Aurora*," I emphasize my full name, "and I'll be your server this evening. Can I get you started with an appetizer? Perhaps some wine?"

Mascen's eyes dart up to me, surprise evident on his face. Quickly, the surprise melts into anger. Even his nostrils flare.

Come on, Wade, what is it you're so pissed about?

He angles his body toward me, his date's hand falling away. In fact, he basically blocks her like she's not even there.

"What are you doing here, Rory?"

"Actually, it's Aurora," I correct him. He has no right to call me Rory, not when he looks at me like he wants to kill me. "And I happen to work here. I don't normally walk around dressed like this and holding an order pad just for fun." I motion to the tray tucked under my arm, the pad clasped in my hand. Holding the pen against the paper I arch a brow. "Now, what can I get you?"

His jaw ticks, that elegant, sculpted from stone bone actually moves, reminding me he's a real breathing human being despite his cold-eyed gaze.

"All right then, *Princess*. We'll take a bottle of your most expensive wine. Don't care what kind it is. I'll also have the house draft. Alessa, you look like the kind of girl who likes those prissy umbrella drinks," he says to his date. "Am I right?" I manage to see her nod, her eyes darting back and forth from Mascen to me like she's watching a tennis match. "Okay, so bring Alessa a strawberry basil limonata. For an appetizer we'll have the crab dip. Also, bring new silverware while you're at it. This is dirty."

I open my mouth to question how it's dirty when the dick face knocks it off the table.

"Got all that?"

"Absolutely." Picking up the cutlery from the floor I turn on my heel, suppressing the need to scream. He infuriates me like no one else and this only makes *three* encounters with him.

I enter the order into the system and swipe new silverware from the basket in the kitchen, breezing by the table to drop it off. If he knocks it off again I might shove a fork up his ass. It's guaranteed to get me fired, probably arrested, but I don't care.

"Here are those drinks, Rory," Aldo calls out, when I pass by.

"Thanks." I smile at him and he winks. Grabbing the tray with the beer, fruity drink, bottle of wine, and two glasses, I reluctantly head back to Mascen's table. I set everything down, managing to keep a smile on my face as I do, and open the bottle of wine, filling each glass halfway. "Have you all decided what you'd like to eat?"

I bet Barbie gets a salad.

"Umm," Barbie leans around his big body, batting her eyes up at him, then looking at me, "I'll have the berry salad."

I knew it.

"And for you, Satan?"

Mascen's lips twitch and he attempts to hide the movement behind his fingers. "I'll have the steak marsala. Rare."

"Bloody unlike your cold dead heart. Got it." A choked laugh stutters out of his throat and he quickly turns it into a cough. "I'll put that right in."

I turn around, my ponytail swinging. Putting their order in I check on my tables and greet a man who just sat down. I don't feel tired yet, but I know when it's time for me to clock out the exhaustion will hit. It'll be worth it to have money and not worry. Unfortunately, grocery shopping will have to take place tomorrow.

When their order is up I grab it. Someone else might spit on his food for what a dick he's been since I saw him outside Cole's room, but I'm better than that. Somewhat.

I slide the salad in front of Barbie and then lift his steak off the tray.

"Here's your bloody rare steak, Hannibal Lecter. I hate to tell you it's from a cow and not the human corpses you normally gnaw on, maybe the local morgue can help you out or there's always murder."

His date is once again looking between the two of us. I can't blame her for what's going on and honestly, she's probably a nice girl and I should stop calling her Barbie, even if it's only in my head.

"Such a mouth on you. Bring me another drink." He lifts his empty beer glass.

"Right away, Dracula."

As I'm walking away I hear his date ask what's going on with all the nicknames and if he slept with me or something. I'm too far away to hear his reply. What a shame. I do give my eyes a hard roll though at the preposterous idea of the two of us ever bumping uglies. Mascen is wealthy. I'm the hired help.

"Aldo, another of the house draft." I tap the bar as I walk past.

"You got it, Rory."

I drop the check off at one of my tables and come back for the beer, taking it to Mascen. His date is missing, the bathroom I assume, so I set down the glass and walk away.

Heading into the back I fix my ponytail and sip some water. Catching my breath is impossible with so many people out there, so I turn back around, smile ready, and get back to work.

When I finally make it to Mascen's table, Barbie is still gone and he's almost finished eating.

"Where'd your date go, Heartless?"

Those gray eyes flick up from his plate to look at me. I swallow past the lump in my throat that's suddenly lodged there.

Why does it feel like he can see all of me, the dark pit of my heart, my fears, the rejections.

Mascen Wade is crawling his way under my skin and I don't like it one bit. The last thing I need to do is get involved with a rock star's son in any capacity. My life is better off simple. Normal. If I wasn't crushed under his boot by him, the media would do it for him.

"Why are you staring at me, Sleeping Beauty? Are you hoping I'll kiss you and wake you from whatever walking nightmare you're living?"

I can't believe I was blatantly staring at him. Fuck my life.

"Where'd your date go?"

"Don't know, don't care. She was annoying anyway. Nice tits, but not worth it. I needed to get out though and A is the first letter in the alphabet, so here we are."

He leans back, flicking his fingers lazily. He's the picture of ease, totally unbothered by his date walking out on him.

I blink at him, at a loss for words as he picks up his beer, taking a sip. I notice the wine is completely untouched. I'm not a huge drinker, despite my actions at Harvey's, but it still makes me sad to see a good bottle of wine go to waste.

"If I were her I'd leave your sorry ass too."

His eyes drift indolently up my body before connecting with my brown ones. "You already did."

That stupid lump is back in my throat. I try to swallow it down but it goes nowhere. "I was eight years old," I hiss, leaning down to him, nearly in his face. "I didn't exactly *choose* to leave. I had to go, and believe me, every day of my life has been as close to hell as it gets."

His tongue barely flicks out, moistening that full, pouty mouth. A mouth I definitely don't find sensual and completely kissable. "Looks like you haven't gotten burned ... yet."

With that, he stands suddenly, and I rear back before his beefy shoulder can knock me in the face. He pulls out his wallet, slamming down a wad of cash on the table that's more than enough to cover the bill.

I watch frozen in place as he turns on his heel leaving the last of his food uneaten and heads out the door.

He never looks back.

TEN

MASCEN

THE CIGARETTE SMOKE CLOGS MY THROAT, NEARLY choking me. I didn't intend to suck down three in a row after walking out of Marcelo's but here we are. Leaning against my car, I know I need to go and stop hanging out in the parking lot like a creep. I wanted to figure out which vehicle belongs to Rory—*Aurora*—but since they're all pretty basic it could be any of them. My first instinct said the yellow Volkswagen beetle belonged to her, but the longer I've stood here in the dark like a fucking creep the more certain I become that it's the clunker truck parked in the corner. Pathetically sad and abandoned just like her.

Finishing the last of the cigarette I toss it to the ground with the others.

Reaching for my car door, I get inside, but I still don't fucking leave. I will myself to put my car in reverse and get the hell out of dodge, but my limbs don't listen. I sit frozen, watching patrons trickle from the restaurant into the lot.

Alessa was the first female contact in my phone, and I remembered briefly her slipping me her number last year after a game. She was a cheerleader—trim body, okay face, nice tits. I thought she'd be a good distraction, and I'd planned to take her to a hotel—I didn't bring chicks home, ever—but I hadn't been prepared for fucking Rory to be working there. Our waitress no less.

It instantly pissed me off seeing her. The whole reason I was there with Alessa in the first place was to get my mind off of her. Then she opened her mouth and started insulting me in amusing little ways. I enjoyed it way too much. I liked her barbs, the way her tongue lashed out at me. God, how I wanted to tame that mouth of hers.

I smack the heel of my hand against the steering wheel in frustration.

I shouldn't spare Rory another one of my thoughts, but I know it's a lie if I say I won't.

She's creeping under my skin little by little—a nagging itch I can't and won't scratch.

My phone starts ringing. Digging into my pocket I pull it out and find my mom calling. I'm not really in the mood or any shape to talk to her, but I answer anyway. She's my mom after all—besides with her super freaky mom powers she'd know if I was purposely ignoring her.

"Hey," I answer, my voice a little deeper than normal.

Her voice comes through the car speaker. "How's my baby boy?"

I grin at her words. Leave it to my mom to make me feel better with only a few words. "Uh ... okay."

I back out of the parking lot, pulling onto Main Street. "That doesn't sound very convincing. Is this a bad time?"

"No, no it's fine."

"I just wanted to let you know I mailed you a care package today. I made blondies since they're your favorite. I also packed some tea packets for you— chamomile, chai, and that sleepytime tea you love. Oh, and I figured out how to make my own blends so I sent you one of those as well to try. If you like it I'll send more."

Her rambling brings a smile to my face. I love that even though I'm twenty and living away from home most of the year, she still looks out for me. Others might find it annoying, but I like that my mom wants to be an active part of my life.

Am I throwing a little shade at my dad? Hell yeah.

"There are some other surprises in there too," she adds when I don't speak.

"Thanks, Mom. It means a lot. I'll keep an eye out for the package."

"You don't sound right—and don't even think about telling me I'm wrong. I'm your mother. I know you better than you know yourself."

The light turns red and I slow to a stop. "It's nothing."

She clucks her tongue. "Mascen, talk to me."

I watch the cars driving through the intersection, knowing with each passing second that she's growing more worried, imagining something far worse than the reality.

"Do you remember Rory?" My voice drops like someone might overhear me.

"Rory?"

"Aurora—Rory Abbott, from next door." Next door is a stretch since there were several acres of land between our homes.

"Oh, the Abbotts," she blurts, her voice ringing with clarity. "Yes, I remember them. You two were good buddies. What about it?"

"I saw her."

"You saw her?" she repeats. "Where? Are you sure?"

"Yeah. Positive."

"Huh…" she trails off, and even though I can't see her I have no doubt that she's wearing her thinking face. "It was so sad how all that happened."

"Mhmm, yeah," I mumble. The light changes and I drive forward.

"So, what about her? I'm assuming there's more," she prompts, like I unfortunately knew she would.

"She goes to my school. She goes *here*. To Aldridge."

It's like I'm trying to remind myself that she's in this town, at my school, in my space.

"Oh, wow." Another pause. "That's surprising."

"Yeah, it is," I agree.

"I'm surprised that poor girl hasn't changed her last name."

"Maybe she has, I know I would." *Sometimes I wish I could. It's harder being a Wade than people realize.* Pulling into the driveway I push the button for the garage and roll inside. "I'm home, so I'm going to go. Coach wants us up for conditioning early."

"All right, I'll let you go then. I love you."

"Love you too, Momma."

When I lay my head on the pillow that night, dreams of a little girl invade my mind, her brown pigtails swinging, pink glasses sitting crooked on her nose.

ELEVEN

RORY

"UGH, I CAN'T STUDY HERE," KENNA GROANS, sitting up and letting the heavy textbook she was reading fall onto the floor with a clatter.

I glance over from my spot in the chair, typing on my laptop. I have a paper due in my English class and I've been putting it off. It's not like me to not get my homework done immediately but the topic, discussing classic poems and how the history of their time overlaps into their meaning and how it can be interpreted differently today, doesn't excite me.

Li peeks over top of her computer, a sour gummy

worm hanging out of her mouth. "Why not?"

Kenna stands up, grabbing a bottle of root beer from the fridge. "I need a change of scenery. If I have to keep staring at these beige walls I'll lose my mind."

"We could go to the library." They both glance at me when I voice my suggestion.

"That's not a bad idea," Kenna concedes. "Li, you in?"

The three of us agreed early in the week to spend Saturday studying and catching up on homework before going out. I've spent several nights this week working and while I would have preferred to work tonight too since it's Saturday, I knew I needed to get this essay done and spend time with the girls. Besides, if all I do is school and work I'll burn out fast and I can't afford that with all the years I have ahead of me. Everyone deserves a night off now and then.

Li chews and swallows her sour gummy worm. "Library means no snacks though."

Kenna's face falls. Brightening she argues, "True, but that'll make us work faster so we can eat."

Li shrugs, her lips flattening. "All right. I'm in."

The three of us gather what we need in our back-packs and head across campus to the massive building.

I've been a few times in the month I've been at school. It's my favorite place on campus. Large and imposing, there are three stories of aisle after aisle of bookshelves. Long wooden tables line the middle for students to work at, with a few smaller tables and chairs tucked into corners.

Trudging up the stone steps into the library, a wistful smile touches my lips. Almost daily I find myself having a moment where I'm overcome with joy because I'm *here*. I did it. I made it. All on my own.

Often times my mom wanted to make me think I couldn't do anything or be anything without her. It was a lie to try to trap me.

Inside, I follow behind the girls, gawking around in awe at the rich wood shelves, glittering chandeliers, and the magic every library has to transport us to another world.

You'd think since I've been here multiple times I'd be over the beauty of it, but I'm not.

"Here's one." Kenna slams her bag down on one of the long tables. There are two people at the other end with plenty of empty chairs between them and us.

Li slides in across from Kenna and I pull out the chair beside her.

Placing my laptop onto the table the three of us get to work, silence stretching between us. Perhaps it's the magical powers of the library, but I'm able to get in the zone and within two hours my paper is done and the girls are finishing up.

I stretch my arms above my head, stifling a yawn.

Closing her laptop Kenna groans. "That's it. I'm finished. I can't even *think* about homework for at least another twenty-four hours."

"Agreed." Li begins packing her things away in her bag.

"Harvey's for dinner and drinks?"

I have to stifle my cringe at Kenna's suggestion. We haven't been back since our first night out and I really don't want to have a repeat. The solution is simple though. No drinking.

"I could use a drink." Li stands, shrugging her bag around her shoulders. "But I need to shower and change first."

"Me too." I sniff discreetly at myself.

"I'm going to third wheel that." Kenna cackles, flipping her hair over her shoulder.

Outside, we walk side by side back to our dorm. The sun hasn't set yet, but it will shortly. For now, I soak in what's left of the sun's rays, knowing it'll be gone by the time we go to the bar.

"How's the job going?" Li's voice breaks me out of my thoughts.

"Pretty good. I like it." Izzy has mellowed out some, she was able to hire two more waiters so that things aren't stretched so thin. I get along well with everyone and the tips aren't bad. I feel like things have worked out better than I could've hoped for.

"Maybe I should get a job," Kenna muses, tilting her head to the side.

"Why?" Li blurts, stifling a giggle. "You're rich."

"My *dad's* rich," she corrects. "Besides, I think a job could be fun."

Only someone with money could think working and going to school *could be fun*. I don't tell her that. I don't want to start a squabble over a trivial comment. She's a nice girl and I know she didn't mean to come off rude.

I reach the dorm first and swipe my keycard, letting us inside the building. We grab the elevator up to our floor.

"Rock, paper, scissors for the shower?" I arch a brow, waiting for their response. Both nod and we stand in a circle. "Rock, paper, scissors, shoot." I do paper and they both do rock. "I go first," I sing-song, adding in a little shimmy.

Stepping back, they go again, Kenna doing scissors and Li paper. Li's shoulders fall dejectedly. "You guys suck. Third it is."

"Hey, it's the fairest way." I flick the end of her braid playfully as I pass her to my room so I can grab my shower stuff. I learned quick to keep it in my room. Kenna likes to 'try' everyone else's stuff.

With my shower caddy in hand I lock myself in the bathroom. I let the water heat up, fogging the mirror, and turn on my music to play.

Stripping out of the sweatpants and t-shirt I wore today I leave them in a pile on the floor. I'll add them to the hamper in my room. I need to make a trip down to the laundry room on the first-floor tomorrow.

Finishing my shower, Kenna hurries inside the steamy room while I lock myself in my room to get ready, putting in extra effort to look somewhat put together.

I blow dry and curl my hair, even taking the time to put on some makeup. I figure if I'm going out I might as well look the part.

Two hours later the three of us are ready and pile into Kenna's car once again.

No drinking tonight, Rory. None whatsoever.

The parking lot of Harvey's is full and as soon as my heeled booties touch down in the gravel parking lot I can feel the thump of the music.

Kenna lets out a little squeal, pointing ahead of her. "Five-dollar margarita night! Yes!" I don't tell her, but back home there were dollar margarita nights. "I'm going to get shit-faced. What about you?" she addresses me.

I hold my hands up in surrender. "Not tonight."

"Excellent. You're the DD then." She passes me the keys to her luxury SUV and I swear even the key fob feels expensive.

Li pats my shoulder, grinning at me. "Thanks for taking one for the team."

"It's not a problem."

Alcohol and I are currently not on speaking terms.

I've spotted Cole a few times on campus and he always smiles when he sees me, but we've never spoken again. I've heard murmurings on campus about him. Apparently, he's a scholarship student here because he's incredible at basketball. The way people talk it's like they expect him to become a legend or something. Like Mascen he's a pretty big deal.

"Time to relax, ladies." Kenna does a little shimmy before opening the door into the bar.

The two of us have very different ideas of relaxing. For me, it's lounging in my PJs, sans makeup, binge-watching a TV show. A loud, chaotic, bar filled with drunk college students does not fall into the relaxing category for me.

Kenna breezes in, pushing her way through the crowd. It seems a lot of people here don't bother with a table, instead opting to stand around and drink while they socialize. The dance floor is empty for the moment, but it's still early in the evening. I have a feeling in the next hour it'll be packed with sweaty dancing bodies.

We find a high-top table with three chairs and snag it. It's near the bar and Kenna raises her fingers in signal. Within seconds a frazzled waitress appears at our table.

"What can I get y'all?"

"Margaritas for us and…" Kenna pauses eyeing me.

"Dr. Pepper for me. And chicken tenders."

The waitress is gone, her hair flipping around her shoulders as she goes.

"Chicken tenders?" Li tries not to smile.

I shrug. "Chicken tenders are my weakness."

And luckily, if memory serves me correct, the food was true greasy bar food, not the gourmet version I was expecting.

The waitress drops off their margaritas and both girls sip happily at them. When half of Kenna's is gone she stands, wiggling her hips. "I'm going to go pick a song from the juke box. Any requests ladies?"

"One Direction," I mutter, totally kidding, but she grins from ear to ear.

"I love them! Li, what about you?"

"Anything that makes me dance is fine by me."

Kenna claps her hands excitedly. "I'll be right back."

I watch her push through the crowd to the opposite side of the restaurant. Kenna is always so full of energy and almost constantly happy. I wish I had a little bit of her pep instead of being so cynical.

Li sips at her drink, tucking a piece of long straight black hair behind her ear. "How are you doing handling school and working?"

"Pretty good, I guess. I have to do it, so I'm learning how to balance my time so I study and get homework done on time."

"I don't think I could do it." She bites her bottom lip lightly. "I kind of envy you for that."

I wrinkle my nose. "For working?"

A light laugh leaves her. "I know I sound like a spoiled brat. I'm lucky that my parents are paying my way and I don't have to worry, but you're so … composed. You have your shit together. It seems like you can handle anything. That's what I envy." Her eyes sparkle with humor. "I certainly don't have my ducks in a row. Those losers are always getting lost and waddling away."

Kenna pops up back at the table, sliding onto her stool. "All right, ladies, I put a song on rotation for each of us. We're going to tear up the dance floor."

"Oh, no, no, no," I chant, swishing my arms in an X shape through the air. "No dancing for me tonight. Nope. Not happening. I'm on babysitting duty."

"Babysitting? There aren't any kids here," Kenna blurts, the rest of her margarita already gone.

Li elbows her. "She meant us."

Kenna's lips part in a perfect O. Pulling her brown hair over her shoulder she grins at me. "I knew that."

Kenna's not dumb. In fact, I think she's one of those deceptively smart people, but sometimes things leave her mouth before she thinks.

"Chicken tenders and Dr. Pepper." The waitress sets down my basket of tenders with honey mustard.

"Thanks." I pick up a fry, chewing on the end of it. Kenna reaches for one and I playfully swat her hand away. "Get your own."

Pouting her bottom lip she gives me puppy eyes. "Please, just one?"

"Fine." I stick my tongue out at her and slide the basket her way. "Li, you want one?"

"Sure." She shrugs, grabbing two and winking at me.

"Ooh, these are delicious. We need a whole basket." Kenna hops up yet again, running off to find the waitress.

Li props her elbow on the table and her head in her hand. "Sometimes I wonder if that girl ever runs out of energy."

"I don't think she does."

Kenna has the personality of someone who always has to be doing something or going somewhere. I don't know her that well yet, it's not like any of us have talked about the deep stuff or dark secrets of our pasts, but sometimes I think that she's running from something.

Munching on a fry, I look around the bar to see if I recognize any familiar faces from my classes. I spot a girl from math class. She catches my eye and waves.

"I put an order in for us, Li." Kenna slides onto the barstool, two fresh margaritas in hand. She gives one to Li, tilting her head to the side as she looks at me. "Are you sure you don't want a drink? We can always Uber home if you change your mind."

"I'm positive."

I shudder at what happened last time, my chicken tenders suddenly sitting heavy in my stomach. I'll never drink that much again. I've learned my limit and I won't exceed it.

It isn't long before the waitress drops off the food for Li and Kenna. They both dig in and I push my now empty basket to the side. Somehow in the thirty minutes we've been here the bar has become even more packed. Soon it'll be standing room only. The press of bodies closing in makes me feel a tad claustrophobic, but I refuse to let it get to me too much.

Suddenly, the opening notes of One Direction's *What Makes You Beautiful* comes on.

"It's your song!" Kenna cries, pushing her basket aside.

"I was kidding about the One Direction thing," I groan as she tugs my hand, pulling me from the chair.

"I don't care, we're dancing."

"No, no, no," I laugh, trying to escape her.

"Come on, it'll be fun." Li joins us, pushing at my back to help her get me on the dance floor.

"Yeah, but you guys are buzzed, I'm perfectly sober."

"Who gives a shit?" Kenna smiles at me, eyes twinkling. "You only live once, so *live*. Make a fool of yourself, make out with a random guy, just *dance*."

"Fine," I agree reluctantly.

Fully on the dance floor now, the three of us start dancing, shout-singing the lyrics while we do. As hard as it is for me, in that moment I allow myself to let go. I'm not the girl whose whole life changed course thanks to a single moment. I don't let guilt weigh me down. And I don't give a single fuck what anyone watching might think.

Sweat quickly dampens my skin from the heat of lights and packed bodies.

I spin in a circle, singing the poppy song at the top of my lungs, when I get a prickle on the back of my neck like I'm being watched.

Turning to face the opposite direction I see Cole sitting at a table, beer in hand. He's laughing at something one of his friends has said, but he's not the one watching me.

Even across the room Mascen's gray eyes have the ability to freeze me in place. A shiver makes its way down my spine and I feel my nipples tighten, probably visible through my shirt now if the way his eyes narrow are any indication.

Everything about him, from his stormy eyes, sharp

cheekbones, and full lips, screams danger. He's everything I should stay away from. Not just because I used
to know him, but because my gut knows he'd ruin me in
every possible way.

He frowns as he watches me, steepling his fingers in
front of his lips. A black baseball cap sits backwards on
his head.

Suddenly, his eyes leave me and that's when I notice
the blonde beside him leaning in to whisper in his ear.
He shakes his head at whatever she says, muttering
something in rapid succession. She rolls her eyes and
gets up, moving to a different guy.

Swallowing, I force myself to look away from him.

I don't feel like dancing anymore and thankfully the
song ends giving me an easy escape.

The girls and I start back to the table, but I don't
make it far before a large muscular arm loops around
me. I spin into the massive body, caught off guard. My
hands flying up to a hard chest. Stupidly, I expect to see
Mascen towering above me, but instead it's Cole. His
amber eyes glitter down upon me, his grin the kind of
smile that should make my stomach do flips but I ... I
feel nothing.

"I haven't seen you around in a while, Rory." His
smile is infectious and I can't help finding myself
smiling back. I hate to admit I'm surprised that he
remembered me. I figured after the day he chased me
down that'd be the last I'd ever see of him. Guys like
him have plenty of girls to keep their interest. I'm not
anyone special.

"I've been busy with class." I tuck a piece of hair behind my ear, my head tilted back to look at him. I don't remember him being so tall. I guess before I was too drunk to notice and the day on campus too surprised by his sudden appearance.

"Yeah, yeah, I get how that is. Been busy too." He chuckles, the sound warm and husky, almost sexy sounding. "You wanna join us?" He points to his table and I glance over, catching Mascen's narrowed gaze.

"I'm sorry." I frown, rocking back on my heels. "I'm here with my friends."

"Right, of course." He continues to blind me with his bright smile. "How about a dance then?"

This time I'm the one to laugh, my cheeks heating. "Well, remember how that went last time?"

Somehow his smile grows impossibly bigger. "All the more reason to dance — I need to give you something to remember me by."

Biting my lip, I glance back in the direction of the table Kenna and Li are at, but can't see them. Blowing out a breath, I nod. "One dance." I wiggle a finger, showing him I'm serious when I say *one*.

"Sure thing, beautiful." He takes my hand, tugging me back onto the dance floor.

I don't even know what song is playing, but I follow his lead.

Cole is a surprisingly good dancer, moving his feet and hips in time with the music. I let him guide me, laughing when I step on his toes by mistake.

"It's okay," he coaxes, "keep going." His large hand

settles low on my waist and he pulls me as close to him as I can get. His pelvis grinds into me to the beat of the song, his eyes never leaving mine. But while I try to return his look, I can still feel the searing gaze of Mascen following us. His eyes feel like a brand on the back of my neck. There's a sting there I want to rub, but I don't dare lift my hand to feel the skin. I know he'd get way too much satisfaction out of the gesture.

I let Cole spin me around, a giggle bursting out of my throat.

I feel free, light, as I dance with him. I never got to experience things like this before. When I wasn't in school I was working. I didn't have time for a social life. The hookups I had were about mutual satisfaction and not about genuinely getting to know each other.

The song ends, bleeding into another. I try to pull away from him anyway, but he grins down at me. "One more, pretty girl."

I nod, because frankly I'm enjoying myself despite Mascen's death glare from a distance. If he's tried to warn Cole away from me it's clearly not working. But from my brief interactions with him in the last month he doesn't seem like the type to say anything at all. No, Mascen Wade is the kind of guy who keeps everything to himself, letting it build until one day he explodes, taking out innocent bystanders in the process.

It ends up being three more songs before Cole and I part. He heads back to his table and after a brief check in with the girls I make my way down the hall to the restroom. Slipping inside there's thankfully one empty stall and I relieve my protesting bladder.

"Did you see Mascen tonight?" One girl says from in front of the mirrors, her conversation impossible not to hear.

"I know! Talk about moody and broody." Another says. "He looks hot as hell pissed off, though."

The first one gives a snort. "He's hot any time. That baseball cap? I want him to fuck me while he wears that."

I have to suppress my snicker as I pull up my pants and flush the toilet.

When I exit the stall they've left, so the sinks are empty. I wash my hands, taking in my flushed cheeks in the reflection of the mirror. A light sheen of perspiration clings to my skin and my hair has definitely looked better. But the smile on my face says it all. It's the genuine happy smile of someone who isn't afraid anymore.

Drying my hands, I open the door to leave the bathroom. A squeak flies out of my throat when a large hand closes around my wrist. The heat of the person pierces my skin, their intoxicating smell hitting me a second later.

Citrus and wood invades my senses, my brain whispering *Mascen* to me.

I find myself yanked into a dark closet and even though I can't see him I feel him. His presence is always overwhelming but in the tiny closet I'm certain I'm going to suffocate from his proximity.

"Why are you *here?*" he growls, his breath fanning across my cheek, the slight smell of whiskey clinging to his lips. I bet it's the most expensive kind the bar serves. Mascen doesn't do *cheap*, and that's exactly what he thinks I am.

"H-Here?" I stuttered, my heart racing—not in fear, but *excitement*. "Spending time with my roommates." Somehow I manage to sound breathy, but sure of myself, my backbone firmly in place.

"Not *here* as in Harvey's. Why are you at *this* school? Why Tennessee? Why are you suddenly in my life again? Invading my space. You're every-fucking-where." His lips are suddenly right beside my cheek, brushing against my sensitive skin with each and every word. I'm thankful for the fact he can't see the goose-bumps pimpling my skin or my hardening nipples begging for his touch. "I can't fucking escape you."

He grows quiet and I realize the questions I thought were rhetorical are in fact very real.

"I … you want an answer?"

"Yes, Sleeping Beauty, I want a fucking answer. That's why I asked the question. I'm not in the habit of wasting words. Life's too short not to say shit you mean."

I can't see him but I know he rolled his eyes at me.

"I … this is the school I wanted to go to." I try to keep my voice calm, but I'm sure he notices the quiver to my words, all because of his proximity. "I got a schol-arship, so here I am. As for bumping into each other…" I gather my breath, because he's stealing all the oxygen in the small room. "It's a large campus, but not *that* large."

"Did you know I went here?"

His words take me aback. "Excuse me? Are you implying I chose this school because I found out you went here? I haven't seen you since I was eight years old. Don't flatter yourself Mascen."

He lets out a humorless laugh. "Still ironic, though, huh, Princess? Out of all the universities in the entire United States you choose this one. Where I am. Reunited once again."

"Why did you really pull me into the closet?" My pulse stutters when I feel the brush of his nose against my neck. "I don't think it was to discuss why I'm attending school here."

His laughter rumbles through his chest and I feel the vibration in mine. "I wanted to tell you to stay away from Cole."

"Why?" My treacherous breath catches when his lips brush against mine. It's not a kiss. His lips are there and then gone.

Against my right ear, he leans in so his mouth touches the sensitive skin with every word. "Because you don't belong to *him*."

The word comes out as a growl, making my breath catch audibly. Before I can find words, he opens the door, light flooding inside for one second, and then he's gone leaving me wondering if he was ever there at all.

Mascen Wade seems more like a ghost than a human.

TWELVE

MASCEN

LEAVING AURORA BEHIND IN THE CLOSET, I WALK UP to the table, downing my fresh drink the waitress left in my absence. Conversation continues at the table, my friends oblivious to my thunderous mood. Slapping bills down on the table, I announce, "I'm out. Enjoy your night. There's more than enough to cover another round."

"Whoa, whoa, whoa. Leaving? Now?" Teddy looks at me incredulously, his large hand wrapped around a beer bottle. He flicks his blond hair out of his eyes, narrowing his gaze. "What the fuck man? Not having any fun?"

"Just not in the mood."

I dig my keys out of my pocket, twirling the keychain around my finger.

I'm not going to stand there and argue with them, so I lift my hand in a goodbye wave. Cole arches his brow, approaching from the bar now with nachos.

"Leaving?" I nod in response. "Cool, see you later."

At least Cole knows it's a waste to try to convince me to stay.

Pushing my way through the crowded bar, I ignore the guys trying to pull me into conversation and the girls hoping to slip me their number.

My car is parked right up front and I slip inside, pulling out in such a hurry that the gravel kicks up a cloud of dust so thick I can't see Harvey's in the rearview mirror.

I should go home, but I know I won't be able to clear my head there.

Instead, I find myself showing up at the local batting cages. I might be Aldridge's star pitcher, but it doesn't mean I don't get satisfaction from hitting some balls either.

The lot is pretty much empty, which bodes well for me. But I've never run into any of the guys from the team here anyway. Hopping out, I grab my gym bag and head inside.

"Hey, Mark." I greet the owner, tossing up my hand.

Mark lowers the motocross magazine he was reading, narrowing his eyes. "What's wrong with you? You only show up here when you're in a pissy mood."

He's not lying. "Just life," I reply with. "You okay that I'm here?"

The gray-haired man lets out a gruff laugh. "You're always welcome here, Wade. Now get in there and out of my hair."

I shake my head at the man, sliding twenty bucks across the counter. He narrows his eyes, since he's always telling me not to pay, but knows better than to argue with me now.

Nodding at him, I open the door, heading for the room with the cages. I pick the one on the far end. It's the one I always choose if it's available.

Setting my bag down, I pull out my gloves, grab a bat and let all thoughts empty from my mind.

———

"DUDE, WHERE HAVE YOU BEEN?" Cole blurts, the moment I come upstairs from the garage. It's late, after two in the morning. Mark lives in a house behind the cages and let me stay as long as I promised to lock up when I left. I look around, half-expecting to see Rory here. Thankfully, it looks like Cole is the only one home.

"Went to the cages." Striding across the room to the kitchen I grab a bottle of water from the fridge, leaving my back to him.

"You didn't want to hang at the bar with us, but you went to the cages instead?"

I roll my eyes, but he can't see. "Would you be as perplexed if I'd been with a girl?"

He makes a noise in his throat as I close the fridge. "You've been weird lately. Weirder than you normally are."

Twisting the cap back on the water I set it on the counter and swipe an orange from the center bowl.

"Thanks, man. I feel the love."

The leather of the couch protests and I know he's getting up. The next moment he stands beside me at the kitchen counter, his arms braced on the stone. "What's going on?"

I look up from the orange peels, meeting my friend's eyes. "Nothing."

This time he's the one to roll his eyes. "You're so full of shit. You think no one can smell it, or they'll overlook it because of your last name. I'm not that person. I'm your best fucking friend. Don't bullshit me."

I twist my lips, my fingers sticky with juice. "I don't want to talk about it."

He shakes his head. "Whatever, dude. You know, sometimes I wonder why I put up with your sorry ass, but then I remember I care about you. You're like a brother, and yeah, you might be pissing me off, but whenever you decide the great Mascen Wade wants to talk about it I'll be waiting."

"I don't talk about my feelings," I bite out when he turns to leave the kitchen.

He looks back, one hand braced on the doorframe. "That may be so, but you need to. I don't know what the fuck you have all bottled up inside you, but some- thing tells me it's more than you want to acknowledge. If you don't one of these days it's going to suffocate you."

I bite the inside of my cheek as he stares at me a second longer. With an exhale, he leaves the kitchen. A second later the TV turns off in the living room. Another second and the stairs creak with his steps.

"Fuck!" I toss the half-peeled orange off the counter. It slams into a cabinet before falling to the floor. I thrust my sticky fingers through the strands of my hair.

Crouching on the floor I pick up the mess, tossing the ruined orange in the trash before wiping a damp towel over the tacky residue left behind.

I have so little control over anything anymore, least of all myself.

THIRTEEN

RORY

I HURRY ACROSS CAMPUS FROM ONE CLASS TO THE
next, a hot tea clasped in my hands because I'm *trying* to
cut back on my amount of coffee. Only, this chai tea
stuff tastes like shit and I'll end up buying coffee
anyway. Honestly, you must be related to Satan to like
the stuff.

I toss the offending cup into a trashcan I pass by
before entering the brick structure my psychology class
is housed in. It's my favorite of all my classes. I've
always loved exploring the human psyche. What makes
people tick, make certain choices, how our personalities

can be determined by our upbringing. All of it is fascinating to me.

Opening the door, I walk down the stairs, sliding into my usual seat by a girl named Julie. She's already seated, laptop up and ready on a new blank document to take notes. I'm not envious at all of the coffee by her side.

Actually I totally am, so much so I'm tempted to steal it, but I refuse to be that much of a coffee fiend.

Lowering my backpack to the ground, I pull my own laptop out so I'll be prepared for the extensive note taking Professor Simmons expects of us. It's not that I mind note taking, but he speaks so quickly that I have to type inhumanly fast to keep up. By the end of the lecture my fingers are always left sore and slightly swollen around the knuckles. I wish I was exaggerating.

I flash a smile at Connor when he sits down beside me. It's funny to me despite the lack of assigned seating we always end up in the same seats.

"No coffee today?" he asks in a sleep-ridden voice. His hair is a mess like he did, in fact, roll out of bed before rushing here.

"Thought I'd try tea." I stick out my tongue and roll my eyes for good measure.

He chuckles. "Big mistake, I take it?"

"You have no idea."

Professor Simmons enters the room, shuffles some papers, and gets straight to his lecture.

My fingers fly across the keyboard as he speaks, not

slowing until he utters the one word I'm not prepared to hear.

Suicide.

My fingers stop all together, my breath held in my throat when my lungs refuse to cooperate.

Over the years, I've learned I can't avoid the topic of suicide. Whether it's referenced on TV, in a book, or any other number of ways. Despite that, sometimes, like now, it hits me harder than other times. Taking me back to eight-years-old when my whole life was forever changed *because* of that word.

Professor Simmons keeps talking, but I don't hear him, not over the rush of blood roaring like an ocean in my ears.

"Daddy! Daddy! Look what I made!"

"...Daddy?"

"DADDY! NO!"

I grab my stuff, my laptop under my arm, and run from the classroom. Heads turn my way and I hear the professor tell everyone to get back to work.

Bursting through the doors, I inhale the first lungful of air I've taken since he uttered that word.

Running down the hall, I stop when I reach the end, leaning against the wall since my body is suddenly too heavy to hold up.

Coming home from school, armed with my A+ project in hand, I'd been so excited to show my father. Ramsey Abbott was known as a Senator by most people, but to me he was just Daddy.

Until that day.

When he hung himself from a beam in our family room.

At first I didn't understand what I saw, but by the time it registered in my child brain it was too late to unsee. My mom came in behind me, her scream shrill at the sight of his limp dangling body.

Sometimes I can still smell the awful scent of human bile permeating the room.

"Hazel! Stay outside," she'd screamed, grabbing me by the shoulders and ushering me back out. "Take your sister!"

Everything happened in a flurry then, people coming in and out of the house, other politicians showing up, and no one seemed to understand why a man as beloved as my father would take his own life.

That is until a week later, during his funeral no less, the news leaked the story of the century all about how my father was taking bribes and covering up dirty crimes.

Senator Ramsey Abbott ceased being a good person in the eyes of anyone that day.

We lost everything.

The house, the cars, every cent.

We were the ones that paid for his crimes.

That day, too, was the last day my mother ever cried. After that, she just stopped caring.

It's funny too, considering the corruption that runs deep in politics that my father was singled out. I guess the difference is he got caught.

A tear drips off my chin, shocking me back into

reality. I hate crying. My mom fed on my tears, said it made me weak. I guess since she never cried anymore that made her the strong one.

I hate that her words get to me even now. She's states away, still in Florida, doing God knows what to keep a roof over her head. As much as I want to say I don't care, I wish that were true. All these years a small granule inside of me, as minuscule as a grain of sand, has loved her despite her flaws and hoped she'd get her life back on track for Hazel and me.

She never has and I know deep down she never will.

After my father's betrayal, she couldn't cope, spiraling out of control.

I know she truly loved him, and his suicide hurt her like a gaping wound, but it was the loss of the money that drove her mad.

I've always vowed to myself to never let money become such a priority in my life. I want enough to own a house, put food on the table, and cover other necessities. As long as I have that I'll be happy.

"What are you doing sniveling in the hallway? Princesses do seem to cry in all those Disney movies. Very woe-is-me-esque if you ask me."

I look up to see Mascen strolling down the hall, jeans hugging his narrow waist and thick thighs, a heather gray t-shirt molded to his muscular torso, and that fucking baseball cap on backwards.

A baseball cap should not be so sexy.

"What do you want, Wade?" I growl out, bending down to put my laptop in my bag. I try to inconspicuously dry my tears, but I know he sees. Mascen Wade seems to see everything. His boots come to a stop inches from my backpack, the heat of his body managing to warm the space around us.

"I was just passing by and saw you crying. It's not *my* fault you're drawing attention to yourself."

I wrinkle my nose, standing up straight. "If you're only here to insult me, go away. I'm not in the mood to trade barbs with you."

He lowers his voice to a husky whisper. "Oh, but it's so much fun." His lip curls in distaste as he continues to stand there.

I huff out a breath and toss my backpack over my shoulder. He won't move, so I'm forced to bump into him as I pass.

He falls into step beside me, causing me to stifle a groan. I want to fall apart in quiet solitude. The last person I want to witness me crumble is Mascen.

Why does he have to be here? Campus is huge, couldn't he be anywhere else?

"Can you go away?" I hiss out, not bothering to look over at him.

"I'm headed this way, Princess. *You* were the one crying. Excuse me for being a gentleman and stopping to console you."

My steps freeze. When he realizes I'm no longer beside him, he turns around, walking back to stand in front of me.

"You call *that* being a gentleman?" I shake my head rapidly back and forth. "Any time we've spoken pretty much every word out of your mouth is an insult." Lifting my chin, I glare haughtily up at him. "What happened to the kind, sweet boy I knew growing up? That boy is nothing like the person standing in front of me." Moving in closer to him, our chests only a centimeter apart, I say, "How would your mom feel if she knew how you talk to me?"

His jaw clenches, the muscle twitching. His lips pinch together while his dark brows draw in. Even glaring at me like he wants to set me on fire, Mascen Wade is the hottest guy I've ever seen.

He ducks his head and my breath catches when his lips press right against my ear. The cloying scent of cigarettes lingers on his skin, masking his normal aroma. "Life happened. You should know that better than anyone." Straightening, he takes a step back. "Dry your tears, Princess. Whatever it is, it's not worth crying over."

With those parting words, he turns, leaving me alone in the hall as he descends the stairs.

His final words echo behind him, and for a moment, in those sparkling gray eyes, I saw the boy I used to know. Not the one I know could break my heart so easily if I don't stay away.

FOURTEEN

MASCEN

How is it possible that Rory is every-fucking-where?

It was chance that I was in that building at this time, having a meeting with one of my professors. As I was leaving I noticed someone crying in the hall. Normally I would've kept on walking, but something clicked in my brain and I realized it was her. I had no idea what had her sniveling. Didn't care either. Princess could cry all she wanted, but those tears meant nothing to me. Everyone has problems. Hers aren't worse than anyone else's.

122

Then why are you still thinking about her?

"Good question," I mutter under my breath, causing some guy on the sidewalk to side-eye me.

I curl my lip at him, heading across campus in the direction of my next class. Farther and farther away from *Aurora*. I hate that a part of me is curious as to what she was upset about.

I have about thirty minutes before class starts, so I opt to get lunch on campus. I could go to the dining hall, even though I don't live on campus I'm still required to pay for the food services, but I'm not interested in dealing with people.

Despite the fact I fall at the top of the social hierarchy at Aldridge it isn't of my own doing as far as being a nice, sociable person. No, the only reason people want to know me is because of my heritage and the fact I happen to be really good at baseball. They hope if they get close enough to me, if I think we're friends, somehow, someway, I'll get them somewhere. Most of these people are rich pricks anyway, or at least their family is rich, but the difference between them and me is *fame*. There are numerous, mega wealthy families that the average joe has never heard of because they stay on the outskirts, their names aren't in the media or gracing tabloids. Not like the Wade name. Even with my dad in his fifties, interest in him and the band hasn't waned. Their old fans remain loyal, and because their music is timeless a lot of people my age are obsessed with them too.

If my dad and his bandmates are kings in the music

industry that makes their children the princes and princesses.

Opening the door to one of the cafés on campus, I get in line, not surprised when more than one student lets me cut in front. I don't protest either, and if you think I offer thanks you'd be wrong.

At the counter, I place an order for some fancy apple and turkey sandwich with brie and a tea. The girl looks at me weird when I order the tea, which makes me glare right back.

Off to the side, I wait for my to-go order. Sitting inside the crowded café to eat my lunch would be like sitting in the fiery pits of hell which gets a big fat *no thank you* from me.

Digging my phone from my pocket, I scroll through it haphazardly using it as a block that says *don't fucking approach me, I'm very fucking busy.*

As soon as my order number is called I grab the paper bag, my drink, and get the hell out, ignoring the stares as I go.

Underneath one of the large maple trees I sit down in the grass beneath the shady branches to eat my sand-wich. It puts me far enough away from people that they're not likely to see me, but it does leave me close enough to watch the goings-on of campus life.

Stretching my legs out, I unwrap the plastic from the sandwich.

It's a sunny day, warm, but there's something in the air, maybe a difference in pressure that you know the days are very soon to get colder.

My phone buzzes and I look at the text from Cole.

Cole: Where r u? Want to get lunch?

Me: Already eating.

Cole: Motherfucker.

I laugh to myself, shaking my head as I bite into my sandwich.

Me: My next class starts soon anyway.

Cole: U making dinner?

Me: It's my turn.

Cole: Sweet.

Finishing the last bite of food, I scrunch up the trash and stand with my tea in hand. I toss the trash when I finally pass a garbage bin—I can't have the karma of littering following me everywhere—and head straight across to the science building.

I should probably be offended by how shocked people are when they learn I've decided to go down the path to sports medicine. I guess they expect me to kick back and live off a trust fund or something, but that's not me. I want to work for what I have. I love baseball and other sports, plus science and math have always come easy to me, so sports medicine just made sense.

I've had people ask why I wouldn't want to go pro with baseball, but I've hated life in the limelight as is, why would I set myself up for even more personal scrutiny? At least with sports medicine it's something I'll enjoy and if things work out maybe I'll still be around baseball but in the background.

Entering the building I head up a floor to my classroom. I'm the first person and I take my usual seat nearest the exit. Pulling out my shit, I set everything up as more students trickle into the room and finally the professor joins us from a side room.

He talks, I listen and take notes, the monotony of it somehow comforting. Or maybe it's only because for a little while I can't think about anything else.

FIFTEEN

RORY

THE CAMPUS IS ABUZZ WITH ENERGY, STUDENTS decked out in the school's colors as they head toward the football field. Despite my lack of sports knowledge even I have to admit I'm excited. There's an infectious energy in the air for the first home game.

"This is going to be so much fun!" Kenna practically squeals. Her face is painted in the school's colors, blue and orange, and she even has the matching ribbons woven through her two braids.

Li tugs on the hem of the tiny short-shorts she borrowed from Kenna. I lucked out with the denim mini-skirt Kenna told me to wear. It's short, but not like the shorts she gave Li. If I was wearing those they'd be so far up my crack they'd never see the light of day again. She did force me into a crop top, which is *so* not my thing. It makes me feel uncomfortable exposing my midriff. When Kenna saw my belly button piercing she asked me why I'd have my belly button pierced if I didn't intend to show it off. I didn't give her an answer, but the truth was it'd been a stupid impulse decision to have some sort of control.

Pushing my glasses up my nose when they slip down, I follow the girls through the crowd of students. Smiling around me, I feel like a true student for the first time. Not that all the homework hasn't been enough of a reminder, but this was one of the things I was most looking forward to when I went away to college. The camaraderie that comes with living on campus.

Kenna flashes our tickets to one of the workers and he takes them, scanning them on his fancy device before ushering us inside.

Kenna lets out a little squeal and shimmies. "Go team!"

A couple people turn to look at her exclamation, but it doesn't faze her a bit.

We walk down the concrete stairs, our seats near the front since Kenna splurged on getting good ones. She also gave Li and I strict orders not to worry about paying her back. It didn't make me feel any less guilty. I wasn't used to being spoiled, and while trying to build genuine friendships with my roommates it felt wrong to let her treat me to something like this. That being said, I clearly took her up on the offer. I need to save every penny I can. So far I've lucked out that the tips from Marcelo's have been decent, far better than the diner I worked at before.

We're almost to our seats when something catches my eye. I look to my right, squinting from the bright sunlight to find Cole waving at me. I give him a small wave back.

Kenna notices too and pauses, smiling at me. "I cannot believe Cole Anderson likes you."

"He doesn't like me," I snort, my eyes sliding to his surly friend beside him.

I wish Mascen didn't capture my attention so much. Logic doesn't seem to matter when I'm inexplicably drawn to him.

Kenna laughs, drawing my attention back to her. "Are you blind? Of course he's into you. I mean, you went home with him that first night at Harvey's and he wanted to dance with you again the second time, now this." She ticks off on her fingers. "He likes you."

"He definitely does," Li agrees as we shuffle the rest of the way down to our seats. "If a guy doesn't like you he's going to ignore you."

Like Mascen, my mind taunts.

I tuck a piece of long dark brown hair behind my ear, once again pushing my stubborn glasses up my nose. Our seats are two rows beneath the guys and on the next aisle over. Trying not to look at Mascen is killing me, but I know he doesn't deserve a second thought. I'm being weak.

Cole is a nice enough guy, especially for being popular on campus, but he doesn't make my heart beat faster. My palms don't sweat when he's near. And he definitely doesn't make me crazy like Mascen does.

Beside me, Kenna turns to look at the guys, letting out a soft moan. "God, Mascen Wade is so hot."

"Mascen?" I blurt, my tone higher pitched than normal from the surprise of her bring him up.

Kenna looks back at me, arching a brow. "Surely you've heard of him. He's like *the* guy on campus. You know, the stereotypical hot jock who pretty much every girl wants to take a ride on his pogo stick." Biting her lip she adds, "I've heard he only fucks from behind, but that could just be a rumor. Apparently he's this amazing baseball pitcher too. I can't wait to witness his fastball in person. Or curve ball. Or any kind of ball." Li snorts at her antics from my other side. "I can't help myself. He's sexy as fuck. That stare … I'd let him do me any way he wanted. He can break my heart, my bed, even my back." She licks her lips suggestively, winking at us. "And as if all that isn't enough, he's basically music royalty. His dad is the drummer in Willow Creek. Like yeah there are a lot of students here from prominent families, present company included," she playfully sticks her tongue out, "but he's basically American royalty. I read in a tabloid once that he dated the First Daughter."

My jaw drops at that last tidbit of information, especially since it hits close to home. At one point my dad talked about running for President one day. Obviously that never came to fruition.

"That's probably just a rumor," I whisper, mostly to make myself feel better.

"What's a rumor?" I jump in surprise, finding Cole's tall lean body towering above us.

Kenna, the subtle person she is, begins to elbow me repeatedly in the arm giving me a look that says *told ya so*.

"N-Nothing," I stutter, caught off guard by his imposing presence. The guy is *tall*. No wonder he's a basketball player. "How are you?" I ask, raising my hand to shield my eyes from the sun. It's too bad I don't own prescription sunglasses, but they're expensive and maybe it's vain of me but I didn't want to wear the ones that fit over my glasses because I think they look dumb.

"Good, good. You ran off the other night."

I'm about to ask him what he's talking about, but then I remember how after Mascen cornered me in the closet at Harvey's I grabbed the girls and left.

"Oh, yeah. I was the DD. I had to get these ladies home." I smile up at him.

My neck begins to prickle like a thousand tiny spiders are crawling up my spine. I *hate* spiders and want to swat at my body, but I know they're not actually on me. Instead, I'm certain if I turn around I'll find Mascen boring a hole into the back of my neck.

"Ah, I understand." His full lips tilt up on the corners, his amber eyes shining down on me. "So, if you're not running off on me then, does that mean if I ask you on a date you'll say yes?"

Kenna lets out a gasp and Li giggles. Worst wing women ever.

"I guess that depends, are you asking?" The words sound far more flirtatious than I meant them to and Cole's grin grows. He might not make my heart pound out of my chest like Mascen does, but he is a nice guy and seems to genuinely like me. Why shouldn't I go out with him? Sometimes chemistry isn't there right away, but it can grow in time as you get to know a person.

Angling his head to the side, he smirks in a playful way. "Do you want to go out on a date with me, Rory?"

I hesitate for a moment, because Cole *is* Mascen's friend and if this would go somewhere things could get potentially awkward. But I'm not about to let Mascen Wade keep me from living my life. "Yeah, I'd like that."

Somehow his smile grows impossibly larger. "Cool. Give me your phone." I pass him my cell and he puts his number in before giving it back to me. "Text me so I have yours." He winks and then smiles at Li and Kenna. "See you guys later."

He heads back up the few steps to rejoin his friends.

Minutes pass, but my neck never stops burning.

———

"YES! RUN! RUN! RUN!" I jump up and down, shouting at the quarterback. Or I think it's the quarterback. That's the only player I know the name of so it's what I'm going with. I've never been a sports person, but witnessing the game in person has me wanting to learn. This is fun. Intense, but enjoyable.

Whoever he is, and whatever position he plays, he manages to make a touchdown, but barely.

Sitting back down, I sip at the soda I bought in the first quarter. It's watered down now, but I don't relish the thought of paying five bucks for another.

"Aren't you glad you came?" Kenna bumps her shoulder with mine. Her face paint is smeared now, and while I'd look like I tried to watercolor my face, somehow she makes it look intentional.

"Definitely." I grin back at her and then at Li.

I was worried I might get stuck with girls who wouldn't like me, or that I wouldn't like *them*, but while all three of us are vastly different, Kenna the outgoing one, Li the more quiet shy one, and me somewhere in the middle, we all click.

I focus my gaze on the field in front of us, trying to ignore the non-stop itching on my neck. I've refused to look, but I know Mascen has stared at me the entire game. He probably knows by now that I agreed to a date with his friend and he's even more pissed off at me for no good reason. It's clear he has a chip on his shoulder, from what I don't know, but he's decided to use me as his own personal punching bag. Too bad for him, I've already been one for my mom and I won't be that girl anymore. I will stand up for myself. He can act like a bully all he wants, but he'll never get me where he wants me.

When the game ends, the stands immediately start emptying out, and with them goes the creepy crawly feeling I endured the whole time. I blow out a relieved breath, smiling and chatting with Li and Kenna as we exit the stadium.

We pick up a pizza and some beer, courtesy of Kenna's fake ID, to take back to our dorm.

Entering the small space, I'm overcome with a sense of peace. It amazes me how quickly this place has become home. I haven't had this feeling of comfort since I was eight. It's something I won't take for granted.

Sitting the pizza box down on the coffee table, I flip open the lid, grabbing a slice of pepperoni before getting comfortable on the couch.

Kenna removes the caps from the beer and passes one to Li and me.

"God, I love pizza," Li hums, nibbling on the end of hers. She always takes the smallest of bites, reminding me of a rabbit.

"Me too." Kenna swipes a slice and plops into the chair.

I'm sure we all look a mess from being outside in the still warm early fall weather. Tennessee heat is no joke. The humidity is enough to take a grown man down.

"Do you know what you're going to wear on your date with Cole?"

At Li's question Kenna instantly perks up. I'm kind of surprised she's going into graphic design with as much as she loves fashion.

"Oh ... um ... I haven't thought about it yet. I mean, he only just asked me."

"Don't worry," Kenna leans forward, her piece of pizza dangling, "I'll take care of it."

I feel like I should be a tad worried about what she might pick for me to wear, but I can't bring myself to care. I'm learning the happier I am, the less I care about any other bullshit. If only I wasn't so afraid that my current happiness is entirely fleeting.

SIXTEEN

MASCEN

COLE TALKED ABOUT AURORA THE WHOLE FUCKING game. I think Cupid shot him with a fucking arrow or something. Cole has never talked about another chick like this before. It's fucking irritating, and why does it have to be *her* of all people? If it was any other girl he was talking about I'd probably be laughing my ass off seeing him all torn up over her but this was *Rory*.

I might not want her, but I saw her first.

Fuck, I sound like a petulant child whining over a toy.

"What's up, man?" Teddy pounds his hand down on

my shoulder, shaking me from my thoughts. His fingers
are wrapped around a red Solo cup, and his smile is that
of a guy who knows he's getting laid tonight. I look
around the party raging in my house. At one point I
actually liked these things. It was an excuse to get shit-
faced and pound some pussy. Tonight, it's more an
annoyance than anything.

"Enjoying the view." I sweep my fingers over the
middle of the living room where a group of girls dance,
gyrating on each other and trying to get attention from
those watching.

Teddy's lips tip up on the corner. "Me too." He takes
a sip from the cup. "I don't see where you're actually
enjoying it, though."

I twist my lips together, trying to think of a response
but frankly I've got nothing since he isn't wrong.

"Maybe parties are starting to get a bit old."

"Or maybe you're getting boring." Teddy laughs,
smacking the back of his hand against my chest. "I'm
going to enjoy myself."

I watch as he lifts his cup in the air, bleeding into
the space between the girls. Several swarm around him
like those dumb bugs that dive straight for a bright
light. I roll my eyes, silently wishing one would get
zapped, because at least that would provide some sort
of entertainment for me.

Emptying my cup I toss it in one of the trash bags
Cole and I set out through the townhouse to encourage
people not to drop their shit where they feel like it.

Turning, I head onto the back deck, digging out the

pack of cigarettes from my pocket as I go. Leaning against the railing, I light up the cigarette, pulling in a long drag to fill my lungs. Shoving my fingers through my hair, I look out at the townhouses behind mine. Row after row, life after life, all perfectly lined up. But nothing is ever truly neat and tidy. I suppose I have to admire the human tenacity to try anyway.

The way I see it, life fucks you over again and again.

No one else is out on the deck, thank fuck for that. I'm not in the mood for the chaos and necessary social- ization. But when am I ever? I've learned to play a part, but it's not me. Honestly, who the fuck am I?

My mom would tell me I'm Mascen Zane Wade. That I'm a great son and brother. A fantastic baseball player. That I care a lot—I would say too much, and that's another reason I'm so fucked up.

Tugging on my hair, a growl rips out of my throat. My insides are in constant turmoil as I do my best to hold onto the last of my sanity. I'm struggling in so many ways, with a million different things I can't speak of.

Standing outside for a few more minutes I smoke another cigarette before heading back in. Immediately the music and chatter is too much to handle. I could go up to bed—we always keep the upstairs off limits—but I would still hear everyone existing in a world I'm no longer a part of.

Slipping through the bodies, I make my way to the bottom level, digging the keys to my truck out of the bowl by the garage door.

I normally drive my Land Rover everywhere, but the cherry red Chevrolet Silverado is what I want to go out in tonight.

None of my friends notice me leave since I don't immediately receive a text asking where I'm going. I'm thankful most of them are occupied for the most part, especially Cole since he notices shit the most. He was playing beer pong with a couple of guys from the football team the last I saw of him.

Putting the garage door up, I back out, disappearing into the night and passed all the cars parked on the street.

Driving out of town a short way, I turn onto an unmarked gravel road. I found it by chance on a night I was stressed and couldn't sleep. I got out and drove and drove, trying to clear my head. I ended up here and it's been one of my favorite places ever since.

Parking the truck in the field, I hop out and grab some blankets from the back seat. Pulling the cab down I hop in and toss the blankets down to form a cushion against the hard bed. Laying down, I look up at the sky.

It's clear, full of stars—a country sky unpolluted by the human population.

This land is probably on someone's farm, but I've never been caught yet, so I keep coming. It's a place that feels entirely mine. Free of judgment and the fear I seem to live with constantly anymore.

What do you have to be afraid of Mascen?
Everything.

But the stars above me? They don't judge me for my

sins, my mistakes, and my misdeeds, not like the entire world does.

SEVENTEEN

RORY

I WIPE DOWN THE LAST OF MY TABLES, THE restaurant lights dimmed since it's after closing time. Aldo counts the cash in the register and Izzy is in the kitchen making sure everything is cleaned and left orderly.

Tossing the rag over my shoulder, I release a breath. It's been a busy night and now that it's over exhaustion has hit tenfold. My feet ache, sweat is dried to my skin, and there's a sting of hunger in my belly.

It's nearly midnight and on top of the chaotic evening Mascen returned with another date. Totally

141

different girl, but same table, and a nearly identical order. My gut tells me he's trying to get under my skin, that he thinks he can hurt me by rubbing other girls in my face.

"Tired?" Aldo asks, closing the cash register. He leans forward on his elbows, his white t-shirt pulled tight over his muscular chest.

"Yeah," I admit, sliding onto the barstool across from him. "Hungry too."

He rubs his stubbled jaw, his lips twisting. "Hold on a sec." He holds up a finger and disappears into the kitchen. I watch after him with a raised brow, wondering what he's up to.

A grin splits my face when he returns a few minutes later with French fries from the kids menu on a giant platter with a cup of ketchup.

"Please tell me you like fries," he practically begs, setting the plate down in front of me. One of the fries falls off the side and he deftly grabs it, tossing it into the bin behind the bar.

"Of course, who doesn't?"

"You'd be surprised."

We both pick up a fry, dunking it into the ketchup at the same time. We exchange twin grins. I have to stifle a moan at how delicious the fry tastes. I skipped dinner since the rush was insane and now I'm paying for it.

"These are yummy." I'm pretty sure anything would taste like heaven to me right now.

"Don't tell my sister these are my favorite thing on

the menu. She'll kill me. My mom too."

"Your secret is safe with me." I mime zipping my lips and tossing the key over my shoulder.

He grins at me, a dimple popping out in the corner of his left cheek.

"Ooh, fries!" Heather, the waitress that had called in sick the day I was hired, breezes over and swipes two fries. "See you later, guys. I'm out." She waves over her shoulder as she leaves, her bright red hair swaying. There and gone in a moment.

Despite my past waitressing experience I've learned a few new things from Heather. The girl is scarily efficient and Izzy would be lost without her.

"I'm going to have to get her back for that," Aldo remarks, leaning his arms on the shiny wood counter. "No one takes my fries."

I pause with one ketchup dipped fry raised halfway to my mouth. "But I'm eating your fries."

He reaches for another. "Yeah, but I chose to share with you."

For some reason color rushes to my cheeks.

Rubbing his hands on a napkin he stands up straight. "I have some things to finish. Leave some for me." With a wink, he turns, heading down to the other end of the bar to clean.

Shaking my head, I scarf down a few more fries before getting up to leave. "Thanks, Aldo."

"See you tomorrow, Rory."

I give him an awkward wave, heading into the back to grab my bag. Clocking out, I exit through the back door into the parking lot reserved for employees.

My truck is parked near the end, closest to the back alley. Not the safest spot, but when I got here it was the only one left open.

With my head bowed, fumbling for the key to my truck I don't notice the form leaning against the driver's side until a cigarette butt comes sailing into my line of vision, falling to the ground right in front of my foot.

I jump back, my hand flying to my chest in surprise, so of course my keys fall out of my hands to the ground, right next to that stupid butt.

"I don't remember you being so clumsy," his deep, husky voice intones. He bends down, that dark head of hair of his nearly close enough to graze me. With one large hand he scoops the keys up, but does he give them back? Of course not. He loops the chain around his index finger, spinning it around and around. Taunting me like a trapped bird.

"I didn't remember you being a stalker." I try to swipe my keys from him, but he has the reflexes of a ninja and deftly lifts his arm high enough above his six-foot-plus frame that there's no chance I can reach them.

Stuffing his hands in his pockets, along with my keys, he draws his shoulders up. He stares down at me, his eyes are black pools in the dark. A shiver courses down my spine, one not from any sort of chill in the air, but the electric forcefield that seems to exist around him.

He keeps staring, not saying a word. Rolling my eyes, my hands settle on my hips.

"What is it, Mascen? Why are you lurking around my car after midnight? I'm tired and not in the mood to deal with you and your bullshit."

He moves so fast I don't have time to react. I find my back pressed against the side of my truck, the rickety door protesting from the sudden contact.

"I don't know why the fuck I'm here," he seethes, his eyes darting down to my lips. "I shouldn't be, that's for hell sure. You should be the last thing on my mind, but lately you're invading every fucking thought of mine." His lips skim over the side of my cheek and dammit if I don't shiver in pleasure from the touch. His hand comes up to my chin, holding my head so I can't move. My heart thunders in an out of control beat, threatening to tumble out of my chest. I bet Mascen wouldn't bother catching it. No, he'd let it fall to the ground and stomp all over it.

Stiffening my spine, refusing to cower to him, I say, "Looks like you've got me right where you want me, if you ask me. Cornered. In your grasp. What are you going to do about it?" His tongue moistens his lips at my words and I find myself smirking. "You want to kiss me, don't you, Mascen? But you're too chicken-shit to do it. That's what all bullies are—*afraid*."

He snarls at me, opening his mouth to speak, but that's when one of the dumpsters clang.

"Rory? You still here?" I hear Aldo's voice coming closer and Mascen slowly registers it too, realizing we're not alone. He lets go of me, shoving my keys in my hand.

"Don't go on a date with Cole."

The words, *you can't tell me what to do,* are right on the tip of my tongue but he bleeds into the shadows, disappearing completely and suddenly I'm alone.

"You okay?"

I turn to find Aldo standing at the back of the truck.

"Yeah," my voice is surprisingly steady.

"What are you doing?" He cocks his head to the side, studying me. I'm sure I look half-insane standing here beside my truck, nearly out of breath from Mascen's shocking presence.

"I ... needed to breathe in the fresh air."

It sounds plausible enough.

"Nobody's giving you trouble out here are they?" He looks around for someone hidden in the shadows, but Mascen's gone, slipped away to whatever cave he hides in. "We get some homeless folks out here from time to time. I always slip them some food—don't tell Izzy, though. She'd have my head." He gives a soft smile.

"I won't say anything." Tucking a piece of hair behind my ear, I locate the key to my truck. "I better get going now."

"'Night, Rory."

"Goodnight." I raise my hand in a wave when he does the same.

Hopping in my truck, Aldo watches as I pull away before heading back inside the building.

I should stop and grab a meal from one of the 24-hour drive-thrus in the area, but I'm suddenly not hungry anymore.

The closer I get to campus, the angrier I become. If Mascen thinks he can tell me who I can and cannot go out with, he's about to learn how wrong he is.

EIGHTEEN

MASCEN

RUNNING NORMALLY CLEARS MY HEAD, BUT TODAY it's fucking pointless.

"Dude, slow down," Teddy wheezes behind me. "You're worse than Coach."

"If you can't keep pace that's not my problem."

And it isn't. He's the one that asked to go for a run with me so I'd push him. If he pussies out that's on him.

"My sides are cramping."

"Then walk."

"You're not even winded," he complains behind me, his steps heavy.

"Because I do this every day."

"And it's too fucking early," he coughs. "It's not even light out. How do you stand getting up this early?"

I don't tell him, but I didn't even go to bed. After I got home from Marcelo's I couldn't go to sleep, too busy cursing myself for hanging around and telling Rory not to go on a date with Cole. Right then and there I showed her and myself that I care.

Not about her, surely not about her.

I let out a growl and Teddy chokes on a laugh. "What the fuck, dude? Are you a bear?"

"Just sick of listening to your whiny ass."

He grunts in response, falling farther behind me. I don't know why he's complaining so much. The loop is only eight miles around town and back to my townhouse.

"Come on, man. Stop being a wuss. You can do this."

When I look over my shoulder he manages to raise his hand and give me the finger.

Shaking my head I pick up my pace again.

Teddy's expletives pick up and I smile.

———

"REMIND me to never run with you ever again, you crazy motherfucker." Teddy shakes his head before gulping down the glass of water the waitress only set down moments ago.

"It'll keep you in shape."

"I *am* in shape." He lifts his shirt, showing off his muscled stomach. "I just fucking hate cardio like a normal, sane person."

"Well, good for you, since you're not invited back. You disturbed my me-time."

He shakes his head, repeating, "Your me-time?"

"Yeah, the time of the day I reserve for me, myself, and I."

He arches a brow, shoving his hair out of his eyes. "Isn't that pretty much every moment of the day for you?"

I wish.

I ignore his question, looking at the menu for the café down the street from my house. I've only been here once before since I normally cook my own breakfast, but Teddy talked me into eating out—claiming I owed him for torturing him.

Apparently I'm a sucker, since we're here.

The waitress comes back with a fresh glass for Teddy and takes our order.

"What's been going on with you?" Teddy asks, picking up the water glass. "You … seem different this year."

Crossing my arms over my chest, I lean back in the chair. "I don't know, honestly. Things feel different than they did before." I guess that's what happens as you get older and grow up, but it's a weird feeling. Like I'm off balance somehow, waiting for things to feel right again.

Teddy's eyes narrow, his head cocking to the side. "I

mean, I know we don't do the whole feelings and shit, but we're friends. You can talk to me if you need to."

"Yeah, I know, man. But really, it's nothing serious. Just life."

Our food comes and talk moves to a safer topic, our shared interest of baseball, because fuck knows I don't do the feelings bullshit.

———

WALKING down the stairs into the classroom, I take my usual seat. Stretching my legs out in front of me I set up my laptop. My mind is elsewhere, definitely not on the lesson that's about to take place. It's unfortunate since I actually like school. It's always been easy for me and something I enjoyed, because the way I see it you can always learn something new.

A few minutes later, almost everyone's filtered into the room, and we're just waiting for the professor to appear. Professor Franks likes to take his time starting class. It's obvious he's one of those teachers who hates teaching.

"Hi, can I take that seat?"

I look up into the pale round face of a girl I haven't seen in this class before.

Wordlessly, I move my legs to let her squeeze into the empty seat beside me. Looking around I find that the rest are indeed full.

"Sorry," she says when her bag hits my leg as she sits down.

"It's okay."

"I just transferred into this class. Is the professor a hardass?" she whispers under her breath.

"Not really, he's lazy which means the class usually has the bare minimum of work so he has less to grade."

She gives a small laugh, setting up her computer. "Well, that's better than what I was expecting. I'm Mallory, but the way."

"Mascen," I mutter, looking at her out of the corner of my eye.

"Nice to meet you." She smiles up at me. There's nothing flirtatious in her gaze which is a nice change.

"You too."

The professor finally comes into the classroom, coffee cup in hand from the stand that I know is on the opposite end of campus. After puttering around for at least five minutes he finally starts the class.

At the end, Mallory and I get up together, walking out at the same time.

"Did you just change classes or are you a transfer from another school?" I find myself asking.

She tucks a piece of brown hair behind her ear and adjusts her bag after some douche bumps into her. "Transferred schools. I just wasn't happy where I was before. Being here brings me closer to home."

"That's cool." Fuck, I'm not good at small talk.

We walk in the same direction in silence. I ignore the stares from girls on campus and I hope Mallory doesn't let the glares aimed in her direction bother her. It pisses me off that if I'm even seen speaking with someone that possesses a vagina it's suddenly news and a reason to put a target on some poor girl's back. I've kept my head down this year, only gone on a few dates for appearances sake more than anything else. I won't lie, the last two years I went a bit wild, but things changed this summer and mindless screws don't sound appealing.

"Do you mind pointing me in the direction of coffee?" Mallory asks, her voice breaking into my thoughts.

"Sure," I mutter.

The dining hall is closest to where we are, and there's a separate coffee area there.

Mallory somehow keeps up with my stride, not bothering to make small talk. Opening the door wide for her to go in, I follow behind, pointing to the area where you can order coffee—these rich kids, like myself, are all too lazy to make their own—there's already a line of ten or so students.

"Can I get you anything?" Mallory smiles up at me as we head toward the line. "It's the least I can do for you showing me the way."

Her words could be taken in a flirtatious way, but the way she looks at me with an aloof expression I know she's genuinely trying to be nice. It's an unexpected change that takes me by surprise.

"Nah, you're new here. My treat." I wasn't going to bother getting a tea before my next class, but since I'm already here why the hell not?

Mallory is quiet beside me. I get the impression she doesn't talk much, which is fine by me.

The line moves slowly, and I try not to let my aggravation show because I don't want Mallory to think it's about her.

Eventually we're able to order, she gets a latte and then gives me an amused expression when I order my tea.

Dropping a few dollars in the tip jar, Mallory and I wait at the side for our drinks.

"What class do you have next?" I ask her.

"Oh … um…" She looks up from her phone, brow furrowed. "Anatomy with Keppler."

"Me too."

Heading toward the doors, I open them wide, stopping dead when I see Rory on the other side.

"Thanks," Mallory says, going through.

Rory looks from Mallory to me as Mallory steps to the side to wait for me.

I can't decipher what's in Rory's gaze, whether it's irritation, or hurt, or something else. She pushes past me, into the dining hall, bumping me as she does.

"Hold up," I tell Mallory.

I don't know what makes me follow Rory, but I can't seem to stop my steps as I go after her.

"What do you want?" She doesn't look at me as she says it, refusing to acknowledge my presence.

She's in line for lunch, picking up items and placing them on her tray. I don't think she's even paying attention to what she's getting. At least, I don't picture her eating a whole burger, pizza, and some weird pasta salad looking thing.

"I don't know." The answer is surprisingly honest.

"Come to warn me away from dating your friend again?" This time she does look at me, raising a brow. "I love the irony of how you seem to go out with every-thing that walks, but I can't go on *one* date with your friend."

I grind my teeth together. I look for words for a response but keep coming up empty. She's seen me on multiple dates now at Marcelo's because I've kept stupidly coming back after I learned she works there. She doesn't realize it, but I'm there for her, not the date. I enjoy our verbal spats way too much.

"Why don't you go find someone else to bug, Dracu-la?" She pushes her glasses up her nose. "Because I'm not in the mood. By the way, I think that girl is waiting for you."

She points to the doors where Mallory is, indeed, waiting for me. I feel bad as the girl shuffles from foot to foot, clearly unsure if she should keep waiting for me or not.

"She's new," I tell Aurora. "We have the same class."

"Whatever, I don't care." Rory swipes her student ID card, carrying her tray to a table. She pulls out a chair and sits down. I stand, hands braced on the chair across from her. "By the way, Cole asked me on a date this morning." She says this all while looking at her bottle of flavored water. Finally raising her brown irises to mine she adds, "I said yes."

It suddenly feels like I've been stabbed in the chest. "I guess it's a good thing I don't care."

She smiles but there's nothing friendly about it. "Aw, Mascen, that's so cute, but you can pretend all you want. Both of us know you care very much."

She winks, taking the top off her bottle and swallowing down some of the liquid.

Shaking my head with my jaw pulsing I mutter, "See you later, Princess."

"Bye, Dahmer."

Walking out of the dining hall, I have to chase down Mallory who got sick of waiting.

"Sorry about that," I say, blowing out a breath as I slow to a walk.

"Girlfriend?" she asks. "I'm sorry, I didn't mean to cause any trouble."

"Uh, no."

"Hmm," she hums.

"What?" I prompt.

She gives a shrug. "It's just ... call it girl intuition or whatever, but trust me, whoever that girl was, she was jealous to see me with you."

I look over my shoulder, back in the direction of the dining hall. "Interesting."

NINETEEN

RORY

STANDING IN FRONT OF MY CLOSET WITH MY HANDS on my hips, I glare at the contents.

It's official, I have nothing cute enough for a date. Holding my robe tighter around my body I peek out into the hallway. "Kenna?"

"In my room."

Padding down the hall, I lean into her bedroom. She looks up from her laptop to find me nibbling on my lip with nerves. "I need your help."

"Sure, with what?" She closes the laptop, setting it aside as she climbs from the bed.

"My date with Cole is tonight and I have nothing to wear."

She squeals so loudly I'm sure the girls on either side of our dorm have to hear. "Oh my God, why didn't you tell me? Li, come here! Our girl is finally going on a date with Cole."

Seconds later, Li appears looking far too put together in a simple pair of cotton shorts and loose tee, while I'd look like a hobo in the combo.

"Ooh, does that mean we get to dress you up?" She claps her hands, her dark hair falling forward like a curtain.

I throw out my arms. "Yes, I'm your doll. I'm clueless. I've never gone on a real date," I admit. "I have no idea how to do this."

Kenna's jaw drops. "You've … never …?"

I roll my eyes. "I have, but not a date."

"Hmm," she muses, moving around me. "Well, we'll have you fixed up in no time."

She isn't lying either, an hour later she's picked out my clothes, done my makeup, and Li did my hair.

"Go check yourself out." She points to her floor-length mirror in the corner.

My jaw drops at the sight of myself. The dark green satin slip dress she put me in makes my skin look tanner and like I have an inner glow. The gold jewelry around my neck helps ground the look, while my long hair curls around my shoulders. For the makeup she kept it simple with a gold and brown smokey-eye, nude lips, and pink blush.

She looks me up and down. "I did good. Cole's going to die."

Smoothing my hands down the front of my dress, I exhale a deep breath. "I'm nervous."

I'll be the first to admit, I agreed to the date to piss off Mascen more than anything, but Cole does seem like a genuinely nice guy and I think he's worth giving a shot. Nothing is ever going to happen between me and Mascen, not that I want it to anyway, he's an asshole. Besides, just because you don't feel a connection with someone right away doesn't mean there isn't one. Sometimes you have to get to know people before you feel something.

Kenna squeezes my arm. "It's okay to be nervous. I think that's normal before any date. No matter how confident you are, nerves are still a thing."

"What will we talk about?" I blurt, my panic rising and with it my temperature. I'm probably going to start sweating profusely in twenty seconds.

Kenna turns me around, leaving her hand on my shoulders so I'm forced to look at her. "Stop over-thinking it. Let conversation happen naturally and go with it. Don't force anything. Okay?" She looks me square in the eyes, waiting for me to agree.

"I'm being dumb, aren't I?"

"Very," she responds. She straightens my dress and tucks a loose piece of hair back into place. "You look beautiful. You *are* beautiful—and smart, and pretty funny when you let loose. Be yourself. It's the only thing any of us can be in the world that's not already

159

been done before." She winks. "Any words of encouragement, Li?"

"Girl, you've got this." She leans against the doorway. "And when you get home Kenna and I will be waiting with snacks so you can tell us all about it."

"Unless of course you go home with him," Kenna adds, sticking her tongue out slightly. "Then ride that stallion all the way into the sweet, sweet morning."

"Oh my God." I stifle a laugh.

"But let us know if you're not coming home." Li grabs my arm so I turn toward her. "We'll worry if you don't."

"I'll keep you updated."

Just then there's a knock on the door.

"Show time." Kenna claps her hands. "You stay here, take a breath and calm down, and I'll get the door."

Kenna breezes past me and Li moves out of her way. The dorm is small enough that in only a few steps I can hear her opening the door.

"Have fun tonight." Li surprises me by pulling me into a hug.

"I'll try."

Giving my hand a squeeze she encourages me out of the room and I step out to find Cole standing just inside the door with a bouquet of flowers, all different kinds and colors. He smiles wide when he sees me. "Hey," he greets, moving toward me.

I meet him halfway, hugging him. "These are gorgeous." I take the flowers when he offers them.

"Here, I'll take them so you can go." Kenna swoops in, my own personal fairy godmother.

"Are you ready to go?" Cole asks, while I'm busy checking him out.

Boots, a nice pair of jeans, and a black fitted button-down shirt tucked into the jeans. Thankfully, I don't feel overdressed.

"Yeah." My voice is a little higher than normal.

Cole's hand glides down my waist to take my hand. "We should go, I have reservations."

I let him lead me to the door, looking over my shoulder to find the girls both grinning at me like fools. Kenna gives me a thumbs up before we're gone.

Outside, Cole leads me to a black Honda Pilot. It's a few years old, not brand new like most of the cars on campus. I remind myself he's like me, here on scholarship, which automatically makes me feel better because it means we're on equal footing.

With his hand on my back, he opens the passenger door for me to climb in.

Jogging around the front of the SUV he slides inside, turning the engine on. "I didn't get a chance to tell you before, but you look beautiful."

My cheeks heat with his compliment. The dress isn't my normal attire and I'd prefer more skin covered, but I do feel pretty in it.

"Thanks. You look good too."

I find myself wishing I had more experience when it came to actual dates and dating so I would know how to make small talk. I feel like I've been dumped into the deep, dark waters with nothing to hold onto.

Cole backs out of the parking space and soon campus is left behind us. We don't talk much on the drive which allows my nerves to grow and fester even more.

Downtown, he pulls into the lot of one of the fancier restaurants, a seafood place I pass on my way to Marcelo's.

"You do like seafood, right?" he clarifies, rubbing his hands on his pants. He seems as nervous as I am, so that makes me feel better. "I should've asked that beforehand, but I didn't think—"

"Seafood is great." I cut him off to alleviate his worry.

"Oh, good."

He hops out and before I can open my door he's there doing it for me. He takes my hand, leading me inside the restaurant. It's decorated nicely, with rich dark colors and hints of gold. I would've been happy going to a diner, but this is definitely much better.

Cole gives his name to the hostess and we're immediately led to a table for two near the back windows overlooking a manmade pond.

The hostess hands us each a leather-bound menu before leaving us.

"Have you been here before?"

"No," he answers, looking at me above his menu. "It's not too over the top is it?"

"It's perfect." I smile at him and his shoulders relax

a tiny bit. "Do you not normally date?" I find myself asking.

He winces, appearing sheepish. "Not really." He twists his lips and I know what he's saying without words, but I'm not judging. I've done the same in the past, so why would I hold someone else to higher standards than I do myself?

"Well, I'm honored you like me enough to take me out on a date."

He smiles back, his amber eyes sparkling. We both grow quiet, perusing the menu to decide what we want. When the waiter comes to fill the water glasses and places bread on the table we give him our order. My stomach rumbles and I reach for a piece of bread, slathering it with more butter than is necessary.

"How are you liking school so far?" Cole asks, sitting his water glass back down after taking several gulps from it.

"It's not so bad." I pick at the edge of my nail trying to avoid eye contact. "Definitely different than high school."

He chuckles, the sound warm and husky, almost cozy like something I could wrap myself in. Once again I find myself wishing that I could like Cole as something more than just a friend, but when I look inside myself I don't feel the warm and fuzzies and I don't think of him in that way. This date is a chance to see if there's a chance of there being more there, but...

"Yeah, it sure is," he interrupts my thoughts.

"It'll be worth it." I wipe condensation from my

glass. "To have my degree, something that's *mine* and no one can take from me."

He angles his head. "What are you studying? I don't think I've asked."

He hasn't. Our brief text exchanges have been little more than checking in with one another.

"I want to be a child advocate attorney."

"That's cool."

He doesn't ask why and for some reason that bothers me. Most people would want to know why you're choosing a certain profession. I don't think it's that he doesn't care, but that he doesn't think it matters.

"What about you?" I ask, grabbing another piece of bread to butter. I can't say no to carbs.

He clears his throat. "Oh, um, I'm studying journalism, but my coach is pretty certain I'll go pro and that's the plan for me. I love basketball and I want to play professionally."

"Wow, really?" I say around a mouthful.

Professional sports doesn't seem like practical thinking to me, but I'm not going to say that out loud. An injury can happen at any time, taking you out, and besides I'm sure most guys playing college sports hold *some* kind of hope that they'll be one of the chosen ones. Granted, I haven't seen Cole play—not that I'd know what I was looking at anyway—so maybe he really is above the rest.

Our food comes, the smell of the lemon and dill coating the fish I ordered is downright mouthwatering.

The small talk continues while we eat.

"Where are you from? Did you live in Tennessee before?"

I shake my head. "No, I grew up in Virginia actually and then moved to Florida."

"Virginia? Where? Mascen grew up there."

My face flushes and I try to think of a way to change the topic but can't. "The Winchester area."

"Fuck, really? That's exactly where Mascen's from."

I swallow thickly, stifling the urge to reply that I know. "Small world." My voice is scarcely above a whisper. "What about you?" I try to speak up. "Where are you from?"

I barely hear his reply, and the rest of the evening I go through the motions, my thoughts now with the wrong guy and not focused on my date as they should be.

When we leave the restaurant he takes me back to the dorm, placing a soft kiss on my lips before leaving.

The girls are waiting eagerly for me to give them every detail, but I fake a headache, removing the makeup and dress before climbing into bed.

When I close my eyes, even my dreams won't let me free of Mascen.

TWENTY

MASCEN

"How'd your date go?" I bite out over breakfast, glaring at the milky depths of my cereal.

"Fuck, man." Cole scrubs a hand over the top of his head, his smile only able to be described as *giddy*. The word alone tastes sour on my tongue. "She's amazing. I love talking to her. She's so cool."

My left hand claws into a fist beside the bowl. "That's … awesome."

Cole doesn't notice my lack of enthusiasm. "Crazy story, though. I asked her where she grew up and she said she lived in Winchester for a while. Can you believe that?"

I bristle, surprised she'd tell him about that. "Huh, interesting."

"Small world, huh? Did y'all ever go to school together?"

"Nope." It's not a lie either. I was homeschooled at that point, so was Aurora.

"I'm going to ask her out again." He fumbles through the drawer, producing a fork for the breakfast scramble he made. "We should go out on a double date. I'd like for you to get to know her. I mean, I'm not planning that far into the future, but there's something special about this girl."

My jaw clenches. "That so?" I bite out. My blood pressure has probably spiked with how angry I already feel. It's fucking stupid for me to feel this way anyway. If Cole wants to date her, so be it, there's nothing I can do about it.

And.

It.

Shouldn't.

Matter.

It doesn't. It doesn't matter to me. I have to keep telling myself that.

"You okay?" Cole asks suddenly. "You're turning red."

I let out a breath. Apparently I forgot the very basic function of how to breathe. "Yeah, I'm fine. I need to go shower."

I push away my bowl of cereal, going up to my room.

The shower doesn't make me feel better, and since it's Saturday I don't even have the excuse of classes to keep me distracted. As I'm putting on my sweats, my phone rings. I expect it to be my mom but I'm surprised to find it's my older sister Willow facetiming me.

"Hey," I answer, smiling genuinely when her face fills the screen.

"Hey, Loser," she responds, sticking her tongue out at me. "What are you up to?"

"Just showered." I point to my wet head like it isn't obvious. "What do you want?"

"I can't check up on my little brother?" She pushes her blonde hair over her shoulder, the same shade as our mom's. It's ironic how much she looks like our mom, while I look like dad, and Lylah is more of a cross between the two. But I get along best with mom and Willow has always been Daddy's little girl. "I miss you," she continues. "We didn't hang out enough over the summer."

Clearing my throat, I look away. "We're both busy with our own lives."

"I guess we are," she sighs sadly with a wistful expression. "How's school?"

"Same old, same old."

"I know it's a while before games start, but Dean and I want to come up to one."

I pause, cocking my head. "Why?"

I'm not trying to be a jerk, but my family doesn't

usually come to my games unless it's an away one in Virginia. I get it, Aldridge is a long ass way from home —nine hours without stops.

"To support you," she says in a *duh* tone. "We thought we could make a little vacation out of it and you could show us around when you have free time."

I rub the back of my head, not sure what to do since she's taken me by surprise. "Uh, yeah, that would be cool."

"Are you coming home for Thanksgiving?"

"Yeah, I will be." Thanksgiving break feels like forever away, but I know it'll be here before I know it. I don't know why she asks, of course I'm coming. I'm pretty sure my entire family—my dad's bandmates included—would hunt me down if I didn't. Liam, my cousin, skipped out on a few holidays a couple years back and now it's mandatory that we're all there. I think the only way we'd be excused from attendance would be if one of us were to die, and even then I think our ghost would be required to make an appearance. I'm not sure my family wants me to haunt their ass. I'd for sure be one of those ghosts that makes life difficult— opening cabinets, throwing spoons, that kind of shit.

"Mascen." Willow snaps her fingers to get my attention like she's standing right there.

"Sorry," I mutter, my apology less than sincere for zoning out on my sister.

"Did you hear what I said?"

"Ah, no." I shake my head sheepishly.

She laughs. "I was just saying how proud I am of

you. God knows I gave the college thing a try and it wasn't for me. You'll be the first of us to finish college. I mean, even Mom and Dad didn't go to college."

I give a shrug. I hadn't ever given that any thought. Going to college doesn't feel like anything special to me, just what I always planned and wanted to do. I try not to give it too much thought considering how many years I have ahead of me of med school.

"Uh, thanks," I reply awkwardly. I don't take compliments well, I never have. Most of the time they've ended with someone wanting something from me. I know that's not the case with my sister, but some things just aren't easy to shake.

"So, the wedding is scheduled for this coming summer," she continues, undeterred by my silence, "we have everything reserved for June tenth."

"Okay?" It comes out as a question.

"I just wanted you to know so you can't miss it."

I narrow my eyes. "I would never miss your wedding—you know that, so what is it you want?"

Apparently even my family does like to butter me up first before asking for something.

"Well, I know you hate attention, but Dean and I really want you to be one of his groomsmen."

"I don't have to be best man?" I raise a brow.

She shakes her head. "Nope, Lincoln will be his best man." Lincoln is her fiancé's younger brother. "All you have to do is walk one of my bridesmaids down the aisle and stand there and look pretty."

"As long as I don't have to plan a bachelor party and do any kind of fancy stuff."

I am not the planning type, more of the show up and have fun kind of guy.

"Well, I mean there will be a rehearsal dinner—" she begins.

"Fuck." I scrub my hands over my face. "I liked it better when you guys talked about eloping."

When Dean's family, and ours, caught wind that the two were considering running off to Costa Rica to elope with baby sloths or some shit, they put a stop to it real quick. Now, it's where they'll go on their honeymoon instead.

Blowing out a breath, I look at the screen, staring into my sister's eyes. "You're lucky I like you. I'll do it."

They hinted before about me being in the wedding, probably to put out feelers to see if I'd flat out refuse, but now that the planning is going on full force she needs a definitive answer from me. I might hate this kind of shit, but my sister, hopefully, only gets married once so I wouldn't miss out on being there for her.

Willow smiles back at me. "Thank you, Mascen. I love you."

"Love you too, sis."

There's a skittering in the background and then her hyperactive Jack Russel terrier jumps on her lap out of nowhere, nearly knocking her down. The dog appeared at her fiancé's mechanic shop and she insisted on keeping him.

"Moo," she groans, grabbing the dog and holding him away. "That's not nice. You could've hurt me."

The rascal licks her cheek and she breaks out in giggles. That dog can't learn anything because she forgives him too easily.

"I gotta go," I tell her, even though I really don't have anything I have to do.

"Sorry, love you."

"Mhmm, love you too," I say again, ending the call.

Grabbing my computer, I leave my room, searching for Cole, but he's either left or in his bedroom.

Grabbing a water I head onto the back deck, sitting down at the table there and opening my computer to get started on homework.

School work has always been easy to me, even with growing up on the road most of the time. There's a misconception that kids who are homeschooled aren't as smart, or are somehow behind other kids their age, but that's a wrong assumption.

Opening up the last document I was working on, I read it over, and start adding to it, researching as I go and citing information. I've always hated the monotony of it. I understand the *why*, but it doesn't mean I have to like it.

As I work, my thoughts drift in places they shouldn't.

Namely, Aurora.

Fucking, Rory, always on my mind when she shouldn't be. Seeing Cole happy should make me happy if I'm a good friend, but clearly I'm not. I don't like the idea of him liking her, and I don't even want to think about what it means if they really start dating.

An hour later, my paper is done, but I'm in a pissed off mood.

In need of a distraction, I grab my phone, scroll to the C's and pick a name.

TWENTY-ONE

RORY

"NEW TABLE IN YOUR SECTION." HEATHER BUMPS MY hip playfully as she passes me in the kitchen. "Requested you specifically. I'd say job well done girl, he's a looker, but he's here with a girl."

I look up from the salad I'm putting together, my lip snarling.

Fucking Mascen, back again.

"Great," I mutter.

He might be a giant pain in my ass, but at least he *does* tip me well. Very well. So I can't complain too much. But I find myself saying anyway, "Why don't you take them, Heather?"

"Uh, because they asked for you, duh." I'm pretty sure if she could flick my forehead she would.

"I know, but just tell them I'm too busy."

"Jealous ex?" she asks.

I'm tempted to lie, because I know she'd cover for me if she thought I needed protecting but I can't. Mascen might be a jerk, but I'm not afraid of him. "No." I exhale a sigh and pick up the finished salad. "I'll take care of it."

Breezing out the door, I drop off the salad before approaching Mascen's table.

"Nice to see you, Joe."

"Joe?" He raises a brow. "Are you hallucinating, Princess?"

"Excuse me?" his date interrupts, clearly offended.

"Exotic—you know, the self-named Tiger King. We don't sell meth here, you'll have to look elsewhere."

His eyes narrow but there's a barely imperceptible twitch of his lips. God, he doesn't want to smile because of me but he still can't help being amused.

"Uh, is something going on here that I'm missing," his date speaks up.

"Sorry, I'm Rory, your waitress this evening."

"Do you two know each other?"

"Obviously," we both blurt at the same time, then glare at each other.

"Now, what can I get you guys to drink?"

Mascen orders his usual house draft and his date orders water.

I let Aldo know what I need before getting the water myself, when I breeze back by the bar he has the beer waiting for me. "Thanks, Aldo."

He grins at me, nodding his head as he reaches down to scoop ice into a glass. There's a bachelorette party lining the bar, and more than one of them is sending flirtatious glances his way. Poor guy has his hands full tonight.

"Here you guys go," I say in my politest tone, setting the glasses down along with a straw for the water. "Are you ready to order?"

"No, not quite—"

"Yes," Mascen interrupts his date, leaning toward me, "we are."

The poor girl frowns, and honestly I can't help feeling bad for her since he's being a dick. Granted, he's always like this so she must've known what she was agreeing too.

"Steak marsala—rare."

"Do you always order the same thing?"

He laces his fingers together, laying his hands on the table. "Yes, I don't like trying new things."

"For you?" I ask the girl. Her head is currently pinballing between her date and me.

Finally, she stops, her eyes landing on him. "Home." She picks up her bag. Giving me a not very nice smile she adds, "I don't appreciate feeling like a third wheel on my own date."

My mouth falls open, but I don't have a response because she's kind of right. If I was remotely attracted to Mascen in a sexual way I would think maybe this is some weird form of foreplay for us, but I don't like him that way. Or any way.

She pauses, waiting for Mascen to stop her I presume, but when he doesn't she huffs out a breath and slides fully out of the booth, walking out.

"Your date left," I announce unnecessarily.

"I can see that." He leans back in the booth, cocking his head to the side.

"Are you leaving too?"

His lips tip up on the corner. "You'd like that wouldn't you? But no, I'm hungry and I want my steak." He makes a shooing motion with his hand, arching a brow when I leave. "Go on, you're the help, put my order in."

My anger flares. I find myself tempted to pelt him in the head with my pen, but if Izzy saw I would certainly be fired. Aldo would just laugh.

But since I can't seem to succeed at being a decent human being I lower until we're eye level, his smirk growing the closer I get to him. "Just remember, this *help* can spit in your food." With that, I turn on my heel to put his order into the system. Will I spit on his dinner? No, I'm not that mean or petty, but seeing the look of surprise on his face makes the threat more than worth it.

I spend the rest of the evening running back and forth to my tables, making sure drinks are filled, orders are out timely, and everyone stays happy. Mascen eats his dinner in silence, and even though we don't trade barbs anymore I find myself continuing to seek him out wherever I'm in the room. When he doesn't think he's being watched there's something melancholy about him. I think it's in the way his shoulders droop and his lips downturn. Something is weighing on him. Something that has nothing to do with me and everything to do with him. I wonder what it is but I know I'll never ask. We're not friends anymore and I don't think we ever will be again. We're too different. He's the spoiled prince and I'm the fallen princess.

The night winds down and I'm more than ready to head home—how funny that I think of my dorm as home now, but it's far more comforting than the trailer I left behind. I haven't heard from my mom once. I wish I was surprised but I'm not.

"Bye, Aldo," I call behind me as Heather and I head for the exit.

"See ya," he replies before the doors close.

Heather smirks at me. "You like Aldo?"

"What? No." I'm so shocked by her question that I worry I sound defensive.

She gives a shrug. "He's cute, you should go for it."

"Uh…" I blink at her. "He's a nice guy, but I don't like him that way. But maybe you should."

She pauses in the parking lot, placing a hand on her hip. "I'm thirty, I don't do young'uns."

"You're thirty, that's hardly old."

"True," she agrees with a grin, "but men don't age as

fast as us, sweetheart. See you later." She waves good-bye, climbing into her red SUV.

At the end of the lot I slide into my truck. The ancient engine sputters and roars. If any of the nearby buildings have apartments, no doubt I've just woken someone up.

Sighing, I brush my hair out of my eyes and back out, the restaurant soon a tiny blip in my rearview mirror.

I'm not surprised to find both girls asleep when I get to the dorm. Kenna, especially, might like to have a good time, but she's surprisingly responsible about getting enough sleep on days she has class.

Taking a quick shower, I change into my pajamas and slip into bed. My body is exhausted and I think I'll fall right to sleep, but of course I'm wrong. While I might be tired physically, my mind hasn't gotten the memo.

My thoughts swirl from Cole to Mascen, to my mom and Hazel, even to my dad, and back again. Covering my face with my hands I blow out a breath, hopefully breathing out my irritation with it. Rolling onto my side, I curl my hands under my head.

Sleep doesn't come easily, but eventually it does overtake me, erasing all my thoughts with it.

TWENTY-TWO

MASCEN

IT'S FUNNY HOW TIME SEEMS TO PASS SLOWLY AND quickly all at once.

Lifting the beer to my lips, I look around the party, most people dressed in costumes for Halloween. The holiday—is Halloween even a holiday?—is still a few days away, but I guess there was some discussion that it'd be celebrated tonight. I missed the memo. Even if I hadn't I wouldn't be participating in a game of dress-up.

The party is being held at one of the frat houses that a large number of football players pledge for. I'm glad to not be the one hosting tonight. I stay on the recesses of the room, drinking more beer than I normally would, watching everyone else mingle.

My eyes find Cole dancing with a girl in the center of the room, but not just any girl.

I watched the two of them sit together at today's game. I saw him make her laugh. Saw her smile at him. Banter. She looked at ease with him, happy.

It makes me angry.

I know it shouldn't, but I can't help it.

I keep telling myself I don't want her, but it's getting more difficult to convince myself that I mean it.

Finishing the beer, I head into the kitchen, and away from the lovebirds, for another. The smart thing to do would be for me to leave. I know if I stay, continue to see them and keep drinking, I'll probably end up doing something I regret—or the very least feel kind of bad about.

"Hey, man, there you are." Teddy smacks me on the back as soon as I enter the kitchen, his eyes glassy from something he smoked.

"Here I am," I bite out, grabbing a beer from the fridge. I know I'm supposed to use the keg, but fuck that cheap watered down shit. Teddy continues to blink at me wearing a goofy grin. "Did you want something?"

Blink. Blink. Blink.

"Ah, fuck, can't remember. I think I just wanted to say hi."

I press my lips together. "Well, you did."

"Mhmm." His eyes follow a girl in a tight jean skirt

leaving the room. He smacks me on the shoulder again. "I'll see you later. I'm going to follow that."

I don't know if he means the girl or just her ass.

"Have fun."

I wait a few minutes, nodding here and there to people who say hello, avoiding girls who get too close and gaining some confused stares in the process, before I return to the large living space where people are dancing. I could go to the basement, play pool or beer pong, or even find a willing girl to head upstairs with me, but I'm not in the mood for any of it. Especially the girl part.

My eyes stray to where Cole and Rory are still dancing, her head thrown back and her hair loose. One of her arms is draped around his shoulder and she's smiling, maybe even laughing. Something flares inside me, and I hate to think it's jealousy, but I know I could never make her smile like that. It's funny how when she first moved away I was so sad and angry. She was my best friend, someone who wasn't family, that I could share secrets with and who just *got* me. When she left it was a long time before I really made friends with anyone again, and even now I keep everyone, even Cole, at arm's length. I've been used too much, especially in high school since I actually attended public school for that, and it's made me jaded. I used to think it was okay to keep people at a distance, that I didn't *need* anyone, but her reappearance is making me question everything and how I might've handled things if I *had* had a friend I could depend on the rest of my childhood. My attraction to her doesn't help matters either, because *fuck*, I want to hate her. I want to blame her for my problems. But that's my issue, I always want to blame everyone else, even my own father, for my problems instead of just owning up to it.

My jaw clenches and out of the corner of my eye I spot Mallory. She's standing in the corner, looking around uncomfortably, but when she catches my gaze she gives a small smile.

Be better.

With a sigh, I set down the rest of my unfinished beer and walk over to her.

"Hi." She gives a small smile, looking around awkwardly. "This isn't normally my thing in case you couldn't tell." She bites her lip, shaking her head. "My roommate and her friends talked me into coming and well, here I am and I don't know where they are."

I wet my lips, fighting my internal conflict. Finally, I offer her my hand. "Wanna dance?"

"I don't normally dance." She eyes my hand warily.

"I don't either. But let's give them something to talk about." I can already feel the eyes in the room on us, the guys now taking notice of Mallory since I have, and the girls taking notice too but in envy.

Mallory's smile is hesitant. She's clearly not used to this scene, probably more the bookish, nose to the grind type.

"Relax," I tell her softly, my mouth close to her ear so she can hear me. "I'm with you."

She gives me a thankful smile and begins to follow

my lead. I try to ignore the persistent buzzing at my back, the one that annoyingly tells me Rory is nearby. It's like my body has an internal alarm system when it comes to her.

A few songs later Mallory smiles up at me. "Thank you."

"For what?" I'm truly confused. It's rare for me to do anything worth thanking.

"Saving me, I guess." She gives a shrug, her hips still moving to the beat of the music. "I thought I'd try to fit in and—"

"And your roommate still ditched you," I finish for her.

"Yeah," she gives a sad sigh.

"People suck sometimes. Especially me."

Her brows wrinkle. "What do you mean?"

"Haven't you heard?" I spin her around and she lets out a giggle. I don't miss the way Rory's eyes flash in my direction, her cheeks heating in embarrassment because she looked this way. "I'm the biggest asshole on campus."

"That's what they say," she replies. "Doesn't mean it's true."

"What all have you heard about me?" I ask, truly curious what some of the rumors and half-truths are. Fuck, some of them are bound to be the actual truth.

"Well, for starters," she blushes, "I heard you got caught having a threesome in the locker room last year." My lips thin and her mouth parts with shock. "It's true?"

"That one is," I reluctantly grumble. "What else?"

"That you smashed your car into the opposing base-ball team's bus."

I cock my head. "Do you think that's the truth?"

She crinkles her nose. "No, you wouldn't still be on the team if that were true. Besides…"

"Besides?" I prompt when she trails off.

"You've been nothing but kind to me, even when you didn't have to be. I'm new here, you could've easily ignored me in class, or told me not to sit by you. You didn't have to walk with me for coffee or to my next class. And look," she adds with a light smile, "I'm not expecting anything from you, so I don't want you to think I've read into any of this. I'm thankful for your kindness then and now. But if you were a truly bad guy you wouldn't be dancing with me right now."

I swallow past the lump in my throat, slowly processing her words. Releasing one hand from her hip I scrub it over my face.

She must sense my internal freak out, because she takes one step back, giving me space. "I'm going to get a drink. See you later?"

She frames it as a question, but I don't give her an answer.

I watch until she disappears from the room and then I do the same, heading upstairs and down the hall to the bathroom that is hopefully empty.

The door is stuck, but not locked, so I give it a shove. A high-pitched shriek greets my ears and I close my eyes, wincing in irritation when I realize it's Rory in the bathroom. Because of course it *fucking* is.

"I locked that!" She yells back at me, wiping her hands on the front of her jeans—much safer than the towel hanging haphazardly beside the sink.

"Apparently you didn't, Princess, because here I am."

She snarls at me, her hackles rising and God if my body doesn't respond in pleasure to it.

"Not on a date tonight?" She arches a brow, leaning her hip against the sink and crossing her arms over her chest. She's trying to appear like she's unaffected by me, but I know she is. I can see it in the way her nipples begin to harden against her cotton t-shirt that's paired with a short jean skirt.

My lips lift in a smirk. "My favorite waitress isn't working."

She narrows her eyes. "How *do* you know my shifts?"

"I have my ways." I cock my head to the side, watching her, waiting for her reaction.

She shakes her head. "I shouldn't be surprised. I'm sure you're used to getting what you want."

I narrow my eyes on her, shutting the door behind me in case someone comes along. I don't want word to get back to Cole that I'm in here with Aurora, especially when nothing is happening.

She looks behind me, her lips pursing.

"Don't worry, Princess. I don't bite. Yet." I stalk closer to her, not missing the catch in her breath when

I'm right in front of her. I should've stayed by the door, the farther away from her the better, but I can't help it. It's like I'm always drawn to her by an invisible string. "Now," I skim my nose along the side of her cheek, relishing in the way she shivers at my touch, "if you wanted me to, that's a different story."

Her body sways toward mine and I grip her elbows in my hands.

With one hand I reach up, gently cradling her cheek. "You can pretend all you want that you belong to Cole, but we both know it's a lie. Your body responds to *me*, not him," I growl, my tone nowhere near as soft as my hold on her. "I'm going to hate fuck the shit out of you, Aurora, and you're going to love it. Fucking beg me for it."

Her brown eyes roll to meet mine, her full lips parted and cheeks flushed. Then, she pulls away, skirting around me so her back is to the door and now I'm in her spot with my back to the sink.

"Funny. I thought you didn't do Cole's sloppy seconds?"

Before I can retort she reaches for the door, slipping out of it and slamming it closed behind her. By the time I cross the room and open it, she's gone.

TWENTY-THREE

RORY

THE STING OF MASCEN'S HAND ON MY CHEEK STAYS
with me for a week. It's not like his touch was too hard,
or anything of the sort, but my body refuses to let go of
the brand left behind from his fingers on my skin.

I keep reminding myself that while my body might
be ridiculously attracted to him, my mind isn't.

Looking out our dorm window, it's pouring down
rain and I groan at the realization that I'll have to run
around campus hoping not to get drenched all day. I
have a raincoat, sure, but it's nothing against this
torrential downpour.

"Ew, rain." Kenna echoes my silent sentiment behind me. "It sucks that the way campus is laid out so you have to walk everywhere."

Parking circles the entire campus, meaning you can't actually park outside any of the buildings. It's a real bummer with weather like this.

"Let's go back to bed," Li jokes, already slinging her bag over her shoulder.

"I wish."

Disappearing back into my room, I grab my coat and zip it on. My stomach rumbles and even though I wasn't going to have breakfast I know I'll need to make a stop by the dining hall.

When I leave my room with my backpack in hand, Li is gone and Kenna is in the bathroom putting on her makeup.

"See you later," I tell her.

"Don't forget it's girls night," she warns. "Cole's hot and all, but we saw you first."

I laugh, pausing by the door and smiling at her reflection as she looks back at me. "I'd never forget girls night."

Outside the dorm, I shrug my hood up to help block against the wind and rain. It doesn't matter though, within seconds my glasses are splattered with water, blurring my vision.

Jogging across campus, I reach the dining hall, releasing a breath when I'm safely inside the warm dry compound.

I grab some breakfast—pancakes with butter and

syrup—and find an empty spot to sit. My first class is in twenty minutes so I don't have long to eat.

As I take my first bite my phone buzzes with a text message.

Cole: Are you in class yet?

Me: No, just sat down in the dining hall. Eating real quick before I have to go.

Putting my phone away, I focus on the plate in front of me, yelping in surprise when two minutes later Cole appears beside me, his lips pressing to my cheek.

"Morning, beautiful." He grins, sliding into the seat beside me.

"Oh, hi," I utter, taken off guard.

I'm even more flabbergasted when the seat across from me is pulled out and Mascen plops into it with a disgruntled expression.

My gaze flickers from one guy to the other. Mascen feigns boredom but I can see in his eyes that he's bothered.

"Is this okay?" Cole leans back in his chair, his smile blinding.

"Oh … uh … yeah," I stutter, my eyes once again going to Mascen. His jaw is tight and he reaches up, rubbing the tense muscle. "I'm happy to see you."

Cole and I haven't put a label on what we are, we've only been on two dates, and neither of those dates has led past kissing, but I *know* he wants more and I don't know what I want.

"Do you want a coffee before class?"

"I'll probably stop and get one on the walk over if

I have time. I'm not a huge fan of the ones here." I point toward the stand in the corner of the room. "That guy makes them too weak and he's *always* working."

"I'll go get you one you like then. Be right back."

"Cole—"

My protest falls on deaf ears and he's up and out of his seat, heading for the exit.

Mascen lets out an amused chuckle, shaking his head with his arms crossed over his chest. He's wearing the black baseball cap again, only today it's pulled forward, shadowing his eyes.

"What?" I snap at him, knowing something sarcastic must be sitting on the tip of his tongue.

"Nothing." He wets his lips, trying to hide his growing smirk.

"Spit it out, Lucifer."

His lips quirk the tiniest bit, his eyes drifting to me half-hidden beneath the brim of the hat.

"It's just amusing how whipped he is." He looks down toward the table and then back up at me. "Must be some damn good pussy you've got there."

My cheeks heat, and embarrassment tightens my chest, but I refuse to cower to him. "What kind of flavor is jealousy?" I snap at him, tilting my chin down as I gather my stuff, my food unimportant since I'm no longer hungry. "Because you look like you've eaten something sour."

Shrugging my bag onto my shoulders, I grab my tray and dump the uneaten food in the trash. What a shame, I wanted those pancakes just ten minutes ago. Leave it to Mascen to steal my appetite.

Pushing the doors open onto the rainy campus, I tug my hood up and walk in the direction of my class.

Footsteps sound behind me and somehow I know it's *him*. But I won't look back. I won't give him the satisfaction.

The steps stop and I keep going.

"Don't be so sensitive, Princess!" He yells after me, his voice a rumbling roar above the pounding rain.

I swing around, ignoring the other students dressed similarly to me, just trying to get to class. "Then don't be an asshole!"

Anger bubbling in my veins, I turn back around, keeping my head down.

I've only walked maybe a minute longer when I hear, "Rory, whoa, whoa, whoa. What's wrong?" I pause, Cole jogging up to me, his blue raincoat slick with the wet stuff, the hood barely shielding his face. "Did you forget I was getting you coffee?" When I blink at him, his face falls. "What happened? You look upset."

I look over my shoulder even though I know Mascen is long gone. "No, nothing. I … I realized I didn't have as much time to get to my class as I thought. I'm so sorry."

He smiles but it looks a little forced. "It's okay. Here, take your coffee. I won't keep you since it's pouring."

I hold my hand out for the coffee and he slips it in,

at the same time ducking his head and sealing his lips over mine. It catches me off guard, but before I can react he's pulling away.

"See you later."

"Thank you," I call after him, lifting the coffee.

He waves, his smile real this time.

I hurry off to class then. By the time I get there, I'm chilled from the rain and my coffee is far from warm. But the chill that's settling in my bones has nothing to do with either.

———

AFTER CLASS the rain has thankfully turned to a drizzle instead of a downpour. I toss the empty cup of coffee into the trash can outside the building and wrap my arms around myself.

If it was a nice day I'd probably sit outside for a bit before my next class, even if it was chilly, but the rain makes that impossible.

I wander into the common building, seeking warmth and shelter. I've only been here a few times, it mostly houses things like study rooms, and indoor extra curriculars.

The classic stone walls are lined with photos of alumni, even the most recent photo editions are edited to look worn and ancient. There's something imposing about all the serious faces looking down at me from above. It makes me feel small, as if I'm being judged here for not belonging. It isn't even my lack of money I feel judged for, it's my parentage. The sins of my father passed to us, and I'm just thankful over time people don't automatically hear my last name and associate me with him or his crimes. It's a conundrum, because while I know my father did bad things, and took his life instead of face it, I still love him. I was only eight. I didn't see or know that side of him. While he wasn't around a lot when he was he made an effort to spend time with Hazel and me. He taught me to ride a bike. He built a tent inside so Hazel and I could camp out. He watched movies with us and even played tea party. It's hard for me to reconcile my memories with the facts.

Drawn farther into the building, I realize the sound of a piano is pulling me along.

I drag my fingers over the wall, heading closer to the sound. Whoever is playing is talented. I'm no musical genius, but I know when someone is good or not.

I should turn around, go no closer, but I can't help but want to see the person who is creating such beautiful music.

Rounding the corner, I see the open door on the left. I drift toward it and pause outside. I can't see who it is, not with the grand piano shielding them. I lean against the doorway letting my eyes drift closed. The music rolls over me, the melody so lovely, so sweet, unlike anything I've heard before. It calms the chaos of my thoughts until all I can focus on is the notes filling the air.

My head moves with the song and as I open my eyes I drift farther into the room rounding the massive piano.

Air catches in my lungs when I see it's Mascen hunched over the piano. His baseball cap sits on the bench by his leg. With closed eyes he gives himself over to the music, his fingers nearly moving in a blur. I've never seen anything like it. It's as if him and the piano are one entity. I can't tell where one ends and the other begins. Music like this is precious and I can't believe someone so ... so assholish could create something this sweet.

Unbidden, I move even closer to him. When I sit on the bench he still doesn't notice. He's lost in the feeling of the music thrumming from the keys through his fingers.

I wish I could record this moment so I could press play on it later, listen and feel all over again. But I can't, so I have to hope I remember this well enough to recall it later.

The music comes to an end. I don't move and neither does he. His posture becomes tense and when he opens his eyes he turns to me slowly. That sharp jaw is rigid enough to cut stone and his eyes are glacier. There is no warmth in them. No softness in the set of his lips.

Something tells me I should be afraid, but I'm not. In fact, I stupidly lean closer to him.

"I didn't know you played piano."

I mean, of course I didn't, why would I?

He cocks his head slightly, eyes narrowed. "Most

people don't." His voice is gravelly and low. My treach-erous body feels that tone *everywhere* and it's wrong, especially considering I've been going out with his best friend, but feelings just *happen*. Chemistry exists between two people. It can't be forced. Mascen and I happen to have it in spades. "Why are you in here? Stalking me, Princess?" He tries to give me a cocky smile, but it doesn't hide the hunger in his eyes.

I want to give him a sarcastic answer, but I find myself telling the truth instead. "I heard the music. It was so beautiful I couldn't help but listen."

"And you decided to sit beside me?" He arches a lone dark brow, angling his head.

I shrug. "I couldn't help it." It sounds insane, but it's true. "Who taught you to play?"

"My mom," he answers, his long fingers stroking the ivory keys but not pressing. His fingers are long and narrow with dark hair peppering the knuckles.

"That's right." I nod with a smile. "I remember watching her play some. You're incredible."

"I'm mediocre at best."

I shake my head adamantly. "No, you're amazing."

His lips twitch into a smile. "Not insulting me today?"

"Eh, the day is young." I inhale a shaky breath. Being this close to him is doing something to me. He moves, his bare arm brushing mine. The black t-shirt clings to the definition of his biceps and chest, tapering at his waist. I drop my eyes to the piano so I don't have to look at him.

I startle when his warm finger touches the bottom of my chin, guiding my head away from the keys so my eyes are forced to meet his. I itch to adjust my glasses, but I don't dare move.

He stares so intently at me that time stretches and thins. The air becomes a pulsing vibrant thing between us, heavy and pulling us closer. The weight of it presses on my back and it must his too, because our lips draw nearer until our breath mingles.

Whatever is about to happen shouldn't, I know it, he knows it, but neither of us makes a move to stop it.

He hesitates, his lips millimeters from mine. "Fuck it," he growls, crashing his lips against mine in a bruising kiss. His hands delve into my hair, holding me against him. Our mouths fight for dominance, neither of us wanting to cower to the other, it makes for a heady feeling. I've never felt anything as powerful as this before.

My hands grip his t-shirt in my fists, the fabric bunching and wrinkling beneath my hold. His hands move down my body to my hips, his left hand hooking around my right thigh to pull me onto his lap so I'm straddling him while he faces the piano.

He deepens the kiss, his tongue tangling with mine. His flavor invades my taste buds, something almost herbal that I can't quite pinpoint mixed with the tang of a cigarette. He pulls me closer, rocking my hips into his and I moan at the feel of his growing length against the heat of my core.

I want to open my eyes, to see if this is real and not a dream, but I don't dare break the spell.

I follow his lead, letting him guide the kiss, for once not fighting against him because this feels impossibly wonderful.

No kiss has ever been this … this *electric*.

It's like there's a current zipping through my entire body. The buzzing spreads through my fingertips as I stroke his freshly shaved cheeks.

My hips continue to roll against his unbidden, seeking more of the delicious friction. My pussy pulses and I feel like I should be embarrassed that I'm this close to climaxing, but the pleasure feels too good to care.

Mascen's fingers tug on my hair, the sting of pain somehow heightening the pleasure. He nibbles my bottom lip, dragging it between his teeth and releasing it with an audible pop before diving back in. My breasts press into his hard chest, my nipples pebbled. His large hands begin to tear at my jacket, shoving it off my body with desperation. I help him remove the article of clothing, letting the jacket fall to the floor.

He pulls away just slightly, his heated eyes meeting mine.

Wordless communication passes between us. He hooks his thumbs in the back of his shirt, yanking it off and over his head. His tanned skin looks like it's sculpted from marble. The muscles too hard and smooth to possibly be real. I barely have a chance to look before he demands, "Up."

I lift my arms up and he slowly, inch by inch, raises my shirt up. His eyes are glued to my stomach and then my breasts when my bra is revealed.

"Fuck," he growls out lowly, the word drawn out.

My breasts, while small, look good in the push up bra I wear to give them a little more definition.

I squeak when he stands suddenly, his hands on my ass. I twine my arms around his neck and he carries me to the back of the grand piano, laying me on top of it. His large body leans over mine. I feel sheltered, protected, and that's definitely not something I should feel right now. Not when it comes to this guy.

But I don't stop kissing him. I don't think I can.

His hands wrap around my stomach and he yanks me closer to the edge of the piano so my center is once again pressed against his. I pant against his mouth, wild with need.

In the past when I've hooked up there's been an almost clinical process to it. It was about mutual release and nothing else. But what's happening with Mascen ... it's something I've never felt before. Explosive. Magnetic. I should've known it would be like this, even when we're at each other's throats there's always that thrum of something beneath the surface, the hint that if we ever act on something it'd end up like ... like what's happening right now.

He bites down on my bottom lip hard enough to draw blood, then soothes the nip with his tongue. I grind against him, gasping as my orgasm builds.

There's a voice whispering in the back of my mind

to stop this, but it's not loud enough. Or maybe I don't want to listen.

When Mascen's fingers dig into my hips, my orgasm finally hits, shooting through me with a vibrancy that's nearly blinding. I cry out, my lips wrenching from his as my head drops back with my moans. Someone's bound to hear. The pleasure seems to go on forever, my pussy pulsing with it and wetness soaking my panties.

Slowly, I blink my eyes open, my skin damp with perspiration.

Mascen still hovers above me, his hands gripping my hips tight enough to hurt. His eyes are shadowed, his jaw clenched, and the look of hatred in his eyes steals the last of my breath and not in a good way.

"M-Mascen," I stutter his name, a broken plea on my lips.

He tears away from me, turning so I only see his profile. I know his brows are dipped down angrily. I stupidly want to know what I did wrong to cause this sudden change in behavior, but I remind myself this is Mascen, and there's no logic when it comes to his mood swings.

He picks his shirt up from the ground, yanking it over his head and down his torso to hide the sharp defined outline of his abdominals. Next he swipes up his baseball cap, putting it on backwards. In the next blink he's at the door, yanking his raincoat from the hanger by the door.

Then, he's gone.

The room is silent save for the erratic beating of my

heart and my panting breath as I struggle to get enough air.

Sliding off the piano, I pick up my things, redressing much slower than he did.

The daze clings to me, refusing to let go. Confusion rattling me. I like being in control, knowing what's what, but Mascen stole that from me and I let him because I'm a stupid girl.

Picking up my backpack I head out the door turning the lights off behind me.

Instead of going to my next class like I should I let Mascen Wade corrupt me further when I return to my dorm, climb beneath the blankets, and cry.

TWENTY-FOUR

MASCEN

Playing Xbox with Cole should be a normal pastime, and it is, except for the detail of making out with his girlfriend weighing on my conscious.

It's been three days since the kiss. Three torturous days where I've weighed whether or not to tell my friend what I did. My selfishness is showing in the fact that I haven't fessed up—selfish because I don't want my friend to be mad at me.

Pathetic fucker.

"I'm going for a smoke." I toss the controller down and Cole glances at me.

"We're in the middle of a match man, you can't leave."

"You'll be fine without me."

He shakes his head with a sigh, but doesn't argue when I heave my body from the couch and dig the pack of cigarettes from my sweatpants. Out on the back deck I light up, leaning against the railing.

I bring the end to my lips, inhaling the nicotine. I keep telling myself I'm not addicted to this shit, but if I'm honest with myself, I'm using it more and more often to steady my nerves and ease my tension. It's just about the only time I'm relaxed anymore.

Leaning forward, I run my fingers through my hair, then down my jaw.

Pulling in another drag, I hold it in as long as I can before releasing the smoke into the night air. I watch it float away like a cloud, disappearing from existence like it was never there to begin with.

"Are you happy, Mase?" My mom asked me when she called yesterday.

"Of course," I answered. What else was I going to say?

"You don't look happy, or sound it. I'm worried about you."

I thought about the mounting pressure on my shoulders—the normal stuff, like school, preparing for the baseball season to start, life in general—and then I thought about Aurora, the way she tasted on my lips like a mix of the best thing I'd ever had and the very thing that could bring me to my knees.

I ended up telling her I had a big test coming up and

it was stressing me out. I hung up with the excuse that I needed to study.

"Fuck," I curse, when the ash from the tip of the cigarette burns my fingers since I stupidly forgot to flick it off.

I put the wasted cigarette in the ash tray I keep on the deck and light up another.

Pulling out one of the deck chairs, I sit down, stretching my legs out as I lean back. I've always found something comforting in being in the outdoors. Growing up, my dad had a treehouse built for us on the property. I spent more time in it than my sisters did, though they used it too, but it became my safe place. A quiet place where I could be alone and think. Too often, even as a young kid, I would sneak out at night and climb the ladder into it so I could lay down on the outer deck around it and look up at the trees, the leaves swaying in the nighttime breeze, with the stars winking in and out of existence.

I guess I'm more of a loner than people realize, even myself. I have to get away to recharge and settle my chaotic thoughts.

The sound of the sliding glass door interrupts my musing and Cole walks out.

"I'm calling it a night," he announces, "but I just talked to Rory and wanted to run something by you."

"Oh?" I sit up, my heart suddenly in my throat.

If she told him about the kiss before I did…

But he doesn't look pissed so it can't be that.

"I told her I wanted to take her somewhere this

weekend but didn't say where. I was thinking bowling and thought it'd be fun with more people, so why don't you come?"

"I'm not third-wheeling your date," I growl, finishing my cigarette.

He laughs, amused by my reply for some fucking reason. "I thought you'd bring a date, too, man. Don't you have an endless roster?"

I think of all the girls' names programmed into my phone, the alphabetical list I've been going through on my dates to Marcelo's.

"I suppose." A part of me doesn't want to commit to the atrocity of a double date with Cole and Rory—not when I can still taste her on my tongue and remember what it feels like when she orgasms, and that's *without* my cock ramming her.

He braces his hands on the back of one of the patio chairs. "Why do you sound unsure?"

Kicking my legs up on the table, I hope I appear unbothered. "Double dates aren't exactly my thing."

"I've never done one either, but come on, dude. It'll be fun."

I could give Cole an entire list on why this *won't* be fun, but that'd be too exhausting and he'd probably still pester me to say yes.

"Fine, whatever. I'll do it."

"Thanks, man." He holds his hand out for me to slap mine against. "I'm going to go tell, Rory."

I tip my head at him. "You do that."

He heads back inside and I know I should too. It's

cold out, in the forties, and I didn't bother to grab a jacket. But I stay for a few minutes longer anyway.

Once I finally go in he's turned the TV and all the lights off.

I drag my body upstairs to my room collapsing on top of my bed. It's plush, the best mattress and covers money can buy, but the way I feel right now it could be a concrete floor and I couldn't tell the difference.

Sleep doesn't come easily, not that it surprises me, and I've probably only had four hours tops by the time my alarm goes off for my morning run.

I heave my body up and change into my workout clothes, heading out into the still dark morning.

Pounding my feet against the pavement helps me clear my head a bit and I start feeling less guilty for kissing Aurora. She kissed me *back*. We were two willing parties and therefore are both guilty. I shouldn't have to shoulder this burden entirely on my own. She could've stopped me, but she didn't. In fact, if *I* hadn't been the one to end it I'm pretty sure she would've let me fuck her right then and there in the practice room.

Making it back home, I enter through the garage, taking the stairs up to the main living space.

"Good run?" Cole shakes a bottle with his protein drink in it.

I nod, still catching my breath. Despite the lack of heat in the air these days, my shirt is wet with sweat. Pointing upstairs to indicate I'm going to shower he nods in reply.

Chucking my clothes in the hamper and giving

myself a moment to grumble over the nearly over-flowing pile and the fact I'll be forced to do laundry tonight, I get in the shower, washing away the sweat.

Turning the faucet off, I step out and grab a towel off the rail, quickly drying my hair and body before I tie it around my waist. At the sink, I brush my teeth, shave, and go about my entire morning grooming process.

The whole time I can't stop thinking about a double date with Rory and Cole. It sounds like the worst kind of torture imaginable but of course my dumb ass agreed so now I'm stuck. I don't know why I do this stuff to myself. It's like I purposely like to make my life miserable.

Once I'm dressed I go down to the kitchen, grabbing a protein bar and apple. It's not much, especially after my long run, but I barely have an appetite.

Cole's thunderous steps echo on the stairs and he rounds the corner tugging on a sweatshirt. "Can I ride with you today?"

"Why?" I ask suspiciously, biting into the apple.

He grabs the counter, standing across from me. "Because my car is making a weird noise and I need to have it looked at. I can get a ride home from someone else after practice."

"Sure, that's fine." What am I going to do? Say *no*? That'd be hard to explain—that I'm irritated with him because I like his girlfriend.

Fuck, I like her. I haven't wanted to admit it to myself, but I do, and it makes me hate her all the more.

"Thanks, man." He turns to the fridge, swiping a blue Gatorade. "Are you almost ready?"

I look at the half-eaten apple. "Yeah."

I chuck the rest in the trash.

———

HALFWAY THROUGH MY classes for the day I'm walking across campus to stop for a cup of tea when I spot Mallory heading the same way.

I'd been planning to go through my roster, as Cole refers to it, for this horrendous double date idea, but as soon as I see her I figure I'd rather ask her. She's nice, and sweet, plus at least so far I haven't gotten any vibes that she wants anything from me. Not a relationship, not bragging rights.

"Mallory!" I call, jogging over to the brunette. She pauses, looking around, a soft smile curling her lips when she sees me.

"Mascen." She clutches her textbook to her chest as I stop in front of her. "What's up?"

I shake my hair out of my eyes, giving her a dazzling smile. I should probably dial the charm back a bit but the fact is I need her to say yes. If I have to take some random chick chances are I'll pluck my own eyeballs out before bowling night is over.

"I have a favor to ask."

She arches a brow, angling her chin. "Oh?"

"My best friend, he's dating this girl and wants to … go on a double date, but I don't have a girlfriend and I don't want one," I'm quick to add, because I don't want her getting a false idea, "but I feel like we're kind of sort of friends, right?" I widen my eyes, hoping she'll take mercy on me. "I was hoping you'd go with me?"

"As a fake date?" I can tell she's amused, not mad, so I take that as a good sign.

"Um, yeah." I smile sheepishly, running my fingers through my hair. It's getting a bit too long but I've been too lazy to get it trimmed.

"Is this like a fancy restaurant kind of double date?"

"No," I blurt quickly. "It's bowling."

She grins suddenly. "Then I'm so in. Prepare to go down, Wade."

"You'll do it?" I sound way too surprised.

"That's what I said. When is it?"

"This weekend. I'm guessing Saturday but I'll have to double check with Cole."

"That should be fine. Let me give you my number so you can send me the details."

I pull out my phone and put her number in, promising to let her know more later.

I feel a bit better about agreeing to go now that Mallory is in, but when I turn and see Rory watching me from across the quad I wonder why I'm torturing myself.

She can never be mine, not when she belongs to him.

TWENTY-FIVE

RORY

"BOWLING?" I ARCH A BROW IN SURPRISE WHEN I pull into the lot of the building Cole directed me to. I put my truck in park, looking over at him.

"Is it a bad idea?" He sounds slightly worried. "I know it's kind of childish, but I thought it might be fun."

"No, no," I rush to assure him. "This is a great idea. It should be a lot of fun."

Getting off campus and having some fun is honestly what I need. With the Thanksgiving holiday and break approaching I've been feeling down. I don't have a family to go home to, not like Cole, or Li and Kenna, or even Mascen. It's not like I've celebrated any holidays with my mom for years. Heck, she didn't even do anything for my birthday or Hazel's. It was up to us to do something for each other. One of my favorite birthday's was when I turned thirteen and she gave me lemon flavored cupcakes from the grocery store and a stuffed turtle. It might seem childish, but it meant the world to me because I knew she cared.

"What are you thinking about?" Cole's voice interrupts my walk down memory lane. "You have this faraway look in your eyes."

"I was thinking about my sister."

"You have a sister?" He sounds so surprised and I instantly feel bad that I've never told him about Hazel.

"Um, yeah." I give him a hesitant smile and tuck a piece of hair behind my ear. "She's older. Her name is Hazel."

"Hmm." He hums, nodding. He rubs his hands on his jeans, looking out the window. My intuition tells me he's upset he's just learning this. It's something I *should* have mentioned in the few weeks we've been going out, but it's not like Hazel is a huge part of my life so sadly it didn't cross my mind.

Climbing out of the truck, the door closes behind me with a clang. Honestly I'm surprised there isn't rust sprinkling the ground.

Cole meets me at the front of the truck and takes my hand, intertwining our fingers, so he must not be too mad or irritated.

Smiling up at him, I let him guide me toward the entrance.

I spot Mascen's Land Rover parked in the front causing bile to rise up my throat.

It could be someone else's. I know in my gut it's not.

Cole sees where my gaze has strayed. "I invited Mascen, is that cool? I thought it'd be more fun to make it a team thing."

"Team?" I squeak, feeling sick, because I'm certain I know where this is leading.

"Us against him and his date."

"Right ... sounds fantastic." If he notices the change in the pitch of my voice he doesn't comment.

I'm tempted to text Kenna or Li, beg one of them to give me an excuse to get out of this suddenly torturous event, but I know I have to deal with it and go on. I can't avoid Mascen forever after our kiss.

I keep trying to pretend it sucked, but the fact is no kiss has ever topped it. It was intense, passionate, full of emotions neither one of us will ever admit to. It was the kind of kiss they talk about in fairytales — one to wake a sleeping princess.

Cole guides me inside the sleek looking bowling and bar crossover. A lot of the people hanging out are dressed nicely, there are even men in business attire smoking cigars in a lounge area. This is nothing like the weed infused bowling alley I used to frequent in high school.

Cole notices my awe and chuckles. "Swanky, isn't it? I guess a rich town calls for a bad ass bowling alley."

"Can you even call this a bowling alley? It's more like a club." I notice a room off to the side, sectioned off with a thick deep blue velvet curtain. I can't help wondering if there are dancers back there.

Cole pays for our rental shoes, which are shiny black and white leather and look brand new, not all used and busted.

He leads me into the bowling area. At the back by the wall Mascen sits with his date. He's leaning back in the chair, legs spread wide in ripped jeans, wearing a fitted white v-neck that shows off the elegant slope of his smooth neck and collar, with a leather jacket tossed on like an after-thought on top. His hair is messy, eyes dark, while his lips are wrapped around a cigar instead of a cigarette. Fuck. It shouldn't be sexy but it is. He sucks on the end of the cigar and blows out the smoke so it clouds his face. On the table beside him sits his baseball cap. I'm used to him wearing it and find it almost lonely seeing it rest on the wooden top by itself.

I force myself to stop staring at him, and instead I take in his date. I startle when I realize it's the girl he danced with at the Halloween party a couple of weeks ago and the one I've seen him on campus with a few times. The flare of jealousy heating my veins sends color to my cheeks from embarrassment. I shouldn't be jealous of this girl for being with him. I should feel sorry for her instead.

With lighter shade of brown hair, pale skin, and a round face she looks sweet, almost shy. I know under normal circumstances this is probably the kind of girl

I'd get along great with, but because she's here with Mascen I feel instant dislike and I hate myself for it. She's done nothing to me and I'm not here for him anyway.

I smile up at Cole, forcing all thoughts of Mascen from my mind. For the moment at least. "This is going to be fun. You had a great idea."

"Thanks, babe." He lowers his head, giving me a peck on my lips.

My stomach rolls with nausea.

You have to stop this, Rory. Cole is a good, kind, decent guy who doesn't deserve to be strung along by the likes of you.

I exhale a weighted sigh, suddenly feeling the need to cry.

Cole truly is a sweetheart and I've been halfway out the door our entire relationship, if you can even call it a relationship.

Sitting down, I switch out my black converse for the bowling shoes, knowing I have to put a brave face on for tonight, even though I know I'm going to have to be honest with him later.

Cole enters our names into the touch screen computer and I silently note to myself that the girl is named Mallory.

She smiles at me, giving a small wave. My cheeks heat again, realizing I was staring at her.

"Hi, I'm Rory," I tell her, extending my hand.

"Mallory." She shakes my hand and then tucks a piece of hair behind her ear before eyeing Mascen shyly. Honestly, she doesn't look that interested in him, merely hesitant and kind of amused.

"I thought it was Aurora." Mascen's deep, throaty voice invades my senses, thickening my blood until it pounds against the walls of my veins.

"Only to you," I mutter.

Mallory hears and gives a small laugh.

"You're up." I turn at Cole's voice and he waves me over.

"I don't want to go first."

"I put your name in first," Cole replies, pointing at the screen. "Sorry."

I lower my head. I suck at bowling. I always end up in the gutter no matter how hard I try. Forcing a smile, I hug his side. "It's okay. I just suck at this."

"I can help you."

He walks over to the wall lined with bowling balls and tells me to pick one that feels right. I end up with one that's lighter and feels easier to handle.

"Can you hurry up?" Mascen snaps, his cigar between his thumb and forefinger as he leans forward, eyes glaring at me from beneath narrowed brows. "We don't have all fucking night."

Mallory glances from him to me, her lips tilting in a speculative way.

"Don't be such a whiner."

His lips quirk with the threat of laughter. "Show us how it's done then, Princess."

"Princess?" Cole looks between the two of us. "Why are you calling her princess?"

"Her name is *Aurora* fuck face. You know, like Sleeping Beauty."

"Oh." Cole nods with a grin. "I get it now."

He urges me forward with a hand low on my waist. Standing in front of the long narrow lane I take a deep breath hoping I don't make a fool of myself in front of my three companions.

Cole murmurs instructions in my ear, his voice low and his lips brushing the side of my face. I feel like I should be getting turned on, but I don't feel anything. Something tells me if it was the man brooding behind us at my side I would be.

Cole takes a step back, giving me space to swing the ball.

My arm flies back and with it the ball. It pops off my fingers, rolling away.

"That's okay. It's happened to me before." Cole heads to get the runaway ball, but Mascen scoops it up before he can.

"Princess, the ball goes the other way." Instead of handing it over to Cole who stands waiting he walks over to me. "Don't over think it," he whispers under his breath. "Just play."

He hands over the ball and walks away. Cole hesitates beside me, probably wondering if I want more coaching or if he should let me go for it.

"I can do it." I figure it's better to let him think I'm confident about this.

Lining my eyes up with the lane I take a breath and swing the ball.

It goes straight for the gutter but at least it made it onto the lane this time. It's not much of a positive, but it's something.

When the ball comes out of the machine, I pick it up for my second attempt. I only knock down two pins. It's better than zero. Cole goes next, getting a spare. Mascen, hilariously, hits the gutter on his first shot — glaring at me like it's my fault — but then knocks down the rest on his next try earning a spare like Cole. Mallory blows us all away by getting a strike. She turns around, pointing at Mascen.

"I told you I'd take you down." She gives a little giggle before sitting down beside him.

I'm not jealous. I'm really not, I chant to myself. I'm afraid it's becoming a screwed up mantra.

It's my dreaded turn again. I'm not surprised when I only knock down five. It's half of the ones I needed to knock down, so I guess that means I'm making progress.

Cole goes up for his turn which leaves me with Mascen and Mallory.

"What's your major?" Mallory asks, angling her chair toward me.

"I'm currently doing my general studies, but I plan to apply to law school when I can."

"Law school? Wow, that's awesome. Good for you."

"Thanks." She seems genuinely nice, but I have no control over my distant tone. It's not her fault I can't get her date off my mind.

Mascen watches the two of us with a relaxed

posture, his lips quirked slightly like he's amused by this whole thing. As much as I've obsessed over our kiss, replayed it in mind, punished myself for loving it, I bet he's completely forgotten about it. He's with girls all the time. I'm nothing special. Never have been, and it won't start now. I wish I could get the cocky bastard off my mind, because he doesn't deserve a second of my time, but I can't stop. I see now why so many girls lust after him on campus, he's sexy and mysterious. The aura that surrounds him is a calling card to women. We can't help it. It's ingrained in us to like the guy we know is bad news. The one with the dangerous smile and smoldering gaze. We know he'll destroy our hearts but we think the pleasure will be worth it.

Was kissing him worth it to me?

I guess so, because I wouldn't take it back.

I'm such a sheep.

Cole finishes and Mascen goes up for his turn. I watch him way too closely. The veins roping his tanned arm shouldn't be sexy, but they are, and it makes me glad he ditched his jacket. He picks up the blue colored ball, his eyes intent as he turns for the lane, his back now to us. He sizes things up, adjusting his stance. His jeans aren't fitted, but they still can't hide his muscular backside and thick thighs. I've never cared much for sports, but now I find myself desperate to know what he looks like in his baseball pants.

When he lets go of the ball I force myself to stop staring at his ass like a pathetic loser—especially since I'm here with his best friend. God, I'm worse than

Mascen. At least it seems like he's honest with his dates, hookups, conquests, whatever you want to call them, but I haven't been with Cole.

The ball knocks down one pin and Mascen curses.

Mallory hops up, her gait almost ballerina-like — smooth, graceful. She says something to him and he shakes his head with a true heart-stopping smile. It might be the first genuine smile I've seen from him. When his ball appears she grabs it before he can and he playfully fights for her to give it back to him. It's cute. A scene right out of a movie.

"I have to go to the bathroom." I hop up before Cole can reply, taking off back in the direction we came. I find the restrooms easily enough and dash inside to one of the sinks, splashing cold water on my face.

"Get a grip, Rory." I hold onto the marble counter for support. "You're being ridiculous."

My eyes are bloodshot in my reflection. Inhaling a lungful of air my shoulders dip further like they bear the weight of the world.

For the rest of the evening, I pretend I'm having fun. I act like everything is normal. But I know by the end of tonight Cole is probably going to hate me.

TWENTY-SIX

MASCEN

"You're here late."

"So are you." I tip my head at Mark as I walk past him for the batting cages.

"Avoiding the Missus," he grumbles, closing the car magazine he's reading today. "Apparently I'm driving her up a wall, but the feeling is mutual."

"Mind if I bat for a while, then?" I pull out some cash and set it on the counter. He eyes it, then gives me the same look he always does when I force him to take the money.

If he's going to be extra chatty tonight then I'll

leave. I'm not here for conversation. "Go on ahead. The door was unlocked."

I tip my head at him and continue down the hall.

I dropped Mallory off at her dorm thirty minutes ago. She beat my ass at bowling like promised, getting a strike every time. I don't care about her defeating me, well all of us, and I actually had fun with her. But the entire time my mind was on Rory, watching her with Cole and how they interact. It was torture. I'm sure it makes me a spoiled brat, but I'm used to getting what I want, and she's the one thing I can't have.

Mallory surprised me when I parked outside her dorm when she turned to me and said, "You like Rory."

I played dumb and muttered, "Of course I do. Cole's my best friend and she's his girlfriend."

She shook her head at me. "I'm not dumb, Mascen. You *like* that girl." She paused then, taking a breath like she was waiting for me to do or say something. "I've been in that spot before. It's a sucky place to be. I'm sorry."

"Nothing to be sorry for. I don't like her."

She laughed. "God, you're stubborn. See you in class."

She hopped out of my car and ran for the building. I waited until I saw her get inside.

Now, I'm here. Hitting balls like my life depends on it. The clang of the ball against the bat soothes something inside me. Over and over I hit the balls as they shoot out at me. I set the machine a tad faster than normal, Mark will probably berate me once he realizes I messed with the machine, but at least tonight I'll be long gone before he notices.

I'm not sure how much time passes, maybe an hour, before Mark comes to tell me I need to go.

I pack my stuff up and head home, despite not wanting to be there. I'm sure Cole will want to talk about the date, and go on and on about how wonderful he thinks Rory is. If that happens I'll probably punch him in the fucking face. I can only take so much.

I pull into the garage and head up, expecting him to be home. The downstairs is dark, but it means nothing. He could be sleeping already. Sleep is one of Cole's favorite things in the world.

Grabbing a bottle of water I jog upstairs, not being as quiet as I should be. His bedroom door is closed. I pause outside of it, listening for any sounds of life, or God forbid him and Rory going at it like rabbits. It's silent. My hand wraps around the knob and I ease it open, revealing his empty bed.

Rage simmers in my blood. If he's not home yet it means he's with Rory, that he's been with her ever since we left the bowling alley. He doesn't have a car so he's dependent on her to get home.

Slamming his door closed the whole wall shakes with the force. I stalk across to my room, my anger growing by the second. I can feel my blood pressure raising and no amount of deep breaths can lower it.

I yank the covers off my bed in my fury, muttering nonsense under my breath.

I keep reminding myself I have no right to be angry that he's not home.

It's late, the smart thing to do would be to shower and go to bed, but I don't think it's possible.

Grabbing the keys to my truck I plan to drive out to my safe space, the one where it's just me, the stars, and silence.

Bounding down the stairs two at a time, I'm shocked to find Cole coming up from the garage. He lifts his head, looking forlorn. Spotting me with my keys in hand, he cocks his head to the side. "Where are you going?"

"Uh ... out."

He presses his lips together. "Hope you had fun tonight."

"It was ... nice."

Fuck, I'm eloquent.

He walks around me, and I'm not a fucking expert at this kind of thing, but I did grow up with two sisters so I know enough to know when something is wrong with someone and Cole is clearly upset about something.

"Did you get bad news about your car?"

He turns around, his brows drawn. "What?"

"You seem upset. Did you get bad news on your car? I can always loan you the money, or you can borrow my car, I'll take the truck."

He shakes his head back and forth. "It's not about the car, or money, or anything like that."

I hesitate, swinging the keychain around my finger. "What's up then?"

He blows out a breath, shoving his hands in his pockets. "Rory broke up with me."

It takes his words a moment to make their way to my brain. "She ... broke up with you?" Even saying the words out loud they're still not making sense.

He shakes his head in a self-deprecating kind of way. "She said I'm a 'nice guy'," he air quotes in a pissed off tone, "and she really likes me as a friend, but she doesn't have any feelings beyond that for me."

I stand there, feeling like a dumbass because I don't know what I'm supposed to say. "I'm sorry."

His shoulders droop and his lips press flat. "You know the worst part?"

"What?"

He straightens, crossing his arms over his chest. "We both know you're an asshole. But girls throw themselves at you. And I'm not saying I'm lacking where that comes from, but the difference is, those girls would drop *anything* to be your girlfriend. You're the bad boy they all want, but they forget that bad boys break hearts. Me? I'm the nice guy and nice guys don't win."

His jaw twitches and I know he's hurt and angry, but I don't have any words of advice. I'm not good at this. I'm not the relationship kind of guy.

Quietly, he turns and goes upstairs.

I don't see the point in heading out to sulk now. It's fucking wrong how my best friend is hurting and I'm celebrating. Rory isn't his anymore. It's not like it's exactly good news for me. I'm not going to make a move on her, but it is a relief to know I won't have to see her attached to my best friend anymore.

Fuck, I'm a selfish bastard through and through.

Even with that knowledge, I can't wipe the smile off my face as I go up to my room.

TWENTY-SEVEN

RORY

"You broke up with him?" Kenna lays back on the couch, popping a cheeseball in her mouth. "Why? He's hot, nice, caring—the whole package."

"Well, something must've been wrong." Li swipes one of the cheeseballs from the container Kenna holds hostage. She perches her butt on the coffee table, the two of them looking at me in the armchair, waiting for some kind of explanation.

Kenna gasps and sits up, some of the little orange balls flying out of the top and onto the floor. "He doesn't have erectile disfunction does he? I know he's young, but that shit happens to guys any age."

"Kenna!" Li laughs, shaking her head.

I blush, hiding behind my hair. "Um, not that I know of."

"What do you mean 'not that I know of'?"

I lift the cup of freshly brewed coffee to my lips, testing the temperature before I scald my mouth. "I never had sex with him."

Kenna chokes on a cheeseball, which doesn't bode well for the gag reflex I've heard her brag about. "You didn't sleep with him? Why? He's hot!"

I shrug, wrapping my fingers around the warm mug. "I wasn't interested in him like I should've been—and he's nice. I've used guys for sex plenty of times but I knew he wanted more from me than that. I didn't want to lead him on."

Li shakes her head, stifling laughter, while Kenna looks flabbergasted.

Shaking her head, Kenna leans against the cushions. "Damn, the restraint you have. I could never."

I look away from her and out the window at the parking lot. I feel bad for breaking things off with Cole. The look on his face when I told him I didn't feel for him the way I knew he did me was heartbreaking.

"Are you sad?" Li, always the mama bear, inquires.

"I'm sad I hurt him. He's a good guy. But I'm not sad I broke things off."

She nods like this makes perfect sense while Kenna

is still flabbergasted I didn't take a ride on his pogo stick.

Finally, Kenna snaps herself out of it. "If you're not sad then we don't have a legitimate excuse to stuff our faces with ice cream and junk food."

I eye the plastic container she's been digging into the for the past ten minutes. "I don't think that's stopping you," I joke.

She throws one at me and I dodge it, but some of my coffee escapes over the lip of the mug. I lick it off my fingers.

"I'm on my period and all I want is junk food."

"You live your best life, honey." I grab the cheeseball off the floor and toss it back at her.

"Now that you're single again does this mean we can go out to some bars and find some guys? Obviously once shark week leaves."

"We do that anyway."

"Don't knock sex on your period," Li blurts at the same time. We both look at her and her cheeks pinken. "It heightens sensation." Her voice softens as her shoulders draw up to her ears. "Besides, don't act like sex isn't messy. The fluids are just usually clear."

"Wow," Kenna ponders her statement, "you learn something new every day. Li likes bloody sex."

"Oh my God." She hides her face, sliding off the coffee table and onto the floor to curl into the fetal position. "I hate you guys."

"Lies, we're the best roommates you could ever ask for." Kenna tosses a pillow at her.

Li grabs it, hugging it against her chest.

"When do you guys leave for break?" I decide to save Li from more torture.

"Friday after classes." Kenna gives me a sympathetic look. She pulled me aside and said I was welcome to go home with her, but while I appreciated her wanting to make sure I'm not alone for Thanksgiving I also didn't want to spend the holiday with people who aren't anything to me.

"Saturday morning." Li sits up frowning. "Are you going to be okay here on your own?"

"I'll be fine." I dismiss her concern. "I love you guys but it'll be nice to get some alone time. I'll have more hours to work too."

It sucks that I don't have a home to go to, but it is what it is. I long ago accepted my situation and I'm okay with it. I'm not the only person in the world with a broken family.

"All this talk of leaving is making me sad. I know it's a short break but I'm going to miss my girls." Kenna pouts, her eyes filling with tears. Her period is clearly making her more sentimental than usual. "Let's put a movie on."

"What are you thinking?" Li gets up, padding into the kitchen. I'm not surprised when she digs in the cabinet and procures a box of popcorn.

"Something sweet and sappy. I'm not in the frame of mind to do anything sad."

"Sweet Home Alabama?" I suggest. It's one of my go-to movies when I want what she's asking for.

She crinkles her nose in thought. "That's the one with Josh Lucas, right?" I nod. "He gave me a country boy fetish from that movie. That accent." She licks her lips, then stuffs a handful of cheeseballs in her mouth. I'm beginning to think I'm going to have to stage an intervention with the snack. "It also gave me a plaid shirt kink."

Li snorts, spitting out the White Claw she just opened. "Plaid shirt kink?"

"It's a thing!" Kenna defends, her bottom lip jutting out. "Don't mock me."

I start the movie and Li comes over with the popcorn, the two of us joining Kenna on the small couch so we're all squished together but can see the TV.

We spend the whole day watching romantic comedies and pigging out on snacks.

I don't tell them, but it's one of my favorite days ever.

———

"ENJOY YOUR MEAL." I smile at the elderly couple who both look ready to dig into their spaghetti.

Breezing by my other tables, I do a scan to see who needs refills, if anyone needs napkins, or who might be ready for their check.

"Busy night," Aldo remarks, shaking up a cocktail.

"It's always busy."

"Thank goodness for that," Izzy inserts, running by.

Heather comes up beside me, tucking her tray under

her arm. "Aldo, think you can do us all a favor and slip something into Izzy's drink to calm her crazy ass down."

He gives a laugh, pouring the blue colored drink into a fancy glass before popping an umbrella in. "I wish, but alas we all must deal with my sister."

"Ugh, that's what I figured." Heather sticks her tongue out and crosses her eyes. She gives me a light tap on my butt and heads into the kitchen.

I grab refills for a few of my tables and drop off the check at two of them. I'm glad the night is busy. It keeps me distracted from the fact that tomorrow is Friday and Kenna will be leaving, and then Li on Saturday. I know I'll be fine on my own, but I will miss them.

For some stupid reason, I keep expecting Mascen to come with one of his 'dates'. But he hasn't shown all week. I've seen him on campus once this week and he was in line for coffee with Mallory. My heart instantly dropped. I've never seen him multiple times with a girl like I have with her. It makes me think maybe they are dating—according to campus gossip he's still free real estate, which is the dumbest saying I've ever heard.

Approaching the elderly couple's table, I ask, "Would you guys be interested in some dessert this evening?"

"Not tonight, sweetheart." The woman smiles kindly at me.

Rubbing his round tummy her husband adds, "I'm stuffed."

"Okay, are you ready for the check then? No rush."

"Bring it by when you have time."

Bustling back to the kitchen I bring out an order for another table and then drop the check off to the couple. He immediately slides a bill into the sleeve.

"No change."

"Thank you. You both have a good evening."

They both stand, the man reaching for his wife's coat first to help her into it. "You're welcome. Good-night," they tell me.

It's another two hours before my shift ends, which is a little earlier than normal. Still, it's dark outside when I walk out to my car. The streetlights are bright, but the lot for staff isn't as well lit.

When I first notice the body leaning against my truck my heart freezes in fear, a scream lodged in my throat. I quickly recognize the body frame and my heart doubles in speed. Mascen must hear my shoes on the gravel because his head flies up and somehow even in the dark our eyes make contact.

"What are you doing here sulking in the dark, Edward Cullen?"

"Waiting for you." He doesn't move away from my truck.

"Why?" I stop a few feet away from him, my purse drawn across my body like a shield. Sadly, the feeble and fraying fabric isn't going to protect me from the heartbreak that is written all over a guy like Mascen.

"Heard you don't have a home to go to."

"Where did you hear that?"

He cocks his head. "I know everything, Aurora."

"So, what? You came all the way to my job to mock me?" An incredulous laugh bursts from my lips. "Wow, you know, despite how much of a dick you are to me you still manage to surprise me."

His lips quirk. "Gotta keep you on your toes, Princess, but you shouldn't insult me when I'm riding in on my white horse attempting to be ... not a prince," he wrinkles his nose like the thought disgusts him even though that's exactly what he is, "maybe a really naughty knight—"

"Is there a point to this?" I interrupt. I'm tired, cranky, and my feet hurt. A shower is calling my name and I plan on stuffing my face with the brownies Kenna made because she feels bad for leaving me.

"You're coming home with me." He grins from ear to ear like this is the greatest news ever.

"No, I'm not."

"Yes, you are."

"*No*, I'm not."

"Yes, Rory, you are."

"Don't call me Rory."

"I'll call you whatever I want."

I throw my hands in the air. "What are we? Twelve? This is ridiculous. Do you even hear yourself? *Telling* me that I'm going home with you? We don't even like each other!"

Lie. I like him very much. At least in a 'I find him very attractive and want to jump his bones' kind of way. As for his attitude and what comes out of his mouth, I don't like that so much.

"Why are you so stubborn?"

I gape at him. The man has lost his mind. "Me? Stubborn? Look in a mirror, bud—or wait, maybe you can't see your reflection. Vampire and all." I give a shrug. "But we're not friends." I wag my finger between the two of us. "Me going home with you makes zero sense. I am fine alone."

"Just because you're okay alone doesn't mean you should be." His lips soften. "It's Thanksgiving, Rory. Do you really want to be by yourself?"

I square my shoulders, my chin rising slightly. "My roommate Kenna invited me to go back home with her and I said no."

"You don't know her family, but you know mine," he counter-argues. Stuffing his hands in the pockets of his school sweatshirt, he leans closer to me, like he hopes his laser-hypnotic gaze can convince me. "Surely you haven't forgotten my mom and dad. Or Willow. Or Lylah."

I look away. Of course I haven't forgotten them. His family was a part of some of my best memories, but that was a long time ago. "I doubt they remember me."

"Sure they do. Do you really want to disappoint my mom, Princess? I already told her you were coming."

His mom was always kind to my sister and me. She was the real motherly type, baking with her kids, teaching them to garden, all kinds of things, and she always let Hazel and I pitch in.

I exhale a lungful of air, looking away from him. I

can't think straight when I'm staring at his annoyingly smug face. "I'm fine by myself."

He lets out a gruff laugh. "Look, I'm not doubting your ability to be fine on your own, but it's a family holiday and you shouldn't be alone when you don't have to be. I'm loaning you my family. Just say thank you and that you'll come."

I look back at him. "I'm scheduled to work. I need the money."

His smirk intensifies. "I already spoke with your boss letting her know I was surprising you with an unexpected trip back home. She told me I was a wonderful boyfriend."

He's so fucking pleased with himself, meanwhile I'm stuck on him saying *back home*, because I haven't been back to Virginia since we left and now that I'm reminded of that fact I do want to go.

"Don't ever talk to my boss again." I try to sound as stern as I possibly can. "But…" His annoying smile grows further, knowing he's about to win. "I'll go."

"I knew you'd see things my way, Princess." He finally moves away from my truck, walking backwards toward his SUV. "Pack your shit. We leave tomorrow after your last class. Psychology, right?"

My mouth pops open. I don't even have to give him a reply. How does he know what class I have tomorrow afternoon? I laugh to myself as he gets in his car. This is Mascen Wade I'm talking about. All he'd have to do is bat his eyes and any number of people would let him know my schedule — my roommates included.

I watch him pull out before I get in my truck, already wondering if there's any way I can get out of what I've just agreed to.

SITTING down in my psychology class the following afternoon, I feel confident in my resolution not to go with Mascen today. I didn't bother packing my bags, because going home with him would be the worst idea ever. I was conned by the potent power that is him last night, but as soon as I got away from him it faded. I'm sure he'll be waiting for me after class and I'll tell him no. As simple as that. He won't argue with me in such a public place.

Pulling out my computer, notebook, and pen, I set up the small workspace in front of me so I'm ready for class.

Someone slides into the seat beside me and I bend down, moving my backpack out of his foot space.

"Brought you a coffee, Princess. Black just like your stained soul. I hope that's how you take it, but if it's not complain to someone else."

My body shoots up quickly from my bent position. I nearly knock over my laptop as I straighten but his large hand grabs it before it can wobble off.

"Mascen," I hiss, glaring at him. "What are you doing?"

He releases my computer, sitting back. Crossing one foot over his knee he waits to answer me. After he's pulled out a notebook and pen, the pen pressed against the side of his lips, he finally puts me out of my misery and replies. "I would think that would be quite clear but you've proven to be ridiculously oblivious. I'm here for Psych one-oh-*one*." His lips exaggerate the word *one*.

"You're not in this class," I state the obvious as the seats fill in around us for the two o'clock lecture.

He mock gasps, throwing a hand to his chest in a fit of dramatics. "You mean I've been in the wrong class all this time?"

"We both know you don't belong here. Leave."

"No can do." He scoots his long legs forward, scrunching down in the seat. "I'm sure you're a flight risk, so I'm here to make sure you don't take off on me."

I square my shoulders, looking straight ahead at the podium standing empty in wait for the professor, willing him to hurry up.

"I wouldn't take off on you."

I would.

"Don't lie Princess or you'll end up as Pinocchio."

I glare at him. "Do you live to irritate the shit out of me?"

He leans back, the cocky grin on his lips too fucking hot for someone so infuriating. "I am beginning to think it's my sole purpose in life."

"This is *my* class, can you go now?"

"Did you pack your bags?" Silence is my only response. "Mhmm," he hums, balancing his pen on his top lip. "You didn't did you? Which is exactly why I'm here. Try to tell me to leave again, Aurora." He moves suddenly, leaning in so his mouth is right by the side of my face. "I. Dare. You." I desperately want to look at him but I know better than to move my head. "You think there are certain things I won't do, but believe me, I won't have a problem throwing you over my shoulder and carrying you out of here kicking and screaming. You agreed to go, you're going. No takebacks."

My breath catches with the last two words and when I look at him his eyes have widened. I'd forgotten it until he said, but no takebacks was something we said to each other a lot growing up.

"No takebacks," I find myself whispering to him as the professor finally enters the room.

Sadly, I don't remember a word of the lesson.

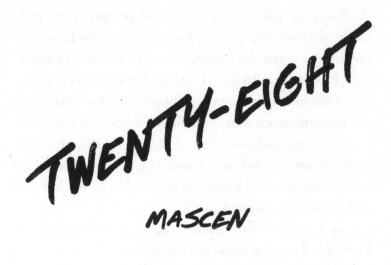

TWENTY-EIGHT

MASCEN

"Do you really need to come into my dorm?" Rory hesitates outside her door. A few girls linger in the hall and I wave, earning a few giggles and flirtatious grins tossed my way. "You could've stayed in the car."

"So you can hole up in here and *not* come out?" I guffaw. "I think not."

She must really think I'm dumb if she thinks I'd let that happen. I don't know why I'm so insistent on her coming, it shouldn't matter, but when I heard that she was staying on campus for the holiday break it didn't seem right for that to happen when I can do something about it.

Sure, my parents are crazy and eccentric, my little sister will probably give me hell, and my older sister will torture me when she's around, but it's family. It's home. And I want Rory to have that. We have the extra room, so it's not like her presence will be disrupting anything.

Rory inhales a deep sigh, finally unlocking the door.

"Oh, hey," a brown-haired girl greets her. "I wasn't sure I'd see you before I leave. Oh, who is this?" Her smirk tells me she knows exactly who I am, but she wants Rory to acknowledge it.

As I follow Rory inside, I recognize the girl from Harvey's. I've seen them there together.

"Kenna, hey. Hi. Um. You know Mascen."

"We haven't met," I interject.

The girl laughs. "Yes, but everyone on campus knows who you are."

I lean against the kitchen counter, my eyes scanning the small pieces of décor, trying to figure out if any of the trinkets are Rory's. Any insight I can get into the person she is today I'll take.

"So, why are you here with Rory? In our dorm?"

Rory looks at me over her shoulder, her eyes desperate and begging for me not to tell the truth.

"Just picking up something of Cole's he left here."

Kenna grins like the cat that ate the canary and I know I'm in trouble. Rory's shoulders droop and she visibly cringes.

"Cole only came here once and *definitely* didn't leave

anything behind, just like he apparently never took a trip down Rory's love canal either."

"Oh my God." Rory covers her face with her hands.

I don't have a response. Normally I would, but I'm too taken aback by the fact that apparently Cole and Rory never slept together.

"Interesting," I finally say.

"So, why are you really here?"

"Kenna," Rory pleads. "Drop it."

Her friend grins, her hand braced on a suitcase. "I have questions and I want answers."

"Rory and I grew up in the same area." I can tell Kenna is the type of person to not let this go. "I told her I'd give her a ride home. Save gas."

"But you weren't going home?" She frames it as a question, eyeing Rory with suspicion.

"I … uh … changed my mind."

Kenna sighs, her gaze swinging between the two of us. "I don't believe either of you. But I have to go. You, missy," she points at Rory like a mother scolding her unruly toddler, "will have explaining to do when we get back. But I have a flight to catch."

Her smile softens and she hugs Rory, brushing past me to leave.

"Treat my girl, right," she calls over her shoulder, closing the door behind her.

Silence entreats on the small living space and Rory keeps her back to me. After a minute she slowly turns. "You never slept with Cole, huh?"

She narrows her eyes. "Of course that's the first

thing you say, but no, I didn't. Not that first night, not ever. But it's not your business who I do and don't sleep with."

I'm on her in an instant, pushing her back against the wall. The breath leaves her in a gasp, her eyes wide with surprise and lips parted.

"We both know that's not true." I skim my nose along the smooth column of her throat. She smells like something floral with a hint of crisp apples and vanilla. It's delicious and I can't help but want a taste. My tongue threatens to take a lick, but I know if I do it'll be even more difficult to get her to come with me. "Deny it all you want, but there's a mutual attraction here." She shakes her head. "When you lie so blatantly it makes me want to punish you."

She writhes against me trying to break free of my hold but then a moan escapes her and she sinks further into me.

"It's okay to hate me and want to fuck me."

"I do hate you, but I don't want to fuck you."

I grin like a wolf about to devour a tasty morsel, and I know Rory would be oh-so-sweet. "I love it when you lie to me. Do it again, and again, and again, because Princess, all those lies are adding up into favors you're going to owe me."

"I owe you nothing."

I chuckle, gliding my lips along her jaw. "Wrong, you owe me everything."

———

"I STILL DON'T UNDERSTAND why you insisted on me coming with you."

Rory sits in the passenger side of the Rover, arms crossed over her chest, and dare I say pouting.

"I told you, no one should be alone on the holidays when there are people they can be with."

"I don't know your family anymore," she argues, looking out the window at the blur of trees in the growing darkness.

I'm quiet for a moment, feeling uncomfortable. "You know me."

I can feel her penetrating gaze, but for once she says nothing.

"We're going to stop around nine and get a hotel."

"What?" she scoffs. "I'm not sharing a hotel room with you."

"Relax, Princess, I'll get you your own room."

She makes a noise that I can't quite decide is in relief or general irritation.

At least twenty minutes pass in silence between us before she breaks it. "I hate your music."

"Don't diss my man Jason Aldean." I purposely draw out my southern twang more than usual. I didn't grow up in the deep south, but that doesn't mean I didn't pick up a slight drawl. "What do you want to listen to? Disney musicals? One Direction?"

"Don't drag One Direction like that. Their music is good."

I keep my eyes on the road despite my desperation to look at her. "I feel like I don't even know you."

It's meant to be a joke, but she replies, "You don't."

I wince. It's sad, but true. I don't know her, but she doesn't know me either. Sure, she thinks she does, but people tend to not dig beneath the surface.

Clearing my throat, I wiggle a bit in the seat, uncomfortable from the sudden tension between us. "Take my phone." I nod at where it rests. "Make a playlist for us. My country ... your ... tween bops."

She hesitates, her hand hovering over the sleek device. "Are you sure?"

"We have two more hours before we stop tonight. We might as well compromise on the music before we rip each other's throats out, though if you want to rip clothes off I'm all for it."

She groans. "Nice try, Bundy."

I glance at her with an arched brow. "In to choking? Kinky, I like it."

She rolls her eyes, finally picking up my phone. I rattle off my password before she can ask.

Drawing her legs up onto the car seat she leans her left elbow on the middle console which brings her closer to me. "Murder is illegal you know."

"Huh?"

"Bundy. Choking." She bites her bottom lip. I shouldn't be staring at her, not while I'm driving, but I can't help it.

Clearing my throat, I force my eyes back to the road. "A little choking in sex never hurt anyone. It heightens pleasure."

"Have *you* ever been choked? Or are you always the one doing the choking?"

I decide to answer honestly, no point in lying. "Yes, I have been."

A little gasp of surprise leaves her lips, making my honesty all the more worth it.

"Did you … like it?" Her voice becomes small, like a teeny tiny little mouse.

"Yes."

"Hmm," she hums.

"What?"

"You didn't strike me as the submissive type."

Her statement catches me off guard and I nearly choke on my own tongue. "I'm not." My tone is definitive.

"Would you let me choke you if we had sex?"

Holy shit this girl keeps surprising me. "Depends, I guess." I adjust my hold on the steering wheel for the sake of being able to do something with my hands when all I want to do is pull the car over and kiss her.

"On what?"

I give her a brief look before returning my eyes to the dark road ahead. "Are you choking me to give me pleasure … or to kill me?"

She busts out laughing, her eyes on the glowing phone screen as she adds song to the playlist. "I haven't decided yet."

She finishes the playlist and plugs my phone back in. The first song that comes on is a poppy tune that's definitely not my taste. The lyrics keep saying something about making you glad you came and I don't think they mean to a party.

"What'd you name it? The playlist?"

She smirks, bringing her feet back to the floor. "Princess and the Vampire Mash-Up."

Laughter bursts out of me. "Catchy. I like it."

I feel her smile rather than see it. "I do too."

———

PULLING into a hotel lot after nine with a sack of greasy fast-food in hand we grab our bags from the backseat, walking toward the entrance.

"Two rooms," Rory reminds me, adjusting her bag on her shoulder. She was too stubborn to let me carry it.

"I haven't forgotten."

The hotel is one of those basic ones you can find off almost any exit of the interstate. The lobby outdated but clean. It'll do for the night. Tomorrow we'll have another four hours to drive to get to my house.

"I can give you money for my room." She grabs her bag, pulling it around to her front to dig in a pocket.

I roll my eyes. "Don't insult me, Princess. I insisted on you coming, I'm paying."

She crinkles her nose, her teeth digging slightly into her bottom lip. "I hate handouts, but since you did practically force me to come I guess I'll make a concession this time."

I snort. "I'm honored."

Heading up to the check-in desk I speak with the

receptionist. She's young, probably twenty-four or so. Her flirtatious words and smiles don't go unnoticed by Rory who crosses her arms over her chest and glares.

When the receptionist tells me what time she'll be getting off I say, "That's enough, give me the room keys."

Her eyes widen in shock and her lips shut. She grabs the keycards, activates them, and passes me the envelope.

"Let's go," I say to Rory, ushering her toward the elevator with a hand hovering at her waist. I don't dare touch her for the fear of her biting my hand off or another appendage I'm overly fond of.

I push the button for the second floor and the heavy sigh that leaves me has my body leaning against the side of the elevator.

"Tired?" Rory arches a brow at my form.

"Extremely."

"Hmm."

"What? I can't be tired?"

The doors slide open and we step out. Deep red carpeted floor with gold wallpaper greets us.

"Hotels choose dark carpets to hide bodily fluids," Rory informs me, she too taking note of the hideous décor. "Blood, urine, semen," she rattles off.

"Semen?" I arch a brow.

"People like to have sex in public places. Hotel hallways are a prime choice."

"Have a lot of public sex, Princess?" I joke, pausing outside my room when we reach the two side by side.

She's silent, not willing to answer me. My brow arches in surprise. "So, you *have* had a lot of public sex? Color me surprised? You didn't peg me for an exhibitionist. You learn something new every day."

She groans, hanging her head. "Don't make this into something it's not."

I lean my body against the door, holding onto the envelope that holds both our keys. "I need more explanation, darlin'."

"Give me my key." She squares her jaw, holding her hand out.

"I hold all the cards here, literally. Why so much public sex?"

She rolls her eyes. "I couldn't exactly do it at home." She crosses her arms over her chest defensively. "When I wanted to have sex I had to get creative."

"You're only eighteen, how much sex have you been having?"

She tosses her head back. "Drop the overprotective older brother act and give me my room key."

My teeth gnash together. "I'm definitely not your brother, Aurora."

A little smirk crosses her lips and fuck it's hot. I dish shit out to her, but man she knows how to use my own weapons against me. "You're just jealous because all the sex I've had hasn't been with you." Effectively rendering me speechless, she grabs the envelope, takes her key, and shoves the other back at me. "Ta ta, Mascen."

TWENTY-NINE

RORY

THE CLOSER WE GET TO HIS HOME THE MORE stressed I become. It might be ten years since I've been anywhere near Virginia, but there's no mistaking the familiar landscape of rolling hills and mountains with endless farms.

"I can feel the tension radiating off of you."

"I'm not tense."

Of course I am. I know it. He knows it. But God forbid I admit he's right.

"Liar," he chuckles, clutching the steering wheel in his left hand. Sobering, he glances at me briefly, enough of a look for me to see that for once he's not being a jerk. "You can talk to me. I know coming back here can't be easy for you, not after…"

"After my dad killed himself in my childhood home?"

He swallows thickly. "Yeah, that."

I look out the window, a minute of silence passing between us as I watch the blurring brown bark of trees passing us by, and the kaleidoscope colors of changing leaves.

"I saw him," I whisper into the quiet.

"Your dad?"

"Yeah." My tear ducts start to burn, but I refuse to let the treacherous liquid fall. "You know what they don't show you in movies and TV shows is how bad a hanging really is. It's not this body just dangling limply there. I was *eight* and I still remember every detail." I bite down on my lower lip to stop the trembling. "I didn't even see him for that long, but it was like time stood still and I saw things in a different way. I wish I could forget it all the time, because that's the last memory I have of my dad and I don't want it."

Mascen clears his throat, probably uncomfortable with the conversation, which I don't blame him. "I'm sorry. Truly."

"I've never told anyone that before," I admit quietly, feeling like he deserves to know that I've chosen to share something with him. Only him.

"Why did you tell me?"

"Because," I sigh as Mascen takes an exit off of interstate 81, "I know I can trust you."

That might seem strange, Mascen being Mascen and all, but it's true. I know he won't tell anyone.

"You trust me, huh?" His cocky grin almost entirely ruins the moment.

"Don't let it go to your head, Freddy Krueger."

"Why do you trust me?"

"You're making me wish I hadn't said anything now." I watch as we pass by a cluster of fast-food restaurants and gas stations.

"I'm serious. I want to know."

I know he won't let it go until I give him some kind of answer. He's a pest through and through. "You're not a gossip, and even if you don't like someone I don't think you'd do anything to intentionally hurt them in any way. Your prickly attitude does a good enough job already."

The signs of city life begin to disappear as we head further into the country. Farms line both sides of the roads with cows and horses wandering in their pastures.

Mascen adjusts in the seat like he's uncomfortable and I worry it's something I've said. "I hurt Cole," he finally speaks, his jaw taut, "when I kissed you."

I stiffen. "Did you tell him?"

"No. It wouldn't make any difference if I did. I know you didn't either."

"How do you know that?"

His gray eyes flash in my direction, something I can't decipher reflected there. "I'm still alive aren't I?"

"Is Cole mad at me?" My voice becomes small. I feel terrible for leading him on. It wasn't my intention. I truly hoped my feelings would grow for him, but when they didn't I knew I had to break things off.

"He's hurt." Mascen winces. "He really liked you."

"I didn't mean to hurt him."

"I know."

Turning onto a backroad with more farmland on either side, I know we're getting close to his house, which means we're close to my childhood home too.

Out here, acres of land separate homes, but you still call each other neighbors. From the direction we're coming I know we'll get to his house first, which means today at least I won't have to see the place.

A few miles later, Mascen slows to turn on to the private drive.

The anxiety I felt earlier expands tenfold. I'm not sure what his parents are expecting from me, what Mascen's told them, and frankly it's nerve-wracking to think that I'll be spending the next two weeks here before we have to head back to school for finals before winter break.

"What did you tell your mom about me? Why does she think I'm coming with you? She doesn't think we're dating right?"

He snorts like the idea is ludicrous. "No. I said you couldn't go home and were staying on campus and asked if she'd care if you came home with me. She didn't. End of story."

"What about your dad?"

"I'm assuming she okayed it with him."

"You didn't?"

"I talk to my mom more." He shrugs like it's not a big deal, but the way his shoulders tense and his brow furrows I think there's more to the story than he's letting on.

Too soon, the road bends and the large restored Victorian home appears. I'd forgotten how beautiful it is, but it takes my breath away. As a little girl I was convinced it was a giant doll house with the eaves and turrets.

Mascen lets out a sigh, one that sounds both relieved and stressed. He eases his car to a stop in front of the garage addition, killing the engine. Resting his hands on his jean-clad thighs he turns to me with a small smile. "Home sweet home."

He undoes his seatbelt and I follow suit, opening the passenger door to step onto the brick paver driveway. I inhale the sweet scent of mountain air. It takes me back to days of running through fields, grass stuck in my hair, playing tag and daring each other to do things we thought were crazy at the time but now seem so silly.

The breeze blows my hair in my face and I go to move it, finding Mascen watching me with a wistful expression, hands in his pockets. The baseball cap is back in its rightful place backwards on his head.

"What?" I lower my hand from my face, wondering why he's looking at me so funny.

"Nothing." He opens the trunk, grabbing our bags.

"I can take mine." I reach for it as he closes the trunk.

"I've got it."

"Mascen," I argue.

"Rory."

The screen door on the front of the house suddenly flies open and we hear a cry of, "My baby!"

A smile I've never seen him wear before, one that lights up the entire universe and bathes the tiny woman running toward him in a glow, takes over his face as he opens his arms, our bags still managing to rest on those wide shoulders of his.

"Momma!"

Emma dives into his arms, squeezing him tight. It's funny how small she is compared to him but still manages to swallow him whole with her arms.

She grabs his lightly stubbled face and plants kisses all over it.

"Ew, mom, stop."

"You're my baby and I'll cover your face with kisses if I want. I had to push you out of my vagina and you had the biggest head I've ever seen. You owe me for life."

He chuckles, kissing her cheek. Her eyes sparkle with happiness at having her son home. It makes my heart ache. I wish I had this. This is what family is supposed to be like, but unfortunately a lot of times it's not this way. Mascen's lucky to have a close-knit family and I hope he realizes it.

A girl steps onto the porch with the same round face

as his mom and blonde hair to match. It's been so long since I've seen his sisters that I can't even make a guess as to which one it is. "Mascen, you're home!"

"Lylah!" He grins at his sister as she runs toward him. He scoops her up and swings her around. Setting her down, he turns to me. "Mom, Lylah, you remember Rory?"

"Of course." Emma turns that beautiful happy smile to me. She surprises me when she opens her arms for a hug. Even though I'm taken off guard I let her hug me. She squeezes me tight, whispering, "It's good to see you, sweetie. It's been too long."

Stepping back, I try to hide my surprise and the stupid tears that want to flood my eyes. "Thank you for welcoming me into your home."

"Of course, sweetie."

"Hi," Lylah gives a wave. "Nice to meet you ... or see you again." She laughs, shaking her head. "Sorry, this is weird. I don't really remember you."

"It's okay. You were really young when I moved away. But I'm looking forward to getting to know you now."

I sound oddly formal, but I guess it's my way of handling this crazy situation.

Emma claps her hands together. "Should we head inside then? I made some snacks in case you guys were hungry. I wasn't sure if you'd stop for lunch."

"Snacks sound great, Mom."

I follow the three Wade's up the porch steps, taking everything in as I go. On the large porch there's a hanging swing, and several white rockers. A wind-chime of metal music notes hangs from a nail, the sweet sound of them gliding against each other filling the air.

Mascen holds the screen door open for us to go inside first. The grand sweeping staircase fills my vision and ghosts of my past, of a giggling girl and boy, run up those stairs.

The screen door clangs shut behind him and he sets our bags by the stairs, following his mom into the kitchen. I don't know why I expected the house to be entirely different in ten years, but it's very much the same. It makes my chest feel tight from the memories — the *good* memories. Somehow I've let myself forget so many of them, dwelling on everything that was wrong instead.

The kitchen is bright and white, stools lining the large center island. There's a built-in breakfast nook overlooking the backyard pool area. I remember sitting there with Mascen, eating freshly made chocolate chip cookies and then stealing more when we had no busi-ness eating more sugar.

On the island, Emma has fruit and veggies cut up, mini sandwiches waiting, and those same chocolate chip cookies from my memories.

"Eat as much as you want." Emma turns for the refrigerator. "Drinks?"

Mascen asks for a Dr. Pepper for each of us and passes me a bottle. I make sure not to touch his fingers when I grab it for fear of even more emotions stirring inside me. He notices my attempt not to touch him and gives me a funny look.

"Thank you," I mouth, hoping to make up for my behavior.

Sliding onto one of the barstools Mascen motions for me to join him. I don't think I've ever felt more awkward in my whole life as I sit by him. It feels like we're enemies on the opposite sides of a battlefield most days, but for now I guess we're calling a ceasefire.

"How's school going, Squirt?" Mascen asks his sister as she grabs a can of Coke from the fridge.

"Senior year is a blast. The teachers don't give a shit. It's easy sailing."

"Lylah," their mother scolds.

"It's true, Mom. We literally fill in the blank on worksheets in most classes."

"What about cheer?" He pops a grape in his mouth. "How's that?"

I reach for a sandwich while the siblings chat and Emma smiles like she's pleased to see me eating.

"You know how much I love cheer. It's a blast. It's sad to know this is my last year."

"You won't cheer in college?" I interject and her eyes swing to me.

"I'll try out, but it's more competitive. I'm not sure I'll make the team."

"You will," Mascen sounds so confident and sure, "I believe in you."

"You go to the local high school?"

"I do, it's nice."

"Once my husband stopped traveling so much with the band it made sense to enroll the kids in public school, give them some kind of normalcy."

"And we thank you for it." Mascen tips his head at her. "Where is Dad anyway?"

"He's at Hayes's studio. They're releasing a special Christmas song next month and are perfecting it."

I know Hayes is the guitar player in Willow Creek, the band Mascen's dad is the drummer in, but I don't think I've ever met him. At least if I did as a little girl I don't recall it.

"This is really good, thank you," I tell Emma, holding up the sandwich I've been nibbling on.

"You're welcome."

"Did Dad know when I was coming?" Mascen asks, tearing apart the sandwich his mom had slid his way.

She bites her lip, hesitating.

Mascen laughs in a self-deprecating way. "Of course."

Lylah frowns, looking between her brother and mom. "What's wrong?"

"Nothing." Mascen stands, swiping two cookies. "Come on, Rory, I'll show you the guestroom."

I finish the last bite of sandwich and stand. He holds one of the cookies out to me, a peace offering—for what I don't know—and I follow him out of the kitchen.

At the stairs he grabs our bags and heads up. Down the hall he goes with me at his heels, munching on the cookie. "God this is good. Remind me to have your mom teach me how to make these before we leave."

He grunts in response. "Here's where you'll sleep." He nudges the door open, revealing a nice sized room with a metal-framed bed covered in fluffy white pillows and blankets. The simple table beside it has a stack of three books with a lamp sitting on top. The walls too, are white, with simplistic line drawings in black ink framed on the walls. The rug covering the original hardwood floors is the only source of color with a swirl of blue, purple, and pink. Mascen sets my bag on the ottoman in front of the bed. "Enjoy your stay at Casa Wade." He forces a smile.

Rocking back on my heels, I stick my hands in my back pockets. "And where's your room?"

His lips lift higher on one end. "Thinking of sneaking in? Morning blowies are a great wakeup call."

I roll my eyes and stand on my tiptoes, swiping the hat from his head and sticking it on mine. "Don't make it weird, Voldemort."

He chuckles, but there's still distance in his eyes like his mind is elsewhere.

"My room is this way." I follow him to the hallway and he points to the door at the very end. He opens it, revealing a set of stairs. "I have the attic. It used to be Willow's but after she moved in with her boyfriend— fiancé," he shakes his head in correction, "I moved up here. More privacy."

"That's perfect for a vampire."

"Why?" He narrows his eyes.

"Attic. Rafters." I wait for him to get it. "Bats, Mascen. Bats are in attics. Vampires turn into bats."

He shakes his head, pressing his lips together to hide a growing smile. "Maybe if you're a good girl I'll show you how I do it."

My pussy clenches at the innuendo he puts into *good girl*. "D-Do what?" I stutter, my lids fluttering closed.

"Transform into a bat."

I open my eyes to find him smirking. With lightning fast reflexes, ones I'm sure help him on the baseball field, he grabs his hat off my head, fixes it back on him and climbs the stairs up into his domain, a world entirely unknown to me.

THIRTY

MASCEN

"What the fuck am I doing?" I mutter to myself, dumping the contents of my bag on the bed. I didn't pack much, just the necessities like deodorant and my shaving kit since everything else I need is here. Picking up everything on my bed I move it to the top of the dresser out of my way.

Taking off my hat, I ruffle my hair, trying to make sense of everything when it comes to Rory. Am I flirting with her? Do I really want to go down this path?

"Stop overthinking shit." I know I look insane up in

my attic room, pacing the length of the space while I mutter to myself.

I'm not ready to go back downstairs just yet so I plop in the computer chair, spinning around and around a few times like a little kid until I face the black wall my bed is against, the one that's actually a chalkboard. Last time I was home I drew a UFO and aliens. Come abduct me motherfuckers, I'm in need of a memory wipe.

Pushing the recline lever on the chair I lean all the way back so I'm looking at the ceiling now. Wooden beams criss-cross the rafters. When my parents remodeled the attic into a room they chose to leave the beams exposed. It's a peek into the bones of the house, the structure holding everything up. Without what's above there would be no house below. Those beams are strong, resilient, and I'm not. Rory is. She's the strongest person I know and I don't even know her anymore, but I know that for her to be the person she is today she's had to be tougher than I'll ever be. So many people think strength lies in the physical, like the muscles cording my body, but they're wrong. Strength lies in what you cannot see, the mind of a person, and some people can handle more than others. I can see in Rory's eyes that she's endured a lot and I selfishly want to get all her secrets.

"Are you sulking Bella in New Moon style? Should I play some sad music? Maybe find the world's smallest violin?"

"Jesus Christ!" I jump, the chair rolling out from

under me so I slam into the floor. "What the fuck, Willow? Give a guy some warning." I rub my bruised tailbone. Unfortunately I can't do anything about my ego. "What are you even doing here?"

"Um … saying hello to my little bro." She stands above me since I've yet to get up from the floor. "I told mom to text me when you got here so I could come over. Didn't you miss me?" She's laughing at me—not with actual laughter, but I can see it in her eyes. She's mocking me in the way only older siblings seem to know how.

"I didn't miss you a bit." I get up, making sure not to flinch, but my ass hurts.

"Liar." She pulls me into a hug which is kind of comical since she's so much smaller than me now. "Ugh, it's good to see you."

I might envy the close bond my sister has with our dad, but I would never envy *her*. Sure we fight like any siblings and mock each other, but Willow is always going to have my back just like I'll have hers.

"How's the almost-married life treating you?"

She steps back smiling, her skin almost glowing. "It's great. I couldn't be happier. Dean is … he's every-thing. I'm so glad we both got our heads out of our asses and decided a relationship was worth a shot over risking our friendship."

"You two have always been meant for each other." I might be a guy, but even I could see that. I've never seen two people better suited for each other. "Is Dean here?"

"He's in the kitchen stuffing the food in his mouth I'm sure is meant for you."

"And Rory."

"Rory?" Her brow furrows. "Who's that?" Her mouth widens. "A girl? Did you bring a girl home? Oh my God, Mascen! Do you have a girlfriend?"

The fact that I'm almost twenty-one years old and this is such shocking news should probably offend me, but it doesn't. I'm not the girlfriend kind of guy.

"Rory is a girl, yes, but she's not my girlfriend. She's *Rory-Rory*," I try to put emphasis on her name, hoping Willow will get what I'm saying. She ends up only looking more confused. "Remember Rory and Hazel that grew up in the house down the road—that Rory."

"I'm so confused," she mutters. "I didn't know you kept in contact with her? You were so young."

I shake my head, picking up the chair from the floor and returning it to the upright position and it's rightful spot in the room. "I didn't. But she's a freshman at Aldridge."

She blinks at me and bursts into laughter. "Wow, what are the odds?"

"No idea, but they have to be slim."

"Why are you hiding out up here then? Shouldn't you be with her?"

"I just showed her to her room and came up here."

"And it looked like you were doing a whole lot of nothing. Come on," she grabs her hand, yanking me forward, "introduce me to this girl you brought home

264

that's not your girlfriend, but we also somehow happened to know a long time ago."

The last thing I want to do is leave the sanctuary of my bedroom, or I guess maybe I should start referring to it as my bat cave.

Peeking my head in the guestroom I find Rory isn't there. The bathroom straight across from her is empty too. I left out the convenient fact that we'll have to share.

"I don't know where she is."

Willow gives me *the look*, the one she perfected at a very young age that says I'm an idiot. "Then I'm sure she's downstairs with everyone else."

Sure enough, we find everyone gathered in the kitchen. The kitchen is the heart of the home after all.

She's laughing with Dean, her head tossed back. She looks at ease, but I don't miss the tight set of her shoulders, so she's not entirely comfortable. Her laughter is genuine, the cadence tinkling and light. I could fall in love with that sound and it scares the shit out of me. Another part of me is furious that Dean is the one making her laugh, but I remind myself he's engaged to my sister and has no interest in Rory.

Dean must sense my sister's presence because he looks over, the smile on his face the one he wears only for her. He immediately heads over to her, wrapping an arm around her waist and pulling her in for a kiss.

Gag me.

I can't imagine ever being that wrapped up in a woman.

Rory watches them before her eyes slowly drift to me. Her smile falters a bit, but it doesn't stop her from coming to stand by my side while the lovebirds reacquaint after their five-minute separation.

"Getting to know everyone?"

"Trying to. It's weird that I used to know everyone except Dean." She shrugs her narrow shoulders. "But we're all strangers now. Time does that."

"Yeah, it does." In ten years people grow, literally, personalities change, things evolve. In another decade we'll all be different varied versions of who we are now in this moment. "Are you guys going to stay around?" I address my sister and Dean.

Willow shakes her head. "We're going to run into town for some errands but we'll have dinner tonight. Mom said she's making your favorite."

"What's your favorite?" An amused smile plays on Rory's lips. "A bloody steak?"

Despite my best efforts a smile overwhelms me. "No, lasagna."

"Interesting."

"Why is that interesting?" Willow's eyes bounce between us, trying to put something together. I don't know what she possibly thinks there is to figure out.

"Oh," Rory clears her throat, adjusting her glasses on the bridge of her pert nose, "I work at an Italian restaurant near campus. When he comes in he always orders steak."

Willow says nothing, still looking between Rory and

I like there's some special road map written between us that only she can see.

"I don't like their lasagna." I tilt my head down to Rory. Sometimes I forget how much shorter she is than me until I'm right beside her and the only way to look in her eyes is to almost completely look down. "My mom's is better."

"I guess that makes sense."

"Well, we're going to head out now. We'll see you later."

Willow taps my shoulder and stands on her tiptoes to kiss my cheek. Dean holds his hand out for a fist bump and we both blow it up. I chuckle at his dorky ways. He really is the perfect match for my quirky sister.

With them gone, Rory slides onto one of the barstools, leaning over to grab another chocolate chip cookie. Her tee rides up, exposing the smallest hint of her creamy midriff. My eyes linger there and I look away in shame when she sits down fully and her shirt lowers once more.

"This is my fourth cookie," she whispers conspiratorially. "Don't tell on me."

I reach for another for myself. "My mom is the best."

"Yeah, she is." Sadness fills Rory's face and she looks away, not wanting me to notice, but it's too late.

"How is your mom?"

She presses her lips together, licking away a piece of chocolate stuck there. "I wouldn't know."

"You don't talk?"

She puts the uneaten portion of her cookie down on the counter and scrubs her palms nervously on her jeans. "No. She wasn't really *there*. I mean, she wasn't even like your mom when things were good and my dad was alive, but she wasn't like what she became. Once we lost everything, we lost her too. Hazel and I were a burden she didn't want to deal with. We raised ourselves after that."

My fists clench at my sides, pissed off at her mother. "Despite what happened, she shouldn't have stopped caring about her kids."

Rory rolls her eyes and picks up the cookie. "Well, she did."

"How bad was it?" I'm hesitant to ask, worried her answer will only piss me off further.

"Bad enough. I'm sure other kids had it worse."

I shake my head, my teeth grinding together. "Did she ever hit you?"

Her face reddens. "Once. A back-handed slap."

"Why?"

Her face, somehow, gets an even darker shade of red. "Um … she found Plan B in the trash. I thought I put it down far enough she wouldn't find it, but apparently she wanted to hide something too."

I suddenly, very much, want to hit something. "How old were you?"

"Sixteen." She turns away from me, picking a crumb off the counter.

"Who was the guy?"

"A nobody. It was literally a one and done deal in the back of his truck."

"And how old was he?"

She tucks a piece of hair behind her ear. "I don't know why that matters."

"It does."

"Because you don't do sloppy seconds?"

"No," I growl, suddenly right in front of her. I brace one of my hands on the counter beside her and the back of the stool she sits in, keeping her from leaving. "But I might have to drive wherever the fuck this guy lives and punch him if he was messing with an underage girl." She bites down on her tongue, turning her head to the side so she doesn't have to look at me. I take her chin gently between my fingers. "Tell me."

"Twenty-one."

"Fuck," I growl, desperate to hunt down and kill this unknown to me guy.

"It was a mistake, among many others." She gives a shrug like it's not a big deal.

"You were sixteen. A kid."

"I'm only two years older now."

"Almost three," I remind her. She looks confused and I crack a smile. "Yeah, I remember your birthday. January fourth. You're a Capricorn."

She raises a brow. "Into astrology now, Lex Luthor?"

I brush my finger over the smooth slope of her jaw. "Not really, but I am a Taurus. The bull. It makes me notably stubborn, so maybe there's something to it after all."

A small smile softens her face, but I can tell from her eyes that she's still far away. "Something tells me you'd be stubborn, Taurus or not."

"You're probably right." I take a step back and hold my hand out to her. "Let's go somewhere."

"Where?" She narrows her eyes suspiciously

Wiggling my fingers, I sigh. "Somewhere you've been before. Trust me."

Her lips pinch, but finally she slides her fingers into mine. With her free hand she grabs the last of the cookie and tosses it in her mouth, laughing in amusement at my expression. "I like sweets."

And I like the way she tastes. The urge to lean in and kiss her is strong, but I don't act on it.

Since it's not exactly warm out I pass her a sweatshirt from the mudroom, it's probably one of Lylah's, and dig out one from my cubby that's been left there from last winter. Holding the backdoor open for her, we traipse past the fenced in part of the yard, heading for the trees quite a way in front of us.

"Are we going to the treehouse?"

I jerk to a stop. "I can't believe you remember." The treehouse had only been finished a few days prior to when she disappeared from my life.

She rolls her eyes. "Of course I remember."

We reach the woods and it's not far from there. The path is still clearly laid out even though I'm pretty sure

I'm the only one who still comes here, and it's not like I'm around much.

The treehouse is nicer than most, with a ladder built into the ground, stabilized with steel rods drilled down into the earth. The ladder leads up to the treehouse, which is basically one square room with an outer deck area. When I was young I felt like a king and this was my castle.

"It's smaller than I remember," Rory remarks, tilting her head to take in the wooden structure.

"You got bigger."

Her laugh fills the air, my chest tightening in response because I made her make that noise. "Calling me fat?"

"No," I blurt, feeling like an idiot. "I meant we grew up."

She smiles over at me, her eyes clearer than before. "I know. I wanted to mess with you."

I groan. "Go up, Princess."

"Fine." She reaches for it and starts up the first two rungs before pausing to look down at me. "Enjoy the view, Farquaad."

"Oh, I will."

I follow after her, definitely enjoying the lovely view of the delectable curve of her round ass. She gets to the top and crawls into the tree house on her knees instead of standing up like a normal human and walking in.

"Whoa, this isn't what I expected." She looks around at the bean bag chairs, rug, full bookcase, and other things I've drug up here over the years. One fall when I was bored I put some of those sticker wallpaper things on the inside that looks like brick.

"It's my home away from home." I plop my ass into one of the bean bags and she does the same.

"You're kind of a loner, aren't you?"

"I suppose you could say that. It's hard to make true friends when most people want something from you."

"You're friends with Cole," she points out.

"Cole puts me in my place. He tells me when I'm an asshole and he's not scared of hurting my feelings. He never asks me for money and gets irritated when I offer. He insists on paying rent to my parents for the town-house, even though they don't want his money. He likes me for me, even when I'm less than tolerable."

"Which is almost always." She leans across the narrow space, nudging my knee with hers. "I can't believe I let you convince me to come here."

We both know she doesn't mean the treehouse. "I'm very persuasive."

"You say persuasive, I say annoying."

"Tomato-tohmatoh."

"It's weird being here," she whispers softly, like she's scared to speak the words aloud, "but it's not as bad as I thought it would be. I missed it more than I realized. I feel at peace here."

"I wanted nothing more than to get away," I confess, looking up at the ceiling with the plastic glow in the dark stars I put there when I was eleven. "I thought if I got away it would solve all my problems, that I'd be happier being independent, but I felt lonely and like I didn't belong. It's better now, but I come home every break whereas when I left I thought I'd never come back."

"Why'd you want to leave so bad?"

"I don't even know anymore. In the beginning it was to prove a point to my dad, I think I wanted him to miss me and I needed to hear him say that, but he didn't."

She sits up straighter. "Are things … bad with your dad? I can't imagine your mom —"

"No, no, nothing like that," I rush to assure her. "My dad's a good guy and he's a great dad with my sisters, but me…" I trail off, not sure how to explain it to her. It sounds crazy when I try to say it out loud. "I've always been closer with my mom. I think when I came along and was more into sports and girls and I wasn't anything like him it was hard. He's the closest with Willow. They're so similar, but I'm definitely the least like him. When I got into baseball, he didn't get why it was so important to me, the thrill I get from it. He didn't come to many games, only one my entire senior year and he left halfway through it. Anything I did wasn't as important to him as the things Willow and Lylah did."

"I'm sorry, Mascen."

"Mascen?" I turn my head, smiling at her. "No nickname this time?"

She rolls her eyes. "Don't ruin the moment."

"Thanks, Princess."

"You know your dad loves you, though, right? I can't imagine him not."

"I know, but sometimes love isn't enough. Surely you get that? It takes action. Being there for someone. Stepping up. Showing them that what they do and who they are matters even if we're different."

"Actions speak louder than words," she murmurs.

"Exactly."

THIRTY-ONE

RORY

DINNERTIME COMES AROUND QUICKLY, SURPRISINGLY. For some reason I expected the day to drag on. But after Mascen and I left the treehouse I took a nap and after I woke up I worked on a paper that's due a few days after break ends. By the time I did that it was time to eat.

Seated by Mascen I'm surrounded by his scent. The intoxicating notes of citrus and woods fills my lungs every time I breathe. At the end of the table is his dad, at the other his mom, with his sisters and Dean seated across from us.

Mascen piles a cut of lasagna onto my plate first before putting another on his.

"Thank you," I whisper under my breath. This might be Mascen but I'm still going to use my manners ... sometimes at least.

He then passes me a piece of bread and takes one for himself after.

In the presence of his parents he's on his best behavior.

"So, you're studying at Aldridge with Mascen?" His dad, Maddox, asks me. "What are the odds?"

I shrug, lifting my hands. "That's what we all keep saying."

"How have you been all these years?"

"Um ... good."

God, this is more awkward than I feared. Things went too smooth with his mom and sisters, of course there had to be some sort of speed bump.

Maddox chuckles, running his fingers through his shaggy brown hair. I know he must be in his late forties, but he's still insanely handsome. Smile lines decorate the corners of his eyes and mouth. There's a sparkle in his gray eyes, the same shade as his son's, that tells me that there's a mischievous side to him. He's different from Emma, who's soft spoken and motherly. He's clearly a troublemaker. But when he smiles at his wife the love in his eyes is undeniable. Even after all these years he's clearly still head over heels. He loves his children too. The first thing he did after he greeted Emma when he got home was kiss all three on top of the head and talk about how happy he was to have all three children under the same roof tonight.

Parents aren't perfect, it's impossible, and I know Mascen's feelings toward his father have to be justified in some ways, but his dad clearly cares. It's too bad it hasn't been in the way his son needs.

"Just good?"

I spear my fork into the lasagna but wait to lift the bite to my mouth. "I mean, you know how things went down. It wasn't exactly easy, but we made do."

I don't want to go into detail about my past with him—with *anyone*. I'd rather forget and move on.

He narrows his eyes and I think he senses there's more to the story. I hate being secretive. Especially when him and his wife are opening his home to me for the break, but there are some things I just won't talk about.

"You're a freshman this year?" I exhale in relief that he's moving on to another topic.

"I am."

I'm an exceptional conversationalist.

"What are you studying?"

Mascen lets out a massive sigh beside me, slamming his palms on the table. Glasses clang and I freeze as everyone's eyes go to him. "What the hell, Dad? You don't need to ask her so many fucking questions."

Silence fills the room. I want to fill it in some way, but I don't know what to do or say.

"I was just getting to know Rory again, I'm sorry

that bothers you." Maddox's voice is calm, but there's something in his eyes, like he's hurt but also pissed.

"That's not getting to know her, Dad. That's an interrogation."

Maddox's brows furrow and he turns his eyes to me. "I'm sorry if it seemed like I was interrogating you. That wasn't what I meant to do at all. But a lot happens in ten years and—"

I hold up a hand to silence him. "It's okay, I get it. I'm not very good at talking about myself and things weren't the best when we left here."

"You're attending Aldridge so it couldn't be so bad, right?" His sister Lylah asks innocently. "You guys still had money and did all right?"

I shake my head. "I'm actually there on a scholarship."

Lylah's eyes widen and her cheeks flood with color. "Oh, sorry."

"It's okay. I wanted to go there and I worked hard for a full-ride. I'm not ashamed of it."

And I'm not. Despite the setbacks I faced I worked my ass off to make it happen.

The rest of dinner is a tad awkward but it could be worse. Mascen remains tense at my side only giving people one-word answers when he's addressed directly. After dinner he immediately disappears to his attic room while I help his mom clean up and load the dishwasher.

Finally, I can head upstairs to shower and go to bed.

I glide my fingers along the shiny mahogany bannister. Despite the less than stellar way dinner went, I don't find myself wanting to run out the door and return to campus.

In the guestroom I grab my toiletries bag and pajamas to change into. I didn't feel tired before but suddenly I'm exhausted from the stressful day. I know these people aren't strangers to me, once upon a time they were a big part of my life, but things have changed so much that I felt like I had to be on my best behavior.

Across the hall I close and lock the bathroom door. Spreading the things I'll need on the counter I turn on the water and strip off my clothes.

The hot water cascades over me, loosening my tight shoulder muscles. Grabbing my shampoo, I lather the soap onto my scalp, humming to fill the quiet. I could stay there all night, but after cleaning my hair and scrubbing my body I force myself to get out and dry off. Tugging on my shorts and a t-shirt, I wrap my hair in a towel, before brushing my teeth and applying my night-time moisturizer. If I don't I'll wake up with skin as dry as the desert.

Spitting in the sink, I rinse out the white foam making sure not to leave a trace behind. I don't want to make myself a nuisance in any way. Letting my hair down from the towel, I gently run the brush through the strands so I don't pull it. I'm taking longer than normal in my nightly routine, stalling for God knows why. Securing my damp hair with an elastic in a low bun I pack up my stuff and open the door. Immediately

I'm shoved back inside. In my surprise I nearly fall to the floor on my ass.

Mascen somehow manages to keep me from falling while simultaneously closing the door silently and locking it behind him.

"M-Mascen," I stutter, looking up at him with wide surprised eyes. "What are you doing?" My back thumps into the wall beside me, his right hand clasping the side of my jaw, fingers splaying down my neck. Satisfaction plays on his lips when he finds the unsteady pulse of my heart.

His gray eyes darken to a color like thunderclouds rolling in on a summer sky and his grip on my face tightens when his hand flexes. "I don't know." Something ripples across his face, like he's surprised by his own honesty, but I don't have time to analyze it before his lips crash to mine.

I'm taken by surprise, but my body immediately surrenders to the call of his. I arch into him, my fingers delving into his hair. It's ridiculous how easily my body gives over to him. We might banter like we want to kill each other, and sometimes I do imagine my hands around his neck, but there's no denying the chemistry between us.

He bunches the fabric of my thin cotton tee in his fingers. It pulls taught against my chest and I know if he looks down he'll clearly see the outline of my nipples and areola. I'm sure he can already feel the hard nubs pushing against him, begging for attention. It's scary how quickly my body reacts to him.

He tugs on my hands and I fight against him. I feel his grin against my lips as we kiss. "I love it when you fight me."

Finally, he overpowers me and pins my hands above my head, using his hips to anchor me against the wall. His erection rubs against my pussy, barely covered by my shorts. The sensitive nub pulses begging for more friction.

His mouth is rough against mine. Demanding. Brash. There's nothing gentle or sweet about it. He's staking claim to me.

Holy shit.

I roll my hips down on him, the friction making me breathe harder. I'm so wound up it won't take me long to orgasm.

"Let me touch you." I hate myself for begging, but I need to touch him. I want to delve my fingers in his hair, hold him to me so he can't leave.

"No," he growls, biting my throat.

I squeak in surprise. There will be evidence left behind in the morning, I know it. He must know it too, because he chuckles and swipes his tongue along the spot like he's soothing it.

He returns to my lips, nibbling on them like they're the most delectable fruit he's ever tasted. His tongue searches for mine and I give in easily. He's a masterful kisser and I try not to think about how much practice he's had. It's not like I've been a saint.

"You drive me crazy." He continues to hold my hands in one of his, lowering the other to grip my neck so he can tip my head up. He bites a spot before kissing it, repeating that down my throat. "You're going to be the death of me."

"Mascen," I pant his name, a shudder lurching through my body. My eyes roll to the back of my head, the pleasure taking over. "Oh, God. I'm coming."

He releases my hands and grips my hips as I ride it out. The orgasm goes and goes, my body shaking as I come down from the high. If I orgasmed like *that* with a makeout session I can't imagine what would happen if we had sex. I might die from ecstasy.

Blinking my eyes open I find Mascen watching me with parted lips, eyes dilated. He licks his lips, dropping his gaze down. I wonder if he can feel the wet spot on my shorts. I'm drenched. He doesn't say anything and I lower my feet to the ground. He keeps holding my hips, which is probably a good thing because I'm not sure I could stand upright on my own.

After a moment, he releases me and steps back, bowing his head so his eyes are on the bathroom tiles. "Get out."

"W-What?"

He points to the door, still looking at the floor. "Door. You. Outside of it."

"Mascen, I don't get—"

"*Out.*"

I don't think Mascen would ever physically hurt me, but at his icy tone my stomach plummets with fear.

I slip out of it and run straight across to the guestroom. I close the door and lean my back against it.

Mascen has to be the most confusing motherfucker to ever walk the planet. He's hot one minute, cold the next, and I never know what to expect. It's exhausting but I'm not sure I can quit this. Whatever *this* is.

Across the hall the shower starts up.

THIRTY-TWO

MASCEN

THE WATER CASCADES OVER ME, DRIPPING FROM MY hair to the floor of the shower. Rubbing my face, I push my hair back, tilting my head up to the ceiling. My cock is hard and throbbing, but I refuse to wrap my hand around it, choosing to punish myself instead. It would've been so easy to move aside the fabric of Rory's shorts pull down my pants and fuck her against the wall. I wanted to. So bad. Especially when she orgasmed just from rubbing herself against me. But I couldn't do it. It feels wrong because of Cole. Few people are loyal to me, and when they are I value them above everything else. Rory might've broken things off with him, but that doesn't mean his feelings for her went away. I know I'd be breaking some kind of guy code by pursuing her.

But I can't seem to stop myself from wanting her.

Gritting my teeth, I can't take it any longer. Wrapping my fist around my cock I stroke it, closing my eyes and pretending it's Rory I'm sinking into and not my fist doing all the work.

"Fuck." My head lolls back. Bracing my left hand against the wall I fist myself harder, almost too hard, but the pain feels good because even though I'm giving in, it's a reminder that I can't do this. When it comes to her I need to get a better grip on my self-control.

I hope the shower is loud enough to drown out my moan as I come. My chest rises and falls rapidly as I struggle to catch my breath. Cleaning up I get out of the shower, wrapping a towel around my waist.

I don't know what made me kiss her like I did. I was waiting outside the bathroom for her to finish and even though I was only waiting a few minutes the longer I stood there the more my brain decided to flood me with images. Ones of Rory standing in the shower. Naked and soaking wet. Her long hair hanging over her breasts.

As soon as she opened the door, I lost it.

Climbing up the stairs to the attic I drop onto the bed heaving a massive sigh. This is uncharted waters for me. I've never liked a girl, had this kind of connection, like I do with Rory. As explosive as our chemistry is, and as much as I want to fuck her, I'm worried even if I did it wouldn't be enough.

When the door to my room opens I brace myself, expecting it to be Rory coming up to yell and berate me. Instead, my dad stands there. His arms are crossed over his chest. "We didn't get to talk much tonight."

I pick up the baseball from beside my bed, tossing it from hand to hand.

"No, we didn't."

He sighs, taking a step closer. His hands fall to his sides. "I'm sorry you thought I was interrogating Rory."

I narrow my eyes. "You were but stop apologizing."

He runs his fingers through his hair in agitation. "I don't know how to talk to you."

Sitting up, I swing my legs over the side of the bed. "You never have, Dad."

His brows furrow in confusion. "What does that mean?"

Standing, I drop the baseball on my bed. "You've always cared more about Willow and Lylah. What they're doing, what they like, showing up for them. But me?" I spread my arms wide. "You're absentee. I can't do anything right for you."

His lips part in surprise. "Mase, I don't know what you mean. I've always been here for you, but you've never seemed to need me like your sisters."

"Really? Because that's not the way I remember it."

"How do you remember it?" His voice is soft, almost crestfallen which only serves to piss me off more. I want to see a fire in him, a fight to understand, not this dejectedness.

"I remember learning how to ride a bike but you were more concerned making sure Willow didn't bust her head skateboarding. When we learned to swim at the sports center you stuck with Lylah and the lifeguard helped me." I'm on a roll now, unable to stop. "When I started baseball, mom took me to practice. She sat in the stands. The times when you came you looked like you didn't want to be there and numerous times you got up and left. My last game as a senior you showed up late and left before it was over. Nothing I've ever done has been good enough for you. You don't ask me about school and how it's going. You still don't ask about baseball and last year Mom, Willow, and Lylah came to a game when we traveled to Virginia but once again *you* didn't. I'm going to be a fucking doctor, but you don't seem one bit proud of it while Willow walks on water and she's a college drop out."

He stands there stunned. My chest heaves. I didn't even realize I'd gotten so heated and out of breath. I knew I'd bottled shit up, but I never intended to explode like this.

He nods up and down, eyes downcast to the floor. If I didn't know better I'd think he was going to cry.

My dad's a goofball, the one always laughing and having a good time. The life of the party. He's a good guy, I know that, but even good people don't always know how to do the right thing.

"I ... um ... goodnight."

He slips out the door, closing it carefully behind him. The tiny click of it shutting feels like a gunshot straight to my heart. I don't want to hurt my dad, I really don't, but it's true—nothing I've done has ever been of interest to him.

And at this point I'm tired of pretending it's okay with me.

———

"OH MY GOD!" Rory's hand flies to her heart when she opens her bedroom door and finds me lurking there. "Don't scare me like that." She swats at my arm.

Amusement curls my lips. "I want to take you somewhere."

It's after lunch and I'm desperate to get out of the house, so I started thinking of things I could take Rory to do. I'm sure she needs to get out as much as I do. Neither one of us has said anything about the kiss. I haven't spoken with my dad either. By the time I got up he was gone to the studio.

"Take me where?" Her eyes narrow in suspicion. She never trusts me, rightfully so, but...

"You don't trust me? I'm wounded."

"You don't give me very many reasons to."

"But you're not saying you don't. You like chocolate right? Ice cream?" She nibbles on her delectable bottom lips and nods. "Then let's go."

She doesn't protest this time, following me downstairs. Passing my mom in the hall I drop a kiss on her cheek and let her know we're going.

Rory doesn't say much on the twenty-minute drive into downtown. Pulling into one of the garages I grab the ticket from the machine and park.

Rory hops out, sticking her hands into the back pockets of her jeans. Her orange Aldridge sweatshirt makes her brown eyes seem more golden. She reaches up, adjusting her glasses like usual, oblivious to me staring at her. Smoothing a lock of brown hair behind her hair she motions with her arm. "Lead the way, Lestat."

Exiting the garage at the other end we walk across the street and through an alley to get to the row of shops on the walking mall. Turning to my right, Rory struggles to keep up with my long-legged stride but I don't slow down.

Sugarland comes into view, the old candy and sundae shop one of my favorite places in the whole town.

Holding the door open for Rory, I can be a gentleman when I want, I enter behind her to see her looking around in awe.

"I remember this place," she gasps, head tilted back as she takes everything in. "My dad brought me here a few times. Well, me and Hazel."

She doesn't talk about her sister much and I wonder what's going on there. Clearly things weren't easy for them, but I would've thought it would have bonded the two girls more closely. Obviously not.

The family owned store hasn't changed much. I can see in her eyes she's been taken back to another time.

She spins in a circle.

Standing back, I stick my hands in my pockets, watching her take it all in.

The red and white checkered floors, the ceiling with fake candy hanging from every inch of space, the old-time soda pop counter, candy stations, and the sundae builder. It's a little kid's dream—but the best part of being an adult is no one can tell us we can't have too much.

The bell on the door clangs as someone comes in behind us. I move out of the way, letting them pass.

Finally, she lowers her head, and meets my eyes. "Thank you for bringing me here."

I shrug off her praise. "It's just ice cream."

She shakes her head, her eyes shiny behind the frames of her glasses. "No, Mascen. It's more."

Placing my hand at the bottom of her waist I guide her toward the start of the line. Her eyes flick up to mine with surprise, forcing me to drop my hand.

"What can I get y'all today?" The lady behind the counter asks.

Rory's eyes go from the menu to me, challenge glimmering in their depths. "Are you buying?"

"That was the plan."

She points. "The Kitchen Sink, then." Eyes back to me, she adds, "And I'm not sharing."

"Are you sure, dear? It's huge."

"I'm positive."

"It's fifty dollars," the lady says, like it's not listed plainly on the menu.

"Don't worry, Mascen can afford it."

The lady looks back at me and pales realizing who I am. Most people in this town are used to my family and don't give us much notice, which is nice. Basically at this point they're so used to us that we're not exciting anymore.

"Of course." She lowers her head, trying to hide her blush.

She grabs the kitchen sink looking bowl they use for the specialty dessert and starts adding in all the different ice cream flavors and toppings. Rory licks her lips in anticipation. I don't think she even realizes she's done it.

After The Kitchen Sink is perfectly prepared it's my turn.

"A banana shake?" Rory protests incredulously when I tell the lady what I want. "That's all? Live a little, Norman Bates."

"I am living, I'm having a milkshake."

"But it's banana," she gasps like this is the most blasphemous things ever. "Everyone knows chocolate is the best milkshake flavor."

"No, banana."

The woman finishes mixing my shake and moves everything down to the antique register. Passing over my debit card she rings everything up and I sign the slip. Rory licks her lips in anticipation and picks up her sink, carrying it to one of the booths.

Elvis Presley's voice croons from the antique jukebox about a hound dog

Sliding in across from her I wrap my lips around the wide yellow straw. "Delicious."

"Mine's better." She digs into the vanilla ice cream portion coming out with a spoonful covered in fudge, sprinkles, and whipped cream. The moan she makes when she licks the spoon clean should be illegal.

"I'd argue mine is better, Princess."

She narrows her eyes and I'm so busy looking in her eyes, enjoying the impromptu staring contest, that I completely miss what she's doing with her hands.

I jolt in surprise when cold sticky ice cream splatters on my face.

Rory doesn't make a move, waiting for me to react, but after only a few seconds she can't hold her laughter in any longer.

"That was cold." The words are monotone. I purposely don't want her to know whether I'm pissed off or amused.

"Oh, I'm sorry." She pretends to frown. "Want me to get that for you?"

She reaches across like she's going to wipe it from my face with her finger.

Dipping my finger in her bowl where she can't see I scoop up some of the ice cream and wipe it down her cheek. She jerks back in surprise, her delectable lips parting.

"You. Didn't."

I pick up my shake taking a sip. "You started it, Princess."

"This is war."

"Shit!" I curse, earning me a glare from a nearby family with their two kids. But Rory pelted me in the chest with a glob of ice cream. "Are you kidding me?"

She giggles, lobbing me with more.

I pick up my shake dumping the contents over her head.

"Ahh!" She screams. "It's so sticky and all over me!"

"That's what she said," I mutter under my breath.

"Ugh!" She throws more ice cream at me. She might be trying to sound irritated, but her grin and laughter says otherwise.

It isn't long, maybe thirty more seconds before our fun is ruined by the squawking employee who served us. "What are you doing? Stop that! You're making a huge mess!" Around us the table, booth, and floor is covered in gooey ice cream, not to mention ourselves. "This is such a disaster! It's going to take forever to clean up! I'm so sorry for the disturbance." She quiets her voice turning to the others seated in the dining area.

"You don't have to worry," Rory speaks up, raising a reassuring hand. "We'll clean it up."

My head swings back in her direction. "We will?"

"Of course," she bites out.

The woman pinches the bridge of her nose. "I'll get you everything you need."

"We're not cleaning." I make to slide out of the

booth and she kicks my shin. "Ow, Princess. Watch yourself."

"We made the mess, we're cleaning up."

"You started it."

"And you participated."

I blow out a breath, the ice cream already drying in a sticky layer on my skin.

The woman, Lorelai according to her name tag, returns with a bucket, mop, and a pile of rags. "Get started."

Her voice is nothing less than pissed off. I know we made a giant mess but let us have our fun.

"Come on, Pretty Boy." Rory slides out of the booth and grabs the mop, passing it to me. "Let's get started."

―――――

"I CAN'T BELIEVE we got banned for life. What a load of bullshit," I grumble, walking through the garage.

We're both still covered in ice cream and I'm kind of sad I dumped my ice cream on her head. I wanted that milkshake.

Rory closes the door leading into the house behind her and follows me down the hall into the open entry.

"Oh my God." My mom's hand flies to her chest at the sight of us as she's walking out of the kitchen. "What happened to you guys?"

"The ice cream exploded," I deadpan.

"Food fight," Rory answers.

"She started it," I add quickly, lest my mother think this disaster is my fault. I'm an angel.

Her eyes flicker between us, one of those sighs only mothers seem capable of pulling off emanating from her. You know the one that says she wants to know more but isn't about to ask.

"Just clean yourselves up." Shaking her head and muttering to herself she heads into the den.

Leading the way upstairs and down the hall the two of us pause outside the bathroom.

Rory takes a step back, eyes narrowed. "What are you doing?"

"We can't share a shower sweetheart?"

"I'm sure there are plenty of others you can use in this house."

"There's my sister's and my parents, but this is *mine*."

"You don't have one up there?" She points at the ceiling.

"Nope. This one's mine and the guest bath. It's an old house, Princess, not a lot of bathrooms."

She works her jaw back and forth.

Lowering my head, I twist a lock of her hair around my finger, my lips millimeters from her cheek. "I'll let you off the hook this time." I tug her hair lightly. "Enjoy your shower, Princess." I swipe my tongue over a spot of dried vanilla ice cream on her face. "I know I will."

Turning my back on her I walk away.

THIRTY-THREE

RORY

"MORNING." EMMA SMILES AT ME WHEN I WALK INTO the kitchen the next morning. "Muffin?" She points to a smorgasbord of muffins spread on the counter, some already organized beautifully on a two-tiered display I'd expect to see in a fancy café. "There's blueberry, cranberry and orange, chocolate chip, and banana nut."

My eyes widen. "You made all of these? Like from scratch?"

She laughs. "I know I went a bit overboard. Sometimes I can't help myself. I honestly never thought I'd be *this* mom." She waves her hands at the muffins littering the countertop. "But here we are."

I reach for a chocolate chip one. I pull a small part off and pop it into my mouth. It's still warm, the chocolate gooey. "Mmm, this is delicious. Thank you."

"You're welcome." She finishes pulling some of the cranberry orange ones from a pan.

"I ... um ... I'm going for a walk." It was the reason I came down here in the first place. I was going to tell Mascen, but he doesn't seem to be down here which means more than likely he's still in his tower as I've dubbed the attic space I've yet to see.

Emma nods, her face softening in a way that's too close to pity for me. She knows without saying that I want to walk by my old home. It's a couple miles down the road and I know she'd probably let me borrow a vehicle, but I'm hoping the walk will help prepare me. I know someone else will live there now, it's bound to look different, but it will still be the place I lived for the first eight years of my life. That home signifies the last time I knew stability.

"Bundle up," she calls after me.

"I will."

In the mudroom area I grab my coat and walk out the side door. The driveway is long and by the time I get to the end of it there's no sign of my muffin left. Turning left I keep walking, wrapping my arms around myself.

This hurts and I'm not even to the house yet. I knew this wouldn't be easy, but it's necessary. I can't be here and not go.

The miles pass slowly and it's forty-five minutes before I stand at the end of the driveway of the massive colonial style mansion.

Tears spring to my eyes and I crumble to the ground.

Inside those walls four people's lives changed forever.

One ended.

One gave up.

One did what was necessary.

One is trying to atone for the sins of her family.

But nothing I do will ever be enough. I have to let go. The past is just that, the past. I have to move on, be the best version of myself I can be. I can still make a difference, but for me, not for anyone else.

Sniffling, I wipe my tears off my damp cheeks, startling when I hear a car pulling up. I nearly roll into a bush to hide, thinking it's whoever lives here getting home from somewhere, but the color catches my eyes and I freeze. Just like that first day on campus I'm nearly face to face with the bumper on the SUV. I can't see Mascen behind the tinted windows, but I know it's him. It wouldn't be anyone else. He rolls the window down, sticking his head out the side. He squints at me on the ground.

He hops out in only a pair of gray sweatpants and a wifebeater. I expect him to berate me, but he surprises me completely by doing no such thing.

He bends down, scooping me into his arms like an infant. With a small grunt he stands, carrying me to the passenger side. Somehow managing to keep a hold on me he opens the door and gently places me on the seat. Grabbing the seatbelt he leans across my body, snapping me in. He starts to straighten and I grab his shirt. I look at the fabric in my hand in surprise, not having meant to grab him, but here we are.

Push. Pull. That's us.

"How did you know where I went?" My voice is barely audible.

His eyes pulse with something that both excites and scares me. What's happening to us?

"Let's say it was an educated guess." He touches my cheek with the back of his fingers like he's reminding himself I'm real.

"It's ghosts," I confess brokenly. "That's all that's left. Of them. Me."

He takes my chin between his thumb and forefinger. "You're not a ghost, Aurora."

"How do you know?"

He licks his lips, his eyes flicking down to mine. "Because you're real to me."

Grabbing the back of his neck I crash my lips to his like if I don't kiss him I might die. It certainly feels that way. I didn't know it could feel so good to kiss someone I hate, but I'm beginning to think hate and love or at least like are synonymous. Such passionate feelings can't be reduced to one simple thing.

He kisses me back, his tongue softly stroking mine as he tries to slow the kiss. We've always been wild about it when we get to this point, but I follow his lead, my touch gentle against his cheek as I stroke the slightly stubbled skin with my thumb.

Pulling away he rests his forehead against mine slightly out of breath. "Let's get you home."

"Home?" My brows furrow.

He cracks the smallest of smiles. "I still hate you, Princess, but you always have a home with me."

Suddenly the word hate feels different. It feels a lot like…

"I hate you too, Mascen."

———

SOMEHOW, in a blink, it's Thanksgiving, which means my stay with the Wade's is close to winding down.

In the bathroom I go about my usual morning routine, but take extra time to curl my hair and apply makeup. I even spray perfume on. Back across the hall in the guestroom I dress in the nicest clothes I brought with me.

When I open the door I'm not surprised to find Mascen there. In the past couple of days it's become a hangout of sorts for him. I told him to stop being a lurker, but clearly my criticism had no effect.

"You look horrible." His tone is flat but at this point I know the dance with him, and it's become a compliment.

"You do too." My eyes drop to the bulge his sweat-pants lie against, teasing me.

He chuckles, the sound silky and rich like my

favorite coffee. "My eyes are up here, Princess." I blush at being caught. "My uncle and aunt are coming for the day. My cousin and his girl too, just so you know. Didn't want you to be surprised."

"Oh, um, thanks for letting me know." I start to walk away, but pause, turning around. "Liam? He used to be over with Willow a lot, right?"

"Didn't think you'd remember him, but yeah. Those two have always been thick as thieves. They drifted apart for a bit there, Liam kinda cut everyone off, he wasn't in a good place, but now he's coming around. I think he knows Uncle Mathias will choke him out if he doesn't."

Tucking a piece of hair behind my ear I ease backward down the hall. "I'm going to go see if your mom needs any help in the kitchen."

He watches me with an amused expression until I finally force myself to turn away from him.

Downstairs, I find the front dining room in a state of chaos. Maddox smiles when he sees me, putting in one of the extender leaves for the table. All the chairs are spread throughout the open dining room and into the foyer.

"Morning, Rory."

"Good morning," I reply. "Do you need any help?"

"Nah." He waves a dismissive hand. "I'm almost done here. Emma might need some in the kitchen. Lylah was supposed to wake up early and help, but..." He trails off, laughing a bit. "She likes sleep more."

"I know how that is."

Heading into the kitchen at the end of the house, I find poor Emma running around trying to make sure everything is taken care of.

Picking up an apron from the rack I tie it around me so I won't dirty my outfit.

"Let me know what I can help with."

She lets out a squeak of surprise. "You scared me. I wasn't paying attention." She gives a laugh with a shake of her head. "Don't worry about it, sweetie. I've got it covered and you're our guest."

Rolling up my sleeves, I place my hands on my hips. "I'm volunteering and more than happy to pitch in. Just point me in the direction you need me most."

She hesitates, looking around at the smorgasbord of food in the middle of being prepared. "Have you ever made a pie before?"

"All the time." Even though I waitressed at the diner I used to work at the owner's wife used to have me help with the homemade pies. Eventually I got the hang of it and could do it on my own.

"Okay, would you mind taking over with those?" She points to the counter she has the pie ingredients on.

"Not at all."

"Thank you." She exhales in relief.

I get to work on them—the ingredients are set out for apple and pumpkin pie—and get lost in my head as I go about the familiar routine.

I don't know how much time has passed when I hear Mascen say, "Hey, Momma. What can I help you with?"

I look over my shoulder in time to see him drop a kiss on her cheek.

She puts him to work on the macaroni and cheese. He rearranges things so he ends up working beside me.

Whenever we catch the other looking our way we exchange a secretive smile. I don't really understand what's happening between us, but it both excites and terrifies me.

Lylah eventually comes down and joins us in the kitchen and an hour after that Willow and Dean arrive. The parade plays in the background on the TV and with the conversation and laughter filling the kitchen I can't help but be appreciative that Mascen basically forced me to come. This is what family should be — spending time together, poking fun at each other, just ... having fun.

Once we've done all we can in the kitchen Emma sends us on our way.

"Want to go to the treehouse?" Mascen asks me, hesitating by the back door.

"Sure," I agree. He holds out his hand for mine but quickly drops it, his face shadowed in surprise.

I can't help but be amused. "I don't have cooties. You can hold my hand if you want," I joke, lightly bumping his shoulder.

"Shut up," he grumbles, opening the French doors.

We head down the deck and around the fenced in portion of the yard.

We don't speak the entire trek to the treehouse.

Mascen pauses at the bottom of the tree letting me up first.

Sitting on the outside of the deck I let my legs dangle over the edge as he settles beside me.

He sticks his hand in the front of his hoodie and passes me a juice pouch.

"Are we five?" I ask, holding up the kid's drink.

He rips the plastic off his straw. "It seemed fitting. Like old times."

I take the straw off the back and remove the covering, stabbing it into the pouch. "Cheers."

He grins. "Cheers." We knock the pouches together and take a sip. Mascen's face screws up in disgust at first but then settles like it's really not so bad after all. "It isn't whiskey, but it'll do."

Chewing on the straw like I always used to do I watch him from the corner of my eye.

"What are you looking at?"

"You."

"Why?" He narrows his eyes.

"Because I want to." His jaw pulses and he looks straight ahead. "Tell me about your cousin. How's he been?"

He looks relieved at the subject change. Neither one of us knows what to do about the change coming between us and I guess ignoring it seems like the most practical route.

"He's doing good now. Married with a baby on the way which is fucking mind-blowing. Better him than my sister. I couldn't handle mini Dean and Willow's

304

running around." Despite his words he smiles like he doesn't actually mind the idea of it so much. I have to admit the idea of Mascen playing with a niece or nephew is a bit too much for my heart to handle. "He lives in Malibu, but the past couple of years he's come for every holiday and usually makes a longer trip at some point in the year."

"What's he do?"

"He's a professional surfer."

"Damn." I take a sip of my juice. "Your family is just full of talented people."

"I promise you we don't have our shit together that well."

"Are you happy?"

I can tell my question takes him by surprise the way his posture stiffens. "I guess. For the most part ... yeah."

"You can talk to me. I know we're not exactly friends now or whatever, but I've been through some shit. I would never tell anyone."

He wraps his arms around one of the barriers to keep people from falling from the deck. Tilting his head my way his eyes are darker than normal—serious. "I know, Princess."

My throat tightens at the way he says *princess*. It's different this time. I feel that word all the way in my core.

He finishes his juice pouch and squeezes the cardboard box up, stuffing it back in his pocket. "We better head back."

We haven't been here long but with the walk I know he's right.

"Okay." I finish the juice and he takes it from me.

Before we get to the ladder to go down Mascen looks back at me, eyes downcast. "Thank you."

I don't really know what he's thanking me for, but I nod anyway.

THIRTY-FOUR

MASCEN

AFTER DINNER, WE LEAVE THE PARENTS BEHIND IN the house and head outside to the firepit. It's a chilly evening but the fire more than makes up for it. Liam sits on the ground with his wife Ariella between his legs, his hands on her small round bump. I don't know how the fuck we got to the point of being the age to start having kids. Dean sits in one of the chairs with Willow in his lap, leaving Lylah, Rory, and me in the other chairs.

"How are things going?" I ask Liam. It was hard to catch up over dinner with so many people and clashing voices.

"Couldn't be better." He smiles conspiratorially looking between Rory and me. "Seems you're not too bad yourself. How's baseball?"

"Good. Things are about to get busy."

Lylah heaves a sigh, rolling her eyes. "Are all guys this lacking in detail when it comes to things?"

Willow and Ariella laugh, blurting a simultaneous, "Yes."

I lift my beer to my lips, refusing to acknowledge them.

"You grew up next door, right?" Liam addresses Rory and she sits up a little straighter.

"I did, but we left when I was eight."

"You and Mascen kept in touch?"

Her cheeks color. "No, just happened to go to the same school and ran into each other. Here we are."

"Interesting." Liam winks at me.

I pull my pack of cigarettes out of my pocket needing to light up the way this conversation is going.

"If you ask me, it's serendipitous. Chances like this don't come around often." Ariella looks between the two of us. I hate being in the fucking spotlight like this.

Sucking on the cigarette, I exhale the air out of my lungs. "Didn't know we asked your opinion on it."

Liam straightens and Ari whispers something to him, but he shakes his head. "Dude, don't talk to my wife like that—and could you put that thing out? Ari's pregnant in case you failed to notice."

I narrow my eyes and stand. "Fine."

Grabbing my beer, I stand. "I'll be over here, smoking on the opposite side of the yard."

Settling under the gazebo on the other end from them in front of the pool I stretch my legs out and lie back on my elbows. The furniture that's normally under here is packed away for the winter months.

Rory walks over sitting beside me.

"You know," I drawl lazily, "you coming over here will only excite them further and stir the gossip."

"Let them talk." She pulls her knees up to her chest wrapping her arms around them. "You're not a very good conversationalist are you?"

"I don't like social gatherings." Crushing the butt of the cigarette against the ground to extinguish it I toss it into the bushes for the landscapers to find later. Lighting up another, I say, "I love my family, but I'm not good at this. I'm too..."

"Secretive?"

"It's not even about secrets." I shake my head. "I just don't like talking about myself. But I guess when you don't like yourself that's what you get."

She stiffens in surprise. "You don't like yourself?"

I roll my head her way. "What's there to like? I'm not a good person."

"Why is it you think you're that way?"

"Didn't know this was going to turn into a goddamn therapy lesson. If I wanted that we could've had this talk in the treehouse."

A smile plays on her lips and she tucks them

together like that can erase her amusement. "Tell me anyway."

"It's easier to know why people don't like me—because I give them a reason to—than to question what I've done wrong."

"You're talking about your dad aren't you?"

I finish my cigarette. "I guess."

"Have you ever tried having a conversation with him about how you feel?"

"Why would I? It wouldn't change anything." I think about how I blew up at him the first night home. He hasn't brought it up and our conversations have been like normal. Short and to the point.

"You never know."

"Don't worry about me. I'll be okay."

She looks at me for a long moment, searching for something but what I'm not sure. "Okay isn't good enough. Not for anyone. Don't settle for it."

She starts to get up, but before she walks away I grab her hand, forcing her to look back at me. "Thank you for coming here with me."

A smile softens her face, her eyes warm behind her glasses. "You're welcome."

Her hand begins to pull from mine and I tighten my hold. "Rory?"

"Yeah?" She hesitates, her smile a little wary.

"Don't settle for okay either."

———

THE DAYS PASS QUICKLY and suddenly it's my last day home. A part of me is relieved to be going tomorrow, but I also don't know how that's going to change things between Rory and me. Here we've been in our own little bubble, a silent truce cast between us, and come tomorrow we'll be entering our old world and I'm not sure what that means.

Walking down the stairs I turn for the hall nearly walking straight into my dad coming out of his hedgehog room—yeah, he has a whole room for his hedgehogs. He tried to convince Rory to adopt one, but I cut him off because no way are they allowing one of his spiky little monsters into a dorm.

"Mascen, I wanted to talk to you."

I jerk back in surprise. "Uh, really? About what?"

"Come on." He opens the door back up, nodding for me to follow him inside. I feel uneasy, like I'm being led to slaughter. Contrary to popular belief I hate confrontation.

Inside he motions for me to sit on the couch. One of the hedgehogs runs on the wheel he custom built for it and I stare at the weird looking little animal so I don't have to look at him.

He sits down in the chair waiting for me to acknowledge him.

"What do you want, Dad?" I know it's better to get this over with than to drag it out.

"I think we need to have a talk."

"Honestly, Dad, it's not necessary. I shouldn't have blown up at you. It's fine." I start to stand.

"Sit down, Mascen."

I plop my ass down immediately. I might be an adult now, but his tone is the one every parent has that the kid knows not to argue with. When your mom or dad uses *that* voice you shut up and listen.

Resting his chin in his hands he seems to be gathering himself.

"I've thought non-stop about what you said. It hurt, I won't lie, but I never saw things the way you did." I open my mouth to speak but he holds his hand up for me to shut up. "I'm not saying you're wrong—everyone has a right to how they feel and a reason they do, me telling you that you're wrong wouldn't change the situation."

Leaning back, he runs his fingers through his hair. "I love music, I love my band, I love making fans happy and being up on stage, but you, your sisters, your mom, that's my real reason for breathing. My family has always meant more to me than that. It's why we chose to stop touring for a while, to give you kids a chance to go to a regular school and live as close to a normal life as possible. But just because we weren't in L.A. as much or touring it didn't mean it changed who I was. Who I am."

He shakes his head, giving himself a moment. "I feel like I'm explaining this all wrong, but I'm trying. You've always been the most independent out of the three of you. Sure, Willow is wild and carefree, but she needs her family to thrive. She needs a tether. Lylah is a social butterfly, but she's still always wanted me and your mom to hold her hand through things. But you were always so stubborn and fiercely independent. You always told me not to help, that you were a big boy and could do it on your own. Even as a toddler you were always saying that. You've always reminded me of my brother in that way. Mathias has never wanted to admit when he needs help or someone to be there for him. He's afraid he's admitting weakness if he can't handle something on his own. You wanted to take on the world and I stepped back to watch, because I knew you could do it. I've always believed in you, son. You talked about your games and me not being there or leaving, and that's on me, not you, and how I felt. I thought you didn't want me there. Any time I was you'd find me in the stands and glare like you wished you could erase me. I figured it was because of the attention I'd get and the disturbance it caused, so I'd leave, and then I stopped coming all together."

He pushes up from the chair and comes to sit beside me. "I'm so sorry if I ever made you feel any less than loved. You kids are my world, the one your mom and I created together."

"Ew, Dad," I protest, not wanting this to jump to a birds and the bees topic.

He chuckles, ruffling my hair like I'm five. "Never doubt that I'm proud of you, Mascen. I'm beyond honored to be your father. We might have different interests, God knows I can't play sports to save myself, but it doesn't mean we don't have other things in common. I love you. So much."

"Don't make me cry, Old Man."

He chuckles, his eyes brimmed with tears and he yanks me into his arms in a tight hug. He releases me from the hug but keeps a hold on my shoulders. "I know words can't make everything better, or change the way you felt, but I'm going to do whatever I can to make it up to you."

I don't even know what to say, but I guess sometimes you don't need words.

THIRTY-FIVE

RORY

MY PHONE RINGS WITH A FACETIME AND WHEN I SEE it's Hazel I can't help but smile even if I am a little peeved with her.

"I'm so so sorry I didn't call you back on Thanksgiving," she says instead of hello. "I feel horrible."

"It's okay." It hurt that she couldn't even say a few words on the holiday, but I've learned not to let it bother me for long. I know she doesn't mean anything personal by it.

"It's really not. I'm the worst sister ever. I'm going to

make this up to you, I swear. Maybe come visit for Christmas."

"Sure," I reply, but I know better than to get my hopes up.

"I swear, Rory." Folding a sweater, I pack it into the suitcase. Mascen wants to hit the road early so I decided to pack most of my things tonight. "Where are you? That doesn't look like your dorm."

I'm surprised she can even remember what my dorm looked like considering we've only Facetimed twice since I arrived on campus.

"I'm staying with a friend." I want to be mean and let that be all the detail she gets from me but I know it's better to be honest. "I'm actually staying with Mascen. Mascen Wade. You remember the Wade's who lived next to us?"

"Oh, wow, I remember them. That's so crazy. How did you get into contact with him?"

"School, he goes to Aldridge too." I grab a pair of jeans and pluck a piece of lint off them. "Small world, huh?"

"Definitely. I can't believe that. Wow." I can tell she's truly surprised by the news. With a laugh, she adds, "Do you remember when I fake married you guys? He actually kissed you. That was hilarious."

I drop the pants into the pile of other packed clothes. "I remember."

She turns to respond to someone in the background of the strip club. "I gotta go, sis. Love you." She blows a kiss and disconnects the call before I can say goodbye.

Tossing the blackened screen onto the bed I pack the last of my things, leaving out pajamas and an outfit for tomorrow. I'll stuff today's dirty clothes in before we leave.

Opening the door I peek into the hallway but Mascen isn't lurking there like he sometimes is. Tiptoeing up to his door, I press my ear against it but hear nothing. I ease the door open. "Mascen?"

I hold my breath, listening.

Silence is all that greets me. He's clearly not up there. A part of me wants to sneak up there, check out his inner sanctuary, but I know it would be wrong to breach his personal space in that way. I ease the door closed and go downstairs, thinking he might be in the family room or kitchen.

He's in neither. Taking a chance, I bundle up in my jacket, heading out into the dark to the treehouse. It's harder to find by myself, so I go slow, but eventually I come to the bottom of the tree.

Tilting my head up, I wrap my hands around my mouth. "Mascen! Are you up there?"

I hear some shuffling and then his form appears, leaning over the railing. "What are you doing out here?"

"Looking for you, duh."

"Come up."

I grab one of the pegs for the ladder and start the ascent up. I'm nearly to the top when my foot slips. My heart lurches in fear as I start to slip. I don't have time to panic too much before Mascen grabs my arm pulling me up. How he manages to do that, I know I'm not the lightest person, is beyond me. He must have Thor-like strength. It would make sense considering he seems to think he's a god.

"Be careful, Princess, I don't need you falling and taking a permanent slumber I can't wake you from with the magical touch of my lips."

I push his shoulder lightly. "I can't help I slipped." He backs inside the treehouse, pulling me inside with him. The middle of the floor is piled with pillows and blankets. "Are you sleeping out here tonight?"

"I was considering it." He lays downs on the pillows pulling me with him. A giggle bursts free from my lips from the surprise.

I roll over onto my back, the two of us lying side by side. If you told me two weeks ago I'd be lying beside Mascen in his old treehouse, not contemplating killing him, I would've thought you were lying.

The silence stretches between us. "This is weird," he finally says.

"Why?"

"We're just lying here saying nothing when I really want to kiss you."

He rolls onto his side, bracing his body weight on his left elbow. His hair falls in his eyes and there's more stubble on his jaw than normal. It makes him look older, more rugged. I itch to reach up and touch him but I keep my hands fisted at my sides.

"W-What did you say?" I stutter out, my thoughts barely coherent with him looking deeply into my eyes.

He wets his lips, eyes dropping to mine. "I said I

want to kiss you." His voice is low and husky. It's the sexiest sound I've ever heard.

"You say that you hate me, but then you apparently like kissing me."

He reaches out, tracing the contour of my lips with his finger. A wicked grin overtakes him and I know then I'm playing with the devil. "I told you I was going to hate fuck the shit out of you."

A moan threatens to slip between my lips at the visual of what he could do to me. "I'm starting to think you're all talk. I'm going to need a demonstration."

His eyes narrow. "That so?" His voice is even deeper than normal.

I nod, words fleeing me. Suddenly the only thing I need in the world is his lips on mine, his body grinding above me.

"You're playing with fire, Princess. Not afraid?"

I shake my head, reaching up to thread my fingers through the hair at the base of his skull. I yank him closer, purposely pulling sharply on his hair. He gasps in surprise, the air hissing between his teeth. "You like it rough? Maybe you're not such a delicate little princess." The same finger he used to trace my lips glides against my cheek. "Should I start calling you Monster instead?"

I tug him even closer so we're nose to nose. "Stop talking."

He listens for a change, but not before one of those smirks that I love to hate makes its appearance. With one hand, he angles my jaw upward, and slowly, gently, with intention, kisses me.

He takes his time with slow nips making my body writhe as I want him to kiss me deeper. I've never wanted to give my body over so completely like I do with Mascen.

He pushes at my jacket and I sit up to remove it completely. He sits back on his heels watching me. His normally gray eyes are nearly black. I start to reach for my shirt but he grabs my hands in his rough grip. "No," he snarls roughly, the sound of the barked order sending a shiver down my spine. "I'm going to undress you."

"Why?" I blurt, my hands still tightly bound in his.

"Because you're mine."

He doesn't give me time to react to that proclamation. He grabs my face between his massive hands kissing me like he's lost all control. I revel in it. I've made the normally stoic and always in control Mascen Wade lose his mind. But I swear to God, if he doesn't take things all the way tonight I might kill him. My body aches for him.

He pushes me back so I'm lying once more. My legs spread, giving him room to settle between. He rocks his hips as he kisses me, the moan that leaves me pathetically loud as I feel him growing hard.

He kisses his way down my neck and sits up slightly. Instead of taking my shirt off he eases it up my stomach lowering his head to swirl his tongue around my belly button.

"Mascen," I plead, my fingers threading through his silky hair. "Please."

I don't even know what I'm begging for. This. More. Everything.

I need it all. I need him.

"Shh," he hushes, tipping my head back, thumb on my bottom lip. "I'll take care of you."

His tongue sweeps against mine, a gentle claiming. He's not as wild as he's been in the past where it was like he had no control. This is purposeful and I know then he definitely won't be stopping tonight.

When my lips are swollen and bruised feeling he sits up removing his shirt. He hooks his thumbs in the back of it yanking it up and over. I watch the way his abdominals flex, my throat growing tight. It's unfair for one human being to be so utterly perfect. I trace the contours of his stomach, down, down, down over the hair trailing from his navel until I stop, popping the button on his jeans open.

He grabs my hand and my eyes flick up to his. They're still darker than normal, there's something eerie about them but I'm not afraid.

"I'm in charge." God, his commanding ways shouldn't turn me on so much, but my hand slackens and he releases it when he knows I'm going to listen. "Arms up." I do as he says, staring into the depths of his eyes the entire time I do. With my shirt gone, he reaches behind me and unhooks my bra. It falls to my elbows and he yanks it off. Cupping his hands around my breasts like he's testing their weight he murmurs out a pained, "Perfect. Fucking perfect."

He lowers his head swirling his tongue around first one nipple and then the other. My back bows and he grips my waist, holding me up since we're both still on our knees.

"I wish I didn't want you so bad," he growls, undoing my belt and then the button on my jeans. "But I can't help it." He kisses me deeply and when he pulls away he keeps a gentle hold on my chin looking into my eyes as he says, "You were made for me, Rory." He pulls off my jeans and underwear taking in my naked body with hungry eyes. I wish he was wearing less but I know better than to open my mouth. "Lie back," he commands. I do what I'm told and he wears a wicked grin.

He lowers his body, grinning at me again before his mouth finds my core. A small gasp leaves me as he rolls his tongue around the sensitive nub of nerves. "Mascen," I moan, trying to keep my body still. I can't help but wiggle, the feelings too much, too consuming.

He presses down on my hips, holding me hostage as his tongue strokes my pussy. He's slow, purposeful. He clearly knows what he's doing and my body can tell. Perspiration dampens my skin. He looks up at me then, his lips glossy and plumper than normal. "I'm not rushing things with you."

I whimper when he sucks on my clit sliding two fingers into my pussy at the same time.

Mascen is going to kill me, I'm sure of it—if not him then the pleasure.

He savors me, his fingers working slowly to build the pressure. When I finally orgasm the spasms feel like they go on forever. My body shakes uncontrollably and he's there to hold me his eyes watching with delight. He just played my body like an instrument and I didn't even mind. I'm supposed to hate him but my body certainly hasn't gotten the memo. Let's face it, I'm not sure I can hate him anymore. There are so many layers to Mascen, and all I've seen for months is the masks he wears to keep others at arm's length. But that's dropping and I like the man underneath far too much.

"Are you ready for me, Princess?"

Is my body ready? Yes. My heart? Not in a million years.

I give him a silent nod. I can't stop this now even if he breaks my heart in the end.

He presses a kiss to my neck right where my pulse races. He stands, having to bend slightly in the tree-house, and takes off his jeans and boxer-briefs. His cock stands out proudly from his body, the hair around it trimmed neatly. He smirks when he sees me staring but I refuse to be ashamed.

He pales, cursing under his breath. Before I can ask what's the matter he blurts, "Please, for the love all that is holy, tell me you're on birth control."

I nod weakly. After my scare with the Plan-B I went to the free clinic and got on birth control. I've never missed a dose. I'm not ready to be a mom.

"Thank fuck." He looks up at the ceiling like he's saying a literal prayer.

He gets on his knees between my legs. Wrapping his fist around his cock he guides it to my pussy, teasingly pushing it in before retreating. A whimper sweeps past my lips. I desperately need him inside of me. It's been too long and I know sex with Mascen will be like nothing I've ever experienced before.

He pushes in a little more than the last time and pulls out.

"Oh my God, Mascen, just fuck me already."

His laugh is raspy. "Don't tell me what to do."

He keeps teasing, building up the anticipation. I whimper and the small sound only serves to empower him.

When he finally plunges all the way into the hilt it takes me by surprise, a scream tearing from my throat. He silences me with a bruising kiss, my scream quickly turning into a moan.

"Fuck, you feel so good. Better than I imagined." He rocks into me, his thrusts deep and slow, so unlike what I expected.

His forehead presses gently against mine, our breaths mingling in the air. I reach up, twining my fingers in his hair. His eyes close momentarily and I take the moment to stare at him without being seen — to absorb the unbridled pleasure he feels because of me.

When his eyes open the stormy gray color nearly takes my breath away. He holds his body weight above me, his large hands braced on each side of my head. I want this moment to go on forever, me and him in this little bubble where nothing else exists.

"K-Kiss me," I beg, my voice barely audible.

"Why?" He teases, never wanting to give me what I want.

With my hand that's in his hair I pull him down to my lips. He doesn't fight me but I feel his smile before he kisses me.

He takes my cheek in his right hand, sliding his hand down my neck. His thumb rolls in slow circles. His touch both calms and ignites something in me—a part that aches for more. I know it's silly and selfish to wish for more from Mascen, for something real, and if all I have is now I'm stupid enough to take it.

"More," I plead.

He shakes his head, the ends of his hair tickling my forehead. "Not this time."

Gripping my hips, he holds them up changing the angle and I gasp as it sends him even deeper.

"Mascen!" I cry out his name, my teeth slamming together as I try to quiet myself.

"You fucking love my cock inside you, don't you?"

"Y-Yes," I pant, out of breath.

"Good girl," he rumbles, his thumb rubbing my bottom lip before slipping inside my parted mouth. "Suck."

I do what he says, wrapping my mouth around his thumb and sucking on it like it's his cock in my mouth.

His eyes dilate, narrowing on my rounded lips. Closing his eyes he mutters out a string of indecipherable curse words, his hips bucking harder against mine.

Lowering to his forearms he frames my body. His hand skims around my left breast, down the curve of my waist, stopping at my thigh where he slips it between us rubbing my clit. My back bows from the added friction. My pussy clenches around him and I know I'm close to coming.

"Fuck," he bites out, "I'm so close. Tell me you're almost there."

I nod since I can't make sense of words right now.

His touch becomes rougher, his hips moving against mine faster.

The orgasm builds and builds until I fall off the edge. He's right there with me, his cock stiffening inside me as he comes. He stays there for a moment, frozen, before finally rolling off of me and gathering my naked body against his. He buries his head into the crook of my neck. I giggle from the feel of his hair against my sensitive skin. He kisses what I'm beginning to realize is his favorite spot on my neck. His arm wraps around my body holding me still so I can't move away.

I never would've thought it, but Mascen likes to cuddle. I've never been much for hanging around after the deed, but I know this with Mascen is different. I haven't figured out in what way. I reach for his hand, twining our fingers together.

It's quiet between us, just our breaths and the sounds of the crickets outside.

"What are we doing?" My lips pressing into the top

of his head the way he's tucked into me, his head now lying on my breast. "What is this?"

He stiffens but doesn't try to move away from me.

"I don't know. Do we need to label it?"

"No. But this is something right? You feel it too?"

He doesn't answer for a while and I'm worried I've pushed too far. This is unfamiliar territory for me and it seems to be that way for him.

Finally, when I think he's fallen asleep, he murmurs, "Yeah, it's something."

THIRTY-SIX

MASCEN

ARRIVING BACK ON CAMPUS FEELS STIFLING. A weight I hadn't realized had left is suddenly back. Here, things are different. People know me one way, but over the last two weeks Rory has unknowingly been whittling away at that version of me. It's both thrilling and terrifying.

I pull up outside her dorm putting my Land Rover in park. She sighs, looking crestfallen, but she doesn't say anything.

That's one of the things I like about her. She's not whiny and she won't beg.

"It looks like this is where we part."

"I can carry your bag up."

She shakes her head. "It's not that heavy and there's an elevator. I can handle it. Besides, I'm sure most girls are arriving back right now and you'd cause a riot." I grin at that, amused by the idea. "Don't be so smug about it," she mutters, reaching for the seatbelt. "You know most of the girls on campus are in love with you. I heard one girl already has personalized wedding invitations printed."

I stare blankly at her. "Please tell me you're kidding."

She rolls her eyes. "You're annoyingly gullible."

She reaches for the door but I pull her back, my eyes searching her face before making eye contact. "I don't ... I don't know how to do *this*." I wave a hand between us.

"How about you don't overthink it?"

"I'm not good at that either."

"Maybe you should practice instead of thinking the whole world and everyone in it needs to cater to you and your sensitivities." She sticks her tongue out at me playfully.

I don't want to say goodbye to her. I know when she gets out of the car everything changes. We're in a different world now. Things aren't the same on campus like they were at my home.

Cradling her cheek in my hand I rub my thumb over her silky soft skin.

"What is it?"

"Nothing," I murmur, lowering my mouth to hers. A tiny mewling sound leaves her throat. I don't think she's even aware of the noises she makes when I kiss her, but I love every single one.

I don't want to let her leave the car, but I know she has to go. I pull away and her eyes slowly blink open, hazy with lust. Last night in the treehouse feels like forever ago. I want her again and again, but I know I have to let go. For now.

"You better get out, Princess. I might corrupt you if you stay any longer."

She shakes her head free of cobwebs, her tiny smile amusing to me. She gets out, grabbing her bag from the backseat. I roll down the passenger window when she pauses outside of it.

"What?"

Her smile grows. "Why do you think it's you that's doing the corrupting?"

She winks and before I can generate a response she's walking away. I think she purposely puts more sway in her steps to entice me. If we were anywhere else I'd be out of this car and on her in a heartbeat, tossing her over my shoulder and carrying her to bed.

————

IT's late at night before Cole gets home. He finds me lounging in the living room watching TV. His heavy duffle bag hangs off his shoulder and he looks tired.

"Fuck," he rubs his eyes, "there was an accident on the highway. It took an extra two hours to get home."

"That's the worst." He's only been home two-point-five seconds and I already feel guilt creeping in. I'm not one to normally feel that way—I do what I want without remorse, but I know if he finds out Rory went home with me it won't sit well. Clearing my throat I turn the volume down on the TV. "Need me to grab anything from your car?"

"Nah." He drops his heavy bag down on the floor. "This was it."

He crosses the room to the kitchen grabbing a beer from the fridge. "Want one?"

"I'm good."

He comes back dropping onto the opposite end of the couch. "How was your break? Everything good at home?"

I cross my arms over my chest, not seeming to know what to do with my hands.

"It was nice, my cousin flew in from California."

"Hmm." He takes a swig of beer.

"What about you?"

"It was nice seeing my parents and sister, but I'm glad to be back." He kicks his feet up on the ottoman. "Don't get me wrong, I love them, but being on my own-or you know, rooming with you—is a lot more peaceful."

"Don't forget no one bossing you around."

He chuckles. "Amen."

My phone buzzes in my pocket and I pull it out finding a text from Rory.

Princess: Hey, Satan—how's the temperature in hell? Not warm enough without me, amiright?

Me: You definitely make things hotter.

I glance at Cole but he's busy looking at the TV.

Me: You get settled all right?

Princess: I just gasped. Are you concerned about me?

Me: It was a question.

Princess: I'm fine.

Me: Just fine? Last night you were screaming my name, you should be fucking fantastic.

Princess: You're not fucking me right now are you? No, so just fine it is.

Me: Are you saying you want me to fuck you right now?

Princess: I'm going to bed.

Me: I was just getting started. We can dirty talk.

Princess: I'm ignoring you.

Me: You're evil. You can't bring up this topic of conversation and just ditch me.

But of course she does just that and stops replying.

"You're smiling, it's weird," Cole remarks. My head jerks up to look at him.

"I'm not smiling." I put my phone away before he can see the screen, not that he'd know who Princess is, but the contact name would still pique his interest.

"You definitely are. Who is it?"

I roll my head towards him playing nonchalant. "Nobody, seriously."

He stands, the empty beer bottle dangling from his fingers. "You know, when someone says nobody it usually means it's somebody special." He walks past me, smacking me on the shoulder. "You deserve to be happy man. Whoever she is don't fuck it up."

I hold my breath as he throws away the bottle and grabs his bag heading up the stairs. Something tells me if he knew it was Rory he'd be singing a different tune.

THIRTY-SEVEN

RORY

"Who knew college would require so much studying?" Kenna breaks the long silence between the three of us. We commandeered a table in the library hours ago and have been studying ever since.

It's been two weeks since we got back from break, which required a lot of explaining on my part to Kenna, and filling Li in on the Mascen situation. I told them about growing up beside him and how we'd both been surprised to run into each other here. They thought it was romantic, some kind of once in a lifetime thing. I wasn't sure about that but I did know my hatred for Mascen had reluctantly melted into like.

"Well, it is college." Li nibbles on the end of a Twizzler she snuck in.

"I was being sarcastic." Kenna tosses a Sour Patch kid at her. "Even with snacks I've lost all motivation."

Closing the textbook, I rest my elbow on the table and my head in my hand. "Motivation left me about an hour ago. My eyes are crossing."

"Finals are a bitch." Kenna slides her laptop away from her like maybe the distance will give her clarity.

"And we have three more years of this." I point out.

She narrows her eyes. "Don't remind me."

Li finishes her Twizzler, turning her dark gaze my way. "Tell us more about Mascen. You guys are still talking, right?"

I wave a dismissive hand like it's really not that big of a deal. "A few texts here and there."

More than a few but I want to keep that information to myself. We haven't seen each other in person since he dropped me off. Thanks to classes and both of us studying non-stop it's been impossible to meet up. He did show up at Marcelo's one evening and sat at the bar nursing a glass of whiskey. The way Heather kept eyeing him and then me I'm thinking he bribed her for my schedule. I'm also certain she's planning our wedding and she doesn't even know our past or that I went home with him for Thanksgiving. If she did she'd move from wedding planning to naming our kids.

"Sexy texts?" Kenna waggles her eyebrows. "Please

tell me they're dirty." Heat rushes to my cheeks and she gasps. "Oh my God, they totally are! Ugh, tell me about them." She reaches across the table laying her hand on mine. "I need to live vicariously. I'm lonely."

"I-I they're not—I—"

"Oh, Kenna, leave her alone. They're still figuring things out."

Kenna frowns. "But we're friends. I need details."

I swipe one of her Sour Patch kids. "There's really nothing much to tell. We're flirting, but I haven't seen him since we got home from break." I mean, I have at the restaurant, but I know she'll read more into that than there is.

"God, you're boring and I need to get laid."

I try not to smile in amusement and open my textbook back up. "Enough goofing off, we have work to do."

———

By the end of the week I'm walking out of my final exam. I feel confident I passed everything, but since you can never really be certain I won't feel better until I know for sure.

I don't get far when a hand wraps around my wrist. A squeak flies out of my throat as my body collides with a very solid chest. My eyes dart up to meet Mascen's. We're around the side of the building, tucked into an archway. Still anyone passing by might see and recognize us. He does have his hoodie up, which blocks his face for the most part.

"You are such a stalker—a true Edward Cullen."

"Don't diss the bloodsucker."

I arch a brow. "You know who Edward Cullen is?"

"My sisters made me watch the movies." He shrugs like this information is no big deal.

"Since you've went out of your way to pull me aside you must want something."

A little smirk dances on his lips. He lifts his hands to either side of my head, boxing me back against the brick archway. I narrow my eyes and his smile only grows larger. When he leans forward his hoodie shadows both of us. Anyone that looks over will see what they think is a couple kissing.

His nose glides along the side of my cheek until his lips are at my ear. "Maybe I missed you, Princess."

A small sound threatens to pass through my lips. I don't want to admit it out loud but I've missed him. Three weeks with minimal contact has been a hell I didn't expect. It's weird, since it's not like we're a couple, we're not even friends, but this 'something' that we are I like a little too much.

"Did you now?" I finally find my voice.

"Only a little. But don't tell anyone. I have my street cred to think about." He brushes his lips against mine, there and gone too quick to be a real kiss.

I weave my fingers into his shirt. "Are you going soft for me?" I arch a brow, fighting a smile.

He growls in my ear, the sound making my stomach dip. "There is nothing soft about me, Princess." To get his point across he presses his body closer into mine, all his hard lines against my soft curves.

"So, you're still an asshole?"

"Yes, but I'm *your* asshole."

"There's a difference?"

He wets his lips. "Definitely."

I wrap one of his hoodie strings around my finger. "What was it you wanted again?"

"Winter break starts this weekend."

"And?" I wait, wondering where he's going with this. He mentioned during one of his evenings at Marcelo's that his family was spending the holiday in L.A. and he didn't want to go.

"Stay with me."

The three words catch me off guard. "Where?"

He rolls his eyes. "My place, Princess, where else?"

"Your townhouse?"

The last time I was inside I was fleeing from Cole's room and yanked Mascen's towel off and the last time I was there at all I was dropping a heartbroken Cole off.

"That is where I live." He presses his lips together. "If you don't want to stay I'm sure I can find someone else to fill your spot, but they won't be you, Princess."

"Don't even play me like that." I push playfully at his shoulders.

"What will it be? Yes? No? Or, my favorite, fuck you, Mascen—as in the literal sense of fuck me please, baby, I miss your pussy."

Laughter bursts out of me from the unexpected turn

of events. I let the string go and it unwinds from my finger. "Yes—to the staying and the fucking."

His grin is nearly my undoing. He places a tender kiss on my nose, the gesture sweet and surprising, and starts backing away. "If anyone was ever going to be my girl it had to be you, Princess."

He pulls his cigarette pack from the front pocket of his hoodie, finally turning away from me. I stay in the archway watching him walk away and the slow furl of smoke billowing behind him.

I think I'm in love.

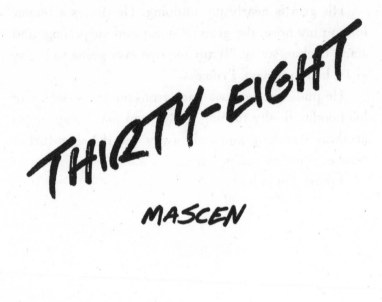

THIRTY-EIGHT

MASCEN

SNEAKING AROUND BEHIND MY FRIEND'S BACK TO have a girl over, *his* former girl, might be the worst thing I've ever done. Then again, probably not, but I do feel like shit over this.

As soon as he's gone I straighten things up—luckily the housekeeper stopped by last week so it's not in too bad of shape—and change my sheets to clean ones. I close Cole's door, my guilt seeping in just by looking inside his bedroom.

With everything in order I text Rory, letting her know she can come over when she wants.

All she replies with is 'okay' which leaves me to meander around wondering when exactly that means.

I'm unhinged because of this girl. I want to hate it but strangely I don't.

Picking up a candle my mom sent me I light it in the living room so the place will smell nice when she gets here.

Fuck, I'm whipped.

How did I get to this point?

Before I can tailspin too hard the doorbell rings.

Swinging it open I can't stop the smile when I see her. "Princess, welcome." I sweep my arm wide to let her pass.

"Thanks, Hans Gruber."

Closing and locking the door behind her, I turn to face her.

"This is your place, huh?" She looks around, eyes wide as she takes it in.

"You've been here before, don't look so surprised."

"In case you forgot I was running away."

"Trying not to turn around and look at my dick more like."

She rolls her eyes toward me. "Of course you'd think that. I was embarrassed as hell and then shocked out of my mind to see you."

I exhale, thinking back to that day. "I was surprised to see you too."

She places her hands on her hips. "Do you have any special plans for us today?"

"No," I reply hesitantly, wondering if I should've thought of something.

"Good," she replies excitedly, digging into the tote bag over her shoulder, "I brought these."

She spreads the DVDs out on the ottoman in front of the couch.

"Silence of the Lambs," she points, looking back at me with a conspiratorial smile, "Die Hard, Twilight, and Interview with the Vampire."

I narrow my eyes. "I notice a trend here." This time, I'm the one who points. "Hannibal Lector, Hans Gruber, Edward Cullen, and Lestat."

She claps her hands giddily and I wish it wasn't so fucking adorable. I like this side of Rory too much, the one where she lets her guard down and she's just herself, unweighted down by her past. "I knew there was a brain inside that pretty head of yours."

"Well, I mean, it's not completely full of air."

She rises of her tiptoes, kissing my cheek. Her lips are soft and warm. Gripping her hand, I pull her closer when she starts to back away, kissing her the way I've wanted since I opened the door.

She melts into me, the heat of the kiss growing. Her small hands push at my chest. With a groan, I pull away.

"Don't think you can distract me from the movie marathon I have planned. I picked up snacks and everything." From the tote bag she pulls out a plastic shopping bag. "Think you can handle this?"

A gruff laugh escapes my throat. "If I can handle anything."

Her mouth drops open and I'm sure she's ready to protest. Swiping the bag, I head into the kitchen before she can start in on me.

I hear her opening the DVDs, ripping the plastic and stickers off, while I dig into the bag pulling out popcorn, Milk Duds, gummy bears, Reese's Pieces, and Reese's Christmas tree shaped chocolates.

"Someone's got a sweet tooth," I sing-song.

"Don't mock me," she yells back at me. "It all looked so good I couldn't leave it behind. It was screaming, 'Take me. Eat me.'"

"I'm pretty sure you're going to be screaming that at me later."

I hear her choke from the other room, on what I don't know. "I can't believe you said that."

I take the popcorn out of the box and pop it into the microwave. While it's twirling around I get the bowl out and another to pile all the various candy and chocolate in. When the pops start to slow I take it out, dumping the steaming kernels into the bowl.

"You ready in there?"

"Yep!"

I carry the bowls in and set them down. "Let me grab some drinks. What do you want?"

"I'm fine with whatever."

From the fridge I grab two sodas and two beers. Setting them both down, I take the spot beside her on the couch. "Cold? Do you need a blanket?"

"I'm good right now."

She hits play on the movie, wiggling around to get comfortable. I pick up the popcorn bowl and set it in my lap.

"I've never had a girl here before," I admit as the opening credits begin.

I feel her stiffen and her head slowly turns my way. "Never?"

I shake my head, looking at the screen not her. "Nope. I mean, sure, some come for parties, but not like this. Not to stay."

"What about for sex?" I can tell the question bothers her but she's mad at herself that it does from the way she toys with a rip in her jeans.

"Nope."

She looks at me in surprise and I force myself to meet her inquisitive gaze.

"Then where?"

"Their place or wherever."

"And by wherever you mean…?"

"The library, locker room, a storage closet, hotel — should I keep going?"

"No," she blurts, "I get the picture." The movie starts to play and it's a few minutes before she speaks. "Just so you know, I don't judge you for those things. I haven't been a saint either."

"Really?" I sound doubtful, I know, but I've learned most girls are pretty judgmental even when they don't mean to be.

She nods. "Want to know a secret?"

344

"Always. Secrets are the best form of currency." I wink at her.

She sticks a piece of popcorn in her mouth to stall. "I've never had sex in a bed." Her confession takes me by surprise. It wasn't what I was expecting. When I don't say anything, she continues, "I know it's super weird, but I couldn't have sex at my mom's place and I wasn't comfortable enough to go to any of my hook ups' place, so…" she trails off. "And then when we had sex it was in your treehouse. So, yeah," she shrugs like she's not uncomfortable at all with the topic at hand, "no bed."

"Pause the movie," I demand, standing up.

"What? Why?" I can tell she's worried I'm pissed, but I'm the furthest thing from it.

"We have a problem to rectify."

"Problem? What problem?"

"Your bed problem, Princess." When she doesn't stand I bend, scooping her up and tossing her over my shoulder. The air rushes out of her lungs.

I'm worried I've been too rough with her when she gives a tiny laugh. "You're crazy."

"Maybe," I agree, starting for the stairs, "but if you're telling me I'm going to be the first to fuck you in a bed I'm all over it."

"Put me down you heathen." She smacks my butt in protest.

"I will. On my bed."

Pushing my bedroom door open I drop her onto the bed. She bounces, glaring at me.

Resting back on her elbows she says, "You could've been gentler about that."

"Princess," I take my shirt off, dropping it by my feet, "you should know by now there's nothing gentle about me."

She wets her lips. "Stop talking then and show me."

Fuck, this girl.

She scoots back on the bed and I lower my body over hers. Kissing her deeply I taste the popcorn on her lips. The past couple of weeks not being able to touch her, kiss her, has been an unexpected torture. Now that I have her here for the entire break I want to do nothing but savor it. I've never had this kind of feeling with anyone before. It's strange and new but not unpleasant. I used to think a relationship would be the worst kind of agony. I've never done well answering to someone else. Rory is making me rethink all that. I like being around her and I miss her when she's gone.

Lifting her shirt up I kiss her belly. She squirms against me silently begging for more. When her shirt is gone her bra follows quickly. I take her firm breasts between my hands paying careful attention to each globe. My tongue flicks over one nipple and then the next, taking my time, savoring her body. I bite the top of her right breast and she yelps.

"Mascen! What the hell?"

I look up. "I told you I'm not gentle." She rolls her eyes. "I'm starting to think I need to spank you every time you roll your eyes at me."

She narrows those pretty brown eyes on me. "Try it

and see what happens." I open my mouth to speak, but she surprises me by curling her leg around my body and pushing me down on the bed with a hand to my shoulder. She wraps her dainty fingers around my throat but doesn't squeeze. "Your fatal mistake is always thinking you're in charge."

"Or maybe I'm manipulative and I wanted to get you on top."

"*Or,*" she grips my face in her hand, digging her nails in, "that's what you're saying so you can still feel like you're the dominant one."

I squeeze her delectable ass in my hands, still wrapped in her jeans. "I'll let you lead … *tonight.*"

Challenge glimmers in her eyes and fuck if that doesn't turn me on more. I know she has to feel my dick rock hard beneath her.

She bites her bottom lip, the picture of innocence. "It's cute you think it's only for tonight."

Her lips descend on mine, taking the lead, and I follow. She rocks against me and I grip her hips, holding her down to increase the friction. A little moan escapes her, the sound so pure and sweet because it's real and not a put on.

"Touch me," she demands, grabbing my hands and moving them from her hips to her breasts. I roll my thumbs over her nipples, eliciting a moan from her again. "Yes, like that."

She kisses her way over my pecs and down my stomach, kissing each indention of my abdominals. When she reaches the top of my jeans she scoots away and starts to undo my jeans, wiggling them down my legs. I sit up to help her and soon both my jeans and underwear are on the floor.

"You next."

"I'm in charge." She waggles her finger, trying to hide a smile.

"You. Next." I repeat, my tone brooking no room for argument. If I don't get her naked soon I might spontaneously combust.

She swallows a lump in her throat, possibly surprised by my tone. Easing off the bed she stares in my eyes the entire time she shimmies her jeans down her hips leaving her in black boy shorts. She takes those off too, exhaling a nervous sigh when she's standing in front of me completely naked. Squaring her shoulders she climbs back on the bed. She wraps her hand around my cock and a moan rumbles in my throat. She lowers her mouth to the tip ready to wrap her lips around me.

"Sixty-nine me." I slap her ass.

"W-What?" she stutters, her hold on my cock slackening.

"Sixty-nine me."

"I don't know what that is," she whispers like someone might overhear.

I grin wickedly. "I'll show you."

She looks at me skeptically as I direct her into place. "This feels weird. My ass is in your face."

"So is your pussy, Princess, and I can't fucking wait to taste it."

My tongue swipes against her core, eliciting a gasp from her. "Oh God."

I chuckle against her.

Lowering her head her hair sweeps forward tickling my skin. I brace in anticipation of her mouth on my cock. I've fantasized about it a little too much in our three weeks apart.

Her tongue swirls around the tip and my hips buck involuntarily. She gives a small laugh and the rumble of her throat against my cock ... fuck, I'm worried I'm going to blow my load early like a complete amateur.

Swirling my tongue around her clit this time she's the one struggling to maintain composure. Payback's a bitch.

"Mascen, oh God." Her legs begin to shake. I know she's close to orgasming, but I don't let her get there. I'm a selfish prick and I want to feel her first orgasm of the night squeezing my cock.

Flipping her off of me and onto the bed the air rushes out of her lungs. Before she can catch her breath I'm plunging inside her. "Oh, fuck." I squeeze her hips, trying to stave off my need to come. She's turned me into a teenager with no self-control.

"Harder," she begs.

"Not yet."

She whimpers with need, but I know if I give into her demands it'll be over.

Grabbing her hair in a tight fist I pull her up until our mouths meet. She bites down on my lip hard enough to draw blood. We both gasp at the metallic taste.

"You fucking bit me," I pant.

She smirks as my arms move to the middle of her body, holding her up as I rock into her. "I told you to stop thinking you were the one in charge." She nips at my ear, her playful laugh rumbling against me.

I pull her back in for a kiss, addicted to her taste.

With her hands on either side of my chest she pushes me down onto the mattress. Breaking from the kiss, she sits up, grinding her hips into mine. She pulls her hair over her shoulder, eyes shadowed behind her glasses. I barely place my hands on her hips when she pushes them away forcefully.

"Don't touch me."

I fold my arms behind my head, listening for once. If she wants to lead I'll damn well let her.

Watching the pleasure on her face makes letting her take control all the more worth it. She's getting off on *me*. On my body. On my cock.

She gives me a little smile, her teeth gently digging into her bottom lip. She almost seems shy and I realize she's probably never experienced this with a guy, this level of control, if she's only every had hookups.

That's the thing about hookups—they're all well and good to scratch an itch, but they lack the intimacy that brings about the real high.

She grips her breasts, squeezing them between her hands and playing with her nipples.

She rocks her hips harder, round and round, up and

down. Her pussy throbs around my cock and I know she's close—thank God since I'm barely hanging by a thread.

"Rory," I warn.

"Almost," she pants, her head falling back, eyes closed.

With a long moan, she starts to come. I can't take it anymore, grabbing her hips and thrusting up into her. Either she doesn't care, or doesn't notice, that I'm holding onto her.

"Fuck, yes!" I cry out, coming inside of her. She continues to move her hips, riding the wave. I collapse, out of breath and my body damp with sweat.

After the last pulses of her orgasm fade she falls on top of me. I wrap my arms around her, holding our bodies together. Pressing a gentle kiss to her forehead, I close my eyes.

This girl.

This girl.

She's *the* girl.

And fuck if that isn't the scariest thing I've ever had to face.

THIRTY-NINE

RORY

STIFLING A YAWN I ENTER THE KITCHEN TO THE SMELL of pancakes.

"You're making me pancakes?" I blurt in awe at the sight of a shirtless Mascen standing over a griddle full of a variety of chocolate chip and blueberry pancakes.

He looks up from flipping a pancake. "I mean, we gotta eat."

I slide onto one of the barstools, resting my elbow on the counter and my head in my hand. "That's for sure." I think back to last night and how after a short nap we were back at it again with another round early this morning. I drifted back to sleep and didn't even notice when Mascen left the bed.

Mascen piles the stacks of pancakes high on a plate then starts to clean everything up.

"I can do that," I protest, getting up. "You cooked."

"You're the guest," he reminds me. "I've got it." I'm ready to argue the matter further but then I think better of it. Mascen and I can both find reasons to bicker over everything, it's time to rise above it. "Grab a plate."

I pick up one of the empty plates he'd already put out and pile three chocolate chip pancakes on it, drenching them in syrup. He looks at me in surprise and I shrug innocently. "What? I'm starving."

I sit back down where I was before, digging the side of my fork into one of the pancakes for a bite. The pancake is light and fluffy, the chocolate melting instantly on my tongue. "This is delicious."

He grins, pleased by the praise. "Thanks, they're my mom's recipe."

He fixes a plate with some of the blueberry pancakes, sitting beside me. His arm brushes against mine as he moves and he smiles.

I feel like it should be weird being here with Mascen, things being this easy and fun between us, but it's not. Despite how things started out I think we were headed this way the entire time.

With breakfast done we clean up the last of the mess together despite his protests. Afterward, he grabs my hips, lifting me onto the counter so he can fit into the space between my legs.

"What are you doing?" I place my hands on his stomach as he comes closer.

"I don't know. I was thinking I might kiss you."

"That so?" I bite my lip to hide my growing smile. Things might've changed between us but that doesn't mean I want to make everything easy for him, even a smile.

"Mhmm," he hums, cupping the side of my right cheek in his left hand.

"What if I don't want to kiss you?"

He arches a brow. "Then I won't kiss you."

He knows I'm playing, but he starts to pull away anyway. I grab the back of his neck. "Kiss me you idiot."

"You're the one who protested," he reminds me a second before his lips touch mine.

Maybe because in the past I've only had hookups, I've never liked kissing too much. I've found it intimate, far more intimate than sex which might sound strange to some, but it's the way I've felt. Kissing Mascen, though, feels natural.

The kiss doesn't last long and I find myself wishing for more.

He lifts me off the counter and I look at him with a curious expression. "What do you want to do today?"

He gives a small shrug. "Anything we want."

———

I'm amazed by how quickly time passes with Mascen. Before I know it two weeks of break have passed and Christmas is days away. The living room of his townhouse now boasts a sparkling Christmas tree after I begged him to go get one. I haven't had a real Christmas tree in too long. Even though he protested I know he's glad we got one and he definitely enjoyed decorating it.

Passing him a cup of hot chocolate I sit down on the couch and curl into his side.

"Mmm," he hums upon tasting it. "That's good."

"I told you that you had to use milk, not water."

"These marshmallows are so tiny."

"Mini-marshmallows are for sure the way to go." I take a sip of the hot chocolate I made for us after Mascen told me he hated it.

Setting the cup on the tray he put on the ottoman earlier, I stretch my legs out and lay my head in his lap. Almost immediately he starts brushing his fingers through my hair and my eyes grow heavy.

I can't believe how content I've become with him. We still haven't talked about what we're doing, tried to put any labels on this. I think we're both too stubborn and maybe too scared.

"If you keep doing that I'm going to fall asleep."

His fingers still for a moment before starting up their ministrations. "You wouldn't dare fall asleep."

"Why not?" I hold back my yawn which is a mighty task.

"I want to take you somewhere."

"Where?" I sit up slightly so I can look at him and his fingers fall from my hair.

"Just a place."

I roll my eyes. "Do you always have to be so cryptic?"

He pokes my cheek. "It's part of the fun."

He starts to get up and I sit up completely. "Wait, we're going somewhere now? What about our hot chocolate?"

"Bring it."

I'm not about to leave my hot chocolate behind so I pick up the mug and follow him. I notice he leaves his and I think he might be lying about liking it this way.

In the garage he leads me to the truck. I've noticed it during my time here, obviously, but he's never taken it out.

When we leave he still doesn't say where we're going. All he does is swing by a Burger King and order a sack of food and keep driving.

"Why the food?"

"We're having a picnic."

"It's December," I remind him. "It's not exactly picnic conditions—not to mention it's *dark*."

"Oh, yee of little faith."

Eventually he turns off the main road and keeps driving for a ways before parking in a field.

"This is where you're bringing me?"

"Yep." He hops out, his boots colliding with the solid ground. He reaches back in for the drinks. "You wait here."

A few minutes later, after digging things out of the backseat and jumping up into the truck bed he finally lets me see what he's up to.

I find the truck bed full of blankets and pillows with our food and drinks in the middle.

"We won't stay long," he promises. "I know it's cold, but I wanted to bring you here."

He jumps up, holding a hand out to help me into the bed of the truck.

"I'm beginning to think you're a bit of a romantic."

Despite the darkness I swear he blushes. He adjusts the pillows and I finally sit down, pulling the bag of food close to me so I can get mine. I wasn't hungry before but suddenly I'm starving and want this juicy greasy cheeseburger more than anything else in existence.

Passing the bag to Mascen he gets his out, lying it in his lap and stretching his legs out.

After we've each eaten a few fries, I finally ask, "What's so special about this place?"

He swallows a bite of food. "It's not really the place but the feeling."

"What do you mean?" I pick up my burger for a taste, wiping the corner of my lip when ketchup gets there.

"I found this place by accident, but I've kept coming back. It's quiet here and I'm alone with my thoughts, the good and the bad ones. But when I look up at the stars and see the entire universe I'm reminded I'm not alone. There's something comforting in that."

Tilting my head back I look up at the stars. The sky is clear, the stars above infinite. "I think I get what you mean. It's impossible to feel alone when all of that exists and there's so much more out there that we don't know."

"Exactly."

I burrow into my sweatshirt more. There's no snow on the ground, but there's a slight wind which makes it feel colder than normal.

"During the fall and spring I can spend hours sitting right here." He pats the space beside his leg. "Sometimes it's hard to leave. Do you have a place like this?"

I shake my head. "No, I wish I did."

"What about before? Where did you guys even move?"

"Florida. For some reason my mom thought the sunshine state would solve all her problems." Picking up a fry I twirl it around between my fingers. "But no, even there I didn't have a place to go to clear my head. Not like you have the treehouse and this." I wave my hand to encompass the dark field.

"I wish you had."

"Hey," I pop the fry in my mouth, "I got out of there. I got this scholarship and I'm doing what I wanted. I won't dwell on the past. That's not good for anyone. It's over and done with—no do overs. Obsessing over it won't change, but I *can* change my future and that's what I've been working to do for years. I want to be somebody, not to prove a point, but because I *can*. I want to improve others lives too so they don't have to work as hard as I have."

He stares at me for a moment, a peculiar look on his face. Finally he says, "You're really something, you know that, Princess?"

"I'm nothing special."

He looks into my eyes so intensely that I start to squirm. "You're special to me."

I blush, looking down.

One thing I remember my mom telling me before everything went to hell was if one person thinks you're special then that's worth more than all the gold in the world.

With the feeling that floods my chest I think she may have been right about that.

FORTY

MASCEN

BREAK IS PASSING TOO QUICKLY. I'VE NEVER IN MY life wanted time to slow down like I do now. I know when Cole gets back and classes start up things will be different. I won't see her every day. I won't wake up with her in my arms. I won't feel ... complete.

Fuck, I never thought a girl would ever get to me like she does. I didn't think I would like the feeling of being so wrapped up in another person, but instead of feeling like I'm leashed I feel freer than I ever have.

With Christmas behind us and New Year's just around the corner there really isn't much time left.

I used to think I had so much of it, time that is, but I'm discovering there's far too little of it when it counts.

"I win!" Rory throws her hands up after counting her money.

"Impossible," I grumble, picking up the money I earned while playing The Game of Life with her.

"Don't be such a sore loser. I beat you by more than a million dollars."

"Let's go again."

"I've won the last three times. You think fourth time's the charm?" She raises a brow and reaches to push her glasses up the bridge of her nose.

"Maybe."

Winning isn't as important as seeing her have fun.

She resets everything and we go again.

———

COLLAPSING in bed beside her that night I wrap my arm around her tiny frame, pulling her against my body.

"Mascen," she wiggles against me, "let me go, I have to pee."

"Not yet." I bury my head into the crook of her neck. She giggles when my hair tickles her skin.

"If you keep holding me like this I'm going to think you like me."

I know it's a joke, but after all our bickering and my harsh words in months prior I feel the need to make it clear to her that I do. "Mmm," I hum against her skin. "I do like you. Very much. More than I should."

She stiffens a tiny bit in my arms and I'm worried I've said something I shouldn't have.

"I like you too," she whispers back. "This is complicated, isn't it, Mascen?"

She pulls my hand off her stomach, twining our fingers together. Her skin is lighter than my tanned hue with a couple of freckles.

"It shouldn't be…"

"But it is," she finishes for me.

She rolls over to face me, tucking her hands under her head. "This might sound cheesy as hell, but I'd rather do complicated with you than uncomplicated with anyone else."

I crack a smile, amused at her declaration. Smoothing a piece of hair behind her ear, I say, "I don't know how to do this. Be someone's … person and … I have my best friend to think about."

"I know." She frowns. "But Cole's a good guy, he'll get over it."

"I'm not so sure," I admit, my voice shaking.

"What do you mean?" Her nose wrinkles with confusion.

I roll onto my back, curling my right arm behind my head as I look at the ceiling. "Look, you know how I am. I'm moody, arrogant, a jerk—most people call me an asshole more than anything else. I'm the antagonist of a story. Cole … he'll think I'm doing this just to be a piece of shit."

"Then explain it to him," she argues like it's so simple.

I don't want to talk about this anymore. Arguing about it will do no good.

Drawing my finger down her cheek, I whisper, "You know I will."

And I'll try, when the time comes, but Cole's seen the way I am for years. He's not going to be easily convinced I care about Rory. And maybe that's a good thing, maybe I should end this before it goes further. I tend to ruin everything so who am I to believe that she'll be any different?

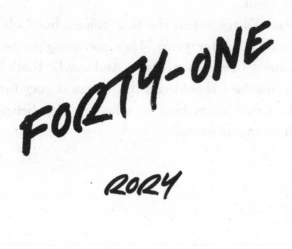

FORTY-ONE

RORY

"WHERE ARE WE GOING?" I ASK FOR THE MILLIONTH time, wiggling in the passenger seat of Mascen's car.

He told me to dress up, which meant I had to go shopping. Mascen offered to buy me whatever dress I wanted for tonight, but I refused. Just because he has more money than me doesn't mean I want him to constantly use it on me.

The fitted deep purple and red sequined dress cost more than I would normally spend on any kind of garment, but I figured for New Year's Eve I'd make an exception. I paired it with heels—God I hope I don't take a tumble and die—as well as a long black coat I borrowed from Kenna when I texted her about my dilemma. It felt weird being back in the dorm to get it after all this time at Mascen's place. Knowing classes will start back up next week is bittersweet.

"A place," he answers, reaching to adjust the volume on the radio.

"A place," I repeat. "That really gives me a lot of information."

We've been in the car nearly thirty minutes heading in the direction of Nashville but that's all I know.

"It'll be worth it." After a pause he adds, "Hopefully."

"And if it's not?" I'm sure whatever he has planned will be fine, but I'm still curious about what he'll say.

"Then we'll leave."

"Just like that?"

"Yep." He looks over at me briefly. "I don't want to stay somewhere you're unhappy."

I swear my heart does a somersault.

Twenty minutes later he exits off the highway, driving through downtown Nashville.

He parks in one of the various parking garages and once we're on the street he takes my hand leading me to one of the older more beautiful buildings. There's a clock inlaid into the top of it surrounded by copper tiling.

"What is this?" I ask him, slightly embarrassed by the giddy quality in my voice.

"I'm not sure if you like country music all that

much, but I thought you'd enjoy a concert."

I stare at him in shock as we enter the building and he passes over two tickets to a guy. He nods and reaches for a set of doors waving us through.

I can hear the music already as we run down a hall, my laughter echoing off the concrete walls.

"We're a little late," he says, pulling me along. I struggle to keep up in my heels. "But our seats are excellent."

"Have you been here before?" I ask, since he seems to know exactly where he's going.

He looks at me like I'm insane. "My dad's in a band, I've been to a lot of different venues."

"Right, I always forget that."

He chuckles as we reach a curtain and he pulls it aside. "That's one of the things I like most about you."

We head down a set of stairs, the music growing to a deafening level.

The dark tunnel we're in starts to brighten and suddenly things open up and we're right beside the stage to the right.

"Mascen!" I gasp, my hand flying up to my mouth. "Holy crap."

"You like this surprise?" He wraps his arms around me from behind and I grab onto them, swaying with him.

"I love it." My eyes are wide, taking everything in. "I've never been to a concert before."

"Another first," he murmurs in my ear, kissing my cheek.

"What do you mean?"

"Bed sex, now the concert. Two firsts of yours that I get to experience with you."

I tilt my head back smiling up at him. "How about that?"

I take in the artist on stage, humming along to the music as Mascen and I sway back and forth.

I was skeptical but this might be the best surprise ever.

————

AFTER THE CONCERT Mascen had plans to take me to a fancy dinner to countdown the new year, but I told him I'd rather go to a diner for fries and a milkshake.

"You really wanted this over a five-star meal?"

I dunk a fry into ketchup. "This is a five star meal to me."

"You're a strange breed, Princess." I shrug, sipping my chocolate shake. He narrows his eyes on the cup in my hand. "You better not throw ice cream at me today." He picks up his shake and winks, tipping the Styrofoam cup in my direction.

"Me? Never."

Across the room the countdown to midnight plays on the TV.

Mascen bites into his cheeseburger, wiping his mouth with a napkin. "You know, I have to agree with you, this *is* better than what I had planned."

"Nothing beats hometown diner food." Picking up a

fry, I twirl it between my fingers. "Do you ever make New Year's resolutions?"

He shakes his head. "Fuck no. There's nothing I purposely want to change about myself, we all grow and change anyway, and anything I want to accomplish I don't need a new year to help me do it."

"Hmm," I hum. "I never thought about it that way."

"Do you make resolutions then?"

"I never have, but I just never gave it much thought. If you were going to make one what would it be?"

He thinks for a moment, truly pondering his answer. "I guess to be more conscious of the things I say and how they can affect people. Your turn."

This time I have to take a minute to think through my answer. "To forgive my mom," I whisper so softly I'm surprised he can hear me, but I know he does from the widening of his eyes. "For me, not her. I guess that's not what a resolution is supposed to be, but..." I trail off, not sure what else to say.

Mascen stares across the table at me, his normally sharp eyes suddenly soft. "I don't think there are any rules when it comes to a resolution, Princess."

On the TV the countdown begins, the chants of the seconds being echoed by other patrons in the diner.

Lifting my shake, I say, "To moving on."

"To moving on," he echoes, smacking our cups together.

In the same moment we lean across the table just as the clock strikes midnight, sealing the vow, and starting the year with a kiss.

FORTY-TWO

MASCEN

I KNEW THIS DAY WAS COMING, THE ONE WHERE RORY would have to return to her dorm for good and classes would resume, and we'd be forced to go back to a life where things are normal.

"Do you have to go?" I wrap my arms around her from behind as she zips up her bag. Cole is supposed to return tomorrow morning so Rory insisted on heading back to her dorm this afternoon to get settled.

"Yes," she giggles, wiggling out of my hold. She turns around, the back of her legs resting against the

369

bed. "If you keep whining about me leaving I'm going to start thinking you like me." She pokes my chest.

I grab her finger, biting it playfully. "Nope, definitely still hate." I kiss the outside part of her hand.

"I hate you too." She reaches up, snatching my baseball cap and planting it on her head backwards.

"I could have lice you know."

"I've had your dick in my mouth. I think I'll take my chances."

"Stay longer," I beg pathetically. "We can order pizza or I'll make dinner if you want and then you go home."

She shakes her head. "Li's coming back tonight and I don't want her to be alone."

"Fine."

Hoisting her bag on her shoulder she reaches for my collar and tugs on it. "Don't worry by tonight you'll realize what an annoying pain in the ass I am and never speak to me again."

"It's possible," I agree.

"Hey." She playfully swats at me. "That was only a joke."

Squeezing her waist in my hands I bend down to kiss her cheek. "You better leave before I change my mind on letting you go."

She rolls her eyes and pushes my shoulder. "It's cute you think you can tell me what to do."

I take a step back from her, watching her head to the bedroom door. An ache fills me I've never experienced before as I follow her downstairs and then out to her truck. The old rickety thing looks like it needs to be in a junkyard, not on the road, but I tried telling her that and she nearly chewed my head off.

She opens the door and it groans in protest like a cranky old man getting woken up from a nap. She tosses her bag on the passenger seat and turns around to face me.

"Where do we go with things from here?" Her lower lip starts to tremble like she might cry. She bites down on it clearly not wanting to let her emotions get the best of her.

We've been avoiding this topic the entire time. Both of us too scared to put a label on things.

I stuff my hands in my pockets, lifting my shoulders slightly.

"I don't really know. I guess take it a day at a time and see what happens."

She nods in agreement. "I hate you for making me feel like this."

I reach out, twirling a piece of her shiny dark hair around my finger. It's soft and smooth. "Yeah, well I hate you for it too, Princess. I guess that makes us even." I wink at her and let the piece of hair go.

"I have to leave," she says more for herself than me.

"I know."

"I don't want to." Her voice is soft, like she doesn't want to give volume to her incriminating words.

"I know."

"Stop!" She breaks into laughter.

I grab her face between my hands kissing her deeply

but keeping it short before I haul her over my shoulder and convince her to go home in the morning.

"See you later, Princess."

"Promise?"

I nod, taking a couple steps back as she gets in the truck. She gives a small wave before putting it in reverse and backing out.

I stand on the driveway until her truck is gone from my sight.

Fuck, it's harder watching her go than I thought it'd be.

Back inside the first thing I do is schedule a pizza to be delivered later for her and her roommate. I'm fucking whipped and I don't know how it happened.

I throw my sheets in the washer and put a clean set on, then wander around the townhouse picking up shit and trying to get things back in decent order. I've never been able to tolerate trash lying around and things out of order.

Flopping down on the couch once I feel like the place is clean, I grab the controller for the Xbox and start playing

Twenty or so minutes later I hear the garage door go up. Pausing the game, I get up, looking out the window to see Cole's car parked in the driveway. My heart drops and I say a prayer that Rory did insist on going back to her dorm today.

The door leading up from the garage opens and Cole steps inside dropping his bag on the floor.

"Hey, man," I greet, more pep in my voice than

usual. I hope he doesn't notice the forced sound. "You came home early."

"Yep." His tone is somber, face angled to the floor.

"Did something happen?" The way he's acting I'm wondering if someone died or some shit, but if that were the case I wouldn't think he'd be returning home early.

He nods, eyes still downcast, and I'm starting to actually get concerned. "Yeah." He rolls his tongue in his mouth. "I think I lost a friend today." The goldish-brown hue of his eyes is glossed over. There's a pissed off set to his lips that I've only ever seen him wear on the basketball court.

"What the fuck, dude? What happened?"

He cocks his head to the side. "You're seriously gonna play dumb with me right now?" He shakes his head back and forth, a coarse laugh filled with disbelief sputtering out of him.

"I'm not playing dumb, I'm fucking concerned."

"Concerned? *Concerned?*" He thunders, suddenly right in my face. The vein in his forehead pulses. I don't think I've ever seen him this pissed off. "Are you for real right now?" He shakes his head harshly, turning away.

"I literally have no idea what the fuck you're talking about."

He stands there, fists clenched at his sides staring at me. "You really don't do you?" He looks shocked by the revelation.

"How could I possibly know what you're talking about?" I try to keep my tone calm and neutral.

He takes a measured step closer. "Rory."

My heart drops. "What about her?"

"Fuck, man." He looks away for a second before getting in my face. "Don't play dumb with me. I saw her truck here."

I've always been good at lying, probably a little too good, so I blurt, "She was picking up something here that she realized she left."

Cole cocks his head to the side, laughing incredulously. "You son of a bitch. You really think you're slick and can get away with anything. The great Mascen Wade is untouchable." He spreads his arms wide. "I saw you kiss her."

Ice slithers down my spine and I grind my teeth together.

"Nothing to say now?" He arches a brow. "No words of defense?" I stand there, letting him say what he needs to. "You know what the worst part is? I'm not even surprised you'd move in on her. This is just who you are and I should've known one of these days your dickish behavior would turn to me. You sabotage yourself every step of the way and that's the real reason you're such a selfish bastard—because it's easier to ruin things and blame it on that than to be a goddamn decent human being and maybe someone just doesn't like you. You want *everyone* to hate you and I've been nothing but a good fucking friend to you." He takes a couple steps back and bends to pick up his bag. "I hope you're happy."

I don't say anything as he heads up the stairs. I don't

defend myself, or explain my past with Rory, my feelings for her, or how conflicted I've been over them
because of him. I just let him go, because all he's said is
true. I am an asshole, one who brings this upon himself.
I don't deserve friends and I certainly don't deserve
Rory.

FORTY-THREE

RORY

L<small>I GETS BACK TO THE DORM SHORTLY AFTER</small> I <small>DO AND</small> after we both unpack we decide to put on a movie for background noise and catch up.

"I miss home but it's so good to be back." She grabs one of the throw pillows from the couch and clutches it against her. "I don't have my mom breathing down my neck. God love her, but it's nice to have some independence. How'd things go with Mascen?"

Instantly heat rushes to my cheeks. "Um, really well."

"That's it?" She punches my arm playfully. "You're always so secretive."

"It was ... nice. Better than nice, actually. We hung out around his place, did some things, I worked some evenings, there's really not a lot to tell."

"But how do you feel about him? Did being alone with him reinforce feelings or are you back to hating him?"

"Things started off rocky, I don't think either of us expected to run into each other here, I mean, I know we didn't, but now it feels like we've always been this way. It's easy. And isn't that how things should be? As easy as breathing?"

Li smiles widely and reaches over to squeeze my hand. "I'm so happy for you. You deserve this. You're so much more lively and vibrant than when classes first started. It's like there's a light in you now that didn't used to be there. And I'm not saying you need a guy to find that light or to be happy, but I think he awakened something in you that you forgot was there."

"Maybe," I agree, afraid to give him too much credit. "Being with him is better than I expected. I never thought this would happen, not the way things were in the beginning, but we click. He's so different once you get to know him. He puts on this front, but God Li, he's just ... he has a good heart, you know?"

Li smiles, releasing a theatric dreamy sigh. "Let me know where I can find a guy like that."

I sigh, feeling a pang in my chest. "Cole's a good guy. I know I hurt him."

"You didn't mean to."

"Even if I didn't mean to it doesn't mean I didn't. He deserved better."

"You can't force yourself to have feelings for someone. They're either there or not. You and Mascen had chemistry from the get-go and I know you liked Cole, but I don't think your feelings ever moved past those of friendship."

I shake my head. "They didn't but I still feel bad."

"I think it's human to feel bad when you know you've hurt someone even unintentionally."

A knock on the door ends our conversation and we both exchange a look, wondering who could be there.

"Mascen?" she asks, pointing over her shoulder at the door.

"I don't think so."

I get up and go answer the door, finding a pizza delivery guy on the other side. "Oh, hi," I blurt out in surprise. "I'm sorry but we didn't order pizza."

I start to shut the door but he stops me. "No, the order instructions said specifically this dorm."

"Oh. Are you sure?"

He tilts his head. "Are you Princess?"

I blush and snatch the pizza from him, closing the door with my foot. The driver cackles on the other side. I hope Mascen gave him a tip, because I'm way too embarrassed to open the door now.

"Pizza?" Li brightens, hopping up.

"A gift from Mascen." The sticker on the side does

indeed include instructions on where our dorm is located and says plainly; To: Princess From: Satan

"Wow, I think I love him too."

My head shoots up in her direction. "I never said I love him."

She smiles conspiratorially and lifts the top of the box, revealing the delicious looking veggie pizza. "Girl, you don't have to say it. I see it in your eyes."

"I don't—not yet. It's too soon."

She plucks a slice out of the box. "Say whatever you want but the truth is written all over your face."

Before I grab my own piece I text Mascen.

Me: Thanks for the pizza, Satan.

I don't get an immediate reply, but it doesn't surprise me. Grabbing two pieces for myself I settle back on the couch beside Li.

"All I'm saying," she struggles to speak around a mouthful, "is if a man sends you pizza, he's a keeper."

———

BY THE TIME I crawl into bed it's after eleven. Stifling a yawn, I reach for my phone for the first time in hours, expecting to see at least a text from Mascen but there's nothing.

Me: Are you okay?

A few minutes go by.

Me: Mascen, you're worrying me.

Me: Hello?

Me: I'm going to bed.

Me: I hope you're all right.
Me: Goodnight.

———

SUNDAY PASSES WITHOUT A REPLY BACK, call, or even a fucking carrier pigeon from Mascen. I've moved from worried to pissed off, because he's obviously ignoring me and I don't know why. His lack of communication is maddening. Did I do or say something wrong? Did he use me as a fuck buddy over break? None of it makes sense. The moments we spent together seemed real and genuine. It makes me sick to my stomach to think he might've been acting to get what he wanted.

Li and Kenna are both in disbelief that he's shutting me out. Li tells me to give him the benefit of the doubt, but Kenna says he's ghosting me.

I have no real idea what to think or feel beyond confused and hurt.

But like a desperate fool I keep texting him.

And to no surprise to anyone, even me, he never responds.

FORTY-FOUR

MASCEN

TWO WEEKS BACK AT SCHOOL AND THINGS SHOULD feel normal, but they're anything but. Even with baseball practice in full swing and Coach nearly shitting a brick over every little thing it doesn't feel right because I'm not talking to *her*.

After Cole confronted me it felt wrong to keep things going. I fucked everything up with my best friend and since I screw everything else up as well it seemed like I might as well end things with Rory too before it got too far. But instead of being a man and telling her that I've given her the silent treatment. I haven't been to Marcelo's. I haven't even seen her on campus—purposely avoiding the areas I know I'm most likely to run into her.

Cole isn't speaking to me either, which means the most socialization I get is with Teddy on the random times I see him, and in class with Mallory. I deserve to suffer in solitude so I'm not complaining.

"Wade, see me in my office after you finish." Coach's hand slaps down on my shoulder, surprising me. Normally I'm more aware of my surroundings but the past couple of weeks I've been zoning out a lot.

I give him a chin dip in response and finish changing into my regular clothes after my shower.

"You wanna go to the bar?" Teddy flicks his damp hair from his eyes, looking up at me as he yanks socks on.

"Not in the mood."

"You never want to go out anymore," he points out. "Come on, it'll be fun."

"Maybe next time." I grab my phone and wallet from the top of my locker and stuff them both in my jeans pocket.

"You said that the last two times." He stands up, closing his locker.

"Well, maybe one of these days I'll agree. For now, no."

"Fine, your loss," he shouts after me as I walk toward Coach's office.

I rap my knuckles against the back of Coach Meyer's door. "Come in."

I push the door open and he swivels around from his desk to face me. "What the fuck was that today, Wade? Forget today, this whole goddamn week."

I clench my teeth together. I knew this was why he wanted to see me, but it still sucks to hear. "I don't know. I've had a lot on my mind."

"Get it off your fucking mind then. Whatever it is isn't as important as the game, you hear me? You're the best pitcher I got but don't think I won't take you out and put Henderson in your place."

Henderson doesn't have half my speed or technique. He's sloppy and has a lot to learn, but I don't blame Coach for the threat. "Understood."

"Tomorrow I expect you here early in the weight room and to be the player I know and expect you to be out on the field."

I jerk my head in a nod. "I will be."

He reaches for his reading glasses. "Good, now get out. I don't want to look at your ugly mug anymore."

Closing the door behind me I return to the lockers and grab my bag. Tossing it over my shoulder I head out of the locker room and gym building to the parking lot outside. My car sits there alone now, everyone else having left. Climbing inside, I'm tempted to change my mind and text Teddy to see what bar they went to, but I know being around that crowd and drinking away my sins isn't going to solve my problems.

Instead, I decide to torture myself by pulling out my phone and bringing up the last text messages from Rory.

Princess: Why are you ignoring me?

Princess: It's been a week. What the fuck is your problem?

Princess: I know we weren't dating, but Jesus Christ Mascen if you didn't want to see me again you could've said so. I'm a big girl.

Princess: Seriously? Nothing? Real mature.

Princess: I hate you—and not in a like you way.

The last text hurt like a bitch, like being sucker punched square in the face. But it's nothing less than I deserve.

Sighing, I put my phone in the cup holder and drive away.

———

"You know, I really don't know what to make of this pouty sad version of you. It's kind of weirding me out." Mallory drops down into her seat beside me. "Here I got you this." She holds out the tea for me. "It's what you always order."

I take it from her, mumbling a thank you.

"What'd you do?" she continues. "You must've done something to be sulking like this. Don't worry, this is a no judgment zone. I'm assuming you fucked it up with a girl and it doesn't take me much guessing to figure out which one." She winks at me.

"I really don't want to talk. Besides, class is going to start."

"After then?"

"No," I bite out.

"You should talk. Talking is good."

I narrow my eyes on her and lift the tea to my mouth, taking a sip. "Are you my shrink now? Because I didn't ask for one."

"You might not have asked, but it doesn't mean you don't need one."

I stare steadfastly ahead. "I'm not good at talking."

"Cool, then you can buy me lunch to make up for my generosity with the tea and I'll do all the talking. All you have to do is sit there and look pretty and listen. You can at least do that, can't you?" I make a noise that is neither agreement nor disagreement. "Perfect. We'll go to the diner. I'm in the mood for burger."

MALLORY RIPS one of her fries into pieces then dunks one of the now smaller pieces into ketchup. "Thanks for lunch."

"You kind of forced me into it," I point out, staring at the BLT I ordered.

"I did, but you looked like you needed a friend."

"I don't need friends. I don't need anybody."

She arches a brow in surprise. "Whoa, I sense some aggression there. Who are you trying to convince? You or me?"

My lip curls and I pick up a fry, shoving it in my mouth so I don't have to say anything. What could I say anyway? It seems like whenever I open my mouth I only dig myself into a deeper hole.

"You know, I get that you're kind of an aggressive guy—total alpha male vibes, but there's a difference in being a protector and a flat out jerk. I'm trying to help you." She stares at me across the table like she's trying to mentally drill her words through my thick head.

"I didn't ask for your help."

She narrows her eyes. "You know what, enjoy your lunch." She tosses her hands up, huffing in exasperation.

She starts to slide from the booth and I grab her wrist. "Wait," I plead, coming to my senses. I can't keep doing this to myself or other people. "I'm sorry. I don't know how to do this ... ask for help ... *talk* about things."

"Really? I hadn't noticed." Despite her sarcasm she gives me a small smile, sliding all the way back into the booth like she was before. "Usually you just start with words, that's what helps me."

"I didn't know you were such a smart ass."

"Well, since I think we're kind of sort of friends at this point I figured it was best to let my true colors shine through. Now cut to the chase, we don't have all day. I'm sure whatever major fuck up you've made to put you in such a dismissal mood requires a long story and my burger is getting cold."

I HATE TO ADMIT IT, and I'll never say it out loud, but talking to Mallory made me feel better. But as soon as I got home and saw Cole's car my mood soured. After I filled Mallory in on my past with Rory, taking her home, and then her staying with me over break, she said I needed to be honest with Cole about Rory but it's easier said than done. My best friend thinks the worst of me now and I know anything I say to him will be interpreted as just another lie and manipulation.

It's been beyond uncomfortable between us these past few weeks. Cole leaves a room almost as soon as I enter it and I know he purposely left his laptop open in the kitchen the other morning so I would see that he was searching for a new place to live.

Climbing the stairs from the garage I open the door. Cole isn't immediately visible but then the deck door opens, the scent of grilling burgers wafting into the townhouse behind him.

He looks up after closing the door to find me across the room. We make eye contact but no words are exchanged. I know I should say something but my mind is empty of words. He shakes his head, a humorless laugh passing through his lips, and heads into the kitchen while I take the stairs.

At the top, I stop looking back down but I can't see my friend—or former friend, more like.

After showering, I get in bed, torturing myself by looking at Rory's last text.

When my mom Facetime's me I nearly don't answer, but this is my momma and I can't ignore her.

As soon as her face appears on the screen I find myself blurting out, "Mom, I fucked up."

"What?" She blinks in shock at me.

I feel bad for catching her off guard and honestly don't know what made me say it. "Don't worry about it."

"No, no, no. I don't think so. I heard what you said, now tell me what you did?"

I prop my phone on the dresser, trying to think of the best way to explain the clusterfuck I've landed myself in to my mom. Rubbing my jaw, I decide to jump right into it.

"Cole was kind of dating Rory before Thanksgiving. She broke things off with him and while we were home things kind of…" I gesture with my hands, unsure how to phrase it proper. "Escalated," I finally settle on. "You know she spent all of winter break here and he happened to see her leaving and now he's fucking pissed at me, rightfully so, because I didn't tell him about her. He thinks I did it on purpose to be a dick to him, but that's not it at all, Mom. I care about her, a lot, and now I've really fucked things up because I haven't spoken to her in weeks."

She stares at me through the screen, blinking slowly. "I never realized what a dumb ass I'd raised. You really are your father's son."

"What?" I sputter.

She shakes her head, blowing out a breath. "Maybe it's a man thing in general, but you guys truly make some of the dumbest decisions ever. You're what?

Punishing yourself by pushing Rory away? Then not being honest with Cole? He's been your friend for over two years now, and a good one at that, stop being such a cry baby and *talk* to him. Tell him how you really know Rory, because I doubt you've said anything about that either, and explain your feelings for her. I can't guarantee he'll forgive you easily, but I think he'll at least understand." She exhales a weighted sigh. "As for Rory, get on your knees and grovel, Mase, because you've really messed up there ignoring her. She cares about you, a lot, maybe even loves you. I saw that when you guys were here in November. Don't throw away a good thing because you're stubborn and scared. Being a decent human being means facing your fears, owning up to your wrong doings, and doing what's right."

She presses her lips together, but I know more words are on the tip of her tongue so I keep my mouth shut.

"You kids know the story of how your dad wasn't honest with me in the beginning of our relationship. Though, I guess honest isn't the correct term, but he didn't tell me he was in a band. I had no clue he was famous. I was a clueless teenager who didn't pay attention to that kind of stuff. I played piano and listened to classical. I didn't read magazines or watch any kind of celebrity television. When I found out I was hurt because I felt like I'd been lied to and used. Rory's probably feeling the same right about now. Find the way to talk to her, or do something, so she knows your real thoughts, feelings, and motives."

"She might not forgive me."

She shrugs, sipping her mug of tea. "She might not, that's her prerogative, but you owe it to her and yourself to apologize and explain. It's better to know than spend your whole life wondering what would've happened if you just said something. Regrets don't tend to go away. They fester in your mind, plaguing you as you go through life. It's better to face things head on in the moment."

I swallow past the sudden lump in my throat. "I'll figure something out."

"Mascen," she says my name softly. "remember, things that are meant to be will be, but that doesn't mean we don't have to work for it."

"Thanks, Momma."

"I have to go for now. I love you."

"Love you too."

She blows a kiss and like always I grab it, pressing it against my heart.

I don't know how to make things right. Not with Cole. Not with Rory.

But I know my mom's right. This isn't a regret I want to live with.

FORTY-FIVE

RORY

I FEEL LIKE I HAVE NO RIGHT BEING HURT. MASCEN and I made no promises to each other. We weren't a couple, not even really friends. It's dumb to feel like I'm owed something, a resolution of sorts, and yet I do.

My anger at him grows day by day, ready to explode and boil over. I know Kenna and Li can see it, probably worried when I do reach that point I'll take it out on them, but they have nothing to worry about. There's only person I plan on unleashing this upon and it's the man who deserves it.

All my life I've been treated like an object. A plaything. Something to pass around. Even as a small child, before things got really bad, our parents would dress Hazel and me up like little dolls to show off.

But I'm a person and I deserve more than that.

Knocking on Kenna's door she calls out for me to come in. "Hey," I greet, crossing my arms over my chest. "I have a favor to ask you and Li."

Li perks up from the couch. "I'm listening."

"The baseball team has an away game this weekend. I need to be there."

Kenna cocks her head to the side. "Are you confronting Mascen or…?" She trails off to let me fill in the blanks.

"Honestly, I have no idea, but I just need to do something. Going to his game seems like a good place to start."

"Well, I'm always in for a good old-fashioned road trip. Li?" She leans off her bed to peer around me to the other girl in the living area.

"Absolutely."

FORTY-SIX

MASCEN

IT'S BEEN A FEW DAYS SINCE I SPOKE TO MY MOM AND she told me in so many words to, "Stop being such a little bitch and talk to Cole."

Working up the courage has been difficult since I'm not very good at apologizing or explaining myself. It feels weak to admit fault in anything, but my mom reminded me the strongest people aren't afraid to be vulnerable.

Knocking on Cole's door I push it open before he can tell me to go away. Not that I'd blame him but I need to get this over with before I lose the courage.

"What do you want?" He sits up in bed, eyes narrowed. He looks skeptical at my interruption and sadly, the way I've been in the past, I can't blame him. But I have an away game this weekend and I'm worried if I don't make things right then I might come home to no roommate and a friendship now beyond repair.

"I need to talk to you."

He slides out of the bed stalking towards me, his body tense like he's poised for a fight. I wish he'd hit me. It'd make me feel better, but that's not Cole's style.

At the end of the day he's right, he's the nice guy and I'm not.

"Shouldn't you have done your talking a while ago? Seems a little late to me now." He raises his hands to his sides and lowers them back. "You've been moping around here like I'm the one who betrayed you."

I clench my teeth and nod. "I know. Fuck, I'm not good at this." I pinch the bridge of my nose.

"Clearly." He crosses his arms over his chest, a look of impatience crossing his face. I know if I don't hurry up and start explaining he's likely to walk away.

"I hate explaining myself or trying to justify my actions. I've always believed in doing things with no regret and owning it, but I'll admit I hated seeing Rory behind your back." I look down at my hands for a moment, flexing my fingers so I don't have to look into his eyes. I fucking hate seeing the betrayed look in them.

"That so?" He arches a brow, his nostrils flaring. He's pissed and has every right to be. "How long was this going on? The whole time I was with her?" His jaw clenches, his hands fisted at his sides like he wants to hit me but I know even now he won't.

I shake my head. "Fuck, man, no. How could you think that?" He gives me a look like he can't believe I just asked that. "Right..." I rub the back of my head awkwardly, blowing out a breath. "Look, there's a lot you don't know that I need to try to explain for you to understand. Do we have to do that standing here?"

He sweeps his arm to the side with a dramatic flourish, like I'm really putting him out for wanting to have this conversation. I know I should've explained things to him immediately. I know he would've still been pissed, but it would've been better than letting this riff grow and fester even more. "Kitchen?"

I nod in agreement and he follows me downstairs. He ends up taking one of the barstools and I stand across from him bracing my hands on the counter.

I know I can't wait long to launch into this or he'll get up and leave, so I get right to it, like ripping off a Band-Aid.

"I've known Rory since we were kids."

His head shoots up in surprise, his face crinkling with confusion and surprise. "What? Why didn't you say anything? Why didn't *she* tell me? I even commented on how you guys grew up in the same fucking place!"

I shrug, not knowing what else to do. The anger in his voice is justified. I should've told him, but it didn't seem important. Not then anyway.

"I haven't seen her in ten years but growing up she was my best friend. I treated her like shit when I found out she was going here. It doesn't help that my first encounter with her in a decade was catching her sneaking out of your room." Cole tenses, but doesn't interrupt. "It's dumb but seeing her again reminded me of how hurt I was by her leaving. Her family moved away when she was eight after her dad killed himself."

His mouth drops open in shock. Scrubbing a hand over his scalp, he shakes his head in dismay. "She never told me that."

"She doesn't like to talk about it. Anyway, we didn't get off to the best start and then you were interested in her which only made me angrier. Looking back, I think I was jealous because the crush I had on her as a boy was still there and I didn't want it to be. Especially when I knew, out of the two of us, you're the better choice."

Surprise colors his face, but it's true. I'm not the best choice for her, or anyone, but it doesn't change my feelings.

"Things changed when I insisted she come home with me. It was practically her second home when we were little and when I heard she was staying on campus for Thanksgiving I..." I look down at my hands, the knuckles turning white where I clench my fists. "I couldn't let her be alone. It didn't make any sense to me at the time, or at least I didn't *want* it to make sense, but things changed with her there. For both of us. And I'm fucking sorry you were caught in the middle of that."

Swallowing thickly I force myself to meet his eyes, hoping he can see the pain in mine for fucking everything up.

"You care about her," he states, his eyes surprised — but there's something else there too, almost like he's pleased. Maybe he's just happy to know the great Mascen Wade isn't completely stone cold. Rory is the one who likes to claim a vampire, and maybe I was, but that was before her. Now, the organ in my chest is very much alive.

"I love her."

The surprise on his face turns to downright shock. "Are you fucking serious?"

"Yeah. Yeah, I am." I feel it, the truth settling inside me.

I hate Aurora 'Rory' 'Princess' Abbott so much that I fucking love her.

"Why the hell are you telling me and not her?" He looks at me like I've lost my mind.

"Uh…" I blink at him, not sure what to do with this turn of events and kind of wishing he'd just deck me so I'd feel better about the whole thing.

"I'm still fucking pissed at you — but if you would've told me this from the start I would've … well, I'd still have been pissed, but after I got over it I would've understood. That's what friends do, Mascen. Stop self-sabotaging yourself. Why do you do this?" He slams a palm on the counter. "It's fucking dumb. Not to mention aggravating."

"I don't fucking know."

He shakes his head in disbelief at my idiocy. "You really care about her, huh?" He grinds his teeth together like the words pain him. I know even with this conversation he's still hurt and angry, but hopefully, maybe he'll forgive me one day. Not that I deserve it.

I exhale a weighted sigh; one I think I've been holding in since the last time I spoke to Rory a month ago. "I do, but she hates me for real now." I rub my jaw in frustration.

"Has she said that?"

I lower my head, her text emblazoned in my mind. "Yeah."

"In the heat of the moment or...?" His voice is tight and I know it's killing him to try to be on my side in this moment. But that's who Cole is, the guy who puts aside his own feelings for others. No one's perfect, but I'll never be as good as him.

"It was a text after I ignored her."

"Fuck." Cole rolls his eyes, slamming his palm down on the counter. "You are the biggest fucking idiot I know. Just tell her how you feel, your real, honest and true feelings. It's not that hard." He shakes his head in disbelief. "I didn't know anyone could be as stupid as you, but here we are."

I roll my tongue around my mouth. "It's easier said than done."

"Dude, what's the worst that can happen? You tell her you love her and she says she hates you for real? Whatever. Move on. But if she feels the same and you let her slip away it'll be the biggest mistake of your life."

"How did this conversation turn from you hating my guts over Rory to you now telling me to get the girl?"

"I still hate your guts ... sort of. But you never apologize for anything and you did this time. My momma always taught me to forgive those who mean it and I know you do. I'm not ready to fully forgive and forget but give me time. You pissed me off and hurt me. Right now I don't trust you like I used to."

"Are you seriously okay with this? With me trying to get Rory back?"

"Not completely," he answers honestly. "But I'll get over it. If Rory and I were meant to be we'd be together. But she's your girl, man. Go and get her."

"I don't know how." I run my fingers through my hair. "Fuck, I've never had to do anything like this before."

"Don't over think it." Cole stands, swiping a water from the fridge like everything is back to normal between us. I know it's not, but it's a start. "Get her some flowers, say you're sorry. It's really not that difficult." He rolls his eyes in exasperation.

I eye him skeptically. After all the shit I've done, I really don't think it's going to be as simple as he says.

———

FRIDAY COMES and I haven't thought of the best way to apologize to Rory. Just saying I'm sorry feels like a bullshit lazy way to go about it. But duty calls, so I board the bus for our first game of the season in Kentucky.

Coach stands outside the bus making sure we all end up on it like we're a bunch of unruly kindergartners he has to wrangle. Unfortunately, that's kind of true.

"Got your head straight, Wade?" He smacks the top of my head like he's cracking an egg.

"I think so, Coach."

"Think so or know so?"

"Know so."

"That's what I want to hear." He pats the back of my shoulder, urging me onto the bus.

I walk to an empty seat, settling against the window. All our bags are being loaded into the bus's storage space so at least that gives me a little more leg room.

"God, I'm fucking pumped for this." I look over to see Teddy plopping into the seat beside me hard enough to make our seats and the ones in front shake. "Nothing beats the high of a game."

Normally I would agree right away but my mind is still on Rory.

"You're always quiet but lately you're quieter than normal," he points out, taking his cap off to fluff his blond hair. "Where's your hat?" he asks, noticing I'm missing my usual one.

"Lost it," I mumble, knowing good and well exactly where it is. My thoughts threaten to drift back to Rory and those last moments I saw her, how fucking hot she looked stealing my hat. She's probably thrown it in the trash by now.

"Lost it?" he repeats in shock, pulling out his Air Pods. "It's not like you to lose something."

I look out the window as the doors to the bus finally close. Up front Coach yells at one of the guys and the bus jerks as it pulls away from the school.

"I've been losing a lot lately," I finally reply to Teddy.

His brow wrinkles as he pops one of his Air Pods in his ear. "Like you've got Alzheimer's or some shit?" I look at him like he's lost his fucking mind. "I'm just kidding man." He knocks his elbow against mine.

He puts in the other ear bud, silencing all further conversation. Normally I'd be grateful not to hear Teddy ramble the entire way but right now I could sure use the distraction. Instead, I lean my head back, letting my gaze drift out the window as I try to figure out how to make things right.

———

"LOOK AT US BEING ROOM BUDDIES." Teddy grins behind me as I swipe the room key.

I look at him over my shoulder as the door beeps. "We always room together."

"Yeah, but isn't it exciting?"

I shake my head, opening the door to the room. "Exciting isn't the word I'd use."

With Teddy around you never know what's going to happen. He's an unpredictable loose cannon. While that used to be fun, it's grown tiresome to me lately.

"Are we going out or ordering room service?"

I set my bag on the bed. "I was going to order in. Go out with the guys if you want."

Teddy claps me on the shoulder. "I can't leave my buddy all alone. What kind of friend would that make me?"

I roll my eyes at him. "Get out of here," I grumble, pushing him away.

He cackles, heading toward the shower. "Order me a steak. I'm being fancy tonight."

"What's the celebration?" I raise a brow, waiting for his answer.

He yanks his shirt off and rolls it into a ball. He throws it at my face but I dodge it easily. "The fact you're buying."

I chuckle and reach for the room service menu. "Of course."

He's still laughing when he closes the bathroom door.

After placing an order for dinner, I sit down at the little desk in the room toying with the paper pad. I have so many thoughts and no way to make sense of them when it comes to Rory or how to explain my feelings. Reaching for the pen I start writing them all down instead.

FORTY-SEVEN

RORY

I DON'T KNOW WHAT POSSESSED ME TO THINK IT would be a good idea to go to Mascen's first game. I had no real plan, just that I needed to be here.

Scooting along to our seats the three of us plop down. Kenna holds securely onto her bag of popcorn already munching away.

"I didn't know baseball games were so popular," I mutter, looking around at the filled seats.

"Me either." Kenna's reply is muffled around her popcorn. "But the way these men look I'm suddenly finding myself very interested in the sport."

Leaning around Kenna, Li says to me, "Do you know what you're going to do or say yet?"

"No. I guess I'm going to wing it."

I figured if I came to the game it would be easier to confront him without giving him an easy means of escape, but my thoughts didn't go much farther than that in regard to how I'd get him alone or even what I'd say. This whole thing was a spur of the moment decision because I refuse to let him off the hook so easily. If he never wants to see me again that's fine but he needs to man up and say it to my face.

"Hey, isn't that Maddox Wade?" Li points toward the bottom of the stands where Mascen's dad, mom, Willow, Lylah, and even Dean take their reserved seats. There are two bodyguards with them as well, one on each side to keep people from bothering them.

"That's him," I confirm, staring down at the family in surprise.

Over Christmas Mascen told me about the talk he had with his dad and I know a conversation doesn't resolve all issues but I knew it went a long way to making Mascen feel better. Misunderstandings have the tendency to snowball into a bigger deal than they actually are. I wish that's all Mascen and I were dealing with.

Settling into my seat I wait for the game to start, trying to ignore the pounding in my chest. My treacherous body is excited to see him. At least my brain is still on the *I hate Mascen Wade's guts* train.

The game gets underway, the racing in my heart only increasing.

"Why are sports uniforms so sexy?" Kenna hisses under her breath, though I'm sure the people around us still hear. "They're all fitted and hot. Look at their asses." She points down below.

"It's a thirst trap for us single girls," Li replies with a smile.

"Ugh, you need to fix things with Mascen so you can set us up with his teammates." Kenna holds the popcorn bag out to me if I want anything but I shake my head in dismissal.

"I'm not the one who needs to fix things," I remind her.

"You know what I mean—after he grovels and kisses your ass you need to find boyfriends for Li and me."

"I'll add that to my to-do list."

"You're the best friend a girl could ask for." My sarcasm goes right over her head since she's too busy drooling at the guys and eating popcorn. She's nearly to the bottom of the bag and the game has barely begun.

Where the dugout is located—at least I think that's what it's called—from where we sit, I can't see the guys on the team at all to see if I spot Mascen. A part of me was worried if I made this trip there could be a chance he wasn't even playing, but the appearance of his family confirms he's definitely here.

Time seems to drag as I wait to lay my eyes on him.

When the teams switch, my eyes eagerly track the players jogging onto the field. Finally, I spot his name embroidered on the back of his uniform as he steps onto the mound.

He rubs his thumb over his bottom lip, his eyes shadowed by a team baseball cap. I'm far enough away that I can't make out his features, but I know from experience that his eyes are narrowed and intense. He's in the zone out there. It may be the first time I've seen him play but it's obvious he belongs there.

I'm so intrigued watching him and his movements as he throws his first pitch that I forget I'm supposed to hate his guts right now. I guess that's our problem, the line between love and hate has always been so thin they're practically the same thing.

"He looks good out there." Kenna nudges my knee.

I don't respond, too consumed in trying to take in every detail. The long lean lines of his body, the sharp cut of his jaw, and the way he holds himself like he's the king and he's on his throne.

Mascen throws his first pitch, the ball so fast I swear it blurs.

I don't even pay attention to what else is going on in the game. He's my sole focus. I begin to understand why I've heard so many rumors about him going pro. I know Mascen doesn't want that, but he *could*. He's incredible out there, like it's effortless. I'm not coordinated enough to jog a mile without running out of breath and tripping over my own feet at some point.

His family cheers down below and he looks toward the stands, surprise coloring his face when he sees them. It's obvious he wasn't expecting them and his happiness hits me like a ton of bricks. I want Mascen to be that happy all the time, even if I want to beat him with a shovel for ignoring me.

The whole game I sit at the edge of my seat and when they win Li, Kenna, and I cheer together.

The stands start to empty out and I hurry the girls so I don't get caught by his family.

"Are you going to wait for Mascen?" Li asks me.

I bite my lip, unsure what to do. "Maybe we should just head back." I'm being a coward, I know, but I'm afraid of what I might do or say if I see him.

"You mean we came all this way for nothing?" Kenna bumps my shoulder playfully. "What a shame. It's a good thing I got to see some men in tight pants. Total consolation prize."

"I need a bathroom break before we hit the road." I point toward the building. "You guys?"

They both shake their heads since they went during the game. I wasn't able to pull myself away.

I watch them walk toward the parking lot before I head inside to the bathroom.

Seeing Mascen reminded me how painfully in love with him I am and I didn't even fully realize it until it was too late. I want to see him, get things off my chest, but I also have to accept that I need to let him go. I won't force someone to be there for me when they obviously don't want to be.

Leaving the restroom I nearly walk straight into a lady entering.

"I'm so sorry," I blurt, stepping aside.

She looks up, her eyes widening, and I curse my luck. "Rory? How are you?" Emma asks with a bright smile. "I didn't know you were here. You could've sat with us. I'm so glad Mascen got his head out of his ass and apologized to you."

I stare at her blankly. "What?"

"He told me he messed things up with you and felt really bad about it. I know he can be hardheaded, but I told him explaining things and apologizing go a long way to mending broken bridges."

I blink at her. "I ... I actually haven't spoken to him in a month. He cut me off completely, but I came here to ... I don't know," I sigh, my shoulders sagging. "I wanted to yell at him and give him a piece of my mind on what an idiot he is, if I'm being perfectly honest. Now, I don't really feel like doing any of that. I just want to go home and leave it be."

Her smile falls a bit but the motherly gleam in her eyes doesn't leave. She touches my cheek briefly before letting her hand fall to her side. "Mascen is a good boy, a stubborn one, and intense, but he has a heart of gold and loves deeply. You have to trust yourself and your own heart, but I promise you, he's worth fighting for."

"Thanks, Emma." I squeeze her hand. "It was good running into you."

The restroom door swings shut behind her and I let out an exaggerated breath.

You didn't come all this way to do nothing you wimp.

Walking down the hall, I pace a few times before

turning a corner. I see some of our players walking out of a room with bags slung over their shoulders. Without thinking, I march through the door figuring the best thing is to just do it and get it over with. If I leave here without talking to him I solve nothing.

"Mascen?" I blurt.

Oh, shit.

I blink at the half-naked guys standing in the locker room.

Oh my God, what have I done?

"I'm so sorry! Wrong room!" I blurt, my cheeks red with embarrassment.

You should've paid attention to where you were going! The men's locker room! Really, Rory!

I turn to reach for the door when one of the guys says, "Looking for Wade?"

Swiveling back around I nod at the blond guy, his smile amused. There's only a tiny towel wrapped around his trim waist. "Y-Yes." My whole body feels like it's on fire and I try to keep my eyes on him since at least he's sort of covered unlike some of the guys around him.

He looks me up and down, tipping his head to the back. "He should be coming out of the shower if you want to wait."

"Wait?" I repeat, my voice high-pitched and squeaky.

One of the guys beside him drops his towel to pull his pants up. My hands fly up to cover my eyes over my glasses.

Suddenly there's a hand on my elbow and I jump. "Relax, I'll take you to where he left his stuff." I recognize the voice as the guy who was speaking to me before.

Keeping my eyes covered, I squeak, "Okay."

He guides me forward, past the guys, some of whom chuckle in amusement. I don't blame them, I'm sure I look insane being led through the men's locker room.

"Just wait here." The guy releases me.

"Thank you."

I carefully lower my hands and find that he's placed me so I'm staring at a wall. I can still hear the guys behind me, but at least there aren't so many pensises everywhere now. Kenna would probably be in heaven.

I'm right beside the showers and knowing Mascen is there somewhere nearly sends me into a panic. Why did I think this was a good idea? I turn to leave, deciding to brave all the penis, and pretend all this never happened when I hear, "Princess?"

A squeal flies out of my throat and I whip around to find Mascen behind me. His hair is damp, the ends slowly curling over his forehead. The towel hanging low on his waist makes my throat go dry.

"What are you doing here?"

"I ... I..." Words completely leave me, tears suddenly stinging my eyes. I haven't seen him since the day I left his townhouse at the end of winter break. I know it's only been a month but it feels like forever.

"I wanted to come see you when I got home. I know I've been a jerk ignoring you and you deserve—"

The words that were gone a moment before suddenly come to the forefront. "No," I push his chest, "you don't get to just wave this whole thing off like it's no big deal, Mascen Wade." He stares at me stoically, jerking his head in a nod. "You fucking ghosted me and I'm allowed to be pissed off about it. What's more maddening than anything is I still have feelings for you even though you are, without a doubt, the biggest asshole I've ever met. If you never want to see me again, say it to my face. I deserve that. Everyone in my life — my dad, mom, even my sister, has treated me like something easy to throw away and dispose of and maybe it's selfish of me to want more than that from you. I don't know why I made this trip all the way here." I throw my hands out wide. "I had no plan, no speech rehearsed, nothing. I thought maybe I'd yell at you and magically feel better but I know that won't change anything. Nothing I say can change you. You have to do it on your own." I poke his chest. "And frankly, I'm not sure if you're capable of caring."

I find myself out of breath from my long-winded rant. But it was all things I needed to get off my chest that have been eating at me.

"I'm not a nobody," I continue, my lower lip trembling with the threat of tears. "I'm somebody. Someone who deserves more than this." I gesture between the two of us. "I won't allow myself to be used by you or anyone else. I got out of the shithole my mother put us in and won't be dragged down for anything, least of all by a man who has his head too far up his ass to actually hold an adult conversation."

"Ror—"

I hold up a hand. "I don't want to hear excuses from you, which no doubt is what you're about to give me. Only you are responsible for your actions. Own them."

I'm flushed, my skin damp with perspiration from my rant and the humid locker room.

Then, because sometimes pettiness is needed, I reach out and yank his towel off just like I did the first time we saw each other.

Some of the guys laugh others cheer and some are silent watching the man behind me.

Holding my head high, I walk out.

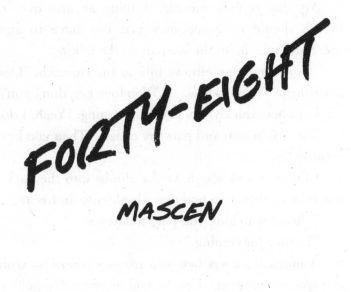

FORTY-EIGHT

MASCEN

"You were so good, Mase. I hate that we have to go." My mom kisses my cheek settling back on her heels beside their SUV.

"I'm just happy you guys came."

Seeing my parents, sisters, and even Dean in the stands had taken me by surprise. But not nearly as much of a surprise as when I saw Rory in the locker room. I still haven't been able to wrap my head around that one.

"Did you see Rory?" she whispers so no one else can overhear. "Did you talk?"

"She talked," I mutter, raking my fingers through my hair. "I mostly stood there."

My dad rounds the car, draping an arm over my mom's shoulder. "Sometimes you just have to stand there and take it, let the woman do the talking."

"Hey," my mom elbows him in the stomach. "Don't eavesdrop." To me, she says, "You love her, don't you?"

I swallow thickly, my chest tightening. "Yeah, I do."

She reaches up and pats my cheek. "Then you know what to do."

I hug her and watch as she climbs into the back of the vehicle, their two bodyguards already up front.

"I loved watching you play today, son."

"Thanks for coming."

A moment passes between us, one where no words are spoken but everything is said anyway. He pulls me into a hug, smacking my back.

"We'll see you soon."

"I love you, Dad."

He presses his lips together, his eyes glassy. "I love you too."

Stepping back, I watch him get inside and the SUV pull away.

Things with my dad aren't perfect and I don't expect them to change overnight, but I think we're headed in the right direction.

"Stop looking like a forlorn poodle without a snack and come say goodbye to your favorite sister." Willow leans out of the Mustang window. Dean, behind the steering wheel, shakes his head and laughs under his breath. "I've seen Goldfish crackers with more depth and emotion than you."

"I would just like to say *I'm* the favorite sister," Lylah pipes up from the back.

I walk over to where they're parked a few spaces down. "Did you guys seriously load up without giving me a hug? Fuck, I feel unloved."

"You'll get over it." Willow sticks her tongue out at me. "We've got to hit the road."

"Me too." I point at the bus waiting in the distance.

"Be careful, and don't do anything I wouldn't do ... which I'll pretty much do anything so shit you have free rein, bro."

I shake my head. "You're fucking crazy."

"Thanks." Willow winks at me.

I bend over, smiling at Lylah in the back. "Love you, Lylah-bug."

"Eh, do you have to call me that?"

"Always."

Leaning through the car window I hug Willow the best I can and fist bump Dean. From the back Lylah grips my hand briefly.

"I'll see you guys over spring break," I promise, stepping back. "I love you."

"Love you, Mase."

"Call more, we miss you!" Lylah yells from the back as the car pulls away.

Watching them leave I feel a pang of homesickness as I head to the waiting bus.

"Thanks for waiting," I tell Coach.

"Don't make it a habit," he grumbles, to which I laugh.

Sitting down beside Teddy he pulls out one of his Air Pods. "Who was the chick who reamed you out in the locker room? She's got spunk. Think she'd go out with me?"

I narrow my eyes on him. "Don't even think about it."

He cackles loudly. "I knew it."

"Knew what?"

"You're in love with that girl, and if the great Mascen Wade's been bitten by the love bug then we're all fucked." He shakes his head, reaching to put his Air Pod back in. "That shit is highly contagious."

I lean my head back against the seat. I don't tell him, but it doesn't matter what my feelings are. Some things are unsalvageable and I don't know if I can fix this with Rory but I damn well am going to try.

FORTY-NINE

RORY

A SOFT KNOCK ON MY BEDROOM DOOR INTERRUPTS my study sesh.

"Yeah?" I voice to whichever of the girls is on the other side.

"Hey." Li smiles, an envelope clasped in her hands. "This was slid under the door. It's for you." She holds it out so I can see my name written on it.

My throat suddenly gets tight when I recognize Mascen's handwriting. I take it from her. "Thanks."

"Mhmm," she hums, eyeing me warily. No doubt

she's figured out who the letter is from. Still, she doesn't say anything and closes the door behind her.

I look down at the envelope, tempted to toss it in the trash. But I know if I did it would be a decision that would haunt me.

I only saw Mascen yesterday, the embarrassment of my locker room meltdown still plaguing me, and I figured I truly wouldn't hear from him again. Especially when he didn't call or text.

Ripping the envelope open, several sheets of paper fall out, one a piece of notebook paper and the others from a small notepad with the logo of a hotel on top. The sheet of notebook paper says *read first*.

Look, I'm not good at talking about my feelings. Articulating them is difficult for me. I wrote the other pages for you Friday evening when I got to the hotel. I planned to give them to you when I got back and let you do with it what you will, but I didn't expect you to come to the game. I'm in the wrong here, I know it, and don't deserve your forgiveness in the slightest, but I hope you do.

I set the piece of paper aside picking up the other sheets. His handwriting is more chaotic on these, like he was in a hurry to get his thoughts down.

My hands shake slightly as I start to read.

I've been racking my brain for a week now to figure out the best way to apologize and explain myself to you but I have none. Flowers are cliché, I'm sure you don't want to hear me out in person, and anything else I think of sounds like I'm trying too hard.

I never expected being with you to be so easy, to feel natural, but it does —did, I guess. At times it felt like you'd always been a part of my life, not like we were rediscovering each other.

Cole came home that last day I was with you and he saw us. It messed with my head. I don't have much in this world I value as much as I do my family and friends. They're everything to me. Knowing I hurt Cole —that he thought the worst of me, that I'd used you to hurt him —fucked with my head. It made me question things, because if my best friend thought the worst of me maybe I am that bad and don't deserve anything good in my life.

Like you.

There's something I've never told you, because it sounds dumb, but that last day I saw you when we were kids, you remember what we played right? Your sister fake married us. I might've been ten, but it felt real to me because I already loved you so much. Even back then I was convinced you were the girl I was going to marry when I grew up. When your family disappeared I felt like my wife had abandoned me. Like I said, it was dumb, but when I saw you again all of those feelings of loss came back but you still felt like mine which scared me even more. Then I had to watch you be with Cole and it was tearing me apart. But we know I'm not very good at actually saying those things.

Look, I know I should've been honest with you right from the start about Cole finding out. I should've just used my fucking words instead of falling into silence. But this is me, and I never do things the right way, and I'm probably always going to be that way. I'm trying to be better, but I can't expect a miracle overnight.

If you never want to speak to me again, I understand, but I

needed you to know this; I hate you, but not as much as I love you. I love you so much it scares me. I didn't know you could feel a love this big, but you proved me wrong, Princess.

--The dragon of the story, the villain, the asshole

I hold the letter, his words, close to my heart—the heart he stole a long time ago and I never really got back.

———

"YOU LOOK LOST IN THOUGHT."

I shake my head back and forth giving Aldo an apologetic smile. "Sorry about that." I take the mixed drink from him. "I have a lot on my mind."

"It wouldn't have anything to do with a guy would it?" Heather breezes by, having overheard our conversation.

I feel my cheeks heat. "No," I blurt.

"Mhmm," she hums. "Haven't seen him around in a while, did something happen?"

I sigh, knowing I need to get back to work. "Things are complicated."

Heather squeezes my arm. "Life is complicated, girly. What's your heart telling you?"

I'm saved from answering her by one of my tables flagging me down. Dropping the drink off at another table as I pass by to see what they need.

"Could we get some extra napkins?" The man pleads, eyeing his toddler. That's when I see the kid is practically taking a bath in spaghetti.

"Yes, of course."

I run over to the stand and grab napkins and some wipes we keep on hand. Taking them back the man smiles gratefully while the toddler protests at being cleaned up.

I'm going through the motions, taking orders, smiling, being my normal self, but my mind is occupied with thoughts of Mascen and the letter. I could feel his honesty in those pages, and it felt good to know that his feelings are real, that this isn't just one sided from me. I'm still hurt and peeved at him ghosting me, but I know we weren't officially together either. We put no label on us and what we were doing.

With my mind otherwise occupied the hours pass quickly and ten in the evening comes quickly. I clock out, saying goodbye to everyone like usual, and grab my bag.

Strolling out to my car I debate whether or not to go to Mascen's townhouse. I want to see him, have a real conversation, but I'm scared.

I'm saved from making the decision when I look up and find him sitting on the hood of my truck. He blows out the smoke from a cigarette.

"Hi," he says softly, sliding off the hood and to the ground. He drops the half-smoked cigarette to the ground and extinguishes it with his shoe.

"Hey." I stop, allowing a few feet of space to separate us.

"Did you get my letter?" I nod. "Did you read it?" I

nod again, unable to form words. He presses his lips together, stuffing his hands in his pockets. "And?"

I close my eyes, centering myself. "And what, Mascen? I-I..." I flounder for words. "I love you too, but at the end of the day does that change anything? You're still you and I'm still me. How do you possibly think we can make this work? What's to say you won't stop talking to me again next week or the next. You're unpredictable and—"

"I know I'm not perfect, Rory. I get that. I'm not denying it. I'm always the first to admit I'm not the best person. But I've never been happier than when I'm with you. I don't know what tomorrow will bring, all I know is I want you in it."

"Why? Why *me?* You could have any girl you wanted. Why out of all of them is it me?"

His Adam's apple bobs. "Because it was you when you were four and I was six and you fell off your bike when you were learning how to ride it and I kissed your scraped knee. Because it was you when we were seven and nine and I broke my collarbone and you stayed over watching all of the Scooby-Doo movies. Because it was you I married at the field that day. Everywhere I turn it's you—in my thoughts, in my memories, and I want you in my future too. I fucked up, I know that, and I'm incredibly sorry for trying to throw us away because I was afraid. I'm an asshole, Rory, but I'm your asshole even if you don't want me, I'll always be that."

I laugh, my face wet with tears. "Only you could think telling me that you're my asshole is romantic."

He shrugs, taking a step closer to me. "It's true."

"Always been me, huh?"

"Always, even when it wasn't." Another step.

"That makes no sense."

"Does to me." He stops right in front of me. "I know I don't deserve your forgiveness, but I'm begging you for a second chance. I'll never be worthy of you, Princess, but I promise I'll damn well try my hardest to get there."

"Okay," I whisper.

"Okay?"

"Okay," I repeat. "But if you fuck things up that's it, Mascen. I won't be treated like less than I deserve. I'll put you in your place."

My heart, no matter how strong of a grasp I've tried to keep on it, has given itself to him. I know he's not perfect, neither am I, but I refuse to throw away the potential of our future because we're both stubborn idiots. I know things aren't perfectly repaired between us, that'll take time, more conversation. But this right here is a start, a step in the right direction for both of us.

"I won't fuck things up. At least not in a big way, because fuck it turns me on when you fight with me, Princess. Are you going to let me kiss you now?"

"I think that might be all right."

He gets the tiniest grin, much more subdued than his cocky one, this one much sweeter and almost shy. He places his hands gently on my cheeks, and the moment his lips touch mine I know for certain that no matter what Mascen and I are meant to be.

Some love stories are a perfect straight line, ours happens to be crooked with plenty of forks in the road.

But I wouldn't have it any other way, because all of it has led us here, to right now, both growing as people, and now with the chance to grow together.

Our lips part and he places a gentle kiss on my forehead.

"Princess?"

"Yeah?"

His eyes glimmer with humor. "Can I have my hat back?"

We both laugh until he kisses me again, getting lost in each other, and the promise of tomorrow.

EPILOGUE

RORY

SUMMER

THE PALE PINK FLORAL DRESS CLINGS TO MY BODY IN the summer heat.

The guests gathered for the wedding sit in anticipation of Willow making her entrance. The wedding is being held in the gardens of a museum, the surroundings lush, green, and colorful.

Music begins, the wedding party starting down the aisle.

Everyone turns to watch, and I smile when I see

Mascen with Lylah on his arm. He winks at me, his hair smoothed back and perfectly tamed for once. A feeling of love floods me as I watch him.

I loved him months ago but that feeling has only grown and intensified. We've worked hard on our relationship, to build it into something strong and unbreakable. There's less fear and uncertainty. We've both grown so much as people, learning from our mistakes.

The music changes and at the altar Dean straightens, inhaling a breath as he looks down the aisle in anticipation of his wife to be.

I turn to watch Willow reach the end of the aisle, her arm on her father's. Poor Maddox is already crying, but as I've gotten to know Mascen's dad better I'm not surprised. The guy is a softy.

He only cries harder when he has to give her away, but she's all smiles, eagerly taking Dean's hands.

Listening to them exchange their vows my heart feels full, and when I find Mascen looking at me I know we're both thinking the same thing.

That's going to be us some day.

———

Mascen

"DANCE WITH ME, PRINCESS." I pull Rory onto the dance floor despite her protests.

She wipes cake from her lips before wrapping her arms around my shoulders. "They look happy." She tips her head in the direction of my sister and her new husband.

"They do," I agree, spinning her around and into my arms.

"Think that will be us some day?" She smiles up at me, her glasses sliding down her nose. She pushes them back up, waiting for my answer.

"Some day? I already married you."

She sticks her tongue out. "I meant *for real.*"

"A piece of paper doesn't make it real, Princess," I whisper in her ear, swaying to the song. "But yeah, I can see us getting married."

"Are you happy?" She plays with my hair at the base of my skull.

"More than I've ever been." I kiss the tip of her nose.

"I've been thinking about something." She bites her lip nervously like she doesn't want to say something.

"What?" I prompt.

She blushes a bit, looking down at our shoes before making eye contact with me again. "That letter you gave me—you said that you were the dragon, the villain of the story, but you're wrong. You're my hero, always, but sometimes we can be the bad guy in our own story keeping ourselves from having the life we really want and deserve. But you slayed the dragon and rescued the princess."

"Hmm," I hum, mulling over her words. "Interesting. I never thought about it like that."

"You know the best part?" She gets a small smile, her eyes sparkling.

"What is it?" I dip her in my arms and back up.

"The happy ending, but the ending is always the beginning, one where you get to write a new chapter, one of your choosing."

I lean down and kiss her, murmuring against her lips, "This chapter is going to be my favorite."

ACKNOWLEDGMENTS

Wow, I never thought I'd be writing a book during a pandemic, but here we are. Times are strange right now and I hope this book brought a little bit of an escape to you.

As always, no book is complete without a lot of help from others.

First off, thank you Emily Wittig for creating the bomb ass cover as well as marketing material. I'm obsessed with everything you create you amazing wonderful unicorn. Love you, wifey! Lol.

Regina Wamba, thank you for providing the most perfect image for Mascen ever. As soon as I saw it I knew he was Mascen and I've been waiting literal years to get it until I actually wrote this book. When it was still available I knew it was meant to be.

To my ARC team, you guys are the real MVPs. Thank you so much for taking the time read and review my books. It means so much.

To my readers in Micalea Minions, I love you guys. Truly. I'm so happy my group is such a positive happy space.

Barbara Saleast Doilies aka B. Celeste aka Big Booty Barb, I don't know what I did without your friendship. You feel like a sister and I'm so incredibly lucky to have you.

Kellen thanks for keeping me sane and going down the 5SOS rabbit hole with me. You've helped keep me sane the last couple of months and I'm sorry for flooding your notifications with Tik Tok's when I should be working. (Okay, not that sorry but whatever)

Lastly, to you reading this, thank you for supporting me and my dream by reading this book. Whether this is the first one you've read by me or the twentieth I appreciate you so much.

All my love,
Micalea